Outstanding praise for the novels of Holly Chamberlin!

THE SUMMER NANNY

"A satisfying and multifaceted story that keeps readers guessing. For fans of similar works by authors such as Shelley Noble and Nancy Thayer."
—*Library Journal*

THE SEASON OF US

"A warm and witty tale. This heartfelt and emotional story will appeal to members of the Sandwich Generation or anyone who has had to set aside long-buried childhood resentments for the well-being of an aging parent. Fans of Elin Hilderbrand and Wendy Wax will adore this genuine exploration of family bonds, personal growth, and acceptance."
—*Booklist*

THE BEACH QUILT

"Particularly compelling." —*The Pilot*

SUMMER FRIENDS

"A thoughtful novel." —*Shelf Awareness*

"A great summer read. —*Fresh Fiction*

"A novel rich in drama and insights into what factors bring people together and, just as fatefully, tear them apart."
—*The Portland Press Herald*

THE FAMILY BEACH HOUSE

"Explores questions about the meaning of home, family dynamics and tolerance."
—*The Bangor Daily News*

"An enjoyable summer read, but it's more. It is a novel for all seasons that adds to the enduring excitement of Ogunquit."
—*The Maine Sunday Telegram*

"It does the trick as a beach book and provides a touristy taste of Maine's seasonal attractions."
—*Publishers Weekly*

Books by Holly Chamberlin

LIVING SINGLE

THE SUMMER OF US

BABYLAND

BACK IN THE GAME

THE FRIENDS WE KEEP

TUSCAN HOLIDAY

ONE WEEK IN DECEMBER

THE FAMILY BEACH HOUSE

SUMMER FRIENDS

LAST SUMMER

THE SUMMER EVERYTHING CHANGED

THE BEACH QUILT

SUMMER WITH MY SISTERS

SEASHELL SEASON

THE SEASON OF US

HOME FOR THE SUMMER

HOME FOR CHRISTMAS

THE SUMMER NANNY

A WEDDING ON THE BEACH

Published by Kensington Publishing Corporation

The Beach Quilt

Holly Chamberlin

KENSINGTON BOOKS
www.kensingtonbooks.com

KENSINGTON BOOKS are published by

Kensington Publishing Corp.
119 West 40th Street
New York, NY 10018

All Kensington titles, imprints, and distributed lines are available at special quantity discounts for bulk purchases for sales promotion, premiums, fund-raising, educational, or institutional use.

Special book excerpts or customized printings can also be created to fit specific needs. For details, write or phone the office of the Kensington Sales Manager: Kensington Publishing Corp., 119 West 40th Street, New York, NY 10018. Attn. Sales Department. Phone: 1-800-221-2647.

ISBN-13: 978-0-7582-7537-0 (ebook)
ISBN-10: 0-7582-7537-4 (ebook)

ISBN-13: 978-1-4967-1881-5
ISBN-10: 1-4967-1881-X
First Kensington Trade Paperback Printing: July 2014

10 9 8 7 6 5 4

Printed in the United States of America

As always, for Stephen.
And this time also for Joey.

Acknowledgments

Endless thanks to John Scognamiglio, the smartest editor ever.

I would like to acknowledge Nancy A. Foss for her dedication to the care and education of women.

Part 1

Take your needle, my child, and work at your pattern;
it will come out a rose by and by.

—Oliver Wendell Holmes

Chapter 1

"Poo," said Cordelia Anne Kane. "Poo, poo, and poo."

The cause of her annoyance or dissatisfaction or just plain grumpiness was right outside the kitchen window. In the past twenty-four hours, inches upon inches of snow had fallen relentlessly, until now, according to the local weather station, there was close to two feet of the awful stuff on the ground. The trees—green pines and bare oaks and white birch alike—were bowed down with the weight of snow on their branches, and the yard was one big sheet of glittering silvery white.

Cordelia turned from the window. Well, what could you expect when you lived in Maine? Snow was what you could expect, and lots of it, along with freezing temperatures, followed by a frustratingly lengthy season of chill and mud. That was followed by a frustratingly short season of sun and warmth. And then, the snow came again. Blah. Cordelia didn't find it pretty or charming at all. Well, except at Christmas. Snow at Christmastime was okay, with the red, blue, and green holiday lights twinkling against it like jewels and the prospect of presents under the tree. In her sixteen years on this planet, Cordelia had found that the prospect of presents made most unpleasant things bearable.

It was a Saturday afternoon in January, around three o'clock, and already the sun, what there had been of it, was fading away and the dark was descending. Cordelia had been in the house all day, totally by choice because a lot of people considered this area of southern Maine to be a sportsman's paradise. You could go cross-country skiing on a golf course about two miles away, and a little bit farther than that there was a stretch of land where you could ride a snowmobile. You could hear the angry roar of the machines from the Kane family's house. It was seriously annoying, like a gigantic buzzing bee.

Anyway, there was no way Cordelia could be tempted to go outside when it was this cold and wet, not even if someone promised to take her to the mall in South Portland or down to the outlets in Kittery. Not even if someone promised her a hundred dollars to spend in one of her favorite stores! Cordelia had her priorities and physical comfort was one of them. She realized that she was very un-Maine-like in this regard. A true hearty Mainer would be outside now, going about his or her business with nary a thought about frozen fingers and a dripping nose. There was a sort of joke about the four seasons in Maine. They were: almost winter, winter, still winter, and road construction. Cordelia didn't find the joke funny at all.

Well, maybe a little bit funny. It was kind of smart and so was Cordelia. Smart, but not the most focused student, so her grades were never quite what they could be. It didn't bother her much. She passed her courses with solid Bs and a sprinkling of As. While she regularly ignored extra credit assignments (unlike her best friend Sarah, who actually liked doing extra work!), she participated in class discussions and was always on time with regular homework assignments, so she managed to be well regarded by all of her teachers.

The reality was that Cordelia really enjoyed school. She got along with pretty much everybody. The bullying types left her alone. The hipsters ignored her but not because they disliked her; they ignored everybody not wearing a wool beanie or raggedy sneakers. The shy and awkward kids appreciated the fact that she always said hello and stepped in when a bully tried to corner one of them. She was aware that she seemed to have a neutralizing effect on whatever group of people she was temporarily a part of. Goths didn't seem so intent upon negativity; jocks didn't seem determined to prove they didn't need an education; nerds seemed a bit more confident in speaking out.

The fact that Cordelia's father, Jack Kane, was principal really didn't matter to anyone at Yorktide High, probably because it really didn't matter to Cordelia. She never expected special treatment and was glad that nobody tried to foist in on her. Cordelia was perfectly content to be just one of the crowd, no better and no worse than anyone else. And her parents, too, seemed proud of their daughter for being who she was, not for who she might be.

Still, there were times when Cordelia supposed that she should start thinking about what she wanted to do with her adult life. After all, she was almost a senior in high school; it really was time to start thinking about college applications and all that went with them. (Ugh! The essays! She could get from point A to point B easily enough, but after that, she found herself jumping all the way to point M and not knowing how to get back!)

But planning of any sort wasn't so easy for Cordelia. Usually when she tried to focus on what career path she might be happy pursuing, her mind wandered to what her mother was making for dinner or what television show she wanted to watch that night. A few times the notion of doing something in the fashion world had struck her as a possibility. Maybe, she thought, she could open a boutique; she already had some notion, if vague, of how to run a retail business, just from working for her mom at her quilt shop, The Busy Bee.

Or maybe she would win a massive lottery, the biggest ever in the state of Maine, and never have to work a day in her life! She would be generous with her winnings, buy a big house on the water someplace warm, like southern California (but not too close to the edge of a cliff because you didn't want to lose your house to a mudslide), certainly not someplace like where her aunt Rita lived—right on a lake, yes, but close to the Canadian border, with no electricity and way, way too many creepy-crawly things. Her parents and friends could come and live with her. They would jet off to Europe a few times a year, and she and her mother would go on shopping sprees to New York and she would donate thousands upon thousands of dollars to good causes that Sarah would research and select for her. Sarah could be trusted with important things like that.

Oh, well, Cordelia thought now, opening the fridge and staring at the leftover slice of pizza she had sworn she would not eat. That was a fantasy. Honestly, she believed that she was too young to worry about the future. In fact, she was pretty sure that the future would take care of itself. Besides, you could make all the careful plans you wanted to and something would come along and make all those plans irrelevant. Like, there was a boy she had gone to middle school with. He had gotten sick with some sort of cancer and had died within months of his diagnosis. That was truly horrible, and Cordelia was one hundred percent sure that Sean had never for one moment planned on dying before his fourteenth birthday. In fact, Cordelia remembered him going on about becoming a famous basketball player one day. The fact that he was kind of short and not a very good athlete hadn't seemed to bother him at all. He had had a dream, if not an actual plan. Sometimes, Cordelia believed, dreams were as good as, if not downright better than, plans. Except, of course, when they didn't come true.

Cordelia shut the fridge on that tempting slice of pizza and trudged upstairs. She tiptoed past her parents' room where her mother was absorbed in the latest title of her favorite series by Alexander McCall Smith. Her father was somewhere out there in the frozen wasteland that was their yard, shoveling snow and scraping ice.

Cordelia's room overlooked the back deck. It had two beds, perfect for sleepovers. The room was decorated in shades of pink and purple. A beanbag chair slouched in one corner. In another sat an antique and rather stately rocking chair, draped in a haphazard fashion with long, silky scarves in rainbow colors. A crazy quilt, one of her mother's earliest efforts, was folded at the foot of the bed Cordelia usually slept in.

Though she was long past the stuffed animal stage, Cordelia still kept a plush, and slightly dirty, unicorn named Pinky on a shelf over her bed. Occasionally, when she was feeling very sad or very stressed, she would take Pinky down from the shelf and bring him into bed. No one knew about this holdover habit, not even Sarah. Cordelia wasn't a particularly private person, but there were a few things she liked to keep to herself.

A state-of-the-art laptop sat on the desk. Cordelia used it for schoolwork but also for browsing the Internet for videos of puppies doing silly things, celebrity gossip columns, street style blogs, and fashion Web sites. She also had the latest version of the iPhone with every app a girl could possibly want and routinely cost her parents too much money by going over the limit for texts. She was always surprised when this happened and always genuinely sorry. Okay, she was a teeny bit spoiled, but that was pretty common with only children, wasn't it?

And it wasn't as if she was a mean or nasty person. She couldn't remember the last time she had spoken back to her parents. And she had certainly never been in a feud with another girl at school! It was weird, but some girls seemed to live for the next round of rumors and hurt feelings and imagined betrayals. Not Cordelia. One of her father's favorite authors was Henry James. He had posted this quote over his desk in his home office: "Three things in human life are important: The first is to be kind. The second is to be kind, and the third is to be kind." Those words had made a really big impression on Cordelia. Besides, fighting and acting all hurtful seemed like such a huge waste of time.

There were not many books in Cordelia's room, but there was a copy of the one classic novel she could never get enough of—*Rebecca* by Daphne Du Maurier. In fact, she had read it three times already. She loved the original movie, too, the old black-and-white one, and every single time she watched it, she felt frightened of creepy Mrs. Danvers, even though she knew she would get her punishment in the end, and a gruesome one at that.

Cordelia opened the door to her closet and studied its contents. It might almost be time to retire the dark skinny jeans she had worn almost every day for the past nine months as they were looking a little worn out. Besides, she had her eye on a pair of mint green jeans that would be perfect for spring (whenever that came!) though she was a tiny bit worried that they might make her thighs look too big.

Cordelia had reached what seemed to be her full height, five feet eight inches, by the age of fourteen. She wasn't skinny and was always bemoaning her weight, much to her friend Sarah's amusement. Her hair was very blond; in fact, some girls at school were convinced she dyed it, but she didn't. Her skin was very white, and she kept it that way by applying super-duper-strength sunscreen year round. Her eyes were very blue and her eyesight was very poor. Cordelia hated to wear glasses, even funky frames; she was convinced they made her look dorky. So she wore contacts most of the time and only wore her glasses in the evening when she was pretty sure no one would be dropping by the house.

Cordelia closed her closet door and plopped onto her bed. She was bored. She wondered what Sarah was doing. Probably tramping through the woods behind her house, totally oblivious to the freezing temperatures and ignorant of watering eyes and chapped cheeks. Sarah was weird that way.

Or maybe she was with her boyfriend, Justin Morrow. Cordelia frowned. She would rather not think about what they might be doing together. Certainly not building a snowman or having a snowball fight! Unlike his girlfriend, Justin was not a nature lover, even though he worked for a local fisherman. In fact, he was pretty much Sarah's opposite. Sarah was smart. Justin, not so much. Sarah was quiet. Justin had a laugh like a foghorn. Sarah had hopes for an important career. Justin was happy living paycheck to paycheck. Well, he *was* good looking, but Cordelia had never known Sarah to be impressed by something as random as a strong nose and big blue eyes.

Cordelia sighed. Maybe Sarah would dump Justin before long and things would go back to normal. It would be just the two of them again, Cordelia and Sarah, best friends since they were still in Pull-Ups.

That, Cordelia thought, *would be awesome.*

Chapter 2

It was such a lovely day, a crystalline wonderland. Sarah Mary Bauer sighed happily as she began to remove layers of wool and fleece clothing. She loved everything about every season, but deep down, winter was her favorite.

It was the same Saturday afternoon in January, almost three o'clock, that found her best friend, Cordelia, bemoaning the frosty conditions. In spite of the bitter cold and the still-falling snow, Sarah had been out for a two-hour tramp and had come home refreshed, invigorated, and with the appetite of a lumberjack.

She went into the kitchen to make a grilled cheese sandwich. Her mother and father had gone to the home of a distant neighbor, an elderly man named Ben Downing. They made it a habit to visit Ben, a widower in his nineties, once a week, to cook a few meals, rake leaves or shovel snow or mow the lawn, and tidy up a bit.

Sarah's thirteen-year-old sister, Stevie (short for Stephanie), was probably in her room with her cat, Clarissa, sewing or reading or listening to music. Stevie was very smart and did really well in school. She was also very creative and had an intense interest in style. Sarah wasn't the least bit interested in fashion. She dressed in jeans and hoodies and T-shirts and hadn't owned a dress since first grade. She was naturally slim, like her father, with long brown hair she usually wore in a ponytail. Her eyes were brown, too. She would be the first to admit that she wasn't beautiful or even pretty. And she didn't see the point in wearing makeup, unlike Cordelia who never left the house without mascara and lip gloss and nail polish.

Sarah took the sandwich out of the toaster oven and ate it in four bites. There was a leftover piece of her mother's award-winning apple pie, and she ate that, too. Sometimes she thought that the hardest thing about going away to college would be having to eat awful cafeteria food.

But she *would* go to college no matter the awful food, and after that, she thought that she would like to pursue a career as a nurse. All these commercials on television talked about the health field constantly growing, what with the huge ageing population. Then again, the law interested her too, especially when it involved the preservation and protection of the environment. Law school was insanely expensive, and it might take her a lifetime of hard work to pay off loans, but it might be worth it in the end, especially if she spent that lifetime fighting for a good and selfless cause. Then again, as a nurse she would also be making a positive difference in people's lives, and in a much more immediate way.

Building a career was going to be really tough. But Sarah knew that she could never be content to work at the sort of job that ended when you left the office at five o'clock in the afternoon and that started up again when you walked into the office at nine o'clock the next morning. She knew that she wanted work that would fill all twenty-four hours of her day. That sort of work had to be fought for and earned.

And her parents were totally supportive of her dreams, even though neither of them had gone to college. In fact, the only family member of her parents' generation who *had* gone to college and then graduate school was her father's brother, Jonas. Jonas and his wife lived in Chicago; he was a corporate lawyer and Marie worked for a bank, managing the portfolios of its biggest clients. Jonas and Marie had a Facebook page; Sarah had told her father about it, but he didn't have any interest in following his brother's life via the computer. From what Sarah could tell, there was no animosity between the two men, just a vast canyon of difference.

It was interesting, Sarah thought, as she put her dishes into the dishwasher, how two people could grow up in the same household and yet decide on two very different walks of life. She wondered if she and Stevie would become another pair like their father and uncle, amicable but also kind of indifferent to each other. That, Sarah thought, would be sad. She would try her best not to let that happen.

Sarah peered out one of the kitchen windows at the snowy scene. Nothing made Sarah happier than being outdoors. She found rain refreshing and thunderstorms exciting. Snow was beautiful. Even high humidity could be borne when the payoff was a vista filled with wild flowers and buzzing bees. Most times, her ambles were solitary because she just didn't know anyone else who shared her passion for the outdoors. Justin, her boyfriend, teased her about being "Nature Girl" (his idea of fun was a beer and a baseball game on TV) and Cordelia vastly preferred to spend her free time shopping or watching movies. Kicking through fallen leaves or climbing over the decaying remains of dead trees or tramping along a stretch of hot white sand did nothing for Cordelia. She didn't care, she said, for extremes of temperature (cold made her skin flake and heat made her hair frizzy) and she found rocks boring (they just sat there).

Sarah turned away from the window and looked around the kitchen with fondness. She loved every bit of her home, from the embroidered sampler over the sink to the old marble lamp in the living room; from the slightly slanted floors on the second level to the way the wind sang through the old, ill-fitting windows in the living room. Every inch, every possession held charm for Sarah, largely because the house was the one in which her father's paternal grandfather had been born. His father and mother had owned it after his grandfather's passing, and Joe Bauer, Sarah's dad, had bought it from his parents when they retired to a smaller place closer to the heart of town.

Though the land on which the house sat was no longer used for commercial farming, Sarah's parents had planted a big vegetable garden, and Cindy, her mom, maintained a lovely flower garden. There had been some talk about raising chickens, too, but when the girls had admitted they would probably not be into cleaning the coop, the idea had been abandoned.

The house was a classic old farmhouse, white clapboard and two stories high with an attic that extended the length of the structure and a big porch out front. The first floor contained the kitchen and mudroom in back, and the living room in front. Stairs to the second floor were against the right wall of the front hall. The second floor contained Sarah's parents' room in front, Stevie's bedroom next, the house's one bathroom, and at the very back of the house, Sarah's bedroom.

The rooms throughout the house were small and the ceilings low by contemporary standards. It felt a bit like a warren compared to the more open plan of the Kanes' development house. There was no central air-conditioning, but there were window units in the bedrooms. As a result, the first floor of the house could feel brutally hot and close in summer. Fans did little to alleviate the oppression of the heavy, still air; most times, the Bauers didn't even bother to waste the electricity.

Sarah went up to her room now to change her socks. They had gotten slightly damp, which meant that she had to waterproof her boots again. If she were lucky, they would last for one more season. Good boots were expensive.

From her bedroom window, there was a perfect view of the extensive vegetable garden and beyond that, a heavily wooded area dense with pines and white birch and oaks. From this vantage point, you could often see deer grazing, and hedgehogs nibbling flowers, and chipmunks scurrying under rocks. On rarer occasions, you could spot a fox sneaking along the remains of an old stone wall not far into the mass of trees. Some years there were coyotes; you heard more than saw them, and the lonely sounding howls usually meant big trouble for the neighborhood cats and small dogs.

And there were parading families of wild turkeys and all sorts of other birds on the wing, from tiny, brightly colored songbirds to impressive birds of prey, hawks, falcons, and even, on occasion, an eagle. At night, you could hear the haunting cry of owls on the hunt. And in the morning, if you looked, you could find the skeletons of the owls' prey at the base of trees. Sarah had pointed this out to Cordelia on one of the rare occasions Cordelia had, reluctantly, accompanied her friend into the woods. Cordelia had run shrieking back to the house. Sarah had not made that mistake again.

The room itself was very simply furnished. There was one bed, one dresser, and a small wooden desk with a chair. On the desk sat an old laptop, which Sarah used for school and research only. She had a very basic phone, and she was very careful about using it wisely.

The walls of the room were painted white and on her bed lay one of her mother's quilts, the one she had made for Sarah right after her birth. It was a magnificent example of something called a log cabin quilt. Every time she looked at it, Sarah was amazed at her mother's skill.

A bookshelf her father had built was crammed with volumes she had collected at yard sales and secondhand bookshops. Sarah loved to read, and it almost didn't matter what the content was—fiction, nonfiction, history, mystery. She read everything but bodice-ripping romance. Recently she had discovered the works of May Sarton. Anne Morrow Lindbergh's *Gift from the Sea* was also a favorite. There was a biography of George Washington that had taken her almost a year to get through, not because it was difficult reading but because schoolwork came first. When her history teacher had asked what famous person from the past she would most like to meet, Sarah chose Abigail Adams. She had read a biography of her, too, and a lot of the letters she and her husband had written to each other. If she ever got married, Sarah hoped she would find a best friend in her husband, like Abigail had found in John.

For now, Sarah had Justin. She really liked him, but marriage was the last thing she could think of, not until she finished school, and that could be eight or nine years from now.

The blare of a horn alerted Sarah to the arrival of her boyfriend. She tossed the damp socks into a hamper in the bathroom, raced downstairs, grabbed her outerwear, and ran down the front steps.

Justin was driving his friend Bud's four-wheel drive truck. There was a raised plow attached to the front as Bud made extra money plowing for his neighbors. He had offered to cut Justin in on the business, but Justin had laughed off the offer. He was the first to admit that he was a pretty lazy guy.

Gosh, he really is beautiful, Sarah thought as she climbed up into the passenger seat. "Where are we going?" she asked.

"How about back to my place? I got a frozen pizza for us."

"That sounds great," she said.

Justin lived in a small apartment above a family-owned hardware store in downtown Yorktide. The apartment was clean enough but kind of messy. It was sparsely decorated with cast-offs from his parents' house and plastic milk crates that Justin used for storage and as surfaces for dirty plates and empty beer bottles.

Well, Justin might not be the neatest guy around, but Sarah thought he was certainly the most handsome one. He made her feel things she had never even guessed existed, a sort of excitement she had certainly never heard her mother, or Cordelia, or any of her teachers talk about. At first, it had terrified her. But over time, she had come to befriend her feelings. Eventually, she had given in to them; she had let them overwhelm all sense of caution or embarrassment. After all, sexual feelings were natural, weren't they? You weren't supposed to feel bad about having them. Her health teacher back in freshman year had stressed that.

"Here," Justin said, holding out a little white paper bag, his eyes fixed on the road ahead. "I have something for you."

Sarah smiled. Every time they met, Justin gave her a little gift. She wished he wouldn't spend his money on her—she knew he didn't earn a lot—but he seemed to get real pleasure out of giving her the tiny stuffed animals and the hair baubles. The hair baubles were more appropriate for a frillier girl, but it was the thought that counted.

Sarah took the bag and peered inside. It was one of those thingies you clipped onto your key chain. It had a green plastic disc on which was printed the image of a grinning chimpanzee.

"You like it?" Justin asked. She heard the unmistakable note of hope in his voice.

"I do," she said. "It's wonderful. Thank you, Justin."

Justin smiled, and Sarah felt an intense rush of warmth. She couldn't wait to get to his place, and the pizza had nothing to do with it.

Chapter 3

Later that same wintry Saturday afternoon, thirty-eight-year-old Adelaide Kane, Cordelia's mother, was sitting at the small island in her kitchen with a fashion magazine and a cup of orange-and-cinnamon-flavored tea, enjoying a few minutes of downtime before she would have to start dinner. Cordelia was taking a nap, and Jack, Adelaide's husband, had been out shoveling snow since about two o'clock.

Adelaide's hair was dark blond, and she wore it in a swingy bob. Her eyes were very blue. Cordelia had inherited their color and also her mother's poor eyesight. Unlike her daughter, Adelaide was comfortable wearing glasses. She was a little taller than Cordelia and over the years had put on a fair amount of weight. But she had made peace with it. She was always fashionably dressed and was very smart about what suited her. She glanced at the slinky sleeveless minidress advertised on the page in front of her and laughed. *That* was not going to happen.

For the past ten years, Adelaide had owned a successful quilt shop called The Busy Bee: Quilts and Quilting Needs. She had first gotten interested in quilts in college when she had taken a class called American Women and the Domestic Arts. Though she did occasionally make quilts, over time she had become more focused on restoring, preserving, and selling other people's work. Opening her own business had been a scary enterprise, but she had proved to have a good business head, and with Jack helping her with what heavy labor was required to get the shop in shape, The Busy Bee, which occupied the front rooms of an old house on Meadow Street, had soon become a success. Her dear friend Cindy Bauer helped her run the shop. She was an expert quilter who had learned the craft from her mother and grandmother before her. The fact that Cordelia and Cindy's older daughter, Sarah, were best friends, was, Adelaide thought, the icing on her professional cake.

Adelaide took another sip of her tea and thought about how different her upbringing had been from Cindy's. While Cindy had grown up locally, Adelaide had been raised in a pretty suburban town in Connecticut, the only child of well-to-do professional parents. She had gone to excellent private schools. She had spent summers swimming at the Olympic-sized pool at her parents' country club and school holidays skiing at fancy resorts in Vermont. The family had traveled to New York City once a year, just before Christmas, and stayed in an old and very respectable hotel on the Upper West Side. Every Friday night until Adelaide was a teen, the three of them had dinner at a four-star restaurant in a neighboring town. Adelaide had never wanted for anything, and until much later in life, she had been only dimly aware that other people—many other people—were less fortunate than she was.

She had met her husband, Jack, while on vacation in Ogunquit the summer after she had graduated from college. He was living in the neighboring town of Yorktide and working as a teacher at the local middle school. They began to date long distance; six months later, she moved to Yorktide, and another six months later she and Jack were married with no protest if, equally, no enthusiasm from her parents. If Mr. and Mrs. Morgan would have preferred their daughter marry someone at least equal to their own social and financial standing, they chose not to say. Adelaide couldn't help but think that after her "near miss" at seventeen (she had heard her mother call it that) they were simply relieved to have her safely deposited with a decent, noncriminal man.

Adelaide got up to make another cup of tea. Cindy always boiled water the old-fashioned way. Adelaide used the microwave. Well, what was the point of *having* a high-end appliance if you weren't going to use it?

The Kane house was one of a development called Willow Bay Estates. It was the second smallest of five different plans that had been available to the new owners, a two-story structure with a back deck off the first floor and a finished basement. The ceilings were high. The first floor was organized on an open plan, with the kitchen, dining room, and living room flowing into one another. In the living room, there was a large gas fireplace with a deep flagstone ledge. Sure, it would have been more romantic to have a real fireplace, but Adelaide wasn't a big fan of the mess logs made, so a gas fireplace it was. In the spring, the house felt welcoming and airy. Central air-conditioning kept it cool even on the hottest summer days. In the fall and winter, a zoned heating system and the roaring fire in the living room made the house feel toasty.

There was a contemporary feel to the structure though Adelaide had decorated with lots of antiques. Painted wooden chests of various sizes were stationed throughout the house. A lovely old spinning wheel had pride of place in a corner of the den, a room that doubled as Jack and Adelaide's home office. A collection of unique ceramic pitchers lined a shelf in the kitchen. And, of course, there were quilts. They were hung on the walls and draped over the back of the living room couch and laid across the foot of each bed. Her collection included sampler quilts, appliquéd quilts, postage stamp quilts, and even a few "art quilts," or, as some people called them, works of fiber art.

Art quilts aside, which were meant to be admired and not used, Adelaide loved the fact that quilts were both beautiful and practical. In the days of the pioneers, they were hung over cracks in wagon walls to keep out the cold and rain and dust; they were hung from the ceiling to partition off a large room; they were used as coverlets on beds to keep the sleepers warm.

Most touchingly, they were used as shrouds when burying loved ones who died in the middle of a desolate nowhere.

No doubt about it, Adelaide was proud of her home. Her mother, too, was house proud, though Nancy Morgan had a lot more disposable income with which to decorate. And Nancy Morgan's interiors were always lifted almost directly from popular home decorating magazines. Individuality wasn't her strong suit. Impressing the neighbors was.

Adelaide heard the front door open and shut. A moment or two later, Jack appeared in the kitchen. In spite of the cold, he was drenched in sweat. He continued to strip off his outerwear—coat and boots had already been abandoned in the front hall—until he stood in a long-sleeved T-shirt, jeans, and socks.

"You look exhausted," Adelaide said.

"I feel exhausted," he admitted. "And a little bit numb. At least, my fingers feel numb. If you can feel numbness. I never really understood that. . . ."

"Something hot to drink?"

Jack nodded. "I'm going to be very adult and very naughty and make myself a cup of coffee liberally laced with Jameson."

Adelaide grinned. "And I won't tell a soul."

Jack Kane, forty, stood at six feet four inches. His shoulders were broad, and his hair was thick and prematurely silver. In striking contrast to his hair, his eyes were intensely blue. He and his wife made an attractive couple; they had been told so often enough, which Adelaide found a little embarrassing, but which Jack took in his stride.

Though he had been born and raised in upstate New York, Jack had lived in southern Maine since graduating from college in Boston. He was popular with everyone, energetic and dynamic. Now the principal of the local high school, he had twice been asked by a group of local business owners to run for the office of town comptroller. It was a responsibility he wasn't ready to take on yet, but Adelaide was sure it was in her husband's future. For the past few years, he had played on a local bowling team and he enjoyed an intense game of chess once a week with a colleague from a neighboring town.

Jack's parents were retired to Arizona. He spoke to his mother on the phone once a week and at Christmas made sure to send Alice and John Sr. a generous gift basket of fruit, chocolates, nuts, and herb-laced crackers.

He had one sibling, an older sister named Rita, who lived in a tiny camp on the border of Canada. Rita was fiercely independent and a bit of a loner, completely unlike her very social brother. She had journeyed south when Cordelia was born but had not seen her family since. Once a year, Jack and his parents received a missive, written on an ancient typewriter, that chronicled Rita's adventures in living a solitary life with no electricity, water from a well, and a diet that largely had to be cultivated, shot, or foraged. Jack thought the letter made interesting reading. Adelaide and Cordelia did not agree.

"Is your student coming?" Adelaide asked. During the summer months and occasionally throughout the school year, Jack ran a tutoring program designed to help kids prepare for the SATs. Even families with limited "extra" income seemed to be willing to plunk down their hard-earned cash to help ensure their children got into a good college. Not that Jack took advantage of this fact; his fees were reasonable, especially considered against what other tutors in larger, more prosperous towns were charging. Still, this source of income was enough to ensure that the Bauer family could put a decent chunk of money into one of their savings plans.

Jack shook his head. "His mom called. She can't get out of the driveway. Plow guy hasn't come yet."

"That's too bad."

"We'll make up the session." Jack took a sip of his hot drink. "Mmm," he said, "that hit the spot."

Adelaide smiled. "Good thing your student had to cancel."

"Yeah. Whiskey doesn't exactly go with teaching math skills."

Chapter 4

While her friend Adelaide was drinking tea and chatting with her husband, Cindy Bauer was settling in after a visit with Mr. Downing. Sarah had gone off somewhere with Justin; she had left a note, as she always did, saying she would be sure to be home for dinner. Stevie was in her room. And Joe had gone out to his workshop.

The drive to and from Ben Downing's had been treacherous at times, and Cindy was very happy to be home. She was terrified of an accident ever since she had fallen on a patch of ice a few years before and sprained her right ankle. The injury had kept her on crutches for a month. She had felt bad about having to rely so much on Joe and the kids while she was recovering. She took her duties as a wife and mother very seriously; to shirk them for a lesser reason than a sprained ankle would have been impossible to imagine.

Cindy was thirty-eight years old. At five feet two inches, she was a comfortable-looking woman with curly brown hair, wide blue eyes, and a ready smile. Like her older daughter, Sarah, she cared little for fashion, but she put some care into her wardrobe given the fact that she worked at Adelaide's shop and was expected to project a professional image. For Cindy, that meant chinos worn with button-down blouses; cardigans in bright colors; and skirts that came to mid-calf.

Joe Bauer was tall and wiry; both of his daughters took after him in that. His eyes were large and brown; his hair was just beginning to thin and a few strands of gray had only just appeared by his temples. He had a quiet, diffident manner; some people might think he was antisocial, but really he was just private and a bit shy. While much respected in the community, he could count his close friends on half of one hand. His father had been the same. Everybody had liked him but hardly anybody other than his wife had known him. Also like his father, Joe was deeply devoted to his wife and children.

He was just about to turn forty-two, and while he was as slim and as strong as he had been in high school, years of working as a contractor in often brutal weather conditions had left his face lined and his hands scarred. But that was nothing against the fact that for eighteen years his business had grown and sometimes even flourished. Cindy was terribly proud of the fact that he had taught himself almost everything he knew, and what he had had to learn he had learned from watching those who had come before him—his father, an uncle, older men on the job.

Cindy and Joe had married when she was only eighteen and he twenty-two. Twenty years later, Cindy still loved her husband from the bottom of her heart and felt blessed to have met him. Joe was largely alone in the world, but for Cindy and the girls. His parents had died before Sarah was born. His only sibling, a brother named Jonas, and his sister-in-law Marie lived in Chicago. They had no children. Joe had a distant set of cousins in Brunswick; that was the extent of the Bauer family.

Cindy put the kettle on to boil and took a tea bag from a tin in the small pantry. She was very aware of the fact that she had nothing about which to complain and only a very few things to regret. The fact that she had not gone to college was one. Encouraging their only child to pursue a higher education just hadn't been a priority for Cindy's parents. She was a great reader and so in some sense self-taught, though occasionally she would come across a reference to a book or a historical event or maybe even a phrase in Latin or French or German, something whose meaning escaped her, and she would feel frustrated. Nobody knew everything, of course. Still, every now and again Cindy wished she had taken it upon herself to get a degree. Maybe when the girls had finished their schooling, she would venture back to the classroom.

Well, Cindy thought with some pride, as she poured boiling water into a cup, she might not know Latin, but she *could* stitch a gorgeous quilt. She had learned the art from her mother, who had learned from her mother, who had learned from her mother. Unfortunately, neither Sarah nor Stevie had shown much interest in learning how to quilt, but Stevie *was* an expert with a sewing machine as well as with a needle and clearly had a strong artistic bent. If only Cindy could urge her to add quilting to her repertoire.

Cindy's most cherished possessions were two quilts made by her great-grandmother. The larger quilt was a hexagon quilt. The smaller was in the tradition of the Victorian crazy quilt. Cindy had had them framed behind glass for their preservation. One was mounted in the living room, the other, in Cindy and Joe's bedroom.

It was just too bad that her mother couldn't see them have pride of place. Margie Keller, with whom Cindy had been very close, had passed away when Sarah was only seven. It was cancer, already advanced when discovered, and fast moving. Within five months of her diagnosis, she was gone. Some might call that a blessing. Cindy called it unfair, even cruel, but there would have been no point in complaining.

Her father, Mick, was remarried to a woman in her mid forties, widowed, with two teenage children. They lived up near Augusta. Cindy had not seen him since his wedding three years before. They talked on the phone at Christmas and on his birthday—Cindy was the one who called—and May, his wife, e-mailed an occasional photo of Mick on his riding mower or raking leaves or of the two of them posing in front of a perfectly frosted birthday cake. May had one of those determined-looking faces; to Cindy, her smile seemed bent on proving to all challengers that everything in her world was perfect. But maybe that was all in Cindy's mind. Her feelings about her father having married again were complicated.

Cindy looked toward the ceiling. She thought she had heard a thump. Probably just Stevie's cat, Clarissa, being her acrobatic self. One thing Cindy didn't mind about winter was the amount of time she could spend at home with her family. The Busy Bee was opened only two or three days a week from mid-October through December. Like many local businesses, it closed for the month of January and reopened again with limited hours in February. Once The Busy Bee reopened *full* time in late May, she would be spending an awful lot of hours there. But, truth be told, she loved every inch of the place and her personal mark was everywhere to be seen. Almost from the shop's grand opening, Cindy had helped design and update the layout, refresh the stock to meet new needs among the quilting community, and come up with clever marketing schemes.

In short, The Busy Bee was Cindy's home away from home, from its racks of pattern books to the two quilt frames in constant readiness. Cindy led workshops focusing on the basic craft and various techniques for beginners and advanced quilters. Adelaide delivered lectures about the history of quilts and quilting in the United States, improvements over time (like the availability of patterns in books and magazines), and current trends, like the rise in popularity of the modern quilt. A particularly popular lecture focused on Civil War women using their quilts as a means to deliver antislavery messages. Both workshops and lectures were usually well attended, mostly by locals, but also by women from towns as far away as Portland and Portsmouth, New Hampshire. In the summer, the workshops also attracted a few vacationers, women who announced with some pride that they just couldn't stand being away from their own quilting projects and community for an entire week.

The shop sold a variety of fabrics, threads, and needles, as well as books of quilt patterns and magazines devoted to the art of quilting and needlework. Occasionally, they sold an antique quilt Cindy had carefully restored and cleaned; more commonly the shop offered quilts made by contemporary quilters. Customers generally fell into two distinct categories: They were either die-hard quilt collectors and quilting fanatics or summer visitors browsing for pretty, locally made gifts to take home to mothers and sisters and neighbors—little sachets stuffed with fragrant pine and balsam needles, handcrafted soaps, and hand-stitched tea towels. Adelaide was currently working to expand the store's Web site so that they would be able to do more online business during the long and thus far unprofitable winter months.

Cindy heard the back door open and shut. It was Joe, in from his workshop. She smiled when he came into the kitchen.

"I was thinking about making a meatloaf for dinner," she said.

Joe smiled back at her. "Anything you make will be just fine, Cindy. You're the best cook there is."

Chapter 5

"Don't you just love the mall?" Cordelia asked.

She did not expect an enthusiastic response from Sarah, and she didn't get one. Sarah just shrugged. Stevie proved more of a fan. "I like the people watching," she said. "You can see some really odd behavior, if you're lucky."

"And the shopping is good, too, right?"

"Some of it," Stevie admitted. "A lot of it is just boring mass-produced stuff everyone else has."

Cordelia couldn't argue with that. Still, very few things made her happier than being at the mall, even if she didn't have a lot of money to spend.

The weather had improved a notch over the past two weeks, but that didn't mean it was going to stay improved. But for now the roads were clear enough for even the most nervous of drivers to venture out on journeys of pleasure. An intrepid driver, Mrs. Kane had dropped the girls—Cordelia, Sarah, and Stevie—at the mall in South Portland while she went to visit a woman who had contacted her about some old quilts she had to sell. She had promised to be back in an hour.

Stevie went off to meet her friends in the food court. Cordelia didn't know Sarah's little sister all that well, but she liked her. She didn't seem like a typical thirteen-year-old. For one, Stevie was really interested in art, and she used her clothing, and jewelry, and makeup and hair dye (in bright colors like acid green and peacock blue) as a form of artistic expression. That was probably why she found a lot of the stuff for sale at the mall boring. Luckily, Stevie shared her mother's skill with a needle and thread and so she was able to make a lot of her funkier clothing, stuff that would have cost a fortune if you could even *find* it in Maine.

Stevie was even skinnier than her sister though she ate enough for three teenage boys. (This drove Cordelia crazy about the Bauer sisters.) Her eyes were blue and her hair—when in its natural state—was much darker brown than Sarah's. Cordelia's mom had described Stevie as "striking." Cordelia agreed and thought this might partly be due to the intensity of her personality. You got the distinct feeling that an awful lot was going on in Stevie Bauer's head, much more than just a concern with outrageous hair dye.

Oh, and then there was Stevie's cat. Clarissa was one of those uncanny beasts, the kind of cat that made Cordelia (and a lot of other people) nervous. She had a look about her that made you suspect she was going to break into human speech at any moment and predict your future or something. Stevie and Clarissa were mostly inseparable, like a good witch and her familiar. The only reason Clarissa wasn't with her now, at the mall, was that Clarissa didn't care for traveling in cars or on buses.

With Stevie off to meet her friends, Cordelia dragged Sarah (literally, her hand on Sarah's elbow) into one of those determinedly hip stores, complete with dim lighting (Sarah tripped the moment she passed the threshold), wall-sized photos of gorgeous young men and women in little or no clothing ("But doesn't this store want to sell its *clothing*?" Sarah asked), and unbearably loud dance music.

"Um, Earth to Sarah?" Cordelia shouted. "Are you okay?"

Sarah startled and looked at Cordelia almost as if she was surprised to see her. "Oh," she said. "Yeah. I'm fine."

"You looked like you were a million miles away."

"Oh. Sorry."

"So, what I was saying was," Cordelia said, continuing to shout, "isn't this T-shirt awesome?"

"I guess."

Cordelia sighed and returned the T-shirt to the pile of similar shirts. "Well, it's my own fault for asking. I don't think you've ever found any piece of clothing awesome."

Sarah managed a smile. "Guilty as charged. I mean, it's only a T-shirt. It doesn't seem to justify such a serious adjective. The night sky is awesome. The ocean during a storm is awesome. The laws of physics are awesome. God, if you believe in one, is awesome."

"Well, I think a T-shirt can be awesome."

"If we're going to have a real conversation, can we please get out of here? I think I'm going deaf."

Cordelia sighed (she wasn't really annoyed; the music was getting to her, too) and taking Sarah's hand, led her through the maze of clothing racks and highly self-conscious teenage boys and girls, and out into the brightly lit mall.

"Deaf and blind," Sarah said, blinking.

"They're trying to create a mood," Cordelia explained. "An atmosphere."

"Oh, I get that. It's just an atmosphere I could do without."

"Well, I'm not thrilled with the music, either," Cordelia admitted. "But I like the clothes."

"Aren't they way overpriced?"

Cordelia frowned. "Yeah. That's why I never buy anything there."

"Then why do you even bother to go in?" Sarah asked.

Cordelia sighed. Sarah had absolutely no concept of the joys of shopping. "You're not quite normal, you know that?" she said with a smile.

Sarah shrugged. "Maybe. Let's go to the Hallmark store. My dad's birthday is coming up. I need to get him a card."

Cordelia agreed. The Hallmark store sometimes had cute, inexpensive jewelry.

It was funny, Cordelia thought, as they walked through the mall, how she and Sarah had so little in common but how they got along so well. Ever since the day they had first met, back when they were little girls, they had been the best of friends. It was probably a case of opposites attracting. Cordelia wasn't at all sure that would work in a romantic relationship (no matter that old cliché, and no matter Sarah and Justin!) but in a friendship, it seemed to work just fine.

Once in the store, Sarah hunted for the birthday cards while Cordelia scanned what she called the "fun stuff." A few minutes later, Sarah rejoined her, a card and envelope in hand.

"Oh, my God, Sarah," Cordelia cried. "Look at this pair of earrings! They're awesome!"

Sarah shook her head. "Awesome? They're just little plastic owls."

Cordelia nodded. "Yeah. And they're totally *awesome*."

"Okay," Sarah said. "You win."

Chapter 6

Sarah sat on the edge of her bed, looking around her room and seeing nothing. In the space of a very few minutes her entire life had changed irrevocably.

In the past few days she had tried to hide her worries, but she hadn't been entirely successful. Cordelia had noticed that something was on her mind, and if Cordelia had noticed, then it was likely Sarah's mother had, too. Sarah was sorry for that. She had hoped not to alarm her friends or her family until there really was something to be worried about.

The fact was that she had missed her period. Now, this was not entirely unusual; she had never been really regular, something to do with her being so thin a doctor had said, but now, because she and Justin had been having sex for the past two months, this missed period was a huge and very frightening thing.

So that morning she had asked Justin to drive her to a drugstore a few towns away. He had not asked her why she wanted to go to that particular store. Justin wasn't a very curious person, and for once, Sarah was grateful for that.

She had been in an agony of embarrassment and shame as she got out of his car. She wasn't even sure she would be allowed to buy a home pregnancy test. Did she need to be eighteen? Did she need to have a parent with her? How, she wondered, could she not know these things? She was sure the health teacher at school must have talked about what rights a teen did and did not have, but for the life of her, she couldn't recall a single word on the subject.

Once in the store she stood before the selection of home pregnancy kits. How did you *choose?* Every brand claimed an accuracy of close to one hundred percent. Were they lying? Finally, Sarah chose the brand that cost the least. The girl behind the counter made no comment on her purchase, whether through ignorance or politeness Sarah didn't know and didn't care.

"Got what you wanted?" Justin had asked when she slid into the passenger seat beside him.

Sarah had managed a smile. "Yes," she said. "Thanks."

When he asked if she wanted to get something to eat, she had claimed a chore her mother had asked her to get done sooner rather than later. Justin had just shrugged and driven her home. There was, she knew, a football game on television that afternoon. Little else mattered to Justin when there was a football game on television.

She returned to an empty house. Her mother had left a note saying she had gone over to the Kanes and that Stevie was at a friend's and wouldn't be home until dinner.

Slowly, Sarah had walked upstairs to the bathroom. She felt like how she thought a prisoner might feel going to her execution, hoping for but not expecting a reprieve.

Minutes later, she learned that she was pregnant.

She knew without a doubt that it was true. Even though the sensible thing to do would be to confirm the news with another test, the kit hadn't been cheap and why bother when she knew as well as she knew her own name that this test result, however unwelcome, was fact.

She wrapped the evidence in toilet paper and buried it in the trash can in her room. Of course, her parents would have to know, but the last thing she wanted was for them to find out by accident.

This wasn't how her life was supposed to be at all. She was not supposed to be having a baby with someone now, especially someone who was not John Adams to her Abigail. She did not love Justin. She had liked him. She *still* liked him. He was goofy and funny, by accident or by design Sarah couldn't always tell, but she found that she really enjoyed that about him.

And she had been so intensely, insanely attracted to him. She still was.

Until she met Justin, she had never thought she was the type to be shaken so thoroughly by passion. It wasn't the sort of person people in Yorktide knew her to be. She was reliable, responsible Sarah Bauer. She was not the sort to lose her head over a boy. Cordelia Kane, unkind people might say, was just the sort, a bit shallow minded, a bit ditzy. And very unkind people might say that she looked the part, blond and voluptuous.

But no, plain, skinny, serious Sarah Bauer had been the one to fall madly in lust with a nineteen-year-old goof-off. She had managed to hold Justin off for almost four months before his increasingly ardent advances and her own strong emotions had finally led her to agree to have sex. Not the kind they had had a few times already. The kind that could make you pregnant. The kind that *had* made her pregnant.

And now, she would have to tell him. She didn't know exactly what he would say, but she knew that he would not be happy.

Sarah put her hands over her face. A pregnancy was beyond her worst nightmare. Honestly, her worst nightmare had only involved disappointing her parents by not getting into a good enough college. And with great bitterness Sarah realized that like all sixteen-year-olds—like all *children*—she had believed herself to be invincible; she had believed, against all reason and proof, that she might very well live forever, certainly not die in a fiery car crash because she was texting, nor fall through the ice on a pond where it was illegal to skate and drown along with her friends, and certainly not get pregnant because she hadn't been extra, extra careful. Or because she hadn't said no.

"Stupid," Sarah muttered behind her hands. "You are a stupid, stupid girl."

Chapter 7

Adelaide, her hands on her hips, surveyed the empty shop. The Busy Bee would reopen soon, with limited hours of course, but there was still much to be done in preparation for the opening. It was amazing how much dust could gather even in a closed space, and the shop needed to be aired out, too.

She began to unpack the bag of cleaning supplies she had brought with her from home, her mind wandering back to an article she had read recently on The Huffington Post. The writer had gone on at some length about the American culture of easy, irresponsible sexuality. In the writer's opinion, sex had been systematically devalued to the point where it was a nasty and not very funny joke.

Look at all the celebrities and politicians acting badly, she had pointed out, taking pictures of themselves half naked in suggestive poses and sending them out to the masses via social media. Even the ones who were married and parents, or worse, underage, indulged in what the writer called "irresponsible and downright cheap" behavior.

The article had made Adelaide wonder. Did people really still believe that a woman's power was solely associated with her ability to seduce men, not with intellectual and financial success, not with the accumulation of wisdom? A brief look at the magazines being sold at the grocery store would seem to confirm that a lot of people still *did* believe this. It was a sickening, not to say embarrassing, state of affairs.

And Adelaide was worried about her daughter coming of age in such a trashy culture. She and Jack had always tried to arm Cordelia with information so that when she was out there alone in the world and faced with decisions regarding her well-being, she would know enough to make the right choices.

But sometimes, well, more than just sometimes, Cordelia just didn't *think*. Adelaide looked at the bottle of bleach in her hand and remembered the time Cordelia had decided to do a load of laundry and had mistakenly used bleach rather than detergent. Everything in the load had been ruined. And just about a month ago, she had seen the mail truck coming down the road and, eager for a package from Zappos, she had run out to meet it, locking herself out of the house in the process. Frankly, Adelaide dreaded the day Cordelia would get her driver's license. It wasn't that she would be purposefully reckless. It was just that she might not be as cautious as she should be.

Cordelia was a wonderful person with a very big heart, but Adelaide worried that very heart might lead her into trouble. Cordelia might rush into a situation where someone with a bit more common sense—someone like Sarah—might spend a moment studying her options before deciding to act.

Still, Adelaide was reassured by the fact that Cordelia wasn't boy crazy. She *liked* boys, but she didn't seem to want to date them yet. Whatever the reason—a slow-to-develop libido or a high sense of self-esteem—Adelaide was grateful for it. Unless, of course, Cordelia was afraid of sex. A certain degree of fear, mixed with a certain degree of curiosity, was normal. After all, sex was an unknown, and the unknown should be approached with a degree of caution. But an inordinate, paralyzing fear might prove disastrous for her future. Adelaide wanted her daughter to have a healthy, normal sex life, one unencumbered by superstitions or shame.

And then Adelaide laughed out loud. Superstitions? Shame? Cordelia was as normal a kid as you could get! And she wasn't a rebellious type, either. Even when she was a toddler, she had been remarkably easygoing, and her passage into the teenage years had been outstandingly free of trauma.

But here was an interesting question, one also posed by the irate author of the article. Was sex still considered rebellious, or was it so ubiquitous that to *not* engage in sexual activity at sixteen was seen as odd? Adelaide didn't really know the answer to that question. People lied all the time about their private behavior, and for all sorts of reasons. Some might claim they were having sex when they were not. The opposite might be true for others. It seemed a wonder that scientists could ever learn anything useful from their human subjects.

Enough speculation. Adelaide picked up the feather duster, attached its long handle, and got to work on the upper shelves and light fixtures. Housework of any sort could be mind-numbingly boring, but it did have the advantage of also being mind-soothingly easy.

Chapter 8

"Can I have the milk, please?"

"May I," Cindy corrected.

Stevie rolled her eyes but smiled as she did it. "May I have the milk, please?"

The Bauers made it a point to have dinner together. It was something that Cindy's family had done, as well as Joe's, and it seemed like a good tradition to maintain. At the very least, it was an easy way to keep tabs on their children. Like this evening, Sarah seemed subdued, not that she was the most high-spirited of girls normally. Still, Cindy thought she had something on her mind.

"Are you feeling all right, Sarah?" she asked.

"Oh, fine," Sarah said promptly. "Yes."

"Everything okay at school?"

Sarah nodded. "Everything's great."

Cindy let it drop. She hoped that all was well between Sarah and her boyfriend, Justin. He seemed like a nice enough young man, respectful of Sarah as far as she could tell, and polite to her and to Joe the few times they had met him, but Cindy had never really been able to understand what Sarah saw in him. She was clearly more mature than he was and much, much smarter. By his own laughing admission, Justin had barely made it out of high school. Still, he had a decent job with a small commercial fishing concern; it required some skill and a lot of brawn, and he had that in good measure. Cindy knew nothing bad about his family, nor did Joe. In fact, she really didn't know much of anything about the Morrows. No news was good news, it was said.

Frankly, Cindy and Joe both felt pretty confident that once Sarah finished high school and set off for college, she would break up with Justin. The idea of an early marriage had never once occurred to either of them. The idea of their responsible older daughter getting pregnant had also never once entered their heads. Cindy had talked to Sarah about abstinence and birth control, and the schools had provided information and even free condoms. (Joe had mixed feelings about that.) A smart, educated girl like Sarah just wasn't at risk.

Still, Cindy would have preferred that Sarah hadn't gotten involved with Justin Morrow in the first place. A smarter boy would have been better, and no boy at all would have been ideal. (Look at Cordelia Kane, for example. She was just fine without a boyfriend.) But children had minds of their own, and no matter how disconcerting that fact was, it was best to accept it sooner rather than later.

"Pass the butter, please?" Joe asked. "And don't let Miss Clarissa get at it on the way."

Clarissa, as was her habit, sat on a stool next to Stevie's chair. Joe's warning was a joke; Clarissa's table manners were impeccable. She liked to drink her water from a glass, not a bowl. She was a terribly sophisticated feline.

"Oh, I'm going to need new cleats for soccer this spring," Stevie said, after giving Clarissa a bit of her halibut. "I can't squeeze my feet into the ones I have now."

"Why is sports equipment so expensive?" Cindy asked rhetorically. "Well, if you need them, we'll get them. You can't be running up and down a field with blistered feet."

"This girl on my team had a really bad blister, and it got infected. She had to go to the emergency room to have it lanced or something. She said it was unbelievably painful."

"Maybe we shouldn't be talking about lancing blisters at the dinner table," Cindy suggested. "Sarah?"

Sarah looked up from her plate. Her peas were now all in a straight line. "I'm sorry?"

"Are you sure you're feeling well? You're awfully quiet this evening."

"I'm sure." As if to prove that she was indeed feeling well, she scooped up the line of peas with the aid of her fork and knife and put them into her mouth.

Well, there was no point in pressing Sarah when she didn't want to share her feelings. The girl could be beyond stubbornly quiet. She was in that way like her father, but to the nth degree.

"Dessert anyone?" Cindy asked brightly. Unlike the answers to lots of questions in life, Cindy thought, the answer to that question was always simple and straightforward.

Chapter 9

"Grrr," Cordelia said to her bedroom.

She was sitting at her desk, supposed to be doing her homework, but her mind kept wandering. This was not unusual—her mind enjoyed wandering; in fact, it was one of her greatest skills!—but at this particular moment, Cordelia found it annoying. And it was all Sarah's fault.

Really, she had been so distant lately. Not exactly moody but less like she was actually paying attention to what you were saying. Cordelia wouldn't be surprised if it had something to do with Justin the Idiot. Sarah had been seeing him for over five months now. Five months too long! Okay, it wasn't as if Sarah spent all of her time with Justin. She and Cordelia still hung out a lot. But the fact that Justin existed as Sarah's boyfriend was like—like an itch you just couldn't reach no matter how hard you tried. Cordelia frowned. Well, something like that. She had never been good with metaphors or similes.

Frankly, Cordelia didn't know why Sarah had ever bothered with him. Okay, he was cute in that hunky sort of all-American way (like Channing Tatum), but he had absolutely no sense of style! Well, neither did Sarah. They both pretty much lived in construction boots and no-brand jeans. No matter how often Cordelia had tried to tempt her friend into buying a T-shirt that actually fit or a pair of sandals with heels, she had failed.

Now, Stevie, on the other hand, looked awesome pretty much all the time. Not that Cordelia always liked what Stevie was wearing (those black bracelets with all the spikes were, in Cordelia's opinion, kind of harsh for life in an idyllic small town in Maine), but at least Stevie *cared* about her appearance. At least she used her appearance to make a statement about herself. Well, to be fair, Cordelia thought, maybe that was what Sarah was doing, too. And Sarah's statement was: My appearance doesn't matter to my sense of who I am. Cordelia thought that was a bit boring, but she would never voice her opinion to her friend. It would sound as if she was criticizing, and Cordelia really believed that people should live and let live.

Except when they went out with the Idiot.

Well, Cordelia certainly couldn't predict the future, but she had a pretty strong feeling that Justin Morrow wouldn't be around for that much longer. Sarah was going to go on to college next year, and she would be so busy with her course work and new activities she just wouldn't have time for a boyfriend who, Cordelia thought, probably couldn't even spell his name correctly. Okay, maybe that was a bit unfair, but her point was well taken. In Cordelia's opinion, her best friend had it in her to do pretty much anything she wanted in life. She could probably even become president of the United States except for the fact that she was kind of a loner and didn't like crowds. Someone like that just didn't stick around with a guy whose greatest ambition was to meet one of the players from the Red Sox or the Bruins.

Not that Cordelia wouldn't mind meeting, say, Robert Pattinson in his vampire makeup, or Johnny Depp in his pirate makeup. She most definitely would, but it was not her highest or her only ambition.

At the moment her only (if not highest) ambition should be to finish the homework still not done, but now, for some reason, all she could think about was the half of a homemade chocolate cake sitting in the fridge. Even a small slice would do. Maybe a medium slice.

"A girl's gotta do what a girl's gotta do," she said aloud, and went down to the kitchen to put the beast to rest. One large slice ought to do it.

Chapter 10

The stars seemed very high and very bright, like brittle shards of glass, like a sprinkling of crystals. Sarah looked up at them through the window of Justin's car and was amazed that given the dread secret she was keeping she could still respond to the beauty of the night sky.

Justin had picked her up after dinner. He had wanted to go to his apartment, but Sarah suggested they go to the diner in the next town of Taylor's Well. While she wanted privacy for what she had to tell him, she also feared being alone with him. She simply couldn't trust herself. He might talk her into another act of foolishness—sex—and that would only drag her further down into an already terrifying emotional hole.

Justin had obliged (he was easygoing; you could say that about him), and now they were sitting in a small booth at the back of the diner. There was an old farmer at the counter nursing a cup of coffee. A couple about twenty-five years old or so sat at a table near the door eating pancakes. Otherwise the diner was empty.

Only one waitress was on duty, a stout, older woman named Jackie with a ready smile and an air of reassurance about her. She immediately reminded Sarah of the Aunt Bee character on those really old Andy Griffith shows. For one insane moment, Sarah wondered what Jackie would say if she spilled her secret to her, if she begged her for help, for a secret place she could hide until the baby was born and then . . .

"What can I bring you?" Jackie asked brightly.

Sarah ordered a cup of tea, though she doubted she could swallow anything; she had hardly been able to eat her dinner. Justin ordered a soda and a piece of devil's food cake. Sarah waited until Jackie had brought their drinks and Justin's dessert and gone off to check on the other customers. She had to clear her throat twice before the words would come out.

"Justin," she said. "I have something important to tell you."

"Wait a minute, babe. I'm getting a text from Buck."

"Justin," she said, feeling her heart begin to race. "Please. It's really important."

Justin sighed, smiled, and put his cell phone on the table. "Okay. I'm all ears. Whassup?"

Sarah leaned forward over the table. "I'm pregnant."

She leaned back. Justin's expression remained fixed for a long moment. He still wore that anticipatory smile. He must be in shock, she thought. She wondered if she should say it again, but then, the smile was gone.

"Oh, shit," he said.

"Justin."

"Okay. Sorry. I mean, wow."

"Yeah," Sarah said with a small, bitter laugh. "Wow."

Justin shook his head. "But I thought that when nothing happened right after the condom broke . . ."

Sarah bit back an angry reply. *God,* she thought, *how stupid can he be?* What had he thought would happen? That her belly would immediately swell to gigantic proportions? Oh, what had she been thinking?!

"Have you told your parents yet?" he asked now, toying with his fork.

"No. I wanted you to know first."

"Oh." Sarah thought he looked confused, as if he truly couldn't understand why he should be so privileged. "So," he said after a moment, "are you going to keep it?"

"Not 'it,' " she corrected, still holding firmly to her patience. It would serve no purpose to fight with Justin, not now.

Not now when she needed him. "The baby. And yes, I am going to keep him. Or her."

Justin put down the fork. "Huh," he said. "Look, are you sure you shouldn't consider an abortion? I mean, that would solve everything. And I could help with the cost. I have some money saved, not a lot, but how much could it be, right? A couple hundred dollars?"

"I don't know," Sarah admitted. "I think it's more than that. But—"

"And I could ask my boss for an extra shift or something," he went on, excitement in his voice. "Maybe pick up another job at night for a while, just until I get enough money to pay for, you know, it. My buddy Jim's uncle runs an overnight delivery service. I think he ships lumber. He sometimes needs guys on a Saturday night to drive trucks down to Vermont."

Sarah looked at his flushed and expectant face and sighed. "No, Justin," she said.

"Why not?" Justin smiled. "I like wood."

"It's not about the lumber, Justin. It's that an abortion is out of the question."

Justin sat back heavily in his seat. "Oh. Are you, like, one hundred percent sure? Because you wouldn't even have to tell your parents about it. We could keep it a secret, right?"

Sarah felt slightly sick to her stomach. She realized that she had no clear idea of the legalities involved. Was she too young to have an abortion without her parents' permission? Would everybody, even strangers, have to know? But those questions were irrelevant.

"I'm not having an abortion, Justin," she repeated. "That's final."

Justin sighed. He rubbed his face. Sarah noticed that his nails were dirty. He had forgotten to clean them again. Still, they were wonderful hands, masculine, and . . . Sarah closed her eyes, remembering his hands cupping her face when they kissed.

"Okay," Justin said. "Then I'll marry you."

Sarah opened her eyes. For a moment she wondered if she had heard him correctly. But she knew that she had. She also knew beyond a shadow of a doubt that he really didn't want to get married to her or to anyone at this point in his life. He was only nineteen; he had laughingly admitted more than once that he didn't act very mature for his age. His boss had told him that, too. So had his teachers in high school.

More to the point, Sarah thought, *she* didn't want to get married to Justin or to anyone else, either, not at the age of sixteen. The idea was appalling. Marriage, if it happened at all, was for *after* you went to college and traveled to someplace exotic and then came back and got a good job.

Still, a part of her was touched by Justin's offer, as insincere and impulsive as it probably was. After all, it *had* come only after he had urged her to get an abortion.

"Oh, Justin," she said finally, her eyes tearing just a little. "Thank you, but that won't work."

"Why not?" he asked, leaning forward again. "I mean it. I'll marry you."

"I know that you would. But . . ." And for one little second, Sarah hesitated. It might be all right, at least for a time. A solution to the problem of having a baby all alone. But then what? Where would they be five years down the line? Forget about five years. What about five months? "No," she said firmly. "It wouldn't be right for either of us."

Justin picked up his fork again and stabbed it into the devil's food cake on his plate. "So what are you saying?" he asked, scowling down at the mess he was making.

"I . . . What do you mean?"

"You don't want me around the kid. That's it, right?"

Sarah shook her head. "No, Justin, that's not what I mean," she protested. "I just . . . I just don't want to get married."

"To me."

Sarah couldn't speak for a moment. Finally, she said, "Yes. To you."

"The father of the kid."

"No, Justin—" Sarah reached across to take Justin's hand, but he pulled it away. The fork clattered to the table. Sarah flinched.

"Well," he said finally, refusing to meet her eye, "I guess I'm supposed to say something like, don't worry. I'll be there for you anyway."

"Yes. I mean, if you want to say it. I know I'm going to need help, a lot of it, but I don't really know what kind yet."

"Right." Justin suddenly looked up and around the diner. Sarah wondered if he was afraid someone had overheard the conversation. Well, what if they had? It wouldn't be long before everyone in Yorktide and even in Taylor's Well knew that Sarah Bauer was pregnant.

"I think I'm probably due some time in August," she said.

He briefly looked back to her. Then he made a show of checking the time on his cell phone. "Look," he said. "I gotta run now. I forgot I got a work thing." In one swift move, he was on his feet.

Sarah swallowed painfully against the lump suddenly lodged in her throat. Justin didn't work in the evenings. He was lying to get away from a supremely uncomfortable conversation. If only *she* could run away from the conversation—from everything—so easily.

There was one more thing she had to ask, though she would have bet all the money she had that she already knew the answer.

"So," she said, when he was about to turn away. "I guess we're not going out anymore."

Justin gave a bitter little laugh, and his face flushed with what Sarah was afraid was anger. "Uh, well, yeah. I mean, you don't want to marry me. Why should I hang around to be your boyfriend? Why should I hang around at all?"

"Because . . ." But how could she explain to him what he should already know? "It's okay," she said. "Anyway, I'll let you know about—things."

"Sure, whatever. Take care of yourself, Sarah."

And then he was gone.

Sarah sat alone in the booth, very still, for some minutes, before she became aware that the waitress was hovering over her shoulder.

"You okay, honey?" the woman asked. "Your friend left in kind of a hurry."

Sarah managed a smile. "He had to go to work," she lied. She paid their bill, leaving Jackie a generous tip. Justin seemed to have forgotten they owed money for their drinks and cake. He also seemed to have forgotten that he had driven her to the diner in Taylor's Well and that short of calling her parents to come and fetch her, she had no way to get home other than to walk the four miles in the cold and dark.

Or maybe he hadn't forgotten at all. Maybe he was punishing her. Maybe he was really, really angry that she had turned down his offer of marriage. Maybe he was really, really angry that she had ruined his life.

Sarah zipped up her parka and pulled her wool hat down over her head. She walked slowly out into the frosty January night and turned toward the Yorktide road. She had gone only a few yards, just out of the welcoming lights from the diner, when a huge sob escaped her. *Oh, please,* she prayed, to whomever was there to hear. *Please don't leave me all alone!*

Chapter 11

Adelaide was going through her closet, looking for just the right thing. She and Jack were going out to dinner at one of the few restaurants that stayed open all winter. They didn't go out often, but they both believed in what Jack called the "restorative power" of a good, old-fashioned date. After more than fifteen years together, their sex life was still vibrant. The biggest fight they had ever had had been over tying up the garbage bags. Jack had insisted that knotting the ends of the bag was the way to go. Adelaide had argued that using a twist tie was safer. Afterward they had both laughingly admitted to having been really, really hungry when the argument broke out.

Adelaide wasn't entirely sure why they got along as swimmingly as they did (she loved that expression), but she wasn't about to waste time analyzing the relationship. If it ain't broke, don't fix it, that was her motto, at least when it came to her marriage.

She chose a navy silk blouse to wear with a tan wool skirt. Classic, elegant, and if she left the top buttons of the blouse unbuttoned, a wee bit provocative. A memory of her mother wearing a navy silk wrap dress popped into her head. She remembered feeling in awe of her attractive mother, and a bit shocked at the sexy figure the dress had shown her mother to have. Her parents must have been going out somewhere very special.

Nancy and Tom Morgan had often gone out alone together

in the evenings. They had taken vacations alone, too, leaving the teenage Adelaide at home with a neighbor. From the time she had been old enough to be conscious of her role in the family, Adelaide had felt like an afterthought. Not unloved, just—unnecessary. She supposed that she had been a "mistake," or, if not, that soon after her birth her mother and father had realized that she was a sort of third wheel, a sometimes cumbersome part of what had been a smoothly functioning unit of two. It explained the fact of Adelaide's being an only child.

For Adelaide and Jack, having only one child had come down to a financial decision. They had wanted a certain lifestyle for their family and though all sorts of unexpected things might happen along the way to undermine that level of comfort, by choosing to limit the size of their family they could exercise some small control over the future. One education, one person to feed, clothe, and indulge, one wedding, maybe even one trip to Europe—it would all cost a lot less than providing for two or three people. The principal of a small-town high school and the owner of a small, seasonal shop were never going to bring in the big bucks.

Adelaide finished dressing and went over to the jewelry box on her dresser. She chose the pearl stud earrings Jack had given her for an anniversary, her favorite long gold chain, and a gold link bracelet her parents had given her when she graduated from college. The black pumps would have to stay home; winter boots were the only logical choice. Adelaide smiled when she thought of how Cordelia grumbled so loudly about being forced to live in big ugly boots for four months a year. She wouldn't be surprised if someday her daughter moved to Los Angeles just so she could wear sandals and heels year round.

So unlike Sarah! Since the age of three, Cordelia and Sarah had been inseparable, opposites who seemed to thrive on their differences. Cordelia had been a chubby, cherubic toddler and had never entirely lost that air of cuteness and innocence. Sarah, on the other hand, had always been spare and lean and serious, an old soul in a child's body. At sixteen she carried herself with the air of a much older person. Standing next to Cordelia, she looked years older, rather than only months.

It would be wonderful, Adelaide thought, if the girls always remained friends. Things would change over time and maybe drastically, but that didn't mean they would *have* to abandon the relationship. Of course, that happened so often in life. Adelaide couldn't even remember the name of her best friend from grammar school and they had been joined at the hip for eight years.

Marriage was one of the factors that might come between the girls, and for all sorts of reasons. Sarah, she thought, would probably marry later in life if ever. She wanted to make a real difference in the world, and marriage could still inhibit a woman's freedoms. It was sad, but true.

On the other hand, Adelaide suspected that Cordelia would be married by the time she was out of her twenties. She would probably have two or three children eventually and be super active with the PTA and . . .

Adelaide almost laughed out loud. It was a total waste of time to guess at the future. For all she knew, Cordelia would suddenly undergo a spiritual revolution and run off to Tibet and become a nun, if American women were allowed to become Tibetan nuns. It was doubtful, but you never knew in life. The future would sort itself out in its own way no matter how much input you gave it.

There was a knock on the bedroom door. "Adelaide?"

She opened it to find Jack, dressed in the tweed blazer and dark slacks that she loved and looking very handsome and dapper in that English gentleman sort of way.

"You look lovely," he said, reaching out to take her hand.

"Thank you," she said with a smile.

Chapter 12

Cindy was in a very good mood. Joe had just gotten paid by one of his biggest clients—and on time at that!—putting them a bit ahead of the game, and the night before they had talked about using the money to replace the fridge and very possibly the oven. Both had been repaired more than once, and the warranties had long been out of effect. A new fridge and oven were hardly glamorous purchases, but Cindy was excited nevertheless.

Life was really pretty good. The girls seemed happy and were doing well in school. If the family didn't have a new car every two years and if they couldn't afford to take vacations very often (well, who needed them when you lived in such a pretty place?) and if putting the girls through college was going to take almost superhuman effort, so be it. Cindy and Joe had each other, a nice house, good kids, and steady jobs. And, soon, they would have new appliances!

Cindy gave the coffee table a final wipe with the polishing rag and left the living room for the kitchen to make a cup of tea. *Good old fridge,* she thought, taking the milk out of it. Whatever features came with their new one, the most important would always be the door on which Cindy could post photos.

She smiled as she looked at the picture of Cordelia and Sarah taken on the first day of kindergarten. Cordelia's mouth was wide open in laughter. Sarah stared directly at the camera, her mouth closed. They had made a funny little pair, Cordelia bubbly and always chattering away, Sarah pensive and quiet. Still, they seemed to thrive on what the other offered. Cordelia made Sarah laugh with her unconsciously dramatic personality. Sarah kept Cordelia from bumping into furniture and running out into the street without looking first for cars.

Cindy poured a bit of milk into her tea and took the cup to the table. The girls had been so good about letting Stevie tag along with them once she was mobile. But that stage hadn't lasted for long. Stevie had always been independent, even more so than Sarah. Though she made friends easily enough, she had never been terribly close to any of them. Even now, Stevie didn't have a best friend; she got along equally well with a group of three girls with whom she spent her free time. Cindy smiled. Correction. Stevie *did* have a best friend. The best friend had four legs and a tail and could leap onto the top of the bookcase in Sarah's room in a single bound. Cats really were pretty extraordinary, Cindy mused. She had never lived with one until the year Stevie was three and Joe had brought home from the local shelter a six-year-old orange tabby in need of love and attention. By the time Stevie was five, she was in complete charge of Orangey (the name had been her decision), and even when his kidneys began to fail a few years after that, Stevie had proved to have nursing talent well beyond her years. When Orangey died, Stevie had mourned, but within a month she had asked her father to drive her to the shelter. They had come home with Clarissa, that very pretty little tortoiseshell with the very big personality.

Stevie had never talked about what she wanted to be when she grew up, but Cindy thought she might become a veterinarian. She guessed that with people's obsessions with their pets, Stevie would eventually be financially secure.

Sarah, of course, would also be successful, whether she went into the law or nursing. There was never any doubt in Cindy's mind that her older daughter would do something important with her life. There was also never any doubt that both girls would marry men like their father, kind and decent and hardworking. Cindy hoped they would stay in Maine, if not in Yorktide itself, but her girls were smart and curious and creative. They might not find the perfect opportunities waiting just down the road. She would hate to live far away from her grandchildren and miss the small and special occasions of their growing up, but Sarah and Stevie would know what was best for their families.

Cindy shook her head at her own folly. What was the point of worrying about or trying to predict the future? The right now kept her busy enough.

Chapter 13

"Hey, Cordelia!"

"Hi, Cassie!"

Cordelia loved the social aspect of school. She had gone only a few yards down the hall after leaving French class and already she had been greeted by three people. Really, the friendliness made any negatives seem not so bad after all. Even gym class was tolerable because she could sneak a commiserating chat with the other kids in the class for whom sports were boring, embarrassing, or downright impossible.

A harsh laugh alerted Cordelia to a knot of kids up ahead by a stand of lockers. She knew it meant trouble even before she identified one of the kids as Corey Bohan, a notorious bully who, unlike a lot of male bullies, was usually smart enough not to get caught. "Not this time," Cordelia muttered under her breath as she strode toward the group.

As she grew closer, she saw the object of Corey's unwanted attentions, a freshman named Martin something or other. *Poor kid,* Cordelia thought. He had bully magnet written all over him, from his too skinny arms to his bad haircut (clearly his mom or dad had done it), from his mouth full of braces to his too short pants.

"Hey, Martin!" she said loudly, causing both Martin and his would-be tormentor to jump. "I was looking for you. I need help with my laptop. Do you have some time to look at it now?"

Martin smiled gratefully and nodded. Corey (*and really,*

Cordelia thought, *he could use a better haircut, too, not to mention a shower*) glared at her for a moment, and then abruptly walked off. His cohorts trailed behind him, muttering empty threats. *Idiot,* Cordelia thought. She would bet money that Corey would be spending his adult life stuck in some minimum wage job he would barely be smart enough to keep.

"Great," she said to Martin. "Let's go."

Cordelia led Martin toward the library. Fact was she really did need some IT help, but even if she hadn't, she would have lied to get Martin safely out of a bad situation. Her father had talked about something called "moral proximity" one night at dinner, and it had really struck a chord. It was the idea that when you were faced with someone in need of help, you had a moral obligation to help them simply because you were there and a witness to the situation. Well, her father had put it more eloquently, but Cordelia didn't need to talk about it, just to put the idea into action. She hoped that if someday she were witness to something really horrific, like what those people at the Boston Marathon had experienced, seeing people blown apart just feet away, she would have the courage to act.

Martin worked his magic on Cordelia's computer and left the library blushing with the pleasure of an accomplishment recognized and valued. Cordelia followed soon after and headed for her final class of the day. Along the way, she kept her eye out for her father.

She hardly ever saw him during the day, but on occasion they would catch each other's eyes across a crowded hallway. Seeing him always made Cordelia smile. Her father was a great guy; even the kids who regularly got in trouble thought so. Well, if they thought otherwise, they weren't telling her, but Cordelia knew that his methods of correction (he didn't like the word *punishment*) were fair and most often they worked.

Cordelia stopped outside the door to geometry class. It most definitely was *not* her favorite subject. Still, there were only four and a half months left of school and then no more sine and cosine and problematic angles and complicated formulas.

Sure, she would probably have to work at The Busy Bee during the summer, but not every day. There were far worse places to work, but she kind of enjoyed grumbling about it anyway. Her mom knew she was only kidding around.

And then, senior year would begin, and it would be so much fun. She and Sarah had been looking forward to it since the start of junior year. Well, it was mostly Cordelia who had been psyched about the parties and the prom and the overnight trip the class would take to Augusta. Sarah was much more subdued a person. She was the sort who calmly took each day as it came, although she was also the sort to plan ahead and to always have a few Band-Aids in her backpack "just in case." In short, of the two, Sarah was the more mature one; everybody could see that.

"And now *I've* got to be mature," Cordelia murmured, "and go inside!"

Cordelia survived the class, as she knew of course that she would, and left the building with a spring in her step. *Wow,* she thought. *Look at that!* The sun was actually shining through the gray cloud cover. Okay, it wasn't as if you could feel its warmth, but there it was, if you looked hard enough. Summer was still a very long way off, but nevertheless, Cordelia's spirits lifted. Better times were coming, and by better, she meant warmer and brighter weather and some awesome new clothes to go with it.

"Hey, Cordelia!"

"Hi, Thomas!"

Cordelia waved and headed toward the waiting bus.

Chapter 14

Cindy and Joe and Sarah were in the kitchen, seated around the table. Stevie had gone to a friend's house after dinner to watch a movie. It was only six thirty, but it had been dark since four. The house felt very quiet.

Sarah noted that her parents looked tired. Her mom had been at the quilt shop most of the day, cleaning for the reopening. Her dad never took a day off, unless he was really sick, and as far as Sarah could remember that had happened only once. He had even gone back to work hours after he had broken his wrist a few years back.

She took a steadying breath. This was the hardest thing she would ever have to do. By comparison, telling Justin that she was pregnant had been a breeze. And that was because she truly loved her parents. She respected them. She cared what they thought of her, far more than she cared what Justin thought of her. What Justin *had* thought of her, once upon a time.

Her mother spoke. "You said you wanted to tell us something."

"Yes." Sarah squeezed her hands together in her lap. She looked at her mother; she couldn't bear to look at her father. "I'm going to have a baby," she said.

Neither parent said anything. There was a dull and uncomprehending look on her mother's face. At least, that's how Sarah read her expression. She still couldn't look at her father.

"I mean," she went on, "that I'm pregnant."

Her mother twitched, as if a switch had been thrown, bringing her back to life. "I know what you mean," she snapped. Then she slumped a bit in her chair. "I'm sorry. I shouldn't have . . . oh, God, Sarah, are you sure?"

Sarah nodded. "Yes," she said. "I took a test."

Her mother leaned forward. "A test? Only one? So that means—"

"No. I mean, I know. I'm sure. I just am."

For what seemed like an eternity, no one moved or said a word. Finally, Sarah's father shifted in his chair and her mother put her hand to her chest as if to calm the beating of her heart.

Sarah felt tears spring to her eyes. "I'm so sorry," she cried. "I don't know what else to say. Except, please, please forgive me."

"Now, enough of that," her father said, in what Sarah thought was a remarkably even tone. She glanced quickly at him, and he gave her the ghost of a smile.

"Is the . . . is Justin the father?" her mother asked.

Sarah nodded. "Yes. I told him a few days ago."

"And? What did he say?"

"He offered to marry me."

"Oh, Lord!"

"Don't worry, Mom," Sarah said hastily. "I said no. I knew he really didn't mean it. And I don't want to be married to him, either. And he offered to help pay for an abortion, but I told him I was going to have the baby."

Sarah glanced again at her father. His lips were now compressed into a fine thin line.

"Where do you stand with him now?" her mother asked.

Sarah looked down at her hands, folded in her lap. "Nowhere, I guess. We're not together, if that's what you mean."

"So he's walking away?"

Her father's voice was tight now. Sarah was surprised he hadn't burst out with a violent stream of abuse against Justin. Not that she had ever seen her father lose his temper, not even when another driver cut him off or when a client cheated him out of part of his fee. But this was something far worse.

"He said he would be there for me." Sarah winced at the lie. That wasn't what he had said, not really.

"What does that mean, exactly?" her mother asked.

"I don't know." *But that's a lie, too,* Sarah thought. She knew very well what it meant.

There was another terribly uncomfortable silence until finally, her father spoke. "Well, that's that," he said. "Cindy, you get Sarah to a doctor. We've got a lot of planning to do, what with a new baby coming along."

He got up from his seat and leaned down to hug Sarah where she sat hunched beside him. Then he squeezed his wife's shoulder and left the kitchen.

The worst, Sarah thought, as a shudder of relief ran through her, *is over.*

Or else, it had only just begun.

Chapter 15

How in heaven's name did a person accumulate so much stuff? Adelaide sighed and tapped the stack of papers that would go into the recycling bin. Even though she straightened her desk several times a week, there always seemed to be a handful of unwanted and unnecessary—well, garbage.

But this advertisement for a college loan program could stay. She and Jack had been saving since Cordelia was born, but there was never any harm in reevaluating their game plan. Adelaide hoped that the Bauers were being as proactive as she and Jack were with Sarah's education fund. But it wasn't something she could ask without sounding as if she were criticizing.

Anyway, figuring out how to fund a college education sometimes felt like learning an exotic and very slippery language. Adelaide doubted anyone could really tell what would happen. Sarah, for example, had the better grades, though Cordelia, with her involvement with the school newspaper (she wrote the weekly social column) and her participation in the Teens and Elders program (once every two weeks a group of kids were bused to a local home for seniors where they read to the residents or played cards or simply talked), might be considered more well-rounded and might therefore be more eligible for scholarships. Cordelia's family had more money than Sarah's; Sarah might be considered more eligible for financial aid. But who knew? They would just have to wait and see which girl was awarded what opportunities. *One thing is certain,* Adelaide thought with a smile. *Neither girl is ever going to get an athletic scholarship!*

Adelaide looked at the framed photo of the girls on the shelf over her desk. Next to it sat a photo of Cindy and Adelaide at The Busy Bee, on the occasion of the store's fifth anniversary. *Hmmm,* Adelaide thought. Maybe the four of them—or the five of them if Stevie were interested—could take a girls' excursion before the summer season hit hard, and Adelaide and Cindy would be glued to the shop. Just a day trip, maybe to the Farnsworth Art Museum or to the Winslow Homer Studio in Prouts Neck, or even just up to Portland. They could easily spend a full day in the city, visiting the museum, shopping, taking a tour of the Longfellow House, and having lunch somewhere fun. There was a good French-style bistro she had read about, though it might be a bit too pricey for Cindy and her girls. *Well,* Adelaide thought, *there is nothing wrong with fish and chips!*

The thought of fish (if not chips) brought to mind Sarah's boyfriend, Justin. *He* hadn't gone to college. In fact, to hear Cordelia talk, he had barely graduated high school. There was certainly no love lost between Cordelia and Justin Morrow. She called him the Idiot.

"Now, Cordelia. Why would Sarah go out with an idiot?" Adelaide remembered asking.

Cordelia had just shrugged. "Don't ask me. But she is."

True, the relationship was a bit curious, but Sarah seemed happy, so she must be getting something from all the time she spent with Justin. Sarah wasn't the sort to waste her time with someone entirely lacking in merit.

Yes, Adelaide thought, she would suggest to Cindy that the five of them take a day trip some Saturday. And if Saturday was the day Sarah usually spent with Justin, well, it wouldn't kill her to change her plans this once. Boys and men could wait.

Adelaide hefted the stack of wastepaper she had gathered and headed down to the basement, where the recycling bins lived.

Chapter 16

It was almost two in the morning, and Cindy was wide-awake. Joe was in a characteristically deep sleep; the man always slept soundly, no matter the worries of the day gone or ahead. Still, this time might prove an exception, so as not to disturb him with her tossing and turning and sighing, Cindy had gone down to the living room and was sitting there now in the dark, alone with her troubled thoughts. She didn't know how Sarah was sleeping and half expected to see her daughter glide into the room, wrapped in her warmest robe, a fuzzy orange thing she had found at Goodwill a few years back.

It seemed like a century since Sarah had told them she was pregnant, though in reality it was only a matter of hours. But in those few hours everything had changed radically. Assumptions had been proved faulty, assurances had been shown to be empty, and certainties had turned out to be uncertainties.

Cindy felt another wave of guilt overcome her. She had talked to Sarah about protection, but she hadn't forced her to go to the doctor to get a prescription for the birth control pill. She should have. She simply had never considered the possibility of Sarah's having sex without being completely prepared.

She had been stupid, Cindy thought now. And ignorant. She had put too much faith in her daughter; she had assumed Sarah was more mature than she had proved. Sarah was a teenager. No matter how smart and responsible she was she was still a child. Children weren't equipped to make the best decisions for themselves. That's why they were legally dependent until the age of eighteen. And even then they could act wildly and irrationally, take dangerous risks and shrug off the possibility of disaster. The sense of being fully human—flawed and mortal—didn't come until later in life. It just didn't.

"Oh, Sarah," Cindy whispered into the dark. "How could you have done this?"

The purchase of new kitchen appliances she and Joe had planned would have to be postponed, maybe for quite some time. *It was odd, wasn't it?* Cindy thought, staring into the dark. Only a day or two earlier she had been thinking about how she would hate to live far away from her grandchildren. And now, her first grandchild would be growing up just down the hall.

She was sure that for as long as she lived she would never forget the moment in the kitchen when Sarah had told them her news. Cindy had watched her husband's face carefully. He was the mildest of men, but neither of his children had ever been in such a situation before. She had felt suddenly afraid, as if for the first time in their marriage she had no idea of what her husband might do or say.

And Justin! He had told Sarah that he would be there for her. It probably meant nothing. Of *course* it meant nothing. Cindy felt a flare of anger so intense she thought for a moment that she would pass out. *Thank God Joe is retaining his composure,* she thought. *Because I'm not sure that I can.*

Cindy rubbed her eyes. She supposed that she should tell Adelaide the news very soon. Adelaide was her friend, she would support her through any trial, but still, telling her was going to be difficult. She didn't really believe that Adelaide would judge Sarah. It was just that . . . just that Cindy had never, ever expected the words "my sixteen-year-old daughter is pregnant" would be coming out of her mouth.

But they would be. And Cindy was sure that nothing would ever feel halfway normal again.

Chapter 17

"Could I have the carrots, please?" Cordelia asked.

"You can and you may," her father said, passing the bowl to her.

"How's Sarah?" her mother asked.

"She's fine," Cordelia said, spooning the carrots onto her plate, but she wasn't really sure that Sarah *was* fine. She was still being strangely quiet, not that she was ever boisterous, and Cordelia was now a wee bit annoyed. She had thought she was Sarah's closest friend, so why wasn't Sarah telling her what was wrong instead of making her guess and worry?

"It's just that I haven't seen her much in the past week."

Cordelia shrugged. "You know how she is. She gets—quiet—sometimes."

"I've been thinking," her father said now. "This family deserves some time off together, an entire week someplace this summer. That is, Adelaide, if you think you can leave the store in Cindy's hands."

"What a wonderful idea," Adelaide exclaimed. "And I think Cindy's totally capable of running the shop on her own. She might even enjoy the opportunity."

Cordelia restrained herself from clapping. Her mother had asked her not to clap at the table as she supposedly did it quite loudly. "Dad," she said, "that would be awesome! Maybe we could rent a house on the beach somewhere. But with a cool town right nearby, with great shops."

"Or we might rent a house on a lake," her mother suggested. "After all, we have a gorgeous beach right here. A change of scenery might be nice."

"As long as it's a lake with no bugs and a cool town nearby with great shops."

Jack grinned. "I'll do some research, get some ideas that work within our budget, and then we'll take a vote. I wouldn't mind a lake with a cool town nearby with a good sports bar. You guys can shop while I watch baseball. And sorry, Cordelia, but I don't think there's a lake on this planet without its share of bugs."

"Or there's Montreal," her mother said. "I've always wanted to go there."

"I might be able to use my French," Cordelia added. "But maybe not. Canadian French isn't the same as what we learn in school, is it?"

"No. But you'll still know more than I will, with only my half forgotten high school Spanish."

"And, of course," Jack said, "we'll have to be sure Cindy agrees to our little scheme."

"I'm sure she'd appreciate the extra money. Because, of course, I'd pay her for the extra duties."

"And she'll have Sarah to help her," Cordelia pointed out. "She's the most responsible person I know. Next to you guys, of course."

"Nice save, kiddo."

"Thanks, Dad. But really, this is going to be so much fun. When was the last time we all went away somewhere? I can't even remember!"

"Well, we did have that weekend in Boston last spring," her mother pointed out.

"Oh, right! The aquarium, the MFA, that seafood place. And the shopping!"

"Does having fun necessarily involve shopping?" Her father shrugged. "I'm just asking."

"Yes," Cordelia said firmly. "It most certainly does!"

Chapter 18

Sarah knocked on the open door to her sister's bedroom. Stevie, seated at her sewing machine, turned her head.

"Can we talk?" Sarah asked.

Stevie nodded and turned fully around. Sarah went in and sat on the edge of her sister's bed.

"Mom told me," Stevie blurted

"Okay." Sarah felt relieved. Breaking the news to Stevie was not something she had been looking forward to. Still, it would have been nice if her mother had let her know that she had already talked to Stevie. Was the pregnancy her mother's news to tell? Maybe it was. Sarah wasn't at all sure how much say she had in this situation. By being so careless, she might in effect have relinquished all control over her own life. It was a disturbing thought.

"I'm sorry," Stevie said now. She patted her leg, and Clarissa, who had been sitting at her feet, jumped onto her lap.

"Thanks. I mean, don't be sorry for me."

"Why not?"

Sarah struggled to find an answer that made some sense. "It's not all bad," she said finally. "I'll have a baby. I mean, I always knew I was going to have kids someday. Just not so soon."

Sarah became very aware of Clarissa staring at her, round green eyes steady and boring into her own eyes.

"Is he going to be around?" Stevie asked.

"Justin?" Sarah looked away from the unnerving gaze of her sister's cat. "No. I don't think so, anyway. Why?"

Stevie shrugged. "Just curious."

Sarah wasn't really sure what to say next. "You're going to be an aunt," she said finally.

"Yeah."

Stevie's tone was neutral. At least, Sarah couldn't tell if the idea of being an aunt appealed to her sister or not. Did being an aunt—a quasi figure of authority—mean anything to a thirteen-year-old? Should it?

The silence dragged on. Sarah realized that she felt embarrassed. Clarissa was still staring fixedly at her and that didn't help.

"I like your bracelet," she blurted. "Is it new?"

Stevie glanced down at her wrist. "Sort of. I made it a few weeks ago. They're amethyst beads. Mrs. Kane got them for me wholesale."

"That was nice of her. I wish I were creative like you."

"It's no big deal. Anyway, I guess a lot of stuff around here is going to change."

"I guess," Sarah admitted. "I'm sorry for that. A lot of babies keep everyone up all night. But I'll try to figure all that out before anyone goes crazy."

"I can wear earplugs."

Sarah smiled. "I'll buy you a whole box of them. And I'll never ask you to change a diaper."

"What about school?" Stevie asked. "What are you going to do about school?"

Sarah flinched. She suspected that an awful lot of people were going to be asking her that question. "I don't know yet," she said. "I want to finish high school. I have to. But college . . ."

"A lot of people go to college when they're adults. There are those places like Kaplan University. And you can get a degree online, too. Even a PhD I think."

All of that was true, and Sarah was thankful for Stevie's support, but it wasn't what she had planned; it wasn't what she had wanted. "Yeah," she said with an obvious lack of enthusiasm. "We'll see what happens."

Clarissa suddenly took it into her mind to leap off her perch on Stevie's leg and bound out of the room. Sarah startled.

"She always surprises me when she does that."

Stevie smiled. "Cats change their minds very quickly. They give no notice of it. None that humans can see, anyway. But I'm used to it."

I'll never be used to change, Sarah thought. *Not now. It will always be something I'll fear.*

"How do you think Clarissa will feel about the baby?" she asked. "I don't think cats and babies mix very well. And animals can get jealous of a new baby in the house. That's what I've read anyway."

"Oh, she won't sit on his face and suffocate him, if that's what you're thinking. But when he's able to crawl around, I think Clarissa will stay way off the ground."

"And it's you she loves, anyway," Sarah added. "Not me. She won't be jealous of the baby with you there to pay attention to her."

Stevie nodded. "She pays as much attention to me as I do to her. We take care of each other. Some people might not understand that."

Sarah thought about it. A baby was not the same as a cat or a dog; the relationship between a human and her pet was not the same as that between a human and her child. Still, like Stevie and Clarissa, Sarah and her baby would be in a relationship all their own, utterly unique, necessarily intimate, and even to some extent, mutual. She couldn't deny that it was a pretty exciting—and terrifying—prospect.

"I'd better get back to my homework," Sarah said, rising.

"Me too. Sarah?"

Sarah, at the door, turned back.

"It'll be okay," Stevie said.

Sarah felt tears prick her eyes. "Thanks," she said, and went back to her own room.

Chapter 19

Adelaide was concerned. Earlier in the day, she had found Cindy crying over her work. This was very unusual behavior; Cindy was probably the most emotionally stable person she knew. When Adelaide had asked her what was wrong, Cindy had just shook her head, wiped her eyes, and gotten back to her stitching.

But the tears began to leak again before long. "Why don't you cancel your afternoon lesson and go on home?" Adelaide, now truly worried, had suggested. "I can reschedule with Mrs. Brown for you."

"No, no," Cindy had protested again. "I'm fine. Sorry." Obviously determined to fulfill her duty, she had soldiered on through the remainder of the day, even instructing Mrs. Brown with a smile and her typical patience.

Adelaide thought it best not to mention Jack's idea of the Kane family taking a vacation that summer. Cindy didn't seem in the right mood to be receptive to the idea of running the shop on her own for an entire week. Besides, there was plenty of time. They hadn't made any definitive plans yet; they hadn't even decided if a house on the water (with nearby shops and a sports bar) was preferable to a week in Montreal.

And boy, by mid-summer she would need a break. She loved running The Busy Bee, but as with any business, there were innumerable stresses that could really add up to one giant pain in the neck. Difficult customers, orders gone missing, random plumbing issues (her landlord wasn't always great about keeping the building in good working order), unexpected overstock, and competition from sometimes surprising places.

No, owning your own business wasn't easy. And owning a retail establishment in a small town, even one that doubled as a destination location, meant that you had the added potential stress of dealing with any unhappy customers face-to-face outside of the shop, like in the grocery store or even in church.

Thank God Adelaide had Cindy as her right-hand woman. Adelaide shot a glance at her friend, wrapping up the lesson with Mrs. Brown. Her eyes were a little red and swollen, but otherwise there was no sign of her earlier distress.

Maybe, she thought, *Cindy was just having a very bad headache. That would explain it all.*

Chapter 20

Mrs. Brown had taken her leave with many thanks and a smile of accomplishment.

"She's so enthusiastic," Adelaide commented as they prepared to close up the shop for the day. "It must be gratifying to teach someone with such a positive attitude."

"Yes," Cindy said. It *was* gratifying, but Mrs. Brown's positive attitude didn't seem to matter much at the moment.

"Back when Jack was still teaching, he used to tell me how frustrated he would get when a student just didn't want to engage with the subject."

Cindy cleared her throat. "Yes. Adelaide, I have to tell you something."

Adelaide looked up from a piece of fabric she was folding. "What is it?"

Cindy took a deep breath. It was better to rip off a bandage than to slowly peel it back and prolong the agony.

"Sarah is pregnant," she said.

Adelaide's face paled. She dropped the bit of fabric and put her hand over her heart. "Oh my God."

"And she's going to have the baby and live with us."

"I'm sorry." Adelaide shook her head. "I'm having trouble taking this in. I never in a million years . . ."

"I know. On some level, I still think it's all a bad dream."

"The father . . ."

"Justin. Yes." Cindy managed a lopsided smile. "He offered to marry her. She said no."

Adelaide reached out and put her hand on Cindy's shoulder sympathetically. "No wonder you were crying earlier. I would be crying, too."

"It wasn't the first time I've broken down, I'm afraid. And it won't be the last, though I'm trying to be strong around the girls."

"How is . . . how is Joe handling this? He must be devastated. God, he must want to kill Justin. I know Jack would, if it were Cordelia."

"You know Joe," Cindy said, retrieving the fabric Adelaide had dropped. "He doesn't talk about what he's feeling. But I know he's heartbroken. I know he wants desperately to make everything better. I know he's horribly frustrated, too."

"Have you told anyone else?" Adelaide asked.

"No. Not yet. Well, except for Stevie. And Sarah said she would tell Cordelia soon, as well. Unless you think you should be the one to tell her?"

"No," Adelaide said promptly. "Let the girls talk about it first. I'm sure Cordelia will come to me afterward."

"And Jack will need to know, of course. Not only because he's a friend."

"Right. As principal of Sarah's school, well, she's one of his responsibilities, at least during school hours." Adelaide paused and shook her head. "My God, I don't think he's ever had a pregnant student before. Not that I know of, anyway."

Cindy failed to prevent a grimace. *And who,* she thought, *would ever have imagined that my daughter, reasonable, reliable, and straight-A student Sarah Bauer, would be the first?*

"I don't think there's a reason she couldn't continue on, at least through the end of the school year," Adelaide was saying. "And then certainly she would be welcomed back in the fall. Maybe it would be different if she were due during the academic year. She's not, is she?"

"I don't think so. Sarah estimates that she's due sometime in August. But we'll see what the doctor says."

"Yes, of course. Oh, Cindy, I wish I could . . . I wish I could wave a magic wand and make everything . . . different. Turn back time, something."

Cindy felt the tears begin to come once again. "But you can't," she said, "can you? None of us can."

Chapter 21

"So, I thought, well, I can justify spending forty dollars on a pair of mint green jeans if I use them as a neutral and not only as an accent. That way I get, like, twenty outfits instead of maybe only ten. Right? Sarah, did you hear a word I said?"

Cordelia frowned at her friend, who was sitting across from her on the second bed in her room.

"I have something to tell you," Sarah said.

I was right, Cordelia thought. *She didn't hear a word I said.* "Okay. What?"

"It's pretty big."

Cordelia regarded Sarah closely. She couldn't read her friend's expression and there was something tentative in her tone of voice. And she had been so—well, so weird—these past few weeks.

"What?" she said. "The suspense is killing me."

Sarah took a deep breath and said, "I'm pregnant."

Pretty big? This was colossal! Cordelia felt sick to her stomach, and tears seemed to spring from her eyes; if she had been wearing her glasses she was sure they would be wet.

"Oh, God, Sarah," she gasped. "Are you sure?"

Sarah nodded.

"Oh, God," she said again, "what are you going to do?" Congratulations, Cordelia felt sure, were not in order, not in this case. Sarah couldn't have wanted this, she simply couldn't have!

"I'm going to have the baby," Sarah said simply.

"And then what?" Cordelia asked, aware that there was an odd tone of pleading in her voice. "Are you going to keep it? I mean, him or her?"

"Yes. My parents agreed. I'll—I mean, we'll—live with them."

"Is . . . is Justin the . . ."

"Yes. Who else would it be?"

"I'm sorry."

"He offered to marry me."

"Oh." Cordelia really didn't know what to make of that. Maybe Justin wasn't such a bad guy after all. But . . .

"And I said no."

Cordelia nodded. She was still not entirely sure she wasn't having a particularly vivid nightmare. She wiped at her cheeks to clear them of the tears. "You're so young!"

"Well," Sarah replied sharply, "there's nothing I can do about that."

"But what about college? We wanted to go to the same college. What about our plans?" *Was that a childish and self-centered question?* Cordelia wondered. Probably, but she *was* childish and self-centered, so what? And suddenly her best friend was leaving her. . . .

Sarah looked down at her hands, resting flat on her knees. "I don't know."

Neither girl spoke for some time. Cordelia couldn't imagine what Sarah was feeling, but she knew for sure that what she, Cordelia, was feeling was bruised and beaten.

"I can't believe this is happening," she said finally. "Not to you of all people." *And,* Cordelia added silently, *not to me.*

Sarah laughed, but it was not a pleasant laugh. "Why not to me? I'm just like everyone else after all. Nothing special. Definitely not smarter."

"Don't say that."

"Well, it's true, isn't it?" Sarah snapped. "If I was smart, I wouldn't be in this mess, would I?"

Cordelia felt that whatever she might say right then would probably be wrong. She didn't like feeling so confused, so out of her depth. It made her feel as if she were on the verge of a panic attack. She had never had one, but she knew they could be seriously frightening.

"Do you know if the baby is a boy or a girl?" she asked after some time. It seemed like a neutral question, but what did she know. This was all violently new to her; this was the sort of reality that wrenched you from your safe and comfortable place in the world and threw you into a place that was dangerous and irritating.

"Not yet," Sarah said.

"Do you want to know?"

Sarah shrugged. "I haven't thought about it."

"Oh. How do you feel?"

Sarah laughed a bit again. "Fine. I'm not sick, you know. Just—" Her voice broke.

Just pregnant, Cordelia said to herself. *Just going to have a baby. Just going to be a teenage mother.* No, there was no *just* about it.

"I'll help you, you know," she said then. "With the baby, I mean. I'll do anything I can."

Sarah put her head in her hands and began to weep, long, deep sobs that tore at Cordelia's heart. She wanted to call out for her mother, for Sarah's mother, for anyone who could make it all stop, make this new and dreadful reality go away.

But she knew that no one could work such magic.

Hesitatingly, Cordelia crossed the room and sat next to Sarah on the bed. Sarah had never really been comfortable with demonstrations of affection. Cordelia remembered the time when they were little, maybe in kindergarten. They were in the public playground, and she had taken Sarah's hand like all the other little girls were taking the hands of their best friends. But Sarah had yanked her hand away. Cordelia had burst out crying. All these years later, she couldn't remember how they had gotten past that unhappy moment, but somehow Cordelia had come to understand that Sarah didn't really like to be hugged and kissed like so many other girls did. It didn't mean that she didn't feel love; it just meant that she could be awkward expressing it.

Now, Cordelia took a chance and put her arm around her friend's shoulder anyway. Maybe, with the old reality so exploded, Sarah would welcome the gesture.

She did. Sarah slumped against Cordelia, and after a time her sobs quieted. And Cordelia realized that in the space of a few moments she had become the strong one, the comforter, in their relationship.

Chapter 22

Sarah looked at her reflection in the mirror over her dresser. She didn't *look* pregnant. Her stomach and breasts were as flat as they ever were. It was so hard to believe there was a very tiny life growing inside her.

She turned away from the mirror, embarrassed by her own gaze. She had woken that morning to a feeling of intense resentment toward her unborn child. She had been horrified by the ferocity of those feelings and ashamed. She knew that this resentment was misplaced. No, worse, it was morally wrong. You could rarely say to another person, "It's all your fault that my life is a mess," and be right. How much more ridiculous was it to say that to an unborn child? The baby hadn't even been conceived when she had agreed to go to bed with Justin!

The baby, her baby, was the only completely innocent one in this entire mess and should never be made to pay for the mistakes of the adults. When a child was made to suffer for sins he had not committed, well, that was called child abuse, and it was absolutely and entirely intolerable.

Sarah felt sure that even Justin would admit that. He was not a bad person. He had even offered to marry her. But, for all his good nature, he was a coward.

She put her face in her hands, ashamed in her own presence. How could she have agreed to have sex with someone with such a weak character? It was disgusting. It was that "smart women making stupid choices" syndrome all over again. Would women ever break that pattern of self-sabotage and destruction?

Of course not. Women were human. Humans were seriously flawed. Sarah had never been in doubt of that.

She thought back to the first time she and Justin had had sex. It had almost happened before, but she had always pulled back at very nearly the last minute. Justin had always been so patient, so nice about it. At least, he had pretended to be. And then, when she had finally said yes, okay, it was Justin who had said no, let's wait until next time. And the next time they were together at his apartment he had brought in flowers from the grocery store and had lit a few half-burned-down candles and had even offered her a glass of white wine. She had said no to the wine but had been touched by his efforts to make the night romantic. And then, he had been so attentive. . . .

Now, the memories of that night brought only embarrassment. Cheap flowers, old candles, and wine offered to an underage girl hadn't meant romance at all. They certainly hadn't meant love.

Sarah lifted her face from her hands and with a sigh continued to dress for school.

You reap what you sow. Sarah thought about those words as she pulled a sweatshirt over her head. The effect was the result of the cause. The pregnancy was her responsibility; she was its cause. So was the pregnancy also a punishment of some sort? Or was that superstitious thinking? If so, where had it come from? She had never succumbed to superstitious thinking before.

You made your bed; now lie in it. Was that sort of the same thing? You made a choice, so whatever the result of that choice, it was yours to own and survive.

Sarah reached for her backpack and checked that it contained the books she would need for that day's classes. Such a mundane activity, when her entire world was spinning out of control!

She wasn't sure she had ever felt real guilt in her life before now. Sure, she had felt sorry on occasion, like when she disobeyed her parents (that had only happened once that she could recall) or the time she had tripped that girl in second grade (it had been an accident, Sarah hadn't seen her coming, so she hadn't brought her foot out of the aisle and back under her desk), but not real guilt like she felt now. She knew how hugely her pregnancy would affect her parents' lives. And she was so, so grateful to them for having accepted it the way that they had. But at the same time, she was so, so ashamed to be causing them such trouble.

"Sarah! Breakfast is ready!"

Sarah cringed. How strange it felt, her mother making her breakfast as if she were still a child. But of course she was still a child, one who would be making breakfast for her own child before long.

She had absolutely no appetite, but for the baby's sake, for *her* baby's sake, Sarah went down to the kitchen and cleared her plate.

Chapter 23

Jack and Cordelia had left for school, Jack at six thirty, in his car, and Cordelia some time later, on the school bus. Adelaide sat alone at the kitchen table. Her head ached. She had taken three ibuprofen and had drunk a second cup of coffee, but the pain persisted. Well, of course it persisted. Its origins weren't physical. No amount of stimulants or anti-inflammatory medications were going to budge a pain that had its source in her heart.

Adelaide was in awe of Cindy's relatively calm acceptance of her daughter's situation. She wished that *she* could be so sanguine. But that was impossible because the news had sent her headlong into her own tumultuous, largely secret past.

At the age of seventeen, Adelaide had gotten pregnant.

To say that she hadn't had parental support would be an understatement. Her parents had been furious that she had "screwed up" and were completely unwilling to disrupt their own lives to raise a grandchild. To be fair, they were in their mid-fifties at the time, still working hard to build a good retirement nest egg, and enjoying a healthy social life, which included travel with other couples whose own teenage daughters were definitely *not* pregnant.

Adelaide had barely graduated from high school when she learned the devastating truth. It had come as a sickening shock. She had been looking forward to starting college in the fall. She had lined up a good summer job as an administrative assistant in a local accounting firm to boost her savings. And now, everything was ruined.

Her boyfriend, on his way to Harvard that autumn and already planning a career in international journalism, had wanted nothing to do with the baby. In fact, he had offered to pay for an abortion. After dumping her, of course. An abortion was something Adelaide's mother also had encouraged.

Thinking back, Adelaide realized that she wasn't sure her father ever knew that his wife had been urging their daughter to have an abortion. He wasn't the type of man to talk about "feminine" things. In fact, he hadn't said a word directly to her during those awful months of the pregnancy, other than "Good morning," "Where's your mother?" and "Good night." Safe verbal offerings that couldn't be misinterpreted or misunderstood even by the most emotionally distraught person.

Adelaide had felt she had no choice but to go through with the pregnancy and arrange to give the baby up for adoption.

It had been very, *very* odd, carrying a child she would never come to know as a person. It had been very, *very* difficult. At times, she had felt frantic for the baby to be gone on his or her way to the adoptive family. At other times, she had thought, wildly, that she would abandon her plans for a "normal" life and run away to raise the baby on her own, far from the condemning eyes of her parents.

And during those long months, people would ask her questions, innocuous in themselves, that made her feel as if she had been hit by a brick. "Oh, are you having a boy or girl?" "Have you chosen a name yet?" "Do you have the nursery set up?" And all she could do was to shrug and shake her head and silently answer: "There is no future here. What you're looking at when you see me is soon to become the irretrievable past. The baby is going to be someone else's future. He or she will be someone else's child to name and to nurture."

It had almost driven her mad.

She had hardly left the house in the final months of the pregnancy, so miserable was she, so desperate to hide herself away from probing questions and curious looks, and worse, the pity she suspected too many people felt for her. The pity she felt she didn't deserve.

In the end, of course, she had toughed it out and survived. And after the baby had been born and taken away, Adelaide had begun her college career, a semester late and more determined than ever to succeed in building a life for herself.

But over twenty years later, she was still wondering if her decision had been a selfish one. Of course, to some extent it had been, but it also had been made in the baby's best interest, too. Or, what Adelaide deemed would be in his best interest. *His* best interest. Though she hadn't wanted to know the sex of the child, she had found out when a chatty nurse let the bit of information slip. This had upset her terribly. She had felt that the less she knew about the child, the easier it would be to let him go.

Adelaide sighed and rubbed her temples though she knew the attempt to ease the pain was futile. These thoughts and memories would come, and she had learned that it was better to let them visit without protest.

So many times over the years Adelaide had been tempted to search for her baby's father. She wondered if Michael Baker had succeeded in becoming a journalist of renown. She had never come across his name in print, but then again, she wasn't entirely familiar with international news sources.

But each time the curiosity had arisen, she had asked herself what good it would do to know that her baby's father had married, fathered children, gotten divorced, and then remarried to someone significantly younger. What good would it do to learn that he had won a prestigious prize for his work and written a best-selling book? What would any of that information gain her? The answer was—nothing. Michael Baker hadn't wanted anything to do with her or the baby all those years ago.

He certainly wouldn't want anything to do with either of them now. *Leave it be, Adelaide,* she had told herself. *Leave it be.*

It was better that Michael Baker forever remain a figure of Adelaide's long buried past. Except when he came vividly to mind, like he had now, with the news of Sarah's pregnancy.

Slowly, Adelaide got up from the table. She would go back to bed for a while. She was very, very tired.

Chapter 24

"Cindy? Good to see you."

It was Mrs. Armstrong. Cindy knew her from The Busy Bee as well as from a reading group she had belonged to briefly. (She had dropped out because she hadn't liked the choice of novels. She had found most of them very depressing. Why did some people equate literature with misery?)

"And you, as well," Cindy replied, forcing a smile. Ann Armstrong was a perfectly nice woman, but Cindy just wasn't in a mood to talk to anyone.

"Seems like the grocery store is our entire social life in winter, doesn't it?" Ann noted. "What with most of the restaurants closed until spring and the bad weather keeping us indoors most days."

Cindy agreed, and Mrs. Armstrong moved on in search, she said, of some sort of marginally healthy food that would entice the appetite of her terribly fussy seven-year-old daughter.

Cindy wheeled the cart down the aisle stocked with diapers and wipes, jarred food, formulas, supplements, and snacks that promised everything from increased mental powers to physical perfection. She tried not to look too interested in the products; if anyone she knew saw her, suspicions would be aroused and rumors would start to circulate that one of the Bauer females was pregnant. Still, she looked closely enough to determine that none of it was inexpensive, neither the necessary items like food, nor the optional items like wipes soaked in moisturizing lotion.

Cindy moved on. At the end of the next aisle, she spotted the reverend from the local Episcopal Church. Quickly, she turned her cart around.

Before long, everyone would be asking her about Sarah. Some would hesitate before speaking, painfully aware of the delicacy of the situation. Some would offer ready sympathy and support. Others, the gossips, might just be looking for any bit of information, good or bad, they could spread to others. And there would be pity.

And why not? Cindy believed that Sarah deserved to be pitied.

Cindy checked her shopping list. She still needed cat food, bread, and paper towels. On her way to the paper products, she passed the aisle containing greeting cards, magazines, wrapping paper, cheap stuffed toys, and Mylar balloons. There were cards for grandmas and grandpas. There were cards for grandchildren. Blue bears and pink bunnies, yellow flowers and happy sentiments, glitter and scrolling print.

Cindy walked on. She had always expected to be a grandmother at some point down the line—she assumed that most mothers did—but certainly not before her fortieth birthday. It seemed somehow . . . what was the word? Well, it definitely seemed odd.

In fact, to some degree, it seemed like only yesterday that she had been caring for Sarah and then Stevie as small children. She remembered how much energy it had taken, how much patience and courage it had required. She remembered the nasty colds and the bouts of fierce flu and the raging fevers; she remembered the routine bumps and scrapes; she remembered the time Stevie had broken her arm falling out of a tree; she remembered Sarah's sprained wrist the time she had fallen off her bike. She remembered the easy times, too, the fun times, but they loomed less large at the moment.

And now there would be another small Bauer to care for

and watch over. Because even though Sarah would be willing, Cindy knew that so much of the baby's welfare would be up to her. She felt tired just thinking of what lay ahead.

Cindy wheeled her cart to the check-out counter. She had only two coupons today. She would be using a lot more coupons in the time to come. Now, she haphazardly stuffed them into her wallet where they often remained until well after their expiration date, but maybe she had better get serious about creating a filing system and carrying it with her.

The sky looked ominous as Cindy left the store. Hurriedly, she loaded the bags in the trunk of her car and slid behind the wheel. As she pulled out of her spot, she saw a teenage girl pushing a shopping cart onto which she had balanced a baby carrier. Was the baby hers? Or, maybe, it was her mother's child or a sister's or even an aunt's. Maybe the girl was babysitting.

But Cindy didn't think so. Something told her that this teenager was the baby's mother. The girl and child disappeared through the automatic sliding doors as Cindy turned the car toward home.

How would the girl pay for her food? Was she married? Had she had to drop out of school?

That will be Sarah someday soon, Cindy thought, her lips compressed tightly, her hands gripping the steering wheel. And people would wonder what had brought that tall, skinny girl to that point of being a parent. They might wonder if the girl's parents had abandoned her. They might shake their heads in pity or in self-righteous smugness. And there would be nothing Cindy could do about the speculation, however kind, however mean.

Chapter 25

Cordelia was lying on her bed, staring up at the ceiling and wishing for the umpteenth time that she could have a dog or even a cat (though she would rather have a dog, a smallish one with white fur like that unbelievably adorable one in the dog food ads). If she had a dog (or even a cat) to cuddle with right now, she just knew she wouldn't feel so lonely. If only her mother wasn't so insanely allergic!

Pinky, her old stuffed unicorn, would have to do. Cordelia had taken him off the shelf where he lived and brought him into bed with her. She looked at him now with fondness. His horn was a bit askew, and cuddling had permanently flattened some of his fur. She still thought he was beautiful.

And a lot easier to take care of than a baby! Everyone knew that a baby took every single moment of a mother's attention; a baby required constant and vigilant care. Everyone else in a mother's life fell by the wayside, at least for a while. Fathers didn't have it quite as bad. Fathers who stuck around, that is. Not fathers like Justin Morrow. *And let's face it,* Cordelia thought. *Even though Justin had offered to marry Sarah, no one who knew him even a little bit could believe that he would go through with it.*

Cordelia sighed. Why couldn't everything just have stayed the way it was? Now, when she and Sarah went back to school in the fall, Sarah probably wouldn't have the time or the money to participate in all the fun senior year activities with her. Cordelia would have to make new friends. . . .

And how exactly would *that* happen? By senior year, everyone was already paired up or embedded in a tightly knit social group. Sure, Cordelia knew she was well liked, and she didn't have any doubt that some of the other girls would probably welcome her along when they hung out at the mall or went to the movies. Which was fine, but Cordelia was not someone who could live without a best friend with whom she could share secrets and jokes and the boring little details of daily life and celebrity crushes and all the other essentials, both large and small, that best friends shared.

Cordelia sighed again. No, it just wasn't fair.

Okay, she knew this wasn't about her, and yet, it *was* to some degree about her, wasn't it? Everything you did or said or experienced in some way affected the lives of the people close to you. It certainly wasn't like Sarah had set about getting pregnant, but she *had,* and so now her parents and her sister and her best friend and even her best friend's parents were involved whether they wanted to be or not.

Like babysitting. Cordelia supposed she would be doing her share of that, like when Sarah had to be somewhere, like at work or at the dentist. She supposed that for the first time ever she would absolutely have to act responsibly. You couldn't take chances with a baby. You couldn't forget that she was in the room and use bad words in case somehow they got absorbed in her unconscious and left a negative impression. You couldn't play your favorite music too loud when a baby was around because you might damage his hearing. You couldn't smoke or drink alcohol (not that she did either) when a baby was in your care, for all sorts of obvious reasons. You couldn't take a sleeping pill or a painkiller, even one prescribed by a doctor, because you might not wake up if the baby was choking to death on one of his toys.

Cordelia pushed Pinky's horn back into place. It flopped back again. She wondered if her mother knew about Sarah yet.

If she didn't, she would soon. Maybe it wasn't Cordelia's news to share, but she needed to talk. Maybe her mother could help her make some sense of it all. But what could her mother say—what could anyone say?!—to make Sarah un-pregnant? And Sarah *not* being pregnant was the only thing that would cause the world to make sense again.

With a sigh, Cordelia got off the bed. She really had to start work on that paper for English class. It wasn't, as her father would say, going to write itself. She reached up to put Pinky back on his shelf, but then changed her mind and set him against the pillows on her bed. She had a feeling she was going to need more of his plushy companionship in the weeks and months to come.

Chapter 26

It was very cold, well below freezing. Sarah was dressed in a thermal undershirt, a wool sweater, a parka, long johns under heavy jeans, wool socks under boots, a hat, scarf, and gloves, and still the cold had made it through such defenses and into her bones. What was exposed of her face burned, and her fingers were beginning to feel dangerously heavy and numb.

She didn't feel the sense of peace she usually felt when she was out alone in the woods behind her house. Maybe that sense of peace was gone forever. *Don't be silly,* she told herself. *Don't be so gloomy. Of course things will get better again.* But only after they got much worse. At least, much more difficult than they had been.

And all because she had screwed up very, very badly. How had it happened? How had she acted so outrageously out of her nature?

Sarah's foot slipped on an icy stone, and she grabbed a dangling branch to steady herself. She caught her breath and continued on. *Maybe,* she thought, *that nature hadn't been real.* Maybe she had appropriated it, like an actor assumes a role. Responsible. Cautious. Reasonable. Maybe that had never been the real Sarah Bauer, only a facade, only the words other people had used to describe their version of her, and she had believed them.

Could that be true? Or could she be mentally ill? Could she have a split personality or schizophrenia? Because in all of her sixteen years, she had never felt so massively disoriented, so horribly alienated from the self she thought she had been.

A cardinal alighting from a branch on a tree just up ahead caused a fall of powdery snow. Once, she would have delighted in that sight, a slash of intense, living red against a background of gray and white. Today, she seemed to be seeing it through a murky veil.

Only that morning, while still in bed, she had asked herself if having sex with Justin could have been an unconscious act of teenage rebellion. No, she had decided, it *couldn't* have been! What was there to rebel against? She had had everything she needed, and more importantly, everything she wanted. And she had *not* wanted to get pregnant. Oh, why hadn't she said no to Justin? Why hadn't she waited, at least until she was eighteen and out of high school!

Sarah felt a little sob escape her. Well, she knew the answer to that question. She had been so very attracted to him, so compelled to be with him, to touch him and to be touched by him, that in the end she hadn't been able to say no. She hadn't *wanted* to say no.

She knew that Justin should never have suggested they have sex. He was the legal adult. He should have acted like a man and not a boy, but he hadn't. He hadn't cared enough about her to resist his own impulses. He had been thrilled when she had finally agreed. He had told her that she was awesome.

That word again!

Sarah carefully negotiated a jumble of stones that had once been part of a wall marking off a farmer's land and felt a surge of righteous indignation flood her veins. Just because she had committed an irresponsible *act* (having sex with only a condom), didn't mean she was an irresponsible *person*. It was on the order of, I told a lie, but I'm not a liar; I committed a crime, but I'm not a criminal. A person couldn't be entirely defined by one action, could she? No. That wouldn't be fair at all. And there was context, too, and background to consider. Pressures a person was under, a precipitating crisis, even unexpected physical duress might propel a person to do something out of character.

Or was that all lazy rationalization?

She was so, *so* worried that the people she had known all her life—her teachers, the regular customers at The Busy Bee, the man who owned the local fish market where her family shopped, the senior librarian at the public library—would assume that because she was a pregnant sixteen-year-old she was unaware of the enormity of her situation. She was so, *so* worried that those people would see her as only a negative stereotype.

She had never realized until now just how conscious she was of her reputation. It should be enough—shouldn't it?—to know that you were a good person. Why was it so terribly important that you prove it to virtual strangers?

But maybe that was just human nature. People needed to be viewed as decent and upright even when they were neither—or maybe, especially when they were neither.

Oh, *why* couldn't you turn back the clock after you made a big mistake?! Why?! Everyone deserved one big erasure, one complete do-over, didn't they? But no one in this world got one, unless they were extremely powerful and had the money and the connections to buy back the appearance of innocence and virtue. Like politicians and celebrities.

Sarah came to an abrupt stop and buried her face in her gloved hands. She stood there for a long time, her mind sinking into a kind of torpor. Finally, the throbbing of her frozen fingers and toes got through to her sluggish brain, and she turned around and headed toward home.

There was nothing out here for her, she realized wearily. Not the vast blue sky or the trees laced with snow or the birds on the wing. Nothing.

Chapter 27

Adelaide shifted on her stool. Her back had been hurting her a lot lately; it might be time for a newer pair of Duck Head shoes. She had given up heels years earlier, keeping only two pairs, one black and one tan, for "occasions" that never seemed to happen. And honestly, even if someone they knew did decide to throw a big party for a graduation or a milestone birthday, "occasions" in Maine didn't usually require heels or anything resembling formal attire.

Adelaide realized that she had been stirring her cup of tea for several minutes. It was probably lukewarm by now. She considered putting it into the microwave for a moment but didn't have the energy to get up and cross the room. These past days, since she had learned about poor Sarah, she seemed to be alternating between brief states of frantic energy and long periods of great lassitude. And then, there were the headaches.

Heavy footsteps alerted Adelaide to Cordelia's impending arrival. "Mom," she said when she arrived in the kitchen, "I need to talk to you about something. I mean, I have to tell you something."

Before Adelaide even saw the look on her daughter's face, her tone of voice, almost sepulchral, told her what she needed to know.

"I think I might know what it is," Adelaide said. "Come, sit down."

Cordelia dropped onto the stool next to where her mother sat. "I don't know how to say it. It's awful. It's the worst thing that's ever happened."

"Let me help you then," Adelaide said. "I had a long talk with Cindy, with Mrs. Bauer."

Adelaide watched as her daughter literally sagged in relief. "So you know about Sarah?"

"I do."

"I thought I was going to throw up at first. I mean, I don't think I ever felt more shocked in my life."

"Shocked is certainly the word," Adelaide agreed. "I know it can happen to anyone but . . . Sarah? It just doesn't seem possible. But it is, and we have to do all we can to help the Bauers."

"Sarah said she's keeping the baby."

"I know."

Cordelia clutched her head with both hands. It was a gesture she had been fond of since she was a little girl. "I . . . I can't imagine it. Having a baby at sixteen. Well, I guess she'll be seventeen by then but still. It seems—surreal. Is that the right word?"

"It'll do. It's a life-changing thing," Adelaide said, as if speaking to herself. "Well, having a baby at any time changes everything, but especially when you're so young and alone."

"But Sarah *does* have her parents. She's not really alone."

"Oh, yes, of course. They'll be a huge help." *But,* Adelaide thought, *the toll it will take on them will be enormous.*

"I wonder how Stevie feels about it," Cordelia said.

"Oh, Lord, I'd forgotten all about Stevie! Poor thing, I hope she doesn't get entirely lost in the mix. Not that Cindy and Joe would purposely ignore her, but their attention is certainly going to be focused on Sarah."

"And on the new baby."

It was suddenly twenty-one years earlier. Adelaide's baby, only moments new to the world, a helpless, howling little being, was at that very moment being taken from her. Adelaide put a hand over her eyes in a futile attempt to hide the tears coursing down her cheeks.

"Oh, Mom, don't cry! If you start, I will, too!"

"I'm sorry," she managed after a moment. "It's just so sad."

"I guess you've told Dad."

"Of course," Adelaide said, wiping her eyes with a tissue. "Sarah's not only a family friend, but she's also one of his students. He's devastated. And knowing your father, I'm pretty sure he feels he's in some way responsible."

"But how could he be?" Cordelia asked, shaking her head.

"He isn't, but he'll think he should have paid more attention to the fact that Sarah was dating an older boy. And a boy like Justin, too. So—so silly. Your father remembers Justin from when he was a student a few years back. Always goofing off. Well, maybe we all should have paid more attention. The adults, I mean."

"So you think Mr. and Mrs. Bauer feel guilty, too?" Cordelia asked. "I mean, for letting Sarah date Justin."

Adelaide desperately wanted to steer the conversation away from the topic of parental responsibility. It would only bring on more bad memories of how her parents had virtually washed their hands of her and her "stupid mistake." "Maybe," she said. "Well, I hope that they *don't* feel guilty. They're wonderful parents to those girls. And they couldn't have known. . . ."

"Yeah." Cordelia groaned. "Mom, I just don't know what to do. I mean, how am I supposed to help? Maybe Sarah doesn't even *want* my help, but I feel like I need to do something, not just sit around and . . . and wait!"

Adelaide put her arm around her daughter's shoulder. "I think we're just going to have to take things as they come. There's no game plan for a situation like this."

"That's for sure. But you know what? There *should* be! There should be a huge book of game plans somewhere, with the solution to every problem that could ever come up!"

Adelaide couldn't help but laugh. "Maybe someday there will be," she said. "But I doubt it."

Chapter 28

Cindy had finished cleaning the bathroom and was almost done vacuuming the upstairs hall. She didn't mind vacuuming, but cleaning the bathroom was her least favorite household chore. Still, it would be good to have a second one. In a few years' time, there would be a fifth person using the one toilet and shower and sink.

Cindy sighed. If only they had enough money to add a powder room or, better yet, a half bath on the first floor. Joe could do the job for less than it would cost if he had to hire a contractor. But they would still have to pay for the fixtures and the services of a professional plumber and where would they *put* the bathroom, anyway? Well, Joe could figure that out, too—if they had the money for the project.

Cindy turned off the vacuum, wrapped the cord around the handle, and placed it back in the hall's narrow linen closet. She closed the closet door and looked from one bedroom to the next. Where would the baby sleep? Well, in Sarah's room, of course. There was just room enough for a small crib. Then again, maybe it would be better to have the crib in the master bedroom. Joe probably wouldn't mind, and Sarah would have a bit more peace and quiet to do her homework, because she would have to finish high school. There was no question in Cindy's mind about that. Of course, a crib on wheels would allow them to move the baby from room to room. . . .

It was one more question to be decided.

Cindy went downstairs to the kitchen to make herself some lunch. There was some sliced ham and Swiss cheese for a sandwich. As she took the bread out of the breadbox and the mayonnaise out of the fridge, she thought about how the day before she had found Sarah sobbing on her bed. The sight had been disconcerting. Sarah hadn't broken down like that since she had witnessed a tiny bird fly into the living room window and die on the ground below. That had been nine or ten years ago.

Cindy had sat on the edge of the bed, soothing her as best she could, smoothing back her hair, murmuring comforting words.

"Mom," Sarah had said, her voice thick, "I'm so scared."

She hadn't been able to tell Sarah that she, too, was scared, that her father, too, was frightened of what might come. Sarah might be on the brink of becoming a parent, but she was Cindy's child, Cindy's responsibility to comfort and encourage for as long as Sarah needed her. Which looked like it could be for a very long time.

Cindy had felt in that moment just how much she missed her own mother. Oh, how she could use her strength, her calming presence, and her everyday practical wisdom, of which she had had an ample store.

"Are you very sure you want to keep the baby?" Cindy had asked.

Sarah had nodded.

"You don't want to talk about an adoption?"

"No."

Cindy had felt enormously relieved. She believed that adoption was a fine and reasonable option. It just wasn't an option she wanted for her daughter or for their family.

Finally, exhausted, Sarah had fallen into a sleep that Cindy could only pray was peaceful, untroubled by dreams of what might have been or, more frightening, of what was to come.

Cindy brought her sandwich to the table and sat. Suddenly, she felt ravenous. She finished the sandwich in record time and debated making another one. Only the thought that Sarah might want the remaining ham and cheese as a snack when she got home from school restrained her.

Chapter 29

"Those earrings are okay," Cordelia murmured. "But not worth thirty dollars!"

Cordelia was killing time online. A cool pair of sneakers from Zappos and a neon orange statement necklace she found on the *Lucky* magazine site came in at numbers one and two on today's wish list. Still, she wasn't getting quite the satisfaction she usually got from virtual shopping, which was a bummer.

Cordelia exited the Internet and sighed. She felt restless and discontent. Sarah hadn't wanted to hang out with her that afternoon after school (she said she needed to be alone and think about things), and as much as Cordelia had been disappointed, she had also been kind of relieved. The fact was that she felt a bit awkward with Sarah now. It was like her friend had become a stranger overnight, the same on the outside (not for long!) but so very different on the inside.

And *that* was all Justin Morrow's doing!

And the bum was walking around Yorktide like nothing earth-shattering had happened! Sure, he had offered to marry Sarah, but that was a joke. Everyone knew he was just a big goof-off. Cordelia wondered what she would say or do if she bumped into Justin one day. Maybe she would just turn around and run away. It wasn't that she was afraid of him—ha!—it was just that when she thought of coming face-to-face with him a big bubble of anger seemed to well up in her chest.

She felt like she might punch him in the nose! She had never before felt an urge to violence but then again, no one had ever hurt someone she loved so badly. Cordelia Anne Kane, Avenging Angel. It had a certain ring to it. She almost smiled.

Not that she condoned violence as a means to an end, of course. Her parents were strictly pacifistic, and she had inherited their views on physical and verbal abuse. Still, the thought of Justin walking around all innocent as if he had done nothing wrong to Sarah made her furious. And the injustice of it made her feel helpless.

Cordelia went over to her bed and sank down with a sigh. She reached for Pinky and held him to her chest.

Justin had probably thought he was so wonderful, giving Sarah all those stupid little trinkets. If it were she (and no way would it ever be because any guy who wanted to go out with her was going to have to give her *real* gifts, gifts that were worth something, gifts he had to sacrifice to afford!), she would have destroyed every ugly troll doll and every ridiculous plastic heart, torn them apart and then burned them and then buried the ashes. And then stomped on the ground to make sure the ashes never saw the light of day ever again.

Cordelia sighed and remembered the conversation she had had with her mother the previous evening.

"Did you know that Sarah was having sex with Justin?" her mother had asked her.

"I had no idea," Cordelia had admitted. "I mean, I guess I should have known it was a possibility but . . . but I just didn't think it was something Sarah would be doing."

"Because she's so smart?"

Cordelia had shrugged, embarrassed. "Because she's Sarah. I know that sounds ridiculous. I mean, just because someone doesn't act all flirty or boy crazy or . . ."

"Yes. Everyone is a sexual person. Some people choose not to cultivate or to emphasize that part of themselves, but that doesn't mean they aren't sexual beings."

"And she never said anything to me about . . . about what she and Justin did when they were alone."

"Some girls might have been dying to tell all to their best friend," her mother had noted. "But certainly not Sarah."

"Mom," Cordelia had asked, "do you think if she had told me, if I had known what was going on, I could have, I don't know, talked her out of it or made sure she had birth control or something?"

"You might have been able to counsel her, but in the end, it still would have been her decision to have sex with Justin."

"I guess. But what if she had told me she was having sex or even that she was only thinking about it? Would I have been under an obligation to tell you? You know, because she's only sixteen?"

Her mother had considered a moment before answering. "That's a tough question," she had said finally. "You certainly wouldn't have been wrong to tell me, though I'm not sure you would have been under an obligation to say anything. Of course, the question then becomes, would I have had an obligation to tell Sarah's mother? And yes, I think that I would have, as a concerned friend."

Cordelia toyed with Pinky's tail (it was regrettably skinny these days). All the time Sarah had been fooling around with Justin, Cordelia had been in the dark! Okay, it wasn't her business what they did together, she knew that, but still, she felt kind of duped.

Why hadn't Sarah told her? Maybe she had thought Cordelia wouldn't understand, but what was there to not understand! Or maybe Sarah had thought that she was too immature to handle the information without, what, freaking out? Huh. Maybe, Cordelia thought, it was her own naïveté that was bothering her now, not the fact that Sarah had kept her personal life to herself.

Cordelia put Pinky back against the pillows and went to her desk. *Enough,* she scolded herself. *You have got to stop think-*

ing about Sarah and her mess and do your homework. Because if you don't, you'll have your own mess to deal with! She could see the headline in the school paper now. "Principal's Daughter Fails Junior Year. Laziness Suspected." It didn't have a very good ring to it.

Chapter 30

Sarah sighed. She had told Cordelia she needed to be alone, but that wasn't really the truth. She didn't really know *what* she needed.

She was sitting cross-legged on her bed with the pile of gifts Justin had given her over the course of their relationship. Once she had found them charming and sweet. Now she saw them as stupid, useless little things, a collection of tacky knick-knacks that were all that she had left of someone she had fooled herself into thinking was worthy of her.

Worthless trinkets. And yet, she wasn't ready to part with them. Not yet.

Sarah picked up her cell phone and stared at the blank screen. In the last few days, she had sent Justin several texts but had gotten no response. She had called his cell phone, twice, and both times had gotten his voice mail. He had no landline, but she could, she supposed, write him a note and mail it. Assuming, of course, he wouldn't just throw it out unread.

It might be that he wasn't ignoring her. Maybe he was simply very busy with work, out on the boat, too far from shore for a signal to reach him. Which, of course, didn't explain why he hadn't gotten in touch once back on land. *Stop making excuses for him,* Sarah scolded herself. *Just stop it.*

Yesterday after school, she had been on the verge of calling his parents' house, but in the end had felt too afraid of the cold reception she was likely to receive. She had only met Mrs. Morrow once (never Mr. Morrow), and she hadn't struck Sarah as a particularly warm person. In fact, Mrs. Morrow had been almost rude to Sarah the time Justin had brought her by his parents' house. She had barely looked at her, and when she and Justin were preparing to leave, Mrs. Morrow had said good-bye to her son but had ignored Sarah. Justin had not seemed to notice anything odd in his mother's behavior. At least, he hadn't made any excuses for her.

Is it possible, Sarah thought, picking up a stretchy pink bracelet Justin had given her only weeks before, *that I might never see him again?*

Sarah tossed the bracelet to the end of the bed. Anything was possible. She had learned that lesson. It was also possible that . . . Sarah frowned. Maybe she really *had* hurt Justin's feelings by turning down his offer to marry her. And for that, she was sorry. But wouldn't a responsible person, a man, not a boy, put aside his embarrassment or hurt feelings and be there for the mother of his child anyway? At least return her calls.

Sarah heard the back door open. Her mother, back from grocery shopping. Her parents, she thought, must be so very, very angry with Justin. So angry that they would confront him? The thought filled her with a terrible anxiety. They might demand he give them money. They might threaten him.

It was a ridiculous thought. It wouldn't make any sense to seek justice from someone as—well, as immature as Justin. Her parents would know he was incapable of making any significant reparation.

Sarah shuddered. The whole situation was just so—embarrassing.

And maybe the most embarrassing part of all was that in spite of everything she missed Justin. The memories of sex with him haunted her. Being with him had been wonderful beyond words, but now she hated that she had taken so much pleasure in being in Justin's bed. She felt dirty. She felt stupid.

Sex with someone you loved wasn't supposed to make you feel dirty or stupid. Sex with someone you only thought you had loved, sex with someone who clearly had not loved you . . . that had proved another story entirely. Maybe it wasn't "supposed" to make you feel anything in particular, but it did. It made you feel bad.

Sarah rubbed her eyes. She considered going for a walk, but realized she didn't have the energy to get off the bed. For a long time, she sat staring out her bedroom window, fiddling with a glittery pencil with a pink eraser in the shape of a heart on top and seeing nothing.

Chapter 31

Adelaide and Cindy were at The Busy Bee, conducting a final check of inventory and cleaning in preparation for the shop's reopening. The day was overcast, miserably damp, and chilly. On days like this, Adelaide thought she might never be warm again.

"Coffee is ready," she said. "Do you want a cup?"

"Yes, thank you."

Adelaide handed her friend a cup of coffee, and then poured one for herself and added two sugars. Sneaky calories, her doctor called them, but Adelaide had decided she didn't care if the calories were sneaky or overt. She liked sugar in her coffee.

"Are you all right?" she asked when she rejoined her friend.

Cindy sank onto a stool behind the counter and took a sip of coffee before answering. "As all right as I can be, given the circumstances."

"I admire your fortitude. I have to admit I'm still in a bit of shock."

"Me too, believe me. And I'm afraid that when the shock wears off, I won't be able to handle the reality. All the decisions to be made. What to do about Sarah's education. Getting the house ready for a baby. Figuring out how to pay for everything . . ."

Adelaide hesitated. She knew she would have to tread gently. "Have you and Joe talked to Sarah about an adoption?"

"A little bit," Cindy admitted. "But she swears she doesn't want to give up the child."

"But don't you think that you should talk more about it?" Adelaide pressed.

"Sarah seemed very firm in her decision."

"But did she discuss things with anyone before coming to that decision?"

"Well, no, I guess she didn't." Cindy laughed grimly. "And even if she had talked to Justin about adoption, I can't imagine he was very helpful. He tried to get her to have an abortion."

Adelaide winced. She tried to modulate the urgency behind her words. "It's just that bringing a baby into your family is going to upset . . . I mean, it will change everything so radically. Does Sarah realize that?"

"I don't know what Sarah realizes at this point." Cindy sighed deeply. "I know she's scared. I know she's sorry. I wish she wouldn't, but she keeps apologizing."

"Well, that's understandable. Sarah's always been a responsible girl. But you're right. Her feeling unduly guilty at this point isn't going to help anyone."

"How did this happen?!" The words burst from Cindy like steam from a kettle. "I mean, how did this happen to *us?* I never thought that my family was any better than any other family. But I never thought that *this,* of all things, would happen to us. Was I being smug, Adelaide?"

"Do you mean, are you being punished for thinking you would escape a particular problem? No. And no, you aren't capable of being smug. Look, Cindy, everyone rejects the notion of tragedy happening in her own family. If we didn't, how could we get through the day without completely falling apart? Fear would strangle us, we'd be incapable of doing anything good or productive."

Cindy sighed. "I suppose that's true. But it's a tragedy in some ways, isn't it? I mean, the loss of my daughter's childhood. The abrupt end of her innocence."

Adelaide thought of herself all those years ago, alone and very much scared. "Yes," she said. "It is a tragedy. But it could be so much worse. At least Sarah has a loving and supportive family."

"We'll do our best. I just hope it's good enough."

It will have to be good enough, Adelaide thought. *Because your best was all you could possibly do.*

"When are you taking Sarah to see the doctor?" she asked.

"We have an appointment tomorrow morning with an ob-gyn in Wells," Cindy said. "I found her online. She seems to be well regarded. I just hope she doesn't judge Sarah. The last thing Sarah needs is for someone to make her feel worse about herself than she already does."

"Well, if this doctor doesn't work out, you'll take Sarah elsewhere. But I'm sure it will be fine. Sarah won't be the first pregnant teen she's cared for."

"Yes," Cindy said. "That's probably true. It's just—it's just that before and beyond being 'a pregnant teen' Sarah is a person, a unique individual. I hope Dr. Westin and everyone else can believe that."

Adelaide, remembering, hoped so, too.

Chapter 32

Cindy put down the book she had been trying to read. It was David McCullough's *1776*. She was dismayed to find that she remembered so little about the American Revolution from high school. Then again, maybe she hadn't learned very much in the first place. College was where you deepened your knowledge of history and languages and science.

Now, she figured, it was even more unlikely that she would ever be able to go back to school and earn a degree. Not with the prospect of starting over with another baby. By the time he—or she—was out of the house Cindy would be in her fifties and . . .

But maybe she was being overly dramatic. First of all, the baby wasn't *hers*. It was Sarah's and who knew where she would be living when her child turned eighteen. Besides, lots of people got a late start with their education or career. And Cindy didn't *need* a college degree. She just wanted one.

Cindy got up from the kitchen table and looked down at the pad of paper that sat next to the phone. On the first sheet, she had written a phone number. It was June and Matt Morrow's number.

For the past few days, she had been sorely tempted to call June Morrow. She imagined that June might be very upset, embarrassed on behalf of her son, and wanting to talk to Cindy.

But shouldn't *she* be the one to make a call? There had to be an established etiquette for such a situation. This certainly wasn't the first time a teenage boy had gotten a teenage girl pregnant!

Cindy frowned. She really couldn't be sure what, exactly, she hoped to accomplish by reaching out to June Morrow. She really couldn't be sure what she wanted to offer the woman. Friendship? An olive branch? But why? *Sarah* had done nothing wrong.

But Cindy *did* know what she wanted from June Morrow. An abject apology. Still, Mrs. Morrow might not be ready or willing to offer an apology. After all, Justin was an adult. His parents had no legal control over his actions. It was Justin who should be apologizing and making amends. Offering, on the spur of the moment, to marry Sarah and then, when she wisely turned him down, disappearing from her life was almost, in Cindy's opinion, the greatest insult he had inflicted on her daughter.

And then there was the fact that Cindy knew so very little about Justin's mother. She had never spoken to her, just glimpsed her across the aisle at the grocery store and outside the dry cleaners in town. Sarah had met her only once and hadn't had much of anything to say about her. Cindy had no idea of the sort of reception she might receive. It might not be a very happy one.

The heck with it, Cindy thought and picked up the receiver. And then, she put it back down. She suddenly felt irritated, almost angry. She didn't *want* a relationship with Justin's family. She didn't *want* those strangers to be part of her life and the life of her daughter. But now, Cindy and Joe and June and Matt would forever share a bond—a grandchild—whether they liked it or not. It made Cindy feel a bit sick to her stomach.

Let June Morrow come to her. Or let her fall off the face of the earth and take her lousy son with her.

Cindy snatched the McCullough book off the table, walked into the living room, and stuffed it back on a shelf.

Chapter 33

"Oh! Sorry."

Cordelia had not even seen the girl she had just stumbled into as she left French class.

"It's okay," the girl said, and went on chatting to her friend.

Cordelia had been walking through the day as if in a dream. *How,* she wondered, *can all this hustle and bustle around me be real? How can everything go on just as it had—history class, gym class, study period—now that the world has been shaken so violently?* It seemed that the cheering squad would still cheer; the band would still perform; the debate team would still compete, all in spite of the monumental fact that Cordelia's best friend in the entire world was pregnant.

She wondered if Sarah was sharing this feeling of dislocation (Cordelia thought that was a pretty good way of putting it) that was dogging her every step. How could she *not? It must,* she thought, *be like when a person dies, someone you really loved.* The world just went stubbornly on in spite of the fact that you were standing right in the middle of it, in shock, screaming, "Stop! Doesn't anybody care? Doesn't anybody see how everything has changed?"

Cordelia spotted Sarah coming toward her down the hall and waved. Sarah nodded in return. Cordelia wondered if she were too depressed to wave.

"Hi," she said when Sarah had drawn near. There were dark circles under her friend's eyes; they looked like bruises.

"Hi," Sarah said, shifting her backpack.

"You look tired."

Sarah shrugged.

"I didn't see you at lunch."

"I wasn't hungry."

"But you have to eat, Sarah."

"I'll be fine."

Cordelia lowered her voice to a whisper. "Did you tell anyone else? I mean, anyone in school?"

"No!" Sarah hissed. "Anyway, who else would I tell? You're my only real friend."

"Oh," Cordelia said. "Right." Just like Sarah was her only real friend. At least, for now. Cordelia thought it likely that once the baby came, she might have no friend at all.

Sarah glanced over her shoulder. "By the way," she said then, "your father talked with my parents last night about how we'll deal with it all when we have to. Like, telling my teachers. But I just can't face anything yet." Sarah's face worked as if she were trying to hold back tears. "I just can't."

"You'll have to be honest about it once you start to show," Cordelia pointed out, in what she hoped was a gentle tone.

"I know that," Sarah said irritably. "But . . . but maybe I won't show for a long time. And it's still going to be cold for a few more months, so if I'm wearing a sweatshirt maybe no one will notice."

"Maybe." Cordelia decided not to mention that Sarah would have to change for gym in front of her classmates, and what then? Would she even be allowed to take gym, being pregnant? Would it be dangerous for the baby?

God, Cordelia thought, *it's awful, all the secrecy.* If Sarah were an adult, she wouldn't have to hide. This would be a happy time—well, unless she didn't want the baby, but still, she might be better able to handle an unplanned pregnancy if she were older and had some money of her own and a partner who had stuck around . . .

If, if, if. There was no point in fantasizing.

"So, um, have you heard from Justin?" she asked, wondering if that question too was going to irritate her friend.

"No." Sarah spat the word as if it were a curse.

The bell rang, signaling the imminent start of the next class period.

"We'd better get to class," Cordelia said unnecessarily.

"Yeah. Oh, I'm going to the doctor after school with my mom, so I won't be on the bus."

"Good luck. Tell me everything after, okay?"

Sarah shrugged. "I'm not sure what there will be to tell other than what I already know. But sure."

Cordelia watched her walk off down the hallway, her slim shoulders hunched under the weight of her backpack and, Cordelia thought, the weight of her troubles. She had a terribly strong impulse to run after her friend and—

And what? What could she possibly do now that would make any real difference to Sarah?

Cordelia turned toward her next class. She was very afraid that no matter what people vowed to do to help, Sarah was going to be all on her own not only for the rest of the pregnancy but also for the rest of her life.

Chapter 34

The waiting room was pretty much like every other waiting room Sarah had ever been in. Prints in pastel colors hung on the walls—a seascape; a white house with a big front porch; a field of lavender. There were stacks of magazines on the side tables; in this case, Sarah noted immediately, lots of parenting magazines and not many copies of *Time* and none at all of *Sports Illustrated*. A watercooler stood in one corner, next to a large potted plant (plastic). Bland music played softly from a sound system. A jumble of plastic toys and a handful of board books were crammed onto two low shelves, in easy reach of toddlers' grasping hands.

The doctor, the receptionist explained, was running late.

"Doctors are always running late," Cindy murmured, as they turned away from the desk.

They took seats next to each other. Her mother flipped through a home decorating magazine. Sarah couldn't even pretend to pretend interest in anything but her thoughts, not even the homework that was stashed in the backpack she had brought in from the car.

She felt hugely self-conscious. Even though she wasn't showing yet, she wondered if all of the other women in the waiting room suspected that *she* was the one who was pregnant. Her mom wasn't too old to have another baby, but why would a mother bring her teenage daughter to the ob-gyn with her? It probably wasn't unheard of, but it probably wasn't the norm, either. *But then again,* Sarah thought, *what do I know about anything?* And maybe not one of these women cared a whit about her.

Except for that woman across the room, the one wearing a very fluffy sweater Sarah thought might be cashmere. She had definitely shot a smug look Sarah's way. Or maybe it had been a look of pity. Either way, it made Sarah vaguely angry.

"I'm going to the ladies' room," she whispered to her mother. She didn't really have to go—and she thought that she probably should wait in case the doctor needed a urine sample—but she just couldn't sit there another moment longer, speculating.

There was one other person in the ladies' room, a very pretty and very slim woman. She was dressed in a red blouse and a black skirt and black pumps.

Sarah smiled at her. The woman looked away and went into one of the stalls. Sarah didn't take offense. She figured the woman must really need to use the bathroom.

A moment or two later, Sarah emerged from her stall and went to one of the two sinks. The woman in the red blouse stood at the other.

"Hi," Sarah said.

The woman did not respond. She kept her head down and her eyes focused on her hands as she washed them thoroughly.

Sarah was sure the woman had heard her. They were standing less than three feet from each other. So why then had she not responded? Why had she avoided looking directly at her? Did she sense that Sarah was pregnant? It wasn't as if she was contagious!

Cheeks flaming, Sarah continued to wash her hands. Maybe the woman in the red blouse was the sort of person who believed in moral corruption through proximity. Sarah had read about that idea. In the not so terribly distant past a "good" woman was forbidden to socialize with a woman who had "fallen." It seemed truly unbelievable that such an absurd superstition could exist today. But in every age, there was the type of person who rode around on a moral high horse (that was her father's phrase), condemning anyone who had "sinned." Maybe that was what was wrong with the woman in the red blouse. In which case, Sarah thought, there wasn't much chance of her coming around to a more loving mind-set without a good old-fashioned miracle.

Sarah remained at the sink until the woman had left the ladies' room before going back to the waiting room. Her mother smiled at her as she sank into her seat.

"You okay?" she asked. "You were gone a long time."

Sarah nodded. She was far from okay, but what was the point in complaining?

When, she thought, *will the doctor finally see me?* She fought the urge to bolt from the waiting room and run and run until . . .

Stop it, Sarah, she told herself. *Just—stop it.*

Sarah took another quick look at the other women in the room. They were all significantly older than she was. Every one of them had a ring on the fourth finger of her left hand. One woman was dressed more stylishly than anyone Sarah had ever seen in Yorktide, aside from a few of the summer tourists who came into The Busy Bee.

Sarah looked down at her own naked hand and the faded T-shirt and hoodie she was wearing over a pair of jeans her mother had said she could adapt when the time came by sewing in a stretchy panel. There would be no fancy maternity clothes for her. But there was nothing to stop her from wearing a simple band on her finger, was there?

Sarah fought an urge to giggle. She was losing her mind. It was a ludicrous idea. She would be fooling no one. And even if someone *did* believe she was married and asked about her husband, Sarah would be forced to admit that the ring was a ruse. What was that line from Sir Walter Scott one of her English teachers used to quote all the time? "Oh, what a tangled web we weave/when first we practice to deceive."

"Sarah Bauer?"

It was a nurse, a smiling middle-aged woman in lilac scrubs.

"Yes," Sarah said, rising. "That's me." *And that confirms it*, she thought, following her mother out of the waiting room. *Now everyone knows for sure that I'm the mother-to-be.*

Chapter 35

The brown skirt with the forest green blouse and the gold brocade jacket. Adelaide decided that would do nicely for her appointment at the home of a family in South Berwick. Paula Fleming said she had a hundred-year-old quilt she would like to sell. Adelaide half dreaded these excursions. Sometimes, if rarely, the quilts were in good shape. Other times, they were in regrettably poor shape, and sometimes they were simply unsalvageable. No quilt owner wanted to hear that the precious family heirloom had no monetary value. If only more people knew how to properly store and clean and repair fabrics!

Well, Adelaide thought, fastening a pendant around her neck, *maybe this excursion will prove to be one of the more happy ones.* Maybe she would have something positive to tell Cindy upon her return.

Poor Cindy. Adelaide couldn't help but wonder if Cindy had known that Sarah was having sex with Justin. She couldn't help but wonder if Cindy had tried to get her daughter on the pill. But she wouldn't ask. How could she? It would sound as if she was judging her friend, looking for a way to blame her for what had happened.

Still, she couldn't help but feel a bit angry with Cindy. It was a misplaced anger, she knew, it was self-righteousness, not to be acted on unless she wanted to inflict terrible damage to their friendship. And she did not.

But she had told Jack what she was feeling. He, too, was

deeply saddened by Sarah's situation. And the night before, in bed, Jack had also admitted to feeling some anger toward the Bauers.

In spite of her own misgivings, Adelaide had pointed out that a parent could only do so much.

"But *did* they? Did they do enough?" he retorted.

Adelaide sighed. "We can't know that. We don't have a right to ask. Besides, what would we do with the information? Punish them if it wasn't what we wanted to hear? Cut ties with them?"

"Of course not. You're right. I'm just so frustrated."

They had turned out the light soon afterward, but Adelaide had lain awake for what seemed like hours, reliving memories of her first pregnancy, and remembering how vastly it had differed from the second pregnancy, when expectations had been high, knowing the outcome would be so vastly different.

Adelaide checked her watch. She had better get a move on if she wasn't to be late for her appointment. She went down to the kitchen and took three ibuprofen as a precaution against what she had taken to calling her "adoption headaches."

Still, even before learning of Sarah's pregnancy, not a week had gone by, not three days in a row, when she hadn't thought of the child she had given up with such a mixture of hope and despair. She wondered if he had grown up an only child or if he had siblings. Did he have grandparents who had spoiled him and a favorite uncle who took him for rides in his cool car? Had his father coached his Little League team? Had her son been a Boy Scout? Had his mother (and here in her thoughts, Adelaide always flinched) sang him to sleep after a bad dream, bandaged his scraped knees after a fall, sent him off with a note and his favorite sandwich to help ease the fear of the first day of school? Had both parents cheered madly when he graduated from college, which, being twenty-one, he might very well just have done?

Adelaide grabbed her bag off the kitchen counter and checked to be sure the coffeemaker was turned off. Then, she fetched her coat, boots, hat, and gloves from the front hall closet.

God, she thought, as she locked the front door behind her, how she hoped that her son had had a normal, healthy, happy, and loving childhood! If she had inadvertently given him up to a worse life than he might have had with her, well, she was pretty certain she wouldn't be able to live with that knowledge.

Chapter 36

"I picked up the folic acid tablets at the pharmacy today," Cindy said.

Sarah looked up from a pamphlet the doctor had given her on exercise during pregnancy. "Okay. Thanks."

"And it says here you're supposed to be eating lots of fruits and veggies. Well, you already do. And Dr. Westin said you're already in peak health. Blood pressure is a good low and the blood tests all came back fine. I guess you should just keep doing what you're doing."

"It's a good thing I'm not addicted to Twinkies," Sarah said with a small smile.

Cindy pretended to shudder. "You can thank me for that. I wouldn't allow them in the house for a million dollars."

"Really? A million dollars?"

Cindy thought. That kind of money would go a long way toward feeding, clothing, and educating a baby. "Well, okay," she said. "For a million dollars but not for a penny less. Anyway, you liked the doctor, didn't you?"

Sarah nodded. "Yes. I was afraid she might be judgmental or something. But she was so nice."

"And I was glad to know that Dr. Westin has two little ones of her own. I always like when a doctor can share in your personal experience."

"But you wouldn't want your cancer specialist to have cancer, would you?" Sarah pointed out.

"Oh, gosh, no!" Cindy said. "I wouldn't want anyone to be sick for my sake! But when it comes to women's things, it's comforting to be cared for by another woman who knows at least a bit of what you might be going through."

"Yes," Sarah said. "I guess."

Cindy looked with concern at her daughter. "Are you sure you don't want to join a support group for young mothers?" she asked. "There are several very good services nearby. I think it might be a very good idea. So did Dr. Westin."

"I'm sure," Sarah said promptly. "Thanks."

"If you change your mind . . ."

"I'll let you know, Mom."

"Okay," Cindy said, though she doubted that Sarah would change her mind. *One battle at a time,* she thought. *It's all either of us can handle.* "So I was thinking that it would be a really nice idea to make a communal quilt for the baby."

"What do you mean by communal?" Sarah asked.

"I mean that you and I and Adelaide and Cordelia would design and make it together. Sometimes we'll meet to work, and at other times, each of us can do her work on her own."

Sarah looked dubious. "I've never been very good with sewing. I don't have the dexterity or something."

"Well, you could contribute ideas. I really think it would be a good creative project for us all."

"What about Stevie?" Sarah asked.

"Oh, of course, Stevie, too. If she wants to."

God, Cindy thought, *I can't forget about Stevie in all this.* She can't become a victim of neglect. Cindy suddenly remembered a family she knew growing up, a nice family with three kids. When the oldest boy was about eleven or twelve, he had been diagnosed with a fast-growing cancer. By the time he was in remission (and he had gone on, as far as Cindy knew, to high school and college by the time she lost track of him), his younger brother, never a problem until then, had been sent off to a juvenile detention center for a series of offenses, and his sister, a quiet, studious sort, had retreated into a severe case of anorexia that eventually took her life.

Maybe it had all been a coincidence, the two younger siblings falling apart while their parents were completely absorbed in the trauma that had befallen their oldest child. But maybe it hadn't been a coincidence. Cindy wasn't about to take chances with her own family.

"You'll enjoy making a quilt," she said now, taking her daughter's hand. "We all will. I promise."

Chapter 37

Cordelia and Stevie were in Cordelia's bedroom. It was the first time Stevie had been there; in fact, Cordelia was pretty sure it was the first time Stevie had been in the Kane house without either Sarah or one of her parents.

Cordelia had seen Stevie, Clarissa perched on her shoulder, passing her house and had hurried out to say hello. Her mother wasn't at home, so inviting them both in was probably okay, as long as she vacuumed and used that special furniture polish that cut down on animal dander before her mother returned so she wouldn't have a sneezing fit.

Clarissa was a small, slim tortoiseshell with enormous, very round eyes. (Cordelia thought she looked like a lemur, but she kept that opinion to herself, unsure of how Stevie—and Clarissa—would take it.) Clarissa was smarter than a lot of people Cordelia knew; at least, she was more curious and clever. She could open doors and drawers; she recognized words and followed directions (really—you had to see it to believe it!); and she always knew exactly when Stevie was coming home, no matter the time of day, no matter if Stevie's arrival was random and off schedule. Moments before Stevie put her key in the lock, Clarissa was waiting just inside the front door to greet her. Cordelia thought Clarissa's love of traveling around on Stevie's shoulder strangely exotic. Maybe Clarissa was the reincarnation of some much-beloved pet of an Egyptian princess. . . .

"The room's kind of a mess right now," Cordelia explained, gesturing at the pile of dirty clothing in a corner. "Well, actually, it's always kind of a mess."

"It's very, um, bright in here," Stevie said. She was sitting on the edge of one of the beds. Clarissa was still perched on her left shoulder, four dainty paws drawn closely together. Cordelia sat on the other bed.

"You mean all the pink and purple? Yeah. I'm thinking maybe I should change the color scheme. I mean, it's been this way forever."

"Change it to what?"

Cordelia shrugged. "I don't know. Maybe cobalt blue and emerald green? Neon yellow and hot orange?"

"You're not into mellow, are you?" Stevie noted. "Or, like, neutrals."

"Mellow and neutral are not my style. Sarah says the room gives her a headache."

Stevie laughed. "Colors not found in nature, she'd probably say."

"Speaking of Sarah, has she heard anything from Justin?"

"Nope."

"I'm glad he's gone," Cordelia said, "though I suppose it would have been good if he'd stuck around to help Sarah."

"He's too lazy to be of much help," Stevie said with conviction. "He might try, but he'd give up pretty soon."

Cordelia thought about that for a moment. "Yeah," she said. "You're probably right."

"I think he thought I was some kind of a joke."

"What do you mean?" Cordelia asked.

"He was always making these stupid, teasing comments about my clothes and jewelry. He thought I was Goth. I am not Goth. I'm not *anything*. I mean, I'm just me."

Cordelia rolled her eyes. "Yeah, well, Justin isn't the most perceptive guy around."

"And he called me Steve-o." Stevie's disgust was evident in

her tone. "I think that's some guy comedian who blows things up or something."

"Justin is so dumb."

"I still can't believe my sister went out with him."

"Yeah, well, me neither," Cordelia admitted. "But people do weird things all the time."

"Not people like Sarah. Not usually."

"I know." Cordelia, who tried to be a fair person, considered for a moment. "Justin is kind of good-looking," she said then, "if you like that sort of hunky guy thing. Maybe that's why she was drawn to him."

Stevie made a face. "I never thought my sister would go out with a guy just for his looks."

"No. There must have been something else. I asked her, you know. Straight out, what do you see in him? Back when they were dating."

"What did she say?" Stevie asked.

"Not much," Cordelia admitted. "She said that he was nice. And funny. Though I never heard him make a good joke."

"That doesn't seem like enough of a reason to go out with someone, does it? That he's nice and funny."

Cordelia shrugged. "I don't know. Maybe for some people it's plenty. Like if you're lonely or something."

"I never thought of Sarah as lonely. She *likes* to be alone!"

"I know," Cordelia said. "But lonely isn't the same thing as being alone. Anyway, it's too late for explanations. I mean, he's gone and what's done is done and all that."

"Sarah Bauer and Justin Morrow, a mystery for the ages."

Cordelia laughed. "I guess so. Definitely not one of the great love stories, like Romeo and Juliet. Well, maybe that's a good thing. I mean, they both wound up dead."

Stevie reached up to lay a hand on Clarissa, who purred loudly in acknowledgment. "Though Justin will never really be gone, will he?" she said musingly. "You said he was gone, but that's not really true. Part of him will be here with us, in the baby. And he could always decide to come back, couldn't he? He *is* the biological father. He must have some legal rights."

"I don't really know," Cordelia admitted. "Honestly, I don't even want to think about it."

"Me neither. But I can't *help* but think about it," Stevie said vehemently. "And I hate him for it. For coming into our lives and ruining them like this. For doing what he did to my sister. He's like this bad thing hovering over us now. A dark cloud. An incubus. And he'll be there for the rest of our lives!"

Sensing Stevie's agitation, Clarissa had begun to purr loudly and rub her delicate face against Stevie's head.

Cordelia felt bad she had brought up the painful topic of Justin. "Oh," she said. And then, "Look, Stevie, Justin isn't evil. Just stupid. And he's not, like, powerful and brilliant. He doesn't even have any money. He can't boss your family around. He's nothing to be afraid of. I'm not even sure he's worth hating." Frankly, Cordelia didn't think anyone was worth hating. Much.

Stevie clenched her hands into fists on her lap. "You don't understand," she said fiercely. "It's not your sister who's pregnant with his baby."

Cordelia felt a teeny twinge of annoyance—how dare anyone doubt that she was very concerned about Sarah!—but then she thought about what Stevie had said. "You're right," she agreed. "Sarah is my best friend and always will be, but she's not my sister. I can't feel exactly what you're feeling. I'm sorry."

"Oh, you have nothing to be sorry about! I feel like I'm being a total drama queen these days."

"Well, it *is* kind of a dramatic thing."

Stevie gave a harsh little laugh. "Dramatic enough for a television show. *Teen Moms of Southern Maine.*"

"Ugh. What a nightmare."

A long moment of silence followed this pronouncement. Finally, Stevie said, "Maybe you should consider black."

"What?" Cordelia asked, startled out of her thoughts. (In

her mind's usual jumping bean way, she had been thinking not about Sarah, but about what her mother would be making for dinner.)

"For your room. A black scheme, maybe with some white and gray accents."

Cordelia was genuinely appalled. "Uh . . ." she said.

Stevie got to her feet—cat still attached to her shoulder—and grinned. "Just kidding. I'd better be going. It's my turn to set the table and stuff."

"Thanks," Cordelia said when Stevie had reached the door. "For talking."

Stevie nodded. "You too."

Clarissa yawned and flicked her tail.

Chapter 38

Sarah stood in the middle of her room. Her shoulders twitched. The room seemed—odd. Nothing physical had changed, but it was beginning to *feel* strange and unknown. Once, not long ago, it had felt like a refuge, a secure place of calm and peace and rest. Maybe, Sarah thought, it was her perception of the room that had changed. On some level it didn't feel like *hers* any longer. It was a girl's room, not a woman's, and now she was a woman, an adult. At least she had to act like one. Was that it?

If you couldn't suddenly *be* an adult, what did it take to *act* like one?

Sarah walked over to her desk chair and sank into it. She wished she knew the answer to that question because everyone from her parents to her doctor was expecting nothing short of a miracle from her. At least, that's what it felt like to Sarah.

She put her elbows on the desk and rested her head in her hands. She thought about the sonogram Dr. Westin had performed the other day. It had been so unbelievably exciting, seeing her baby for the first time! Even more exciting was the news that from what Dr. Westin could tell, the baby was perfect. Sarah and her mother, who had been there with her, had both burst into happy tears. Of course, Dr. Westin had then pointed out that Sara's baby was going to be beautiful and precious no matter what, but in spite of what the sonogram told them, there was always a possibility of something going wrong at some later point in the pregnancy. "It's important to be aware of such possibilities," Dr. Westin had pointed out. "It's important to realize that you might have to make some very difficult decisions concerning your child."

Sarah's heart had begun to race madly. She felt certain that she was absolutely *not* equipped to make difficult decisions about her child. She had never made a really important decision in her life. Correction. Deciding to go ahead with the pregnancy had been major. But it was something she hadn't really thought about. It was a decision that had made itself.

"I'm only a kid!" she had wanted to cry out to Dr. Westin. But she hadn't. She had just nodded and looked again at the image of her perfect little child on the screen.

Sarah raised her head and took a sip of the glass of orange juice she had brought with her to her room. She had had a dream about the baby the night before. Justin too. The three of them were sitting on her family's old red-and-white-checked picnic blanket in the middle of a field full of spring flowers. The baby was waving a daisy in one fat little fist. Justin was laughing. Sarah was wearing a circlet of pansies on her head. That's all, nothing had happened. They were just a contented little family of three.

For the first moment after waking, still in the peaceful world of her dream, Sarah had felt so very happy. And then, she had remembered who and what she was and the reality was in such stark contrast to the atmosphere of the dream that she had felt physically ill.

Sarah got up abruptly from the chair. If only Justin would get in touch with her! It wasn't that she wanted him back. She *didn't*. It was that she wanted to feel as if she had mattered even a little to him. That offer of marriage had been a joke, she was sure of it now, not a sign of love or affection, no matter what he had claimed.

An odd thought crossed her mind. What if Justin saw her once she started showing—really showing—and, faced with the blatant proof of her situation, had a change of heart? What if he decided he could really and truly "be there" for her like he had only sort of promised? What if love for the mother of his child blossomed in his heart like . . . well, like the daisy the baby in the dream had been holding?

Sarah frowned. It was a stupid thought. She did not want Justin to be her boyfriend or her husband. She did not want his help with the baby. She was sure of that. She was absolutely, one hundred percent sure of it.

She would make those adult decisions on her own. And she would pray that she got things right.

Chapter 39

Adelaide got out of her car and closed the door behind her. She drew her coat more closely around her against the damp. She was not looking forward to this appointment with her ophthalmologist. Her eyes had been troubling her again lately and that probably would not lead to good news.

Out of habit Adelaide scanned the parking lot for familiar faces. In a small town like Yorktide, there was little that went unnoticed, and even something as neutral as a visit to the dentist or the dry cleaners might be noted and discussed. She was used to this dynamic, but still occasionally surprised by it, if it was possible to be surprised by the familiar.

There was no one she recognized, just a tiny, ancient woman crawling out of a car that looked far too big for her to handle. But there might have been someone she knew. Just the other day she had seen Justin Morrow in the parking lot outside the supermarket. For one insane moment, she had been ready to race across the lot and confront him. She had gotten the better of herself with some difficulty. After all, what could she have said to him that would have made any difference? And it was likely that her confronting Justin would have backfired somehow on Sarah and that was the last thing Adelaide wanted.

Still, it would have felt good to make some small dent in Justin Morrow's complacency or smugness or ignorance—whatever it was that was allowing him to walk away and leave all responsibility to poor Sarah. Well, not only to Sarah, but to her parents as well.

Adelaide opened the door of the office, greeted the receptionist, and took a seat in the waiting room. She picked up a home decorating magazine (she was too hungry to look at an issue of *Cooking Light* or the *Food Network Magazine*) but found she wasn't able to concentrate on the glossy photos of magnificent gardens and formal living rooms. Her thoughts were still focused on Justin and his family.

June Morrow, whom she knew by sight, was not a quilter; at least, she had never come into The Busy Bee, so there was little chance of an awkward encounter between her and Cindy. June was a small woman, very thin and probably not much more than five feet tall. She worked as an administrative assistant in a real estate office on Route 1 in Wells. Adelaide seemed to remember hearing that she was a member of a rather offbeat church, a mix of several more established and recognized Christian sects. Other than that, which wasn't much, Adelaide knew nothing.

About Matt Morrow she knew only that he worked at a local branch of a large bank. What he did there, exactly, she had no idea. He was, she knew, a big man, tall and broad. Clearly, Justin had taken after his father in that way. She didn't know if he attended the same church as his wife did. She didn't know if he attended church at all.

As far as Adelaide knew, Justin was an only child. And none of what she knew about the Morrow family gave her any clue as to why Justin had acted as shabbily as he had.

"Mrs. Kane?" Adelaide looked up to see a neatly dressed assistant standing before her. "You can come in now."

Forty minutes later, Adelaide left the ophthalmologist's office, a frown on her face. As she had suspected, her eyes had taken yet another turn for the worse, this time bad enough to require a new prescription. She would keep her frames, but still, filling the scrip for a pair of regular glasses and a pair of sunglasses was going to cost a substantial chunk of change.

Plus, the doctor had thought she had noticed the very tiny beginnings of cataracts, unusual in a person as young as Adelaide. They would require surgery, Dr. Snowman said, at some unknowable point in the future.

Maybe it was better that they didn't take a vacation this summer, Adelaide thought as she slipped behind the wheel of her car. It was weird how life worked out.

Chapter 40

"Is this Mrs. Bauer?"

"Yes," Cindy said. The call had come in on the landline. Cindy hadn't recognized the number, and now she didn't recognize the voice, a woman's, shrill and with an unmistakable Boston-area accent.

"This is June Morrow," the voice went on. "Justin Morrow's mother."

Cindy stumbled back against the sink. She had never placed that call to Justin's mother; she had given up expecting Mrs. Morrow to contact her. She opened her mouth to say something—but what?—when Mrs. Morrow continued.

"I'm just calling to say that I hope you don't expect anything from us, or from our son."

Cindy didn't quite know how to answer that because of course she expected something from the Morrows! At the very least, she felt she had a right to expect courtesy and maybe even an apology. But from what Cindy had just heard, she got the feeling that Mrs. Morrow was not the sort who believed in what Cindy's mother had called "correct behavior." Did anyone have an obligation to believe in correct behavior? Yes. Cindy thought that they did.

When Cindy's answer was not forthcoming, June Morrow went on, her tone harsh. "Well, you had better *not* expect anything, not a single thing, and certainly not money because you're not going to get it!"

"Of course we wouldn't ask you for money!" Cindy protested, horrified.

"Because this is entirely your daughter's fault. My son is innocent in this, I assure you. He's a good boy. For God's sake, he told me he even offered to marry her! And thank God she said no because we never would have allowed such a—such a travesty!"

And a marriage between their children *would* have been a travesty, Cindy agreed with Justin's mother on that point. But to hear her daughter blamed for a situation that had quite obviously taken two to create was too much.

"Now, look here, Mrs. Morrow," she began, but she got no further.

"Your tramp of a daughter had better stay away from my son or else there'll be consequences. Of that you can be sure."

Consequences? What is she going to do? Cindy wondered. *Get a restraining order against Sarah?*

"How dare you call my daughter a tramp!" she cried, aware that her voice was ridiculously high and squeaky. "How dare you!"

And then Cindy did something she had never done in her entire life. She hung up on June Morrow without a word of farewell.

She realized she was trembling. She was hurt, and she was furious.

What a little worm, she thought. She imagined Justin running home to his mother, begging her to fix things, to make everything all right again, to make his big, scary problem go away. God, she hated that boy! No, not a boy. A young and very stupid man. She wanted more than anything in that moment to slap him across the face.

And she was worried, too. What if June Morrow spread the nasty lie that Sarah had gotten pregnant purposely to ensnare Justin into a marriage? That sort of behavior probably wasn't all that unusual; lots of women had probably tried the ruse and succeeded, but not Sarah. Never Sarah. And she *hadn't* wanted Justin Morrow as her husband. She had known he wasn't worthy.

Cindy took a deep breath and then another.

If June Morrow did decide to trash Sarah's character, Cindy could only hope that people's better natures prompted them to think well of Sarah, a girl who had never been in the tiniest bit of trouble since the day she was born.

Cindy sank into a chair at the kitchen table. When Joe heard about the phone call, he would be furious. He might even take it upon himself to pay the Morrows a visit. There was a limit even to his patience.

Maybe, she thought, maybe she just wouldn't tell him about the call. She had never kept anything from her husband—what was there to hide?—but yes, the call from the abusive June Morrow, she would spare him.

Cindy rubbed her forehead. How had her life come to include a virtual stranger who was forcing dishonesty between husband and wife? It was an abomination, that's what it was!

She got up again and put the kettle on to boil. A cup of herbal tea might help calm her. She hoped that something would.

Chapter 41

"Hey, Cordelia. So where are Regan and Goneril?"

Cordelia laughed and thought it was a good thing she had read *King Lear* earlier in the school year. She would hate John Blantyre to think she was stupid. "With Dad, out ranting and raving somewhere," she replied.

John Blantyre was a senior. He looked like a young Tom Hanks. (Her father had pointed that out once.) She had heard that he had applied to a college in California. (Maybe, she thought, he hated the Maine winters as much as she did.) John was very popular, kind of in the way she was, meaning that pretty much everyone got along with him and he got along with pretty much everyone in return. He ran track. Like Cordelia, he wrote for the school paper. He had even tried his hand with the theater club, building and setting up scenery. And, obviously, he had read *King Lear*!

"So, how's it going?" he asked.

"Good," Cordelia replied brightly. "How about you?"

John shrugged. "Can't complain. Except that I'm late on a deadline for the paper."

"Can I help?" Cordelia asked. "I mean, what are you writing about?"

John grinned sheepishly. "I'm supposed to write a review of that new movie about the Arctic. The one playing in town?"

"So what's the problem?"

"Well, I went to see it yesterday, and I kind of fell asleep right in the middle."

Cordelia laughed. "Was it really that boring?"

"I don't know. I can't remember! So I have to see it again after school today."

"Drink lots of coffee before you go. And eat some chocolate. And pinch yourself if you start to nod off!"

"Hey," John said. "I have an idea. Would you—"

Cordelia's smile froze. He was asking her out. He was asking her to be alone with him in a dark movie theater. Suddenly, Cordelia was overcome by an ugly, nameless fear. . . . *No*, she thought. *The ugly fear has a name and it's "pregnancy"!*

She slapped a hand to her head. "Oh my God, I totally forgot! Sorry, John, I've got to run."

And run she did, all the way to the girls' room on the far side of the building, where she rushed through the swinging door, almost slamming into a girl coming out, and, panting (*I really should get more exercise,* Cordelia thought), leaned against the wall under the window.

She was alone. Good. At least she wouldn't have to explain the panting.

What must John think of her? That she was a flake? That she was rude? She really hoped she hadn't insulted him by running off, but she suspected that she had. Poor John. He wasn't Justin after all. But who knew who he might become if they were alone and he got all excited and . . .

Cordelia went over to one of the sinks, wet a paper towel with cold water, and held it to her forehead and cheeks. She could not allow herself to become afraid of guys just because her best friend had gotten pregnant by one of them. Sarah had played a part, too. She had agreed to have sex with Justin. Hadn't she? At least, she hadn't told Cordelia otherwise. She hadn't said that Justin had forced her.

Cordelia tossed the damp paper towel in the trash. Well, even if Sarah *was* partly responsible for her situation, Cordelia couldn't blame her, she just couldn't. Justin was the bad one here, the stupid one. He was the idiot who should have known better.

And if it weren't for what Justin had done to Sarah, Cordelia might have been about to go on her very first date with a really nice guy.

Cordelia took a deep breath and checked her hair in the mirror over the sink. She looked pretty good for someone who felt so agitated. She left the ladies' room and headed for her next class, hoping she would not run into poor John Blantyre again.

Chapter 42

Sarah got off the school bus in Larchside, a few stops before her usual one. She couldn't bear to go home just yet and face her mother and her sorrowing gaze.

There it was, The Bookworm. She went inside. The store had a huge section of discounted paperbacks. Browsing for books was one of Sarah's favorite things to do. Even now, she could almost, *almost* forget the pregnancy, if only for a few minutes, and lose herself in a treasure hunt.

Beyond Three Worlds. Sarah vaguely recognized the title and pulled the book from the shelf. She turned it over to read the back copy.

"That's a great book."

Sarah looked around at the guy standing next to her. "Oh," she said. "I've heard about it."

"Definitely worth a read. Even if you're not really into science fiction, which I'm not. Not much anyway."

"Me neither," Sarah said. "But this is considered a classic, isn't it? A cult classic?"

"Yeah. It was one of the first books Christopher Justice ever wrote, and now it's considered his best."

"That could be difficult to live with," Sarah noted. "I mean, to peak early in your career. It could be depressing later."

The guy nodded. "Funny you should say that. I read that he suffered pretty bad depression the last ten years of his life."

"He's dead?"

"Yeah. This book was written in 1937. He was in his nineties when he died. Or maybe late eighties."

Sarah smiled. "I wonder if it makes much of a difference when you've reached that age. A few years, I mean."

"I'd bet it makes a huge difference. By the way, I'm Philip." He stuck out his hand, and Sarah shook it.

"Sarah."

Physically, Philip was as different from Justin as he could be. He was only about Sarah's height, very thin, with dark hair to his shoulders. He wore black-rimmed glasses, and had several tattoos on his forearms. Around his neck hung a silver chain with a horn pendant. His T-shirt and jeans were black. *His jacket must be on a chair somewhere,* Sarah thought. *It's winter. He would need a jacket.* She almost laughed at the inanity of the thought. What did it matter where he had put his jacket?

Sarah had never seen him before, she was sure of that. She liked his manner, at once earnest and easy.

"You don't go to Yorktide High," she said.

"No. I live in Bayville. I'm a senior at the MacAdams School. It's a charter."

"Oh."

Neither said anything for a moment. Philip stuffed his hands into the front pockets of his jeans. Sarah shifted her weight.

Finally, Philip spoke. "Would you, you know, want to catch a movie sometime?" he asked. "Or, maybe get something to eat? There's an amazing little Mexican place just opened up down the block, really authentic. My dad's been going there every day for lunch since it opened, and he's half Mexican, so I guess that says something."

Sarah's heart began to race. She had never, ever expected this sort of thing to happen.

"I'm sorry," she said, her voice trembling. "I . . . I don't date."

"Oh. Okay." Philip nodded at the book still in her hand. "You really should read that."

"Thanks. I will."

Philip walked off, and Sarah turned back to the wall of books. Her heart was still pounding. Oh, why couldn't guys leave her alone! Why couldn't they bother someone else, someone who wanted to be bothered by them, like that clique of boy-crazy girls at school, Jessica and Berkley and all the others? All they wanted to do was go out with guys, break up with guys, send pictures of themselves to guys, talk about guys, and Sarah guessed, sleep with guys or at least pretend that they did.

Why weren't guys after *Cordelia?* She was tall and pretty and fun and . . .

Sarah put her hand to her head. In truth, she hoped that Cordelia stayed far away from guys until she was much older. Honestly, she would do anything to protect Cordelia from the sort of mess she had gotten herself into.

She took a deep breath. She hoped that she hadn't insulted Philip. He had seemed like a nice person, smart, too. But even the nicest and smartest teenage guy was not going to be into dating a pregnant teenage girl, especially when the baby wasn't his. Not that she wanted to get involved with another guy now. Maybe not ever.

Sarah bought the book less because she wanted to read it and more as a sort of apology to Philip for having refused his offer. The truth was that if she hadn't been pregnant she would have liked to get to know him better. But that was a very big "if."

Chapter 43

The Kane women were in the kitchen preparing dinner. Well, Adelaide was chopping carrots and mushrooms for a soup. Cordelia was sitting at the island, flipping through a fashion magazine. Adelaide had tried on several occasions to interest her daughter in cooking, but Cordelia remained content to focus on the end result—eating.

"I wish Sarah would consider having the baby adopted," Adelaide said, surprised by the words because she hadn't planned on discussing this with Cordelia. But feelings had been welling up inside her, and now the words kept coming. "I've mentioned the idea to Mrs. Bauer time and time again, but she's standing firmly with Sarah."

"I don't think I know anyone who's adopted," Cordelia said, looking up from a garish ad for glittery eye shadow. "Unless it's a secret for some reason."

"Yes," Adelaide said, "well, be that as it may, I can't help but feel frustrated. I just don't know why Cindy won't even *consider* adoption."

"You mean, Sarah."

"Yes, of course. Sarah."

"Oh, wait," Cordelia said, "I do know someone who's adopted. Well, I sort of know her. She's a year ahead of me. She's Korean. Her parents are Irish American, I think, because her last name is Moore. Or is that English?"

"I don't know where the name originated," Adelaide replied shortly.

Cordelia shrugged. "Doesn't matter. Mom, do you really want to do this quilt for the baby? Because I'm not sure I do. I'm having trouble feeling excited or happy about any of this. The other day when we all got together at the shop to talk about it my mind was, like, a million miles away."

Adelaide put down her knife. "Honestly," she said, "I don't feel excited or happy about any of it, either. But if making a quilt together makes Cindy feel better, and Sarah, too, then I think we should show our support."

"What if Sarah *does* change her mind about an adoption? What will happen to the quilt then?"

What an odd question, Adelaide thought. "Then the quilt will go with him—or her. Our . . . our farewell gift, I suppose."

"But what if the new parents refuse to take the quilt?" Cordelia pressed. "What if they don't want any reminder of his real mother? People who adopt can do that sort of thing, can't they? Basically erase all traces of the baby's origins?"

Adelaide shuddered. "Don't think about the awful possibilities," she said somewhat harshly. "You'll drive yourself crazy. And besides, it's not your decision to make—arranging an adoption—so don't . . ."

Adelaide turned away, her hand to her head. She should never have started this conversation with Cordelia. It had taken them both too close to Adelaide's past. And this was Sarah's decision to make, not hers. She knew that. She *knew* that.

"Mom?" Cordelia asked. "Are you okay?"

"Yes," she said, turning back to her daughter. "I'm fine."

It was a lie, but Cordelia seemed to believe it. "Good," she said, flipping another page of her magazine. "Hey, do you think I would look too fat in this dress?"

Chapter 44

The dinner dishes had been cleared, and the leftovers had been put away. Joe had gone to Stevie's room to take a look at her sewing machine; it had been making an odd noise. Sarah had gone to her own room to finish some homework.

The kitchen was quiet. Cindy was at the table reviewing their checkbook and the accounts for Joe's business. It was not heartening work. Her eye wandered to the front door of the fridge. In every single one of the pictures posted there, her children looked so carefree, as children should be and so rarely were. There was Sarah bundled to the teeth, pulling Stevie over the snow on a sled. There she was in her Girl Scout uniform at the age of ten, looking so smart and proud. And there she was, sitting next to Stevie on a big rock on Marginal Way.

Cindy sighed and looked away. It just wasn't fair that Sarah should be ripped from her one and only childhood so brutally. Yes, she had taken a foolish chance with Justin. But did that mean she had to spend the rest of her life atoning for that one foolish decision?

Cindy looked back to the papers on the table before her. There was never much of a cushion; some months they barely got by. If only all of Joe's clients would pay on time! He spent too much energy acting as a collection agency. But if he asked one of his employees to handle that unpleasant task he would have to pay him and where would *that* money come from?

And then there was Cindy's job at The Busy Bee. She had

been wondering how Adelaide would feel about having a baby on the premises. Though some of the quilts the shop sold were worth a small fortune, The Busy Bee didn't have a high-end feel. Children were welcome. Adelaide often put out a plate of homemade cookies and was always ready to chat with a curious customer, even those who were honest about not being there to buy. It was a very nice place to work and a lovely place to visit.

But a baby on site from morning until six in the evening when the shop closed for the day was quite another matter. Even if she slept a good deal of the time, she would need feeding and changing and during those times Cindy would be unavailable to help Adelaide. And often, especially during the summer months, the shop could be super, super busy. A hungry, fussy baby in need of changing would be very disruptive to conducting business.

And what would happen when the baby became a toddler? You certainly couldn't have an active two-year-old stumbling around a shop that sold pointy objects like needles and priceless treasures like delicate old quilts.

Cindy sighed. She would have to investigate day care options and hope there was something local the family could afford. There were a few women in Yorktide who provided day care services in their homes. Cindy had seen their ads in the local paper. Maybe one of those women would be open to the notion of barter. Cindy might provide sewing services or Joe might provide some carpentry. It was worth asking. Because cutting back on her hours at The Busy Bee was simply not an option. She didn't make a lot of money, but what she did make was essential. Somehow they would have to afford health insurance for the baby . . .

This was a troubling thought. What if Adelaide couldn't come to terms with the family's decision to keep the child? After all, she was still talking about adoption. If that were the case, Cindy figured she would have to find another job all together. She could hardly spend her days in the same room as a woman—a former friend—who disapproved of her family's choices. It would be intolerable. But how would she be able to care for the baby properly if she had to work for strangers who couldn't be expected to be sympathetic to her home situation, or if she had to work in an office that frowned upon children on the premises, or if she had to take a job that required she work long and varying shifts? Night shifts might be doable; Joe and Sarah and Stevie would be home for the baby. But then how would she function during the day, exhausted from too little sleep and faced with the constant demands of an infant?

Cindy felt her heart beating uncomfortably and pushed aside the paperwork. Unless she wanted to give herself a heart attack, it was best to make decisions about a new job if and when the time came.

"All fixed."

It was Joe, back from solving Stevie's sewing machine problem.

Cindy got up from the table and went into his arms.

Chapter 45

"It's a pretty decent day, isn't it?" Cordelia said. "I mean, for March."

The girls were at the picnic table in Sarah's backyard. They were dressed in winter gear but without mittens over gloves and a second scarf. The trees were still bare of leaves, but a bird feeder made by Mr. Bauer hung from almost every one. Some were really elaborate, with little towers and turrets like those on an old castle. Others were simple, brightly painted boxes, green and blue and pink. They definitely brought some cheer to the otherwise dismal scene.

Sarah nodded. "If you don't mind mud. And I don't."

Cordelia looked with distaste at her boots. They were *caked* with mud. There was no avoiding it in March and most of April, for that matter. It was all over the place, ready to ruin your day. The fact that Sarah didn't mind mud on her shoes and the hem of her pants only proved how much she and Cordelia saw the world in different ways.

Sarah was eating an ice-cream sandwich. It was her second. Cordelia was eating a diet pudding cup. It was gross. Compared to the real stuff it was tasteless and gritty, but she was trying to be smart about what she ate without actually going on an official diet. The thought of actually dieting was too depressing. She figured that if she cut calories and fat in a bunch of small ways it would eventually add up to success. Hopefully. Because she wasn't keen on exercise, either. Who had come up with the idea that sweating was a good thing? Sweating, Cordelia thought, was even grosser than diet pudding.

Anyway, at the moment there was something far more important on her mind than losing an extra pound or two. Her mother had been very clear about the fact that she thought Sarah should give her baby up for adoption. She had cited all sorts of frightening and seriously depressing facts about the lives of teen mothers and their children. Like, how teen mothers often couldn't manage to keep a steady job and how lots of times they wound up living in abusive homes. And how their kids performed poorly in school. And how the daughters of teenage mothers had a much higher chance of winding up pregnant when they were teens compared to daughters born to adults. And how the sons of teenage mothers were more likely to wind up in jail. Jail!

It was all really terrible. Cordelia couldn't bear to think of her best friend in the world suffering like that for the rest of her life. So she had decided to screw up her nerve and talk to Sarah about adoption. Maybe Sarah would listen to someone her own age. Cordelia hated confrontations of any kind and she was smart enough to sense that this conversation could become confrontational. She would have to be very careful of Sarah's feelings and try not to sound as if she was criticizing her friend's decision, even though she was in a sense, wasn't she?

Cordelia put down the empty pudding cup and plastic spoon. "I've been thinking about stuff," she said.

Sarah laughed a bit. "Haven't we all?"

"Yeah. Well, Sarah, I'm not sure you're making the right decision about the baby. I really think you should think about putting him—or her—up for adoption."

"What?" Sarah spit the word as if it had a nasty taste.

Cordelia quailed for a moment but then went on. After all, this was for Sarah's sake. "Have you thought about how expensive it's going to be, raising a child? And about how you're going to finish high school and go on to college? And there are all those awful statistics about children of teenage mothers. . . ."

Cordelia suddenly felt embarrassed. "Well, about them having a lot of trouble in life."

Sarah visibly bristled. "Of course I've thought about all that," she snapped. "First, I'm not a statistic, and second, I made my decision and it's final. I thought you said you'd support me."

"I did say that, and I mean it. I will. But—"

"But what? But only if I change my mind? Look, Cordelia, this is not your decision to make. It's *my* baby, not yours."

"I know that," Cordelia protested. "I'm only trying to help. My mother—"

"Of course! My mother told me your mother keeps talking about adoption. Did she send you over here to convince me that I'm being stupid?"

"No!" Cordelia cried. She was horrified. This entire conversation had been going wrong since the start.

"Why don't you and your mother keep out of my business, all right?"

"It's just that we care about you, Sarah!"

"Really? It doesn't feel like caring. It feels like you think you know it all. And if you and your mother are so against my keeping this baby, why don't you just drop out of helping with the quilt?"

Cordelia realized that she was trembling. Who was this person who was supposed to be her friend and how had they gotten to this awful place of criticism and accusation?

"I'm sorry," she said, tears trickling now down her cheeks. "I shouldn't have said anything."

"You're right. You shouldn't have."

"I'll go now," Cordelia said, getting up from the picnic table. Sarah didn't say good-bye. When Cordelia reached the road, she began to run and she didn't stop until she reached her own home on Rosehip Lane. She thought that she had never felt so miserable in her life.

Chapter 46

Sarah sat at the picnic table for a long time after Cordelia had gone. She felt really bad about the fight. Deep down she knew that Cordelia had only been trying to help. She knew that she should probably have gone after her, or that she should call her right now and patch things up. But all she wanted at the moment was to be left alone.

Because Sarah believed that for all of her good intentions, Cordelia should *not* be fighting her on her decision to keep the baby. Friendship was about *accepting* the other person for who she was, even when you didn't agree with her decisions or didn't understand her motives. Sarah had always been supportive of Cordelia's choices, even when they hadn't been so smart. Like the time she had decided to try that crazy weight loss supplement without telling her parents. Cordelia had suffered an agonizing few occasions of rapid heartbeat before admitting that the stuff was dangerous.

Sarah sighed. Two large crows were eyeing the remains of the food on the table in front of her. Nasty birds mostly. Their cries could pierce an eardrum. She turned her back on them.

How could she explain to Cordelia why she felt so strongly about keeping her baby when the reasons couldn't be put into words? It was more like she simply *knew* in her innermost self that she wanted to keep the baby. It was more like she simply *knew* there was no way she could survive giving him up even though in some ways it might be the smarter thing to do. She could only hope that by keeping her baby she wasn't going to entirely mess things up for everyone she cared about.

Sarah spotted a neighbor's cat at the tree line. He was huge and white and fluffy, a feline version of a snowy owl. His name was Spike, which didn't seem to fit him at all as he was a superfriendly and very cuddly guy. Seeing Spike reminded her of when just last year another neighbor's cat had had her first litter of kittens. Sarah had watched the mother cat feeding, cleaning, and playing with her babies, and even then, the sight had filled her with awe and envy.

It all was so—natural. Cats and dogs didn't read manuals and pore over magazines and watch Internet tutorials and obsessively read mommy blogs. Cats and dogs didn't mess things up. Then again, kittens and puppies didn't grow up to become lawyers and professors and construction workers and accountants. Kittens and puppies didn't grow up to work in the federal government setting foreign policy and running the country. It took a lot of work to grow a decent and decently equipped human being. These days, people pretty much agreed that maternal instinct was simply not enough.

But where did you draw the line between blindly accepting "professional" information (often contradictory) and acting on your own experience and on your own considered reason? When did you know to trust your own instincts especially when, as in Sarah's case, your instincts had led you to make a colossal mistake?

Sarah had heard someone on the local news criticize mommy bloggers for how eager they were to wag an admonitory finger at other mothers and promote their own ideas as best. She had heard one of Mrs. Kane's wealthier customers complaining that parenting coaches were too eager to take your hard-earned money simply in exchange for telling you that everything you had thought you knew about child rearing was wrong.

Fear mongering led to profit. Sarah was not too young or naive to realize that. But not every person or service offered could be a scam. There had to be some good products, some effective methods, some legitimate advice givers out there. The trouble was in distinguishing between a slick but ultimately empty sales pitch and words and products of genuine quality.

Sarah supposed that every parent—every adult, really—had to negotiate that line for herself. It was a scary thought. There would be plenty of people eager to tell her that her ideas were wrong, and only because she was so young.

After a while Sarah gathered the empty wrappers, pudding cup, and spoon, and went inside. Spike had long since disappeared into the woods. The crows, still watching her closely, would have to scavenge elsewhere. She had promised her mother she would vacuum both floors of the house that afternoon. At the very least it would—she hoped—take her mind off more troubling matters.

Chapter 47

Adelaide had just settled at her desk in the den to balance the checkbook and pay a few bills online. A half hour earlier Cordelia had come home from Sarah's house with a tear-streaked face. She had claimed that nothing was wrong, but it was clear that something upsetting had happened between the girls. Well, that wasn't unlikely, given the situation. Suddenly, Cordelia and Sarah each existed in a very different reality. Cordelia's biggest responsibility was doing well in school; Sarah's was preparing to be a good mother to her fatherless child.

Adelaide opened her laptop and stared at the blank screen. She hadn't told Jack that she had been pushing the notion of an adoption with Cindy. She knew that her husband would not approve. He would counsel her to mind her own business, and he would be right. He would remind her that her own past experience might be unduly coloring her thoughts about Sarah and her unborn child.

And he would be right about that, too. Lately, Adelaide had been feeling that she was losing control of not only her emotions but also of the psychological structure she had built up over the years that helped her put one foot in front of the other. More than ever, there were moments when the pain of her loss felt as keen as it had felt twenty-one years ago.

She wondered if there really were women who had been able to put to rest all regrets and sorrow about the child they had given up for adoption. Well, Adelaide thought, if there were such women, were they brave enough to admit their success? She hadn't gone to a support group since before Cordelia was born, but maybe she should consider joining one again. Maybe.

Right now there were those bills to pay. But they would wait another moment. Because against all reason, Adelaide found herself sorely tempted to do an Internet search for Michael Baker. She hadn't had the impulse in almost a year. If Michael Baker was indeed famous, she should be able to find information about him in just a few keystrokes. Her hands hovered over the keyboard. It would be so simple.

And then she heard the front door open. It would be Jack, home from the hardware store. Suddenly, she was overcome with guilt, as if by even considering looking for the father of her first child she were somehow betraying her husband.

Adelaide slapped her laptop shut and hurried from the den, bills forgotten.

Chapter 48

Cindy stood in front of the closet she shared with her husband. Her clothes were hung on the right side, his on the left. She reached for a pair of chinos and hesitated. *No,* she thought. She couldn't wear those. The hems were ragged. They had already been turned up once and would not stand another turning up. She would have to break down and buy a new pair, and a new white blouse, as well. There was a stain on the sleeve of the one she had had for four years that would not budge no matter how often she presoaked and scrubbed.

She would try the resale shops first, of course, and Reny's. Paying full price for clothing was a thing of the past now that there would be a new baby to feed, not that she had ever been a big fan of spending full price without good reason.

Cindy suddenly felt a rush of intense irritation. If Sarah hadn't gotten pregnant, then the family wouldn't be in this mess! Why shouldn't she be able to have a brand-new pair of pants if she wanted them? Didn't she deserve decent clothing?

Her hands shaking, Cindy sat on the side of the bed. She felt slightly sick. Where had this anger come from? She was *not* angry with her daughter. She was angry with herself and with Justin Morrow and with his parents. But she was not angry with Sarah. She couldn't be.

With effort, Cindy got her emotions in hand. Things could be a lot worse than they were. She had so much for which to be grateful, like the fact that June Morrow seemed to have lost interest in harassing the Bauers. For the past few weeks, Cindy had been living in dread of her next move, but the phone had not rung and Adelaide had not reported hearing any gossip around town. It seemed that Mrs. Morrow's ill will had been satisfactorily spent by that threatening phone call. Maybe reason had prevailed and she had realized that if she pursued a path of punishment against Sarah there was little chance her son would escape with his already tarnished reputation any brighter. It didn't matter why she was keeping quiet. Her silence was golden and the Bauer family secret was safe, for now. Not that Sarah's pregnancy was anything of which to be ashamed. Still, Cindy wanted to retain control over the telling. She dreaded the thought of her daughter's name being bandied about by people who knew her only through the gossip vine. Rarely did gossip paint its subjects in a positive light.

Cindy concentrated on taking slow and even breaths. She was meeting Adelaide at the shop that morning to continue the preliminary work on the baby's quilt, and she wanted to be in a good frame of mind to approach the important project. The beauty of a quilt was that it was a practical item as well as something that would grow in sentimental value. It was art with a purpose that everyone could recognize. And the process of creating a quilt was often a healing experience, especially, Cindy believed, when it involved women working together in a collective effort toward a common goal. The act of creation was the making of history, the stuff of daily life that united human beings over the months and years and decades and centuries.

Her mother had taught her that.

Cindy realized that she was crying. She so wished her mother were still alive to counsel her. She could admit only to her mother, not even to Joe, that she felt resentment toward Sarah for having so carelessly thrust the family into this situation. And she imagined her mother's gentle voice, reminding her that she was not trapped in a bleak art house film or a sentimental Victorian novel. Hers was a twenty-first-century life, being lived in real time, not on a screen or a page, and Sarah was a strong young woman with the full support of her family. Cindy just had to believe that everything would be all right in the end. Difficult, yes, but all right. The baby would be born, and the Bauer family would simply continue on.

That shouldn't be too much to hope for.

Cindy finished dressing and went downstairs to the kitchen. From the fridge she grabbed the lunch she had packed in a brown paper bag the night before. Then she bundled into her coat and boots, hat and gloves and went out to her car, walking very carefully so as not to slide on a tricky bit of mud.

Chapter 49

"I'm sorry I got so angry at you. I know you were only trying to help."

The girls were in Sarah's room after school, Cordelia on Sarah's bed and Sarah in her desk chair. They had been awkward with each other all day (when they saw each other, that is; they did not share every class) until they were on the school bus at the end of the day and Sarah had asked Cordelia to come to her house.

"I mean," she had added, looking down at her lap, "if you want to."

Cordelia had felt an enormous sensation of relief and thankfulness. She knew then that Sarah wanted reconciliation as much as she did. Cordelia and Sarah were *not* meant to be enemies.

"That's okay," Cordelia said. "I was way out of line. I really *was* only trying to help but . . . well, I realized that I have absolutely no right to tell another person to give away her child. I'd freak if someone told me to give my dog up for adoption. If I had a dog."

Sarah smiled a watery smile. "I'm sorry," she said, sniffing back tears. "I'm so sorry I ruined everything."

"Oh, don't say that!" Cordelia begged. "You have no reason to apologize to me, or to anyone else!"

"But everything is such a mess now. I just—" Sarah buried her face in her hands.

Cordelia fought back her own tears. "Please, please don't be mean to yourself! I can't stand it, Sarah, really I can't! If anything is anyone's fault, it's that creep Justin's. He's the one who got you pregnant! I hate him. I've always hated him."

Sarah lowered her hands and looked up at Cordelia through red eyes. "You hated him?"

"Well, maybe not hate. Disliked. I disliked him."

"I don't understand. Why didn't you say anything? Why did you pretend to like him?"

"I didn't want to hurt your feelings," Cordelia explained. "Anyway, I wouldn't say I did much pretending. I wasn't really even nice to him. I just wasn't awful. I mean, I don't think I ever said more than 'hi' and 'bye' to him."

"I guess that was pretty much all he ever said to you, too."

"Pretty much. So what did *you* guys talk about? I mean, no offense, but it seemed like you had nothing in common."

"You and I don't have a lot in common, either, but we always have something to talk about, don't we?"

"I guess that's true. But it's different between girls," Cordelia pointed out. "We can always find something to talk about. Even complete strangers can find at least, I don't know, three things they can chat about right off the bat. What they're wearing, for one!"

"Maybe," Sarah said. "Let's see. Justin and I talked about—well, he liked to tell me about baseball. A lot. All the players' names and stats and baseball history and who was being traded to what team and how much money they made."

Cordelia wrinkled her nose. There was nothing in life she found more boring than sports. Playing sports, watching sports, talking about sports—it was all just a big yawn.

"It was actually kind of interesting," Sarah protested. "Some of it. Once he took me to a game at Fenway, remember? I didn't really like the crowds around the stadium—a lot of people were really loud and drunk—but the game was pretty exciting. A lot more exciting than it looks on television, anyway."

Cordelia was beyond dubious. "If you say so. So what did you talk to *him* about?"

Sarah sighed. "I really can't remember," she said. "Not much, I guess. He wasn't interested in nature. I found that out pretty quickly. And quilts were out, of course. He called quilting 'girl stuff.' He really didn't read much so . . . I guess I mostly just listened. Justin liked to talk."

"And to be heard."

"That too."

"Do you hate him?" Cordelia asked.

"No," Sarah said promptly. And then, "Yes. Maybe a very tiny bit. But not enough to go out of my way to punish him. I mean, what would be the point?"

"It might make you feel better."

"I doubt it."

"Yeah. I doubt it, too. I was just wondering."

"The revenge of the teenage mothers," Sarah said thoughtfully. "I bet that would make a good reality show."

Cordelia smiled and thought of an earlier conversation with Stevie. "You mean, all these young moms tracking down and harassing the deadbeat, irresponsible fathers of their babies?"

"Yeah." Sarah shrugged. "It's a silly idea."

"Are you kidding me?" Cordelia laughed. "Some slimy producer is probably already making it!"

"You're probably right. Too bad I hate having my picture taken. I could be on the show and make some real money. No, even if I was comfortable in front of a camera I would never air my dirty laundry in public."

"What a weird old expression," Cordelia said.

"Yeah, but it gets the idea across. Anyway, are you sure you're not mad at me for . . . for all this?"

Again, Cordelia thought she might cry, but she swallowed hard and said, "No. Way. Girls have to stick together, right?"

"Okay."

Cordelia got up from the bed. "I should be getting home now. I've got a ton of homework for some reason. It's like, every one of my teachers got together this morning and decided to assign a huge amount of work just to annoy us!"

"Do you want me to see if my mom can drive you home?" Sarah asked.

"No, that's okay. I could use the exercise. Blah!"

Sarah grinned. "Exercise is proven to make you happy."

Cordelia grimaced and left the room.

Chapter 50

It was early March, still winter, but every so often, if you really tried, you could detect a hint of the coming spring. But not today. The sky was thick with lead-colored clouds and the air had a damp bite to it. Still, the roads were clear enough to allow Sarah to ride her bike to the grocery store. True, some stretches were rough, the asphalt eaten up by repeated layers of ice and salt, but Sarah rode slowly and defensively.

And as she pedaled, she thought about Justin. It had been so long since they had last spoken, the night she had told him she was pregnant. She had sent him so many texts, asking how he was doing, telling him that she had been to see the doctor, letting him know that she felt pretty good. But he hadn't once texted back. He hadn't once answered or returned any of her calls.

Maybe he was still angry with her for turning down his offer of marriage. Maybe he was still angry with her for messing up his carefree life. Maybe he was scared.

Whatever Justin's motives for silence, Sarah had finally come to accept that it all boiled down to the fact that he didn't care enough about her to overcome them. She was sad about this but not really surprised. She had pretty much expected to be abandoned. What *did* surprise her was that Justin seemed to have absolutely no interest in the life he had helped create.

But then she guessed that to Justin that life was only a nuisance, an accident to be regretted, and if at all possible, forgotten. She wondered if all guys in Justin's situation felt so little interest in the baby they had made. Maybe. Probably. Maybe if Justin had been in love with her he would care. But he hadn't been. He had never pretended to be, even while asking her to marry him. So really, what could she expect?

Nothing.

Sarah realized that she was coming up upon Justin's friend Buck's house. She had forgotten that he lived along this stretch of road. She rode past the house without glancing to the right to see if Justin's truck might be in the yard. She dreaded the thought of running into him unprepared. It was doubtful he would be full of sincere inquiries and concern. He might ignore her. He might stop to talk but avoid meeting her eye. He might demand she keep the identity of her baby's father a secret. But even if she did, before long everyone in Yorktide would have guessed the truth. It wasn't as if Sarah had ever had another boyfriend.

A car passed her going way too fast on the damaged road, and Sarah felt tears spring to her eyes. It was all such a mess. Every day, no, every moment she felt plagued by a new doubt or worry. She simply wasn't ready for this. She wasn't at all prepared to be a mother. It was ridiculous. It was absurd!

She felt panic sweep through her. The bike swerved dangerously, and with a heavily beating heart, Sarah regained control and pulled over to the side of the road. What if she had fallen and the baby had been hurt? How would she ever be able to handle the fact that she had damaged her own child?

Sarah wiped tears from her eyes with the back of her gloved hand. Maybe, she thought, she *should* consider giving up the baby for adoption after all. What had ever made her think that she was ready to be a mother?

No, she told herself firmly. She had made her decision, and she would stick to it and be the best mother she could be to her child. Slowly, and very carefully, she steered her bike back onto the road.

When she got to the store, she locked her bike to the rack in front of the main entrance. The automatic doors slid back, and Sarah walked inside. She picked up a red plastic basket and headed directly for the produce section. Her mother wanted to make an orange fool for dessert. It was one of her father's favorites. He had been having a particularly difficult week at work, and her mother felt that he deserved a treat.

Sarah noticed two women who were standing in front of a pyramid of bananas, set up just to the right of the bins of oranges and lemons and melons. The reason she noticed them was because unlike most local residents each was very smartly dressed (that was a term her mother used), one in a long leather coat, the other in a knee-length fur jacket. Each carried an enormous, structured leather bag. And each wore what Sarah guessed was real gold jewelry.

She didn't recognize the women, or at least, she didn't think that she recognized them. The one in the leather coat might have stopped into The Busy Bee once or twice, but Sarah thought she might be confusing her with someone else, one of the wealthier summer residents or a woman down from Kennebunkport for the day.

Sarah turned away from the women. Four or five big oranges, her mother had said. And maybe, Sarah thought, she would get a couple of grapefruit as well. Stevie loved grapefruit, especially in the winter. She said it made her think of summer and Clarissa liked to play with the rinds.

"Bill said he didn't even give proper notice," the woman in the leather coat was saying, "just announced he was moving to Massachusetts and off he went."

"Well, Justin Morrow never was known for his sense of responsibility."

Sarah's hand stopped in mid reach. She felt her heart begin to race uncomfortably.

"You know," the first woman went on, "I heard a rumor he got some high school girl pregnant. Maybe that's why he was in such a hurry to get out of town."

The second woman, the one wearing fur, grunted. "I wouldn't be surprised. I wonder who it is. The girl, I mean."

The first woman clucked her tongue. "Poor thing. If she was looking for some help with the baby, she chose the wrong person to get involved with. I don't know what her mother and father were thinking. I would never have allowed my Judith to go out with a boy like Justin Morrow."

Carefully and noiselessly, Sarah placed the red plastic basket on the floor, and head down, hurried toward the exit. She had to get away from those women and their pity and judgment.

Once through the double sliding doors, Sarah stood under the leaden March sky and took a deep breath. She hoped the two women hadn't noticed her scuttling past them, but even if they had, what would it have mattered? It wouldn't be long before everyone in Yorktide knew that Sarah Bauer was the "poor thing" that Justin Morrow had gotten pregnant.

She took another deep breath. So Justin had actually run off. That certainly explained the fact that in the past two months she had never even glimpsed him around town. She was almost able to laugh. She was so, so glad that she had turned down his offer of marriage. There was absolutely no doubt in her mind now that months, if not mere weeks, into a marriage Justin would have bolted. It was so much better this way. Difficult, yes, but better.

In fact, Sarah thought, her heartbeat calming, she felt relieved. With Justin gone from Yorktide, there was one less thing to worry about. He wouldn't be hanging around, annoying her or interfering with her plans or pretending that he cared.

Of course, when the baby was born, he might suddenly reappear, determined to play a part in his child's life. What would she do then? Would she be under a legal obligation to have a relationship with him?

Stop it, Sarah told herself. *Don't dwell on this now, not here alone in this parking lot*. She had to keep in mind that she was not alone on this journey. Her family would deal with Justin's interference if and when it occurred. They would get a lawyer if they had to. Just last year her father had done a big job for a lawyer with a huge house out on Ridge Road. Mr. Jones was a decent guy; her father had said so. Maybe he could help them.

Sarah got onto her bike. She felt bad that she had run out of the store like a coward. She had acted like Justin had; she had run away from an unpleasant situation. But surely, responsibility for buying oranges did not compare to responsibility for raising a child! Still, she was sorry she had let her mother down, but not sorry enough to go back inside the grocery store. What if those two well-dressed women were still there, talking about the Bauers being bad parents?

Sarah began to pedal. There was still a way to make things right. On the way home, she took a detour to stop by a small specialty food shop in downtown Yorktide. There she paid more for four oranges and two grapefruit than she would have paid for a dozen of each in the supermarket.

Chapter 51

Why can't I let this go? Why can't I accept Sarah's decision to keep her baby?

For a moment Adelaide wondered if those words had actually come out of her mouth. She looked around from the rack of perfectly ordered gift cards she had been pretending to straighten. No. The words had not been spoken aloud. Cindy was still studying the stack of paperwork on the counter before her.

"Did you happen to see that special last night on the New Hampshire public broadcasting station?" Cindy asked then, raising her head. "The one on the history of lace making."

"No," Adelaide said. "I didn't even know it was on."

"It was wonderful. You should try to catch it when they run it again. They always run those specials more than once, don't they? I remember—"

"Cindy?" Adelaide took a deep breath. "Are you really one hundred percent certain that adoption isn't something you want to encourage Sarah to consider?"

Cindy nodded. "Yes. One hundred percent."

"Because—"

"We can take care of our own, and we will."

Cindy's tone made Adelaide hesitate, but only for a moment. "Of course, but—"

Cindy slapped the palm of her hand onto the counter. "Why do you keep insisting on this?" she demanded. "Sarah's made up her mind. We've made up our minds, as a family. Now, please, leave it alone."

Adelaide was struck with regret. She had never seen Cindy so upset. "I'm sorry," she said promptly. "Really, I am."

Cindy took a deep breath. "It's all right," she said after a moment. "I know you mean well."

"I do. I did." Adelaide knew it was time. "Look, Cindy," she said. "I want to tell you something. Maybe I should have told you before now, but it's not something I find easy to talk about."

"All right," Cindy said, though her tone expressed some wariness.

And Adelaide told Cindy all that had happened twenty-one years earlier. When she had finished, Cindy's face was pale.

"And all these years," she finally said, anguish in her eyes, "you've heard nothing of him?"

"That was the way it was planned," Adelaide said carefully, wiping the tears that were coursing down her cheeks. She suddenly felt utterly exhausted. She had never told her story to anyone other than Jack.

Cindy reached out and took her friend's hand. "My God, Adelaide, how can you stand it?"

Adelaide swallowed back more tears. "Honestly, some days the pain of separation feels as raw as it did that day in the hospital when . . . And other days, I find myself not thinking about him at all. But that took time to happen."

"So time's made it easier to bear?"

"Easier?" Adelaide laughed. "I don't know about that. Different, yes. You learn—tricks—for getting through the day. Eventually, you don't have to perform the tricks. They perform themselves. Well, that's an awkward way to put it, but it's all I can manage."

Cindy nodded. "I understand. Something like that happened to me after my mother died. I guess we all cope with loss in whatever ways we can."

"So, again, I'm sorry for harping so much on the idea of

adoption. It's just that I feel so afraid for Sarah. I'm afraid that she'll miss out on opportunities for education and financial security. I'm afraid that she'll miss out on a chance for love, too. If she keeps the baby, she'll never know what it's like to fall in love as an independent woman. She'll always have the baby to consider, and that's a big burden for such a young person."

"But of course I worry about those things, too," Cindy told her. "We're not going into this wearing blinders, Adelaide, I assure you. And yes, I know that no matter how much you prepare for life, it can surprise you in all sorts of ways, good and bad. I know we'll have troubles. But we'd have troubles no matter what Sarah had decided to do about the pregnancy. A different bundle of troubles, but troubles nonetheless."

Adelaide sighed. "You're right, of course. You can't avoid trouble in this life. Every decision is going to occasion both the good and the bad. I'm sorry, Cindy, again. You know you have my full support, Jack's too."

"There's no reason to be sorry," Cindy assured her. "I wish I'd known what you've been through before now, though. I'd have better understood why Sarah's situation was troubling you so much. Anyway, thank you for telling me. It will go no further."

"I'd appreciate that, Cindy. Thank you. Other than Jack, and now you, no one in my life knows. Well, my parents know, of course, they were there, but thankfully it's not something we ever talk about."

Her father, Adelaide thought, had probably erased his daughter's youthful indiscretion (that's what he might call it) from his memory. Her mother . . . well, she really had no idea what her mother had done with the memory of her daughter's youthful shame. Did she ever think about the grandchild she would never know? Adelaide frowned. Why, after all this time, would her mother suddenly care?

"Cindy," Adelaide said, "this just occurred to me. Do you think it might help Sarah in some way if she knew that I had a baby at seventeen, that I put him up for adoption?"

"No," Cindy said forcefully. "I mean, no, I don't think it would necessarily help her."

"Okay."

"I should get back to this order form."

"Yes," Adelaide said. "I think I'll make us another pot of coffee."

Chapter 52

The workday was coming to a close. They hadn't spoken much since Adelaide's revelation, but Cindy felt the silence was a healing, more than an awkward one. This feeling was partly what helped Cindy make her decision.

When the last customer had gone and the door had been locked behind her, Cindy turned to her friend. "Adelaide," she said, "you shared something important with me today. Now, I want to share something important with you."

"Okay," Adelaide said, putting aside the receipts she had been reviewing.

"I lost two babies to miscarriages before Sarah was born. The second one almost cost my life."

"Oh, Cindy," Adelaide cried. "I'm so sorry. And you risked getting pregnant again." Adelaide shook her head. "I don't know if I'm impressed or appalled."

Cindy grinned. "I was stubborn. And determined. And in the end, I was very lucky. Sarah's pregnancy was a bit rocky; I spent the last month on bed rest. Stevie's was a breeze. Can you imagine, after all I'd been through? Anyway, after that, Joe had a vasectomy. I might have been willing to take another risk, but he put his foot down and I realized he was right. No more taking chances with my life."

"Well," Adelaide said, "I must say you're a braver woman than I am."

"Or, more pigheaded. But the point is, I feel so grateful to have my girls; they seem like a bit of a miracle to me. The idea of giving away a child—Sarah's child—who is in some ways my own flesh and blood, is insupportable. I just can't allow it to happen."

"Even if that's what Sarah really wanted?" Adelaide asked.

"Yes. I know that's selfish of me, but that's how I feel. And in some ways, making this quilt for the baby feels like, I don't know, another way to bind him—or her—to us."

"I think I can understand," Adelaide said. "Does Sarah know about the miscarriages?"

"Yes. I told her, leaving out the nastier details, of course. And of course, Sarah's doctor knows, just in case there could be a problem I might have passed along. But Dr. Westin thinks that Sarah is just fine. So far, anyway."

"Well, it seems we both have our traumas to survive."

"Women's traumas. So different from the traumas unique to men."

"What are they, really, I wonder?"

"Traditionally? Having to support a family. Keeping a nicer lawn than the neighbors. Going to war."

Adelaide nodded. "Well, women share all of those responsibilities now. They can join the armed forces, even if they're not allowed into combat."

"That's true. But still, men think differently than we do. They feel differently."

"Yes," Adelaide said. "I suppose they do. That's why we cry at movies that make men yawn with boredom. That's why we ask for help when we're lost and don't insist on driving around in circles, expecting to force the right way out of our brains."

"All the old clichés. All, or mostly, based somewhat on fact. Or on what we've come to agree is fact."

"It's a bit depressing, if you ask me."

Cindy shrugged. "It's just the way life is. I don't think the differences between men and women are worth getting depressed about. Or angry about, for that matter."

"Well, maybe you're right," Adelaide said. "The differences do make life interesting."

But then Cindy thought of Justin, of how he had so blithely walked away from his child—and the mother of his child. Of course there were women who abandoned their children. Of course there were. But they were a small minority among a vast majority of women who would never dream of walking away when things became inconvenient or even when they became terribly difficult.

Cindy regarded her friend. Not that she considered Adelaide one of those cold and irresponsible women. Still, Cindy didn't want Sarah to know that someone she very much admired had made the choice for adoption. It might make her rethink her own decision.

"I had a few ideas about the baby's quilt," Cindy said now. "I'll bring the sketches into the shop tomorrow."

Adelaide smiled. "Good. I'll look forward to seeing them."

Chapter 53

Cordelia frowned. "How do you eat so much and not gain weight?"

Stevie shrugged.

The girls were in the Kanes' kitchen. "It must be metabolism. I mean, what else could it be? It's not like you run five miles every day. Do you?"

Stevie raised an eyebrow. "Are you kidding? I mean, I like soccer, but I only play it because the school says we have to play a sport."

"Ugh. I know. I think it's cruel and unusual punishment. I mean, do you know how many nails I've broken trying to catch a stupid ball?"

Stevie smiled, but Cordelia wasn't really sure she had heard her.

"You know," Stevie said suddenly, "it's kind of weird. I was the one who played with dolls and dressed my cat Orangey, the one I had before Clarissa, in bonnets and took them all for walks in a plastic stroller. Not Sarah. And now she's the one having a baby."

"An unplanned baby," Cordelia said. "Which is not the same thing as a planned one."

"No. It isn't."

"Do you want to have kids someday?" Cordelia asked.

Stevie shrugged; Clarissa stayed firmly aboard Stevie's shoulder. "Maybe. I don't really think about it."

"Good. You're way too young to be thinking about those things." Cordelia grimaced. "Sorry. Didn't mean to sound like a mom."

"That's okay. What about you? Do you want to have kids?"

Cordelia laughed. "*I'm* even too young to think about it! All I know is that if I was going to have a baby I'd definitely want to be married first. There's no way I would choose to be a single mom. I'm way too lazy."

"My mom always says never to say never."

"Well, believe me, in this case I am saying never and meaning it!"

Stevie's face suddenly darkened.

"What's wrong?" Cordelia asked. Stevie's mood could change as quickly as Clarissa could leap across a room.

"Nothing. Just something I was thinking about the other day."

"You can tell me."

"It sounds really awful but . . . well, do you think Justin, you know, forced Sarah?"

Cordelia didn't answer immediately. The fact was she had wondered the same thing herself. After all, Justin was so much bigger and stronger than Sarah. Worse, she had read online that seven percent of girls who had sex before the age of twenty reported that it was "nonvoluntary." Worse again, that sort of thing was more likely to happen if the guy was two or three years older than the girl. Seven percent might not sound like a lot, but it was seven percent too much in Cordelia's opinion! And what about the girls who didn't admit to having been forced, the girls who were too afraid or embarrassed or ashamed to tell the truth?

Still, for all of Justin's faults, and there were many, Cordelia didn't see him as a rapist. Nothing Sarah had ever said or done while she had been dating him had ever struck Cordelia as in the least bit worrisome, a clue that she was afraid.

"No," she said finally. "I really don't think that's what happened."

"Good." The relief in Stevie's tone was unmistakable. "Because if it were true, I don't know how I could look at the baby without thinking about . . . what had happened."

Cordelia felt the same way, but she decided not to voice her agreement.

Stevie went on. "This probably sounds crazy but . . . I don't know. If a baby is born that way, because the man forced the woman, does that somehow . . . Can the baby grow up to be a good person? I mean, some people have criminal parents but aren't criminals themselves. It just seems like . . ."

"Like a disgusting burden to pass onto a child," Cordelia blurted. "I know. But the child is innocent, one hundred percent. Just because his biological father was a jerk doesn't mean that he will be. Or she."

"I guess you're right. Sometimes my thoughts get really dark."

"That's where you and I differ. I hardly ever have really dark thoughts."

"You're lucky, I guess."

Cordelia shrugged. "Am I? Maybe I'd be smarter, more intellectual or something, if I did have dark thoughts."

"Misery doesn't mean brilliance."

"Did you just make that up?"

"I read it somewhere," Stevie said. "But I think it's true."

"Well, you're probably right. There's this Goth guy in my grade who mopes around all the time, and he failed two classes last semester."

"But maybe he's just pretending to mope around," Stevie pointed out. "Maybe his thoughts are all totally shallow."

Cordelia laughed. "It's official. You are just way smarter than me!"

Chapter 54

Sarah sat at the kitchen table, looking glumly at her bank statement. Her mother had opened the savings account for her when she turned twelve, and Sarah had been putting money into it regularly. She had almost a thousand dollars in savings, but it didn't look as if she would be making many significant deposits for some time to come. Not with the loss of all of her significant babysitting clients.

Just last Saturday Sarah had shown up at the Blanchard family's house as arranged only to find another girl, someone Sarah recognized vaguely from town, already there to watch little three-year-old Mylie and Kylie while their mother went to her tennis lesson.

"We no longer require your services," Mrs. Blanchard had told her at the front door, a frown on her perfectly made-up face. "I must say that your—situation—doesn't say much for your intelligence or for your sense of responsibility. My husband and I simply cannot allow you to be in charge of our children."

Sarah hadn't even attempted to argue or to plead for understanding. She had simply turned away, face burning, and walked back down the manicured drive.

Mrs. Blanchard had a right to decide who would watch her children, but why had she let Sarah make the trip to her house a half hour's walk from her home? Why hadn't she simply fired her over the phone? Why had she felt the need to humiliate her in front of that other sitter?

Two days after that, another client had sent a curt note of dismissal. And just that morning, Mrs. Hill, the last of Sarah's longtime clients, had called Cindy to say that Sarah's services as a sitter were no longer required.

"Those were the exact words she used?" Sarah asked, unwilling to believe she had heard correctly. "She wants someone unencumbered by pregnancy?"

"The exact words. She feels that it wouldn't be fair to ask you to run after and pick up a toddler when you were—encumbered."

"Oh."

Sarah bit her lip. This obvious lie was worse than the out and out disdain and the judgment of Mrs. Blanchard.

Now, with the defection of Mrs. Hill, an important source of income had been entirely cut off. Staring morosely at the bank statement, Sarah couldn't help but wonder if this were a sign of financial distress to come, of a social stigma she would be compelled to live under for the rest of her life. Had things really changed for women, or were they still subject to the old stereotypes—Madonna and Whore, Good Girl and Bad Girl? Could one mistake or accident made early in your life necessarily overshadow whatever good you accomplished in later years?

"I'm sorry, Sarah," her mother said then, putting a hand on her daughter's shoulder. "For what it's worth, Mrs. Hill sounded sorry, too."

Sarah shrugged off her mother's touch. Mrs. Hill's feelings of guilt were worth nothing to her. What she needed was a job, not someone's discomfort with her own prejudice.

"It's fine," she said. She got up from the table.

"I made some sketches recently, for the baby's quilt," her mother said. "Would you like to see them?"

"Not now."

Part 2

Friends are the threads of gold in the quilt of life.

—Anonymous

Chapter 55

Adelaide looked at the calendar on the kitchen wall. June twenty-fifth. *Where,* she wondered, *has the time gone?* The spring really had seemed to fly by with astonishing speed. Adelaide had had plans to accomplish a host of little chores but so many remained undone. Like the pair of curtains she had meant to wash and the Adirondack chair she had meant to repaint before the summer season. At least she had kept up with her portion of the work for Sarah's baby's quilt. The five of them—Stevie was very much in on the project—had had their first real work session together just after the school term had ended and the girls had a little more free time on their hands.

The Busy Bee was once again open full time, though business wouldn't really pick up until well after the July fourth holiday. Still, it was nice to see familiar faces after so many months of near hibernation. Some of her customers had returned from second homes in Florida and were sporting tans. Adelaide felt ever so slightly jealous of these women, in spite of her better nature. Everyone had her troubles and concerns, even someone with money enough to afford a second home and winter sunbathing.

Adelaide turned away from the calendar. Speaking of troubles and concerns, the reality of Sarah Bauer's pregnancy had sunk in, though maybe not fully. There were still moments when Adelaide—and Jack, by his own admission—felt that they were going to wake up one morning to find that life had gone back to "normal." There were still moments when Adelaide forgot that Sarah was pregnant and only remembered when Sarah came through the door. It was always a shock, this visible proof.

It was confirmed that Sarah was due in late August. She was doing well. At least Adelaide hoped that she was. Physically, she was thriving. Emotionally . . . well, from what Adelaide could glean, she was doing as well as could be expected. Whatever, exactly, that meant. Certainly, she was enthusiastic about their quilt project.

Cordelia, too, had seemed to settle into acceptance of her friend's situation. Adelaide had been a little worried that Cordelia's school performance was going to suffer as a result of the upheaval in her personal life, but she had pulled off her usual good grades.

As far as Adelaide knew, there had been no word about Justin Morrow after he had defected to Massachusetts back in March. At least he wasn't around to create more trouble. If Sarah missed him at all, she certainly hadn't made it known to the Kanes, not even to Cordelia. Adelaide had seen Justin's mother in the bank one afternoon about a month earlier. She had watched her chatting pleasantly with the teller and had wondered what sort of a woman would allow her son to abandon a girl he had gotten pregnant. But maybe June Morrow had no moral or emotional control over her son. Maybe his father was his son's champion and had convinced his boy he had no responsibility to anyone but himself. Or maybe both Matt and June Morrow had pleaded with Justin to do right by Sarah—if not to marry her, then at least to help pay for the baby's prenatal care—and he had simply fled the scene. Adelaide assumed she would never know the answers to any of those questions. If only she could stop speculating on them!

Adelaide took a pitcher of iced tea from the fridge and poured herself a glass. She and Jack had decided to put off a vacation until the following year. They felt it would be unfair to burden Cindy with the running of the shop with Sarah due in August. Besides, there had been the unexpected expense of Adelaide's new eyeglass prescription, as well as unforeseen repairs to the dishwasher and washing machine. The family deserved a vacation together, but people didn't always get what they wanted, let alone what they deserved. The challenge was to accept what you did get—or what you could manage to wrangle—and make the best of it. Wasn't it? Or was that sort of attitude defeatist, an excuse to embrace resignation?

Adelaide realized she wasn't in the mood to give the answers much thought. Instead, she got on with making dinner.

Chapter 56

The months had passed, March, April, and May slipping by in rapid succession until it was now almost the end of June. School was out until just after Labor Day and Cindy was back to work full time at The Busy Bee. Joe's business was in full swing, and he was, as the saying went, making hay while the sun shined.

Cindy was in the kitchen, preparing a chicken for dinner. Even after a busy day at the shop, she enjoyed making a meal. Cooking soothed her. And it allowed her mind to wander while she worked.

Sarah was showing, though from behind, she still looked almost as slim and narrow as she had back in January. Her breasts were fuller, as, of course, was her belly, but she could still wear much of her usual clothing. She had escaped the curse of morning sickness and was eating an astonishing amount. There had been no alarming mood swings. Her energy level was high, at least until the evenings, and she was still able to keep up with her chores around the house and in the yard.

Still, Cindy wondered if Sarah really felt as strong and capable as she seemed, or if she was just very determined to prove that she was still someone who could be relied upon and trusted. There wasn't any way to tell; Sarah would never admit that she was trying to regain a love she was afraid she had jeopardized.

To everyone's relief, the baby continued to develop right on schedule and without any signs of trouble.

Mrs. Morrow was keeping her silence, and Cindy had heard nothing further about her wayward son. She assumed he was still working for his uncle in Massachusetts (that had been the story put around) but who knew where he really was hiding. Joe, too, had heard nothing except for a few disparaging remarks thrown about by some of his employees right after Justin had gone off. It seemed that no one in Yorktide had ever thought very highly of Justin Morrow. The consensus was that he was a nice enough kid but not very smart or reliable.

Well, Cindy thought, *the Bauers could vouch for that!*

Sarah's pregnancy hadn't been a private matter for months. Mrs. Wade, their nearest neighbor, had been one of the first to approach Cindy, months earlier. Cindy hadn't seen any point in denying Sarah's pregnancy. Besides, Mrs. Wade was a good old soul; her pity was earnest and her pledge of support was, Cindy believed, genuine.

In fact, on the whole, people had been kind and supportive. If they were also judgmental and critical (Cindy thought of Mrs. Blanchard and Mrs. Hill and the other women who had dropped Sarah as a sitter), they were mostly keeping those attitudes to themselves, and for that small favor Cindy was grateful.

The family had learned that Sarah was having a boy, though Sarah had yet to decide upon a name. At first, Cindy had thought that knowing the baby's sex would help them in designing the quilt. Boys liked trains and cars, didn't they? Well, some did, but others didn't. Maybe Sarah's son would prefer flowers to dinosaurs or yellow to blue or writing stories to playing sports. In the end, Cindy and Sarah had decided on a seaside theme. The five of them were tasked with creating images of red lobsters, cobalt blue fish, tan shells, gray and white seagulls, fanciful purple starfish, and beach roses in deep pink, all of which would be placed against a cream-colored background. There was some degree of design beyond that, but the unspoken agreement seemed to be that the baby's quilt would be—how to put it nicely? A bit more haphazard than it might have been had Cindy and Adelaide had their way.

Joe was not so secretly excited about the upcoming addition of another male to the Bauer household. He had already bought him a tiny Red Sox cap and had dug out from the attic a set of hand-carved wooden building blocks that had belonged to his father. Of course it would be some time before his grandson would be old enough to join him in his workshop or to play ball with him in the backyard. But it made Cindy happy to see him anticipating the birth so wholeheartedly. She hoped that it made Sarah happy, too.

As for Stevie, well, she seemed to be okay, though she had been spending less time with her friends in the past weeks. When Cindy had asked if the girls had had a falling out, Stevie had said that no, everything was fine. How far, Cindy wondered, could you press for a particular answer without making it clear to your child you thought they were lying?

Anyway, Stevie and Clarissa were still inseparable, and since Stevie took complete care of the cat—grooming her, cleaning the litter box several times a day, monitoring her diet—Cindy had no cause to complain. She would have preferred that Clarissa not join them at the dinner table, but no one else seemed to mind, so she let it be. Besides, Clarissa had proved to be a magnificent mouser. Not that Cindy's house was at all dirty, but they did live in what amounted to a field and the occasional wee mouse was known to find its way inside. Clarissa dispatched them with speed and deposited them well away from the house. She was a kitty of refinement.

Cindy slid the chicken into the oven to roast. For the moment things felt relatively stable and sure. But in a matter of months, there would be a new member of the Bauer family. And then the world would shift once again, and they would all have to regain their footing on new land.

So be it.

Chapter 57

"Your room is really cool," Cordelia said.

It was the first time she had been in Stevie's room since . . . well, come to think of it, she had never actually been inside Stevie's room, just glanced in from the hall on her way to Sarah's room.

Cordelia had gone to the Bauers' house to see if Sarah was around. She had found the front door unlocked, as it often was, and gone inside. There was no one on the first floor, so she had gone upstairs and found Sarah's room empty. And then Stevie had called out to her.

The room was smaller than Sarah's, but somehow it felt big, which Cordelia thought was weird. Maybe it had something to do with Stevie's personality. Stevie was only a kid, but she was one of those genuinely cool people, not an artificially hip sort. (There were some of them in school, and they were so studied and self-conscious! Really, Cordelia thought that they must be exhausted by the end of the day!)

There was a lot more stuff in Stevie's room than in Sarah's. On top of a big old dresser, there was a large shallow box filled with bangles and beaded bracelets. Next to it was one of those earring trees, hung with all sorts of funky earrings, some with dyed feathers, shiny glass beads, and bits of leather. Next to the display of earrings sat a slightly creepy glass head on top of which was perched a fanciful pink and orange silk hat, covered in some sort of netting. Stevie said that it was from the 1950s.

A stack of books leaned against one wall, the largest volumes on the bottom, the small paperback novels on top. At the very bottom of the pile were a few big art books. Stevie said she had gotten them from one of those fun secondhand bookstores that seemed to be all over the place now. She also had a large collection of books filled with sewing patterns and a handful of graphic novels. Cordelia had always thought that only boys read graphic novels but maybe not. Maybe they were very different from comic books, which were definitely a boy thing from what she could tell.

The bed was covered with a quilt Mrs. Bauer had made when Stevie was born. It was a crazy quilt, a kind of patchwork without a repeating pattern. Cordelia thought that the style suited Stevie. Things looked kind of jumbled at first glance, but when you took another look, you realized there was some method to the madness.

A plush panda bear was propped up against the pillows. Stevie explained that it belonged to Clarissa. "She likes to chew on his ears," Stevie had said, and indeed, the panda's ears were ragged.

Clearly, Stevie's most precious possession was her sewing machine. It lived atop a sturdy wooden table in the very center of the room. Stevie explained that the machine was kind of old and didn't have some of the features she wanted, but that it worked just fine. Her mother had gotten it for her at a yard sale for only ten dollars.

Cordelia thought it was a tiny bit crazy to sew your own clothes when you could just ask your parents to take you to the mall, but she totally admired Stevie's skill and creativity. There was this one jacket she had made that was beyond awesome. It was a gorgeous shade of dark purple, like one of the wines Cordelia's mother liked, and the sleeves, which were tight from the shoulder, flared out at the wrists. If Stevie weren't so much slimmer, Cordelia would definitely have asked to borrow it.

At the moment, Stevie was sitting at the sewing table, one of the unfinished pieces for the baby's quilt in front of her. Clarissa was draped across her shoulders like a furry shawl. The cat's eyes were closed, but Cordelia wasn't sure she was actually asleep. She suspected that Clarissa was listening intently to everything the girls said. Maybe she even understood some of it. Clarissa was an eerie creature, no doubt about it.

"Where's Sarah?" Cordelia asked. "I thought maybe she'd want to hang out."

"Out on one of her walks," Stevie explained. "She'll probably want to walk to the hospital when she goes into labor."

"Ugh. Don't worry. Your parents won't let her. I won't let her!"

"Oh, I know." Stevie shrugged and Clarissa grumbled. "I was just exaggerating."

Cordelia plopped down on the bed. "Hey," she said, "did you like Justin?"

"No," Stevie said promptly.

"Oh. Good. I mean, neither did I. This one time I got a weird feeling that he was looking at me a bit too, you know, closely. Like, maybe he thought I was hot or something."

Stevie grimaced. "That's gross. Did he say anything to you?"

"No," Cordelia admitted. "I thought afterward that maybe I imagined it. I mean, how awful if it were true. Anyway, mostly he just ignored me, which was fine."

"I always got the feeling that Sarah kept him away from us, I mean, Mom, Dad, and me, on purpose. She never even invited him for dinner though my mom asked her to a lot of times."

Cordelia thought about that. "Maybe Sarah thought he was afraid of your dad," she suggested. "Your father might be kind of intimidating to a guy like Justin."

"Justin is too dumb to be intimidated."

Cordelia considered this, too, and decided that she agreed. "Do you think Sarah was embarrassed by him?"

"I don't think Sarah's the kind of person to be embarrassed by someone. I mean, she'd think it was unkind or something."

That is true, too, Cordelia thought. Stevie was so smart. "Well," she said, "maybe she just wanted Justin all to herself."

Stevie looked doubtful. "But why?"

Cordelia shrugged. "You know that saying, 'Still waters run deep.' Maybe that describes Sarah. She looks all calm and ordinary, but there's a lot going on beneath the surface we just can't see."

"Yeah. Actually, that does sound like her."

"Well, it doesn't matter now. I mean, whatever was going on in Sarah's head when she fell for Justin."

"But maybe it does," Stevie said after a moment.

"What do you mean?"

Stevie frowned and looked down at her hands. "I shouldn't even say this. It sounds so horrible. But if Sarah could make this really big mistake once, I mean, going out with a guy like Justin in the first place, someone who was so wrong for her, and then . . . and then, getting pregnant, maybe she'll make another really big mistake. Then what will happen to her life? What if Mom and Dad aren't around? Who will take care of her then? Who will take care of the baby? I guess I could, if I was old enough. . . ."

Cordelia frowned. Poor Stevie. She wondered if Mrs. Bauer knew how worried she was about her sister. She wondered—maybe unfairly—if anyone in the Bauer house even noticed Stevie anymore.

"I don't think you should worry about needing to take care of your sister or the baby," she said finally. "Anyway, I think Sarah learned her lesson, like my father says. I'd be surprised if she ever goes out with another guy again!"

Stevie smiled but halfheartedly.

"Seriously," Cordelia went on. "It's not your job to do anything else but be Stevie Bauer right now, this very minute. Just be almost fourteen."

Stevie smiled more fully now. "What's the job description for being almost fourteen?"

Cordelia smiled back. "Be moody, eat a lot of sugar, and sleep late on weekends."

"Oh," Stevie said confidently, "I can do that!"

Chapter 58

"Here's your change."

"Thank you," Sarah said, taking the twenty-seven cents the woman behind the counter handed her.

Sarah's mother had dropped her off in downtown Ogunquit while she ran an errand. Sarah had been craving chocolate, and her mom had given her ten dollars to spend at Harbor Candy Shop.

"If you're going to indulge," she had said to Sarah, "do it right."

So Sarah had bought a cellophane bag of nonpareils (she would give half to Stevie) and two cashew and chocolate turtles (she would eat them both herself) and a big piece of bark studded with nuts and dried fruit. She had spent almost the entire ten dollars and felt a bit bad about that, but a bite of a turtle magically erased all guilt.

Sarah took her purchases outside. Tourists were beginning to flood Ogunquit, but Maine Street was still passable. Later in the season, it would be impossibly dense with people and the road would be jammed with cars moving at a snail's pace.

It was hard to believe that it was summer already, and that in two months her baby would be born. The past few months had been challenging, especially as her pregnancy had become general knowledge. There had been some unpleasant moments, like what had happened with Mrs. Blanchard, and one incident at school had really hurt her deeply. But Mr. Kane had acted swiftly, and the girl who had taunted Sarah with an abominable word had been punished without the whole school knowing what had happened. In fact, Cordelia hadn't even learned about the incident. If she had, she might have done something silly. You could say that Cordelia sometimes acted irrationally, but you could never say that her heart wasn't in the right place.

Sarah chomped on a nonpareil. Physically, she felt pretty good. Maybe that was a consequence of being young and healthy to start with. And emotionally or psychologically, well, she was definitely in a better place than she had been back in the winter. She was still terrified of the prospect of becoming a mother at such a young age, but now, she was also excited about it. Maybe not all the time, but sometimes, like when she and her mother and sister and Mrs. Kane and Cordelia were working on the quilt together. And she only felt depressed or panicked a few times a week now.

Suddenly, Sarah noticed a girl halfway up the street. She looked about Sarah's age, and she was definitely pregnant. She was staring at the window display in one of the high-end gift shops. Her blond hair was dolloped with areas of green dye, but other than that she looked totally ordinary in a pair of jeans and a T-shirt.

Sarah bit her lip. From the start, she had shied away from being around other girls in her situation—no support group for her—and she had come to regret it, not a lot, but a little. She knew that she had been unfairly judging all other pregnant teenagers. There *had* to be some who, like her, were aware of the gravity of their situation. Like maybe that girl staring at the fancy handmade soaps and overpriced throw pillows.

It couldn't hurt to say hello, could it? Maybe they would strike up a conversation, just a brief one, but one that might make them both feel good. After all, they were united by some pretty important factors. They were teenagers and they were pregnant. That had to give them enough in common to make a connection. Maybe.

Plus, Sarah, thought, she could offer the girl some chocolate.

Sarah walked toward the girl with a tentative smile but came to a dead halt within a yard when the girl took a pack of cigarettes from her purse. She opened her mouth to blurt something to the effect of, "Oh, you really shouldn't—" when the girl, sensing her presence, turned toward her.

"What are you looking at?" she spat.

Sarah shook her head. "Nothing. I mean, I just—"

"You were just going to tell me I shouldn't be smoking?"

"No. Well, yes, I guess . . ."

The girl stepped closer to Sarah and lowered her voice. "Listen, bitch," she hissed. "Back off. I have a right to live my own life without people telling me what's good for me or bad for me."

"But, the baby—"

The girl laughed and nodded at Sarah's middle. "Like you were smart enough not to get pregnant? You're no better than I am. You have no right to preach to me."

She's right, Sarah thought. *I don't.*

The girl tossed her cigarette at Sarah's feet and walked off.

Numbly, Sarah ground out the burning cigarette with the toe of her sneaker. She couldn't be sure that no one had witnessed the encounter. The street was busy, but people seemed to be minding their own business. She hoped that they were because she felt massively stupid.

She had been right all along. She *was* alone and different. There was no fellowship for her with other girls in her situation. Worse was the fact that in the eyes of society she was a loser, a screwup. She thought back to the last few weeks of school. Just as term papers were due and exams were happening, she had come down with a nasty stomach flu and had been forced to miss several days of classes. Her final grades had suffered a bit as a result, in spite of her concentrated hard work.

Sarah knew that a college admissions board would see this

dip as a sign of laziness. She knew that a college admissions board wouldn't care about cutting slack for a pregnant sixteen-year-old. Why *should* they care?

Sarah had never wanted any special treatment; she had always believed in fair play, and she had always been unusually self-sufficient. She had never been the sort to go crying to Mommy the moment her will was thwarted; in fact, she had often been the one to whom others turned in a time of need.

But now, things were different. Now, at some point in almost every day, she felt the urgent need to grasp for a life support before she drowned in her own chaos. Had she suddenly become a weak person? Could you, in the space of a few months, become a person you could hardly recognize?

It seemed that you could.

"Sarah? Sarah!"

Sarah startled and realized that she had been staring blankly at her mother's car, and at her mother, calling her name and waving.

She went over to the curb and got into the front seat.

"Are you okay?" her mother asked, a frown of concern on her face.

Sarah nodded. "Fine," she said.

"Good. I don't want us to be late for our quilting time with Cordelia and her mom."

"And Stevie," Sarah added automatically.

"Yes. And Stevie."

Chapter 59

The tinkling of the bell over the door alerted Adelaide to the arrival of a customer. Except that it wasn't a customer. It was her daughter.

"This is a surprise," she said. "A pleasant surprise."

"Dad dropped me off." Cordelia looked around the shop. "Where's Mrs. Bauer?"

"She had an errand to run."

"Oh. Good."

"Why is it good?"

"Because I wanted to talk to you about something. I suppose it could wait until tonight when you get home but . . ." Cordelia shrugged. "I'm kind of worried about Stevie."

Adelaide felt a tightening in her chest. "What do you mean?" she asked.

"Well," Cordelia began, looking over her shoulder and then back again. "Promise me you won't say anything?"

"Now, how can I promise that without knowing what it is you're going to tell me? Did something bad happen to Stevie? Did someone hurt her? Because then I'll have to—"

"Oh, nothing bad happened," Cordelia said quickly. "Really. It's just that Stevie told me she's worried about the future. She feels she might have to be responsible for Sarah someday, and the baby, like if her parents aren't around. And, if Sarah makes another—you know, mistake."

Adelaide felt enormously relieved. Her imagination had

scurried into overdrive for a moment. Still, she felt sorry for Stevie. "Oh, the poor girl," she said. "She shouldn't be burdened with fears like that."

"That's what I told her. That she should just concentrate on being a kid while she can. But Stevie's like Sarah. She's a deep thinker." Cordelia smiled a bit. "Unlike me!"

"Well, deep thinking is all well and good until it becomes a morbid obsession."

"Oh, I don't think Stevie's anywhere near morbid obsession! But I do feel bad for her. She told me she hasn't talked to her friends about Sarah's situation."

"Did she say why?" Adelaide asked. *Maybe,* she thought, *Stevie felt embarrassed by her sister. Or maybe she was trying to protect her sister's privacy.*

Cordelia sighed. "Not really. Maybe she thinks they won't have anything helpful to say. But I guess she thinks *I'll* have something helpful to say—someday."

"Well, she trusts you, and that's a good thing. But listen, if she says anything that frightens you, or if you think she's in real trouble, you have to promise to tell me."

"I promise," Cordelia agreed. "Okay, I guess I'll head home now. Or maybe I'll go down to the beach for a while, if you don't need me here."

"No, go ahead," Adelaide said. "Things are slow today. But why don't you come back at six and we can drive home together."

Cordelia waved and went off.

Adelaide *had* noticed that her daughter was spending more time with Stevie than she had before Sarah had gotten pregnant, apart from their quilting sessions that was, but she had supposed they were simply passing the time, talking about trivial things or watching Clarissa do her acrobatics. She hadn't considered that Stevie might be sharing serious emotional concerns. She hadn't considered that Cordelia might be doing the very same thing.

Adelaide paused. She wondered if she should talk to Cindy

about Stevie's worries. But no, that would be breaking a confidence (two actually—Stevie's to Cordelia, and Cordelia's to her) and, quite possibly, interfering where she had no right to interfere. If Stevie found out, she might feel she could no longer trust Cordelia and that would be a bad thing. As long as Stevie had Cordelia in whom to confide—and as long as Cordelia kept her promise to come to her mother with anything that seriously disturbed her—Stevie should be okay. At least, Adelaide hoped that she would be.

Chapter 60

Cindy was making a pot of coffee while Joe sat at the kitchen table, flipping through a catalog of construction materials. He still hadn't told his family in Chicago or in Brunswick that Sarah was pregnant. Cindy wasn't sure about the wisdom of this. Not telling could easily be construed as hiding, which would imply shame or embarrassment. But as she knew they would, matters had come to a head quite on their own.

"I heard from Ben this morning," Joe said. "Seems word of Sarah's situation has reached Brunswick."

"Oh." Cindy kept her tone neutral though she felt her heart race a bit. "What did he say exactly?"

"Wanted to know if it was true, what he'd heard. I said, if what you've heard is that Sarah is having a baby come August, then yes, it's true."

"Well, we knew the truth would spread at some point," Cindy said. "Everyone will know eventually. You can't hide a baby for long. And we mustn't let people think we're ashamed."

"I could never be ashamed of my own child."

"I know that," Cindy assured him, bringing the coffeepot and two cups to the table. "Let's hope that other people know that, too."

"Ben knows that. He and Jill are family. They understand."

Cindy winced. It had been the fear of her father's condemnation that had held her back from telling him about Sarah's pregnancy. But she had underestimated him. *Lesson learned,* she thought. *Don't presume another person's thoughts. People can* always *surprise you.*

"Ben said he and Jill have a stroller from their last," Joe said then. "Said it's in good shape and we can have it if we want."

"That's good of them. I'll call Jill tomorrow. I owe her a phone call anyway."

"And I suppose Jonas would want to know. About Sarah."

Cindy smiled in what she hoped was an encouraging way. "Yes, I'm sure he would. Marie too. I'll let them know as well."

Joe nodded. "Any more of that coffee cake left?"

Cindy brought what remained of the cake to the table and cut a piece for her husband. "I'd better make another one today. The three of you never seem to get enough of it."

Joe ate the cake, wiped his mouth with his napkin, and got up from the table. "Best coffee cake in this world," he said. He kissed his wife's cheek and left to return to the job site.

Cindy felt tears prick at her eyes. She was truly blessed with this man. She knew he was happy to sacrifice for his family, but she wished that he didn't have to work so hard. She wished there was something more she could contribute to the household.

And then it struck her. Maybe there *was* something more she could contribute. She wondered why the idea hadn't occurred to her earlier. It was so simple! *Well,* she thought, getting up from the table, *better late than never.*

Chapter 61

The girls were in Cordelia's room. Pinky the Worse for Wear Unicorn sat on her lap, and she was absentmindedly stroking him. (It was interesting, Cordelia thought, that she no longer cared about keeping her relationship with Pinky a secret.) Clarissa, who as usual was perched on Stevie—first, on a shoulder, then on her lap, and briefly, on her head—had eyed Pinky with what Cordelia thought was great suspicion. A good sniff had brought her around, and she had ignored him since.

"What do you think will happen?" Stevie said suddenly.

Cordelia frowned. "What do you mean?"

"I mean, do you think things will work out? Sarah and her baby living at home with us and all."

"I hope so!" Cordelia cried. "I can't imagine what else she would do, can you? Unless she moved in with me and my parents!"

"Move up to Portland or to some other city and live in a shelter, I guess."

"Stevie! That's a horrible thing to say!"

Stevie shrugged. "Why? It's what happens to lots of girls who get pregnant and have no place else to go. At least, that's what I've heard. They go to shelters or care facilities of some sort."

"Well, sure," Cordelia said, "but that will never happen to Sarah."

"I hope not. It's good the shelters exist, though. And the other places."

"Sure, of course. Social services are important. But can we not talk about this?"

Stevie shrugged again. "Okay."

The thought of her friend having to live in a shelter made Cordelia shudder. The world of poverty and abandonment had never touched Cordelia's in any close or direct way and now that the specter of it had, Cordelia suddenly felt deeply frightened. Was everyone's security so precarious? Could everything you took for granted, like a home and parents and school and your own phone and computer and nice clothes, fall away so suddenly and completely?

Of course it could, and for all sorts of reasons.

And if that was true, then life was even more precarious than Cordelia had ever thought, even in her darkest moment, which, admittedly, had never been very dark.

"It's weird, but a part of me is angry with Sarah for getting pregnant," Stevie said, breaking the silence. "Like, what right did she have to mess up our family like this? And another part of me is kind of disappointed in her. I hate feeling this way. I mean, I've always really looked up to Sarah as, like, this perfect older sister. And now . . ."

"Now she's proved that she's only human like the rest of us," Cordelia said. "I know. I feel kind of angry and disappointed, too."

"Yeah. I guess it's not fair of me to—well, to punish her for not being perfect. Even though it's only in my head that I'm punishing her."

"It's probably not fair," Cordelia agreed, "but I think it's normal. I mean, I've been doing it, too, and I'm as normal as you get!"

"And all the attention she's getting from my mom and dad . . ." Stevie fiddled with one of her string bracelets. "I mean, it's not like I want the sort of attention she's getting because that would mean

I'd done something bad or irresponsible. But still . . . I guess I just hope that they remember I'm there, too."

"I'm sure they do," Cordelia said, but she really had no idea what Mr. and Mrs. Bauer were thinking these days.

"My mom forgot to pick me up after swim class at the Y the other day," Stevie said abruptly.

"Oh." Cordelia cringed. "How long did you wait around for her?"

"About a half hour. I guess it was no big deal in the end. My friend's mom drove me home. And my mom couldn't stop apologizing." Stevie laughed a bit. "She insisted on making whatever I wanted for dinner."

"What did you choose?" It was an inane question, but Cordelia didn't know what else to say without sounding as if she were criticizing Mrs. Bauer.

"I couldn't think of anything I wanted so badly, so I just said spaghetti and meatballs."

"Oh. Well, spaghetti and meatballs are always good."

"Yeah. My mom's a pretty good cook."

"So what do you want to do for your birthday?" Cordelia asked. "Are you having a party?"

"I don't really like parties. Anyway, it's no big deal."

"A birthday is always a big deal. Besides, you deserve some attention."

Stevie shrugged. "Why? Because I said that Sarah's been getting it all?"

"Well, yeah. And the fact that you only turn fourteen once."

"I do like cake."

"Listen," Cordelia said, and she was very, very serious. "One of my rules in life is this: If there's an opportunity to eat cake, take it."

Chapter 62

"It's nice to be working outside, isn't it?"

Sarah smiled at her mother. "Yes. I'd always rather be outdoors."

The five women were gathered at the picnic table in the Bauers' backyard to work on the quilt. It was a beautiful afternoon. Earlier in the day, Sarah had been to the pond on their neighbor Mrs. Wade's property, enjoying the coolness under the trees, watching little frogs hopping from shore to water, enjoying the antics of scurrying chipmunks, and admiring the various wildflowers that grew near the pond's edge. *The lazy days of summer,* she thought now. Her *last* lazy summer, ever, as this time next year she would be chasing a busy toddler around the yard and watching that he didn't fall into Mrs. Wade's pond.

Cordelia frowned. "I'd just better not get a sunburn."

Mrs. Kane laughed. "Cordelia, you're covered from head to toe!"

It was true. While Sarah, her mother and her sister, and Mrs. Kane were dressed in summer-appropriate clothing—short sleeves, sandals, bare heads—Cordelia was wearing a big, floppy, brimmed hat, a long-sleeved blouse buttoned up to the neck, and long pants. Sarah figured the only reason she wasn't also wearing gloves was that it would be too difficult to hold a needle.

"But the weather guy said the sun was going to be particularly strong today," Cordelia protested. "Or something like that. I'm not taking any chances."

The subject of the sun was dropped, and the five women worked quietly for some time, stopping only for a drink of lemonade or ice water. For her part, Sarah was thinking about the generous check her uncle Jonas and aunt Marie had sent for the baby. The accompanying note, which had been written by her uncle (his handwriting was very distinctive), had said: "We're so happy to welcome a new member to the Bauer family and hope this contribution will be of help."

Her father, Sarah thought now, had seemed a bit embarrassed by his brother's generosity. She wondered if there was rivalry between them. Her father had never said as much, but then again he wasn't the sort to talk about his relationships with people. He just lived them. Anyway, he hadn't told her to return the check, and neither had her mother.

Sarah had been touched. She had only seen her aunt and uncle a few times in her life, so she thought it was awfully nice of them to think of her welfare. She had deposited the check in the bank with the intention of it being the start of an education fund for her child. Well, she hoped that it would last that long untouched. After all, she had no clear idea of how she would pay for her baby's immediate needs, like diapers and food and doctor visits, let alone his higher education. Sarah glanced across the table at her mother. On second thought, she supposed the answer to that question lay with her parents. It would be *their* money that supported both the baby and Sarah until she could get out on her own and take charge, as a parent was supposed to do. Problem was, she had no idea when that would be. Having lost her babysitting clients hadn't helped, and she doubted anyone would hire her back when she had her own baby to watch. Thanks to Mrs. Kane she still had a few hours at The Busy Bee, but it was amazing how quickly money went, even when you were being very careful with it.

"Did I tell you about this awesome bag for sale at the new thrift store in town?" Cordelia asked suddenly, startling Sarah from her thoughts about her financial future.

"Uh, no," Sarah replied. "I don't think so."

"It's dark green suede. It would be totally perfect for fall."

Sarah smiled noncommittally and went back to her thoughts. She wondered, maybe unfairly, if the next season was as far ahead as Cordelia ever thought. She, Sarah, was more and more thinking years ahead—and not always with good results. For example, just the other day, she had had the brilliant idea of making a will. It was only when she sat down to make a list of her assets that she realized she had nothing of value to leave behind to her child. A measly bank account was all, and that was the property of her parents until she was eighteen. She had no valuable jewelry. (What a thought! Even her mother had only her wedding band and a silver cross on a silver-plated chain.) And her books would bring virtually nothing; they were mostly already third- or fourth-hand paperback volumes. It was a slightly terrifying thought, that in a materialistic sense she was worthless. Possessions had never meant anything to Sarah, nor had money (it was necessary for food and shelter, of course), but now, suddenly, she glimpsed one way in which possessions and money were worth something tangible and useful. That she hadn't realized this before made her feel dumb and naive.

"I'm glad Clarissa is inside," Stevie announced. "Look up at the sky."

They did, to see a hawk circling overhead, looking for prey (like small cats!) or maybe just enjoying the fact of flight. Sarah wondered. Did the ability to feel pleasure, not the kind that was only sensual, but the kind you felt inside, require sentience? *Was* that hawk enjoying his afternoon on the wing in the same way she enjoyed walking through the woods? Animals weren't supposed to be sentient, were they, and yet, how odd to try to imagine a living thing *not* being sentient. It was impossible, really.

Oh, Sarah thought, looking back to her sewing, if she were a bird her life would be so much simpler. Maybe it wouldn't be very easy overall. She would have to search for her food every day and build a home and shelter and protect her young from predators, but life would definitely be much *simpler*. She wouldn't have to choose the best schools and select the most affordable health insurance and shuttle her children from soccer to piano to dance practice and . . .

"Sarah?" It was her mother. "Are you feeling okay? You've got this big scowl on your face. Maybe you've been out in the sun too long."

"Told you," Cordelia said.

Mrs. Kane cleared her throat. "And, um, is that a starfish you're cutting out?"

Sarah nodded and looked down at the piece of purple cotton velvet in her hands. "Oh," she said. "How many arms are starfish supposed to have?"

Stevie laughed. "Not thirteen!"

Sarah smiled. Where had her thoughts taken her?! "I guess maybe I *have* been out in the sun too long," she said.

Chapter 63

The bell over the door at The Busy Bee tinkled. It was Cindy. "Morning," she said.

"Good morning to you," Adelaide replied. "Three customers already. Maybe that bodes well for a good day."

"Let's hope so." Cindy put her bag behind the counter. "Adelaide," she said. "I need your help with something."

"Sure. What is it? Is there a problem with the baby's quilt?"

"No, nothing like that. It's that I've decided to sell my family quilts. The ones my great-grandmother made."

Adelaide felt her eyes widen involuntarily. "The ones you framed a few years back?"

"Yes," Cindy said. "Those."

"But why on earth?"

Cindy looked at a point just over Adelaide's left shoulder. "I don't see any point in holding on to them when they might be worth a significant amount of money. Not that I want them to go to just anyone," she added hastily, looking back to Adelaide. "I mean, I would like to think that whoever bought the quilts will really appreciate them for their true value, beyond the financial value."

Adelaide knew how hard this decision must be for her friend. Cindy lived and breathed quilts and quilting! She absolutely didn't want to trample on delicate feelings; still, having to play a part in the sale of beloved family heirlooms made her feel sad and uncomfortable. "Are you very sure?" she asked.

Cindy nodded. "Yes. I've given it a lot of thought."

"Then I'll put out some feelers and let you know what I find."

"Thank you, Adelaide. I'm going to get a cup of coffee."

Cindy went off to the back room. While she was gone, Adelaide wondered if there was some way she could talk Cindy out of such a drastic measure. But if she really needed the money, and given Sarah's situation it was clear that she did, then what alternative could she offer?

And then it occurred to her. Maybe The Busy Bee could buy Cindy's quilts. Assuming that they were affordable, and Adelaide wouldn't know that for sure until she did some research. Anyway, if the shop owned the quilts, then someday Adelaide might be able to return them to Cindy or sell them back for a token amount. Unless Cindy would see that as unwanted charity and be offended.

Or maybe she could give Cindy more hours at the shop, at least until the baby was born. She would have to take a closer look at the books, see if the business could afford it without damaging her bottom line. If it *were* possible, then maybe Cindy would drop the idea of selling her family's heirlooms.

She wished there was *something* tangible she and Jack could do for Sarah and her family. True, her first responsibility was to her own family, her husband and daughter, but . . .

"Don't look now," Cindy said, coming back out front. "But here comes a van worth of customers."

She was right. A group of at least eight or nine women began to file through the door, exclaiming over the quilts hung on the wall and making a beeline for the quilt frames.

"I guess," Adelaide said, "that this is our lucky day."

Chapter 64

On the way home from The Busy Bee later that evening, Cindy stopped for gas. Prices were up again. Once the girls started driving and the family had to get a third vehicle, the expense of daily transportation alone would probably eat up within months whatever money she would get for the quilts. And—this was the first time this had occurred to Cindy—she should probably give part of whatever money she got from the sale to Adelaide. After all, Adelaide was handling the sale and it was The Busy Bee's reputation that would help place them with a buyer. Adelaide might even *expect* a cut of the profit.

Rats, Cindy thought. She had lied to Adelaide. She hadn't given the decision to sell the quilts much thought at all. She hadn't even told Joe about her intentions. Not that the quilts were his—strictly speaking, they had been left to her specifically—but she was afraid he might try to argue her out of letting them go. He would point out that the quilts were precious heirlooms better kept to hand down to Sarah and Stevie.

And he would be right.

It occurred to Cindy now that this was the second time in months she had kept something from her husband. First had been the menacing phone call from June Morrow. What was next?

A black Mercedes-Benz convertible glided up to the pump directly across from Cindy's car. She watched as a slim, well-dressed woman about her own age slipped out from behind the wheel. Her sandals were silver. Her hair was an astonishingly beautiful shade of strawberry blond. Her jeans were white.

Cindy looked away from the dazzling sight as a spark of resentment flared again inside her. She didn't *want* to have to let go of her precious quilts. She shouldn't *have* to make this sacrifice!

Cindy paid for the gas, got back in her car—old and a bit rusty—and pulled out onto the road. She felt foolish. She had never rushed into a big decision before, but after that conversation with Joe the other day, selling the quilts had seemed like such an obvious way to help the family's financial situation. They would probably each bring several thousands dollars, money that could pay off the part of Sarah's doctor and hospital bills that were not covered by their insurance.

A memory of her mother formally presenting her with the quilts came to her then. It was shortly before Margie Keller had died. She had been so terribly weak, mere skin and bones. And yet she had had the strength to pass the torch, as it were, to her daughter, to symbolically ensure the continuation of a legacy.

Cindy felt sure that in spite of her mother's great emotional attachment to the family treasures, she would have understood her daughter's motives for letting the quilts go. She was also sure that her mother would have been very sad and very disappointed. She might also have pointed out that Cindy was sending a very mixed message to her own daughters—on the one hand, she was spearheading the making of a quilt for the next generation; on the other hand, she was casting off those that had been made by the generations before. Where was the sense of family history and continuity in that?

And the decision was made, for real this time. Cindy would withdraw the quilts from the market. She had acted rashly, and it had led to an interesting if disturbing revelation. As it turned out, there were some things she simply *wasn't* willing to sacrifice for her husband and children. What that said about her, she wasn't quite sure.

Chapter 65

The girls were on a break from work. It was two in the afternoon, and they were sitting on a bench at the top of the beach. It was a glorious day; Cordelia thought that *glorious* was an even more appropriate adjective than *awesome*. The air was warm, but there was a good breeze off the water. And someone not too far away was grilling burgers and the smell was fantastic.

Cordelia waved her iPhone in front of Sarah's face. "I can't wait to show you the cool sneakers I just ordered online. I mean, they're totally awe—"

"You know," Sarah said. "Sometimes I feel like I'm going to be the worst mother ever."

Cordelia laughed. "Come on, Sarah. You'll be great. So, anyway, these sneakers—"

"I mean, I'm a good babysitter—in spite of what some people say!—but that's different. You're with your charges for a few hours at most, and you aren't expected to make any big, life-altering decisions, other than knowing when to call nine-one-one and how not to give peanut butter to a child with a peanut allergy and how not to leave a baby in the bath unattended. And then the parents come home and you're set entirely free of responsibility until the next time the parents want to go to a movie or out to dinner."

"Right. And you get paid for babysitting, which you don't do for being a parent."

"Intermittent responsibility I can handle," Sarah went on, as if she were talking to herself. "I've been proving that for years. But ceaseless responsibility? That's something very, very different. I'm just so worried that because I'm so young I'll get it all wrong with my own child."

Cordelia stifled a sigh. "I'm sure you'll be fine, Sarah. I mean, you're a smart person."

Sarah frowned and squinted up at the sky. Cordelia suspected that Sarah hadn't heard a word she had said since they sat down.

"There's just so much to know!" Sarah cried. "There's all this information about how to teach your child to read by the age of two and how to make him a musical genius by the age of three and how to make your own organic, gluten-free, vegan baby food. And it all makes you feel that one little mistake could ruin your baby's chances for a normal life. It's like disaster is around every corner, just waiting for you to trip up. And I'm just so afraid I'm going to trip up."

"You won't trip up," Cordelia said. Wasn't that what Sarah wanted to hear? "Well, I mean, everyone makes a small mistake here and there but—"

"What if I'm giving the baby a bath and he slips out of my hands and falls onto the floor and bashes his head and has brain damage? What if I'm changing him and I pull the diaper too tight and he gets a painful rash?"

Cordelia raised her eyebrows. "Is that even possible? I—"

"Thank God no one uses cloth diapers these days, the ones you have to fasten with a pin." Sarah shook her head as if in disbelief. "A pin! Can you imagine how many babies were inadvertently jabbed by their doting mothers?"

"A lot, I suppose. Look, Sarah—"

"These days you have to be a diagnostician to be a parent. You have to be Dr. House! You have to learn how to recognize an entire host of symptoms because if you ignore any of them it could result in total disaster. I mean, when is a runny nose just a runny nose and when is it a sign of brain cancer?"

Cordelia laughed. "Sarah, that makes no sense. Come on!"

"My point is valid," Sarah insisted. "I am just so *scared*. I mean, I've never been the worrying sort, but then again, I never had anything to worry about. Other people have always taken care of me. This is totally different. Now, *I'm* going to be responsible for taking care of someone else. And who am I to take on such responsibility?"

"You're—"

"I'm just some sixteen-year-old, unmarried kid in a small town in Maine. It's not like I'm in my twenties and married and have a good job!"

Cordelia wasn't at all sure what she could say to that, so she kept silent.

"I'm just so glad I have my mother to help me. On the other hand, I don't want to depend too much on her, or on anyone else, really. It would be shirking my duty, letting others clean up the mess I made, and my parents didn't raise me to foist my responsibilities off on other people."

"No, of course—"

"I mean, my father didn't build a successful business because he let someone else do the hard jobs. And my mother didn't develop her incredible sewing skills by giving up when she had to learn a really complicated stitch. No, I just won't let anyone but me bear the full weight of the responsibility for my child."

Cordelia's patience—never very strong—finally snapped. "You're so selfish!" she blurted.

Sarah looked thoroughly surprised by this accusation. "Me? Selfish? How can you say that?"

"Because all you talk about is you, you, you. Haven't you even wondered how *my* life's been going?"

"Your life? Your life is—"

"Is what?" Cordelia said. "Perfect?"

"I didn't say that."

"No, because I said it for you. Well, for your information, my life is *not* perfect. No one's is."

"I know that."

"I have challenges, too."

"I know you do. It's just that—"

"It's just that because you're pregnant you think the world revolves around you. Well, it doesn't. Millions and billions of women have babies every day. It's nothing special, you know."

Cordelia stopped short. She felt bad about that last remark. It was childish and mean. "I'm sorry," she added quickly. "I didn't mean that, about it not being special."

Sarah put her hand to her middle, a gesture that had become habitual. "Don't you care at all about my baby?" she said.

"I don't *know* your baby!" Cordelia cried in frustration. "But I do know you, and I care about you, of course I do. It's just that I need you to care about me, too."

"I do care about you!"

"Sorry. Sometimes lately it doesn't feel like you do."

Sarah sighed. "I'm doing what I can. I'm doing my best, I am."

"I know."

"Wait," Sarah said after a moment. "Didn't you say you wanted to show me something?"

"Did I?" Cordelia shrugged. She slipped her iPhone back into her bag. "I forget."

"Oh."

Cordelia got up from the bench. "It doesn't matter. We should get back to the shop."

Chapter 66

Sarah was manning the counter at The Busy Bee. Her mother and Mrs. Kane were also at the shop. At the moment they were deep in discussion about some aspect of her baby's quilt.

Luckily business was slow that morning because Sarah's mind was not on her job. She couldn't stop thinking about what Cordelia had said about her being self-focused. She guessed that she *was* self-focused, but how could she not be? It wasn't like she could forget for even one minute that she was pregnant.

Sarah almost laughed aloud. Cordelia had claimed that her life wasn't perfect. But really, what did she have to complain about? *She* wasn't the one who was pregnant. *She* wasn't the one facing a totally uncertain future. And Cordelia always got everything she wanted, from new clothes each season to a manicure once every two weeks to every new app that caught her fancy. Cordelia wasn't the one who had to work for her pocket money. All she did was bat her eyes at her father or use her little girl voice with her mother and pretty much anything she wanted was handed over to her on a silver platter!

Well, okay, Sarah admitted, maybe not on a silver platter. Still, where was Cordelia today while Sarah was working? On a road trip with her dad to the outlets in Kittery!

Sarah took a deep breath. She knew she was being childish. Mothers were supposed to be responsible adults, not emotionally erratic teens. But that was the very problem, wasn't it? She was *not* an adult, and there was no use pretending to be. Pregnancy didn't confer adult status, and it certainly didn't guarantee mature thoughts and tempered behavior!

In fact, until this summer, she had never felt resentful or jealous of her friend. And Cordelia had done nothing to warrant such feelings of ill will. She, Sarah, was the one who had been careless. Cordelia hadn't changed, and she wasn't the one who had caused their friendship to alter.

"Sarah?" Mrs. Kane said, interrupting her unhappy thoughts. "Would you do a quick inventory of the pattern books on the shelves?"

Sarah grabbed a pad of paper and hurried out from behind the counter. "Sure, Mrs. Kane."

Better to bury herself in the doings of The Busy Bee than to moan and groan about how badly she had screwed up.

A few minutes later, the bell over the door tinkled. Sarah looked over her shoulder to see a woman in her sixties or seventies. Her hair was a stiff halo of a suspiciously dark, flat brown. Her eyebrows, too, were obviously dyed, and shaped into pointy arches not normally found on a human face. Her lips were heavily lined with a dark pink pencil and filled in with a lighter, glossier lipstick. She wore what looked like a pants suit preserved from the seventies, polyester or some other hot and itchy-looking fabric, in a sickly yellowish hue.

Sarah bit back a smile. There was something so clownish in the woman's appearance, something almost to be pitied if not laughed at. Sarah immediately felt bad for thinking this. No one should be laughed at, no one. And maybe the woman was a very nice person. What she looked like shouldn't matter at all. Still, Sarah found herself hoping the woman wouldn't notice her.

But her hope was in vain. The woman's eyes widened when she caught sight of Sarah, and she hurried toward her.

"So you're pregnant!" she cried. "Congratulations!"

"Yes," Sarah said. "Thank you."

"So, honey, when are you due?" the woman asked with an eager smile.

Sarah mustered an answering, though less eager, smile. "Late August," she said.

The woman winked at her. "You must be very excited."

"Um," Sarah said. "Yes."

"So is it a boy or a girl?"

"A boy."

"I knew it! I can always tell. There's something about the shape—" The woman reached out a hand covered in gaudy rings and placed it on Sarah's middle.

She didn't know why the gesture repulsed her. So many other women had done this before. But now, Sarah jerked away from this woman's thoroughly unwelcome intimacy. "Don't touch me!" she cried.

The woman withdrew her hand as if it had been burned. Her eyebrows shot up even farther as her face, under its heavy coating of makeup, registered shock.

"I'm sorry," Sarah said hurriedly. "I'm sorry. It's just . . ." But more words were lost to a sudden flood of tears and Sarah scurried off to the little kitchen at the back of the store. From there she was able to overhear her mother and Mrs. Kane rush to soothe wounded feelings.

"I'm so very sorry," Mrs. Kane said. She was using what Sarah thought of as her professional voice, calm, clear, slightly conciliatory, and pitched a bit lower than normal. "I'm sure she didn't mean anything by it."

But I did, Sarah thought. *I'm not public property!*

"My daughter is a good girl, really," Cindy added. Sarah cringed at her mother's pleading tone. "She's just very tired."

There was a moment of silence before the woman said, "Hormones! They play nasty tricks on us all. I remember when I was pregnant with my first son. Lord, I thought my husband would murder me!"

Sarah waited in the kitchen while the woman purchased some thread and then left. When she had gone, Sarah emerged from her hiding place.

"I'm sorry, Mrs. Kane," she said. "Really. I shouldn't have snapped at her."

"No need to apologize," Adelaide said promptly. "Why don't you take a break, Sarah? Walk down to the beach, get some fresh air."

"Oh, I'm okay, really. I'll get back to taking inventory of the pattern books."

"Are you sure?" her mother asked, concern etching her brow.

Sarah nodded and turned to the bookshelves on the left-hand wall. She felt a whirring in her stomach that had nothing to do with the baby. She was scared. She could not afford to let her mood swings affect her behavior at work. If her boss had been anyone other than Mrs. Kane, she might already be unemployed.

The bell over the door announced the arrival of another customer. Sarah kept her eyes on the pattern books and hoped it was someone who hated babies.

Chapter 67

Adelaide was sitting at her desk in the den. She opened her laptop with the intention of doing some further research on the commercial value of Cindy's quilts. She had put out some feelers to colleagues across the country and already many of them had responded with questions and suggestions and quotes that in some cases were astonishingly high—too high for The Busy Bee to afford.

Heavy footsteps sounded from the hall. Time and again Adelaide had asked Cordelia not to clump through the house, but she continued to clump and Adelaide suspected that she was fighting a losing battle. Not that Cordelia was consciously defying her mother. She just couldn't seem to keep simple requests in mind.

Unlike Sarah. Adelaide felt bad about what had happened at The Busy Bee. Sarah was trying so hard to prove that she was a hard worker and a good person. It was inevitable that she would occasionally break under the strain of all that self-imposed discipline. For the rest of the afternoon, after the departure of that carnival-like woman, Sarah had worked especially diligently, even taking the trash out back to the bins, a task that ordinarily was not hers.

A crash from the kitchen made Adelaide jump in her seat.

"Sorry!" Cordelia yelled. "The broom fell out of the closet. I forgot to put the latch on the door."

Case in point. Cordelia and responsibility were not necessarily in sympathy. God forbid it were Cordelia who was pregnant, Adelaide had no doubt that Grandma would be shouldering most of the day-to-day burden.

What a mean-spirited thought, Adelaide thought, shaking her head. Still, it did make her think about how Cindy and Sarah would divide the decision-making regarding the baby. She suspected they were in for a power struggle no matter how close they had always been. What was that old saying, something about there not being enough room in a house for two women in charge. Well, some might find that sexist, and it probably was, but there was some truth to it, as there always was in those old adages.

What would happen while Sarah was in class for eight hours a day? Cindy would be the one making the moment-to-moment decisions, some of which Sarah might resent or disagree with. Would Cindy become, in effect, a nanny, subject to Sarah's rules and demands? Or, and this seemed somehow more likely, would Cindy naturally assume the mother's role, be more parent than grandparent? Only time would tell, but Adelaide foresaw a degree of messiness.

Well, the entire situation was fraught with messiness. Adelaide thought about the time just before finals in June when a girl in Sarah's grade had called her an appalling name. Jack had been sick about the incident. For one, he had worked very hard in a campaign against bullying of any sort on the school's premises and it was always a severe disappointment when an incident did occur. And, in this case, there had been something more personal at stake. In some ways, Sarah and Stevie Bauer were the Kanes' surrogate daughters. Adelaide and Jack had known them for most of their lives, had watched them grow alongside their own daughter. They had attended their birthday parties and school plays and had taken the girls on excursions to Funtown Splashtown and the aquarium in Boston.

Jack had managed to keep the incident quiet; even Cordelia

didn't seem to know about it. If she had been a witness to the incident, well, Adelaide had no doubt her daughter would have gone in with guns blazing to protect Sarah.

Adelaide's cell phone rang. She didn't recognize the number but as she used the phone almost exclusively for business purposes she answered.

"Hello? Yes, this is Adelaide Kane. Oh, you're calling about the quilts. Yes, they're still for sale. Really?"

Adelaide felt her heart race. Just wait until she told Cindy about this!

Chapter 68

Cindy arrived at The Busy Bee to find Adelaide beaming. And when she beamed, she reminded Cindy a wee bit of a human lighthouse. The fact that she was wearing a red blouse added to the impression of exceeding brightness.

"Good news!" she cried. "We got a very generous offer for your family's quilts from the Museum of Americana."

Cindy's stomach fell. "Oh."

"They're a small museum in Tennessee, only ten years old, and intent on building their collection. The man I spoke to, someone in the acquisitions department, was ecstatic to have found us. Isn't it wonderful?"

Cindy braced herself for what might very well be an understandably angry reaction from her friend. "I'm sorry," she said. "I should have said something sooner. I've decided I just can't part with the quilts."

Adelaide nodded promptly. "I understand."

"You're not going to try to talk me into selling?" Cindy asked. Adelaide's reply had truly surprised her, particularly after her earlier show of great enthusiasm. "After all, you did all the research to determine a price. And you spoke with this person from the museum. I feel as if I've wasted your time. I feel as if I've put you in an awkward position."

"No, of course I'm not going to try to convince you to sell," Adelaide assured her. "And assessing the quilts' value wasn't a waste of time at all. I learned a thing or two."

Cindy felt enormously relieved. “Thank you, Adelaide,” she said. “Really.”

“Actually, Cindy, I know why you were considering a sale, but frankly, I was surprised. Those works of art are a tangible part of your family’s history. If I had something like that from my ancestors, even if it was a really amateurish portrait painted by some great-great-great-grandmother I’d barely heard of, I don’t think I’d ever be able to part with it.”

“You might if you really needed the money.”

Cindy thought that Adelaide seemed a little embarrassed by her comment. “Yes,” Adelaide said after a moment. “Well.”

“I hope I’m making the right decision,” she said.

“I suspect that you are,” Adelaide said, her tone reassuring. “And if someday you come to decide it’s time to part with them, you can easily put them back on the market.”

“Right,” Cindy said, but she knew now there would never be a time when she would be able to part with the quilts. That was okay. Money could be made in other ways.

“I’ll take care of the museum people,” Adelaide said then.

“Thanks. I hope they’re not going to be mad.”

Adelaide shrugged. “Oh, I doubt they’ll be mad. Maybe a bit annoyed and certainly disappointed. But they’ll survive. And I bet you they leave the door open for a future sale. The quality of those quilts is outstanding.”

And, Cindy thought, Adelaide was an outstanding friend. “The girls will be by at the end of the day to work on the baby’s quilt,” she said. “I thought maybe I’d treat everyone to takeout Chinese.”

Adelaide laughed. “You’ll find no argument from Cordelia! And I’ll pay for half.”

Chapter 69

Cordelia was lying on her bed. Pinky was standing, somewhat lopsidedly, on her stomach, his round, blue, plastic eyes staring at nothing from the sides of his head.

"Pinky," she said. "I'm tired of feeling grumpy."

Ever since her last confrontation with Sarah, Cordelia had been feeling bad. Okay, Sarah *was* being self-centered but maybe that was normal and maybe it was even necessary. What was really important was the baby after all, and if Sarah needed to focus entirely on herself in order to be a good mother, well, Cordelia—and everyone else—was just going to have to tolerate her behavior.

Besides, Sarah wasn't *always* going on about herself. It was only on occasion.

Cordelia sighed and glanced over at her dresser, on top of which sat a pile of colorful cotton cloth, her less than perfect contribution to Sarah's baby's quilt. She knew that she shouldn't have lost her temper with Sarah. She really should work on being more patient. A new pair of sneakers, even really awesome ones, didn't compare in importance with having a baby. Still, Cordelia just couldn't imagine trading her interest in—well, in everything!—to concentrate on having a baby at the age of sixteen!

Frankly, she wasn't even sure she *ever* wanted to have children. The thought of childbirth frightened her; she wasn't a fan of pain, even a splinter sent her howling, and she regularly fainted at the dentist before Dr. Horutz even touched her, and they said you never got your body back after you had a baby, and her own body was big enough already, thank you very much! And, more importantly, she suspected that her maternal instincts didn't exist. At least, they certainly hadn't made themselves known. Maybe they never would and she would never have to deal with morning sickness and sore breasts and nasty things like an episiotomy. Cordelia felt faint even saying the word in her head.

How could she be so vastly different from her best friend? Sarah was so weirdly calm about the prospect of giving birth. Unless she was pretending. But why should she lie? Well, why did anyone lie? For a million, billion reasons that often made sense only to the person lying and sometimes, not even then.

Cordelia put her finger on the tip of Pinky's velvety horn. Her mother had told her what had happened with Sarah and that woman at the shop the other day. Poor Sarah. She must feel so embarrassed about losing her temper. And really, Cordelia couldn't blame her. Strangers shouldn't touch each other!

Yes, she would make it up to Sarah as soon as possible, apologize and do something nice for her to show Sarah that she still loved her and that she would always love her no matter what happened or how weird she acted.

"Any ideas, Pinky?" Cordelia asked.

Pinky just stared.

Chapter 70

It was about nine thirty in the evening. Sarah's parents were in their bedroom. She was on her way back from the bathroom to her room when the sound of their voices caught her attention. She had never eavesdropped on her parents before, but now she stopped and held her breath.

"I've gone over the books again," her father was saying. "What with Dave Johnson postponing his renovations until next year, maybe the one after that, cash flow's going to be a problem. Again."

"Maybe we should talk to the bank about a bridge loan," her mother said after a moment. "Just something short term. Or a personal line of credit."

"I don't want to get into debt if we can help it, Cindy."

"Of course not, neither do I. But there's got to be some way. . . ."

Sarah had heard enough. She hurried back to her room and carefully shut the door behind her.

Cordelia had been absolutely right when she had accused her of being self-centered. Having this baby and keeping him was the height of selfish behavior. Something had to be done, and she was the one to do it.

Sarah sat at her desk and opened her laptop. An hour later, she had learned a number of important things about the process of adoption. For one, she had learned that adoptions didn't have to be closed, as they used to be. They could be "open" in a variety of ways. And there were plenty of organizations, many of them right there in Maine, which would help a mother-to-be understand her options and make the decision that was right for her.

And the Web sites Sarah visited were so determinedly optimistic and reassuring. They said that choosing an adoption was not taking the easy way out. They said that choosing an adoption did not mean that you didn't love your baby and want the best for her. They said that by choosing an adoption, you were regaining possession of your life.

It wasn't too late to make arrangements. The baby wasn't due until late August and it was only just July now. . . .

Sarah closed her laptop and lay down on her bed. In spite of the encouraging words she had just read, adoption *wasn't* what she wanted, but the alternative—putting her family through years and years of financial hardship—just didn't seem fair. Somehow, she had to find the strength to make this sacrifice for her parents. And she had to hope that she wouldn't grow to resent them for having "forced" her to put her baby up for adoption. She had to hope that she wouldn't live the rest of her life with a nagging feeling of regret and remorse.

She didn't think that would be bearable. Living with that intensity of pain could very probably drive you to do something drastic, like take drugs or even kill yourself. And if you did manage to survive, if you did manage to get married someday and have another baby or two, would you be able to look at those children without remembering the child you had given up? Would the guilt be too heavy a burden? Would those other children, the ones you had kept, suffer as a result of your misery? Would your husband be driven away by your inability to sustain a reasonable degree of happiness?

Sarah sighed deeply. Adoption was *not* right for her. She knew that. But she would have to *make* it right, for the sake of everyone else involved.

She turned onto her side and slid her hands under her cheek. She had never felt more like a kid than she did in that moment.

A stupid kid who had done a stupid thing even though she had been taught better. Don't touch the stove because it could be hot and you might burn yourself. Don't cross the street against the light because you might get hit by a car.

Don't have sex carelessly because you could ruin your life and disappoint your family and alienate your best friend.

Forever.

Chapter 71

Adelaide was at the Yorktide Library, wandering the section of books that had been acquired in the past five months. She often went to the library with a list of specific titles, but sometimes she just went in to browse. It was always exciting to stumble across a book that turned out to be a treasure. She had found one of her all-time favorite mystery series in this delightfully random way.

Adelaide's attention was caught by a slight commotion in the next aisle where a young woman with a baby strapped to her chest was trying to contain a toddler trying to push her own stroller. "Be careful, Lisa," the woman said to the little girl, who subsequently plowed the stroller into the legs of a middle-aged man. The man laughed, the woman apologized, and the little girl shrieked.

Adelaide looked away. She found herself thinking of Cindy's two lost babies. She hadn't asked if they had been girls or boys or one of each. Sometimes she wondered how she would have felt if Cordelia had been a boy. She wondered if she would have felt as if she had cheated her first son of his birthright. It had the makings of a Greek or a Shakespearean tragedy, didn't it? The older son, the first born, abandoned at birth, returns to the mother who cast him off only to find a second son enjoying the rights and privileges of the heir. Chaos ensues.

Maybe she was being dramatic, entertaining this unhappy possibility that had *not* occurred. But you couldn't always prevent your mind from wandering in all sorts of directions, whether it was the middle of the night when you were wide-awake and feeling very, very alone in the world, which, of course, you were, everyone was, or in the New Books section of the local public library at four o'clock on a sunny afternoon.

"Adelaide, hello."

Adelaide turned to see Maggie Collins smiling at her. Maggie had three children, all now grown, one married and living in Yorktide, one in the army, and another trying to make his way as an actor in Los Angeles. Her husband was recently retired from the gas company. Adelaide hadn't seen Maggie or her husband, Sam, in an age.

"Hi," she said. "How are you, Maggie? You look well."

Maggie smiled. "Can't complain. Sam's underfoot now, but I'm keeping him in line. So how is Cindy holding up?"

Adelaide bristled slightly. "She's fine," she said. "Just fine."

"Oh, good. It's just that it must be so hard for all of them right now. But the Bauers are a strong family."

"Yes," Adelaide said. "They are."

"You know," Maggie said, her voice pitched low, "my cousin's girl got pregnant last year. They live down in New Hampshire. Well, I have to say that my cousin and her husband did just what Cindy and Joe are doing. They rallied around their daughter, and even with ten-year-old twins at home, they're making things work with the baby. Now, I know not everyone can do that, but God bless those who can."

Adelaide managed a smile. "Yes," she said. "God bless them."

Maggie Collins said farewell and took her pile of books to the checkout desk. Adelaide felt a buzz of anger in her head. She hadn't been so lucky, had she? Her parents hadn't rallied around her at all. They had made her feel like a failure and a freak. No one other than a very kind woman at the adoption agency had shown her the slightest bit of sympathy. No one had offered to make a quilt in honor of her baby.

And Adelaide thought, she wanted some sympathy. She *deserved* some sympathy, even all these years after the fact. True, Cindy had been heartbroken when she had learned about the adoption. And yes, Jack had always been there for her but . . .

For the first time in her life, Adelaide left the library without a book. She got into her car and turned it toward home. A thought had occurred to her. She had always assumed that she would tell Cordelia about her first child. Maybe now was the time.

Chapter 72

Joe was sitting at the kitchen table reading the local daily paper. Cindy wasn't sure how he was feeling, but he *looked* perfectly calm. Cindy was a bit envious. She didn't know how he did it, what with all the distressing news lately.

The water bill was higher this month than last and while it was true that it was a pretty dry summer, the bill seemed inflated and would require a phone call. They had heard a report on the national morning news predicting that the economy was still far from a good recovery. And one of Joe's steadiest clients had told them he was moving at the end of the summer. He would recommend Joe to the new owners, but he couldn't promise they would choose his services.

Cindy felt her heart speed up. It was unlike her to panic, and she couldn't help but think of what her mother would say. Worrying was interest paid on a debt that might never come due. That was true enough, but how did you prevent the worrying and the panic from starting up in the *first* place?

And Sarah's pregnancy was by far the most disruptive thing that had ever happened in her life, more disruptive even than the miscarriages and her mother's passing. Still, she had been trying to keep her fears and worries from Joe; he had enough to handle, especially with the extra jobs he had taken on.

The plate Cindy had been drying slipped out of her hand and shattered as it hit the floor.

"Oh, damn!" she cried.

Joe made to rise. "I'll take care of it," he said.

"No, no, it's okay. I broke it. I'll clean it up."

Cindy fetched the broom and dustpan, swept up the broken pieces of the plate, dumped them into a paper bag, and put the bag into the trash can.

"Cindy," Joe said when she was done, "you look exhausted. Come sit down."

She did, and the words came spilling out. "Oh, Joe, I feel so guilty. Somewhere along the line I must have failed as a mother. Why else would Sarah have been so careless?"

"You didn't fail your daughter, Cindy."

"I did, Joe! I should have been able to protect her from this."

Joe shook his head. "I don't know what to say, Cindy. Except that it's my job, too, to protect her. But I don't think it's our fault that she got pregnant."

His words barely registered with Cindy. "It's a mother's job to keep her children safe. And I failed. I wish she had come to me before she had sex with that boy. I'm sure he talked her into it! He might even have forced her! God, she must have been so frightened!"

"Now, there's no good in imagining all sorts of things," Joe said firmly. "Or in wishing you could turn back the clock."

Cindy knew he was right. She felt her anger deflate, but the regret remained. "Oh, I know," she said, "but I can't stop wondering what I might have said or done differently. I can't stop *thinking*!"

"There's a time and a place for thinking, Cindy. And then there's a time when what's required is action. Moving forward."

Cindy laughed unhappily. "Sometimes I feel that I'm doing absolutely nothing constructive for Sarah. Making a quilt for her baby is hardly *doing* anything to make things easier for her."

"It's doing more than you think, Cindy. It's the small things that count. You know that."

Cindy nodded reluctantly. "And poor Stevie. I so hope she's not feeling neglected because of all the attention her sister has been getting."

"Stevie's strong," Joe said. "And smart."

"I know that. I also know that she keeps things to herself. Whenever I ask her if she's okay, all she says is that she's fine."

"Then we just have to believe that she is fine. Until she tells us otherwise."

Cindy sighed. Joe was right. He always was. "Thank you, Joe," she said. "I'm sorry—"

Joe put his hand over hers. "Nothing to be sorry about."

Chapter 73

Cordelia and Stevie were perched on an outcrop of rock by the water in Perkins Cove. Clarissa sat in between the girls, her orange-tipped tail tucked neatly around her front paws.

Cordelia was wearing jean shorts (artfully ripped by the manufacturer) and a navy and white striped T-shirt with a decidedly nautical look. Her sunglasses were enormous (her eyesight was bad enough; the last thing she needed was to burn her retinas or something equally gross). Her flip-flops were white (probably a mistake as they were only three weeks old and already kind of dirty).

Stevie was wearing a pair of black shorts that came to her knees, a long-sleeved chambray shirt, and bright green Converse high-tops. (She told Cordelia she had saved her allowance for almost a year to afford them.)

"It's so pretty here, isn't it?" Cordelia said. "With the sun glittering on the water. Can you imagine, I don't know, a cape that looked like what the water looks like now? A cape fit for an empress!"

"Yeah. Cordelia? If I tell you something, a deep dark secret, will you promise to keep it a secret?"

"Sure," Cordelia said promptly. "I mean, unless you're going to tell me you're a mass murderer or something!"

"Nothing that bad," Stevie assured her.

"Then, of course."

Stevie put her hand on Clarissa's sleek head. "The thing is, I'm gay."

Cordelia felt her eyes widen. "Really?" she said. "I had no idea."

"You didn't suspect?"

"No. Why should I have?"

Stevie shrugged, causing Clarissa to leap into her lap, where Stevie began to stroke her back. "I don't know. It's just that I've been wondering if anyone has guessed."

"Oh. Has anyone said anything to you about being gay?"

"No. But maybe someone's thinking something."

Cordelia frowned. Someone was always thinking something! You couldn't stop people from speculating. She herself did it all the time! "You know," she said, "being gay isn't bad at all. You said the secret wasn't 'that bad.' "

"I know," Stevie assured her. "I'm not ashamed or anything."

"Good."

"Just . . . just that I feel a little vulnerable, I guess. And scared."

"Don't be scared," Cordelia said forcefully. "Just don't. And you're only vulnerable if you allow yourself to be. So don't do that, either."

Stevie laughed. "Easier said than done!"

"I know. But remember you have me. I'm your friend." It was really true, Cordelia thought. Stevie had become a friend in the past few months. And in a weird way, Sarah was to thank for that.

"Okay," Stevie said. "Thanks."

"So, um, have you, you know, gone out with anyone?"

Stevie laughed. "No. You're the first person I've even told."

"Oh. Is there someone at school you like?"

Stevie shrugged again. "Kind of. But even I know I'm way too young to really date. Besides, I don't even know if she's gay, too."

"Right. It's not like you can just ask someone . . ." Cordelia wondered. "But maybe it's okay to ask. I mean, how else would you know?"

"Well, sometimes you can kind of tell . . ."

"Oh. Like if a girl dresses in baggy jeans and plaid shirts then probably she's gay."

"Maybe. Or maybe she just likes plaid!"

"Yikes," Cordelia said. "You're right. I like plaid. In small amounts and only in the winter, but still, I like it. Look, I hope I don't sound like an idiot about this, Stevie. I'm actually really glad you told me. I'm honored."

"Thanks. I guess I'm glad I told you, too."

"Good. And I know your parents are going to be fine with it."

Stevie's eyes widened in alarm. "But you won't say a word, right? You promised."

"Of course not. My lips are sealed."

"Because I don't know when I'll tell them. Maybe not for a long time."

"No problem, Stevie, really. I can keep a secret. But will you tell Sarah soon?"

"Not yet. It's not like she has any time for me. Ugh. That sounded really stupid."

"No, it didn't," Cordelia told her. "Sometimes I feel the same way, like I could shake her and say, 'Hey! It's me, remember?' But I think that's normal. I mean, we're probably not as important to her now as we once were. Maybe once the baby's here and things settle down, she'll have more time for us."

But Cordelia wasn't at all sure that would be true.

"So you don't like boys even a little?" Cordelia asked, hoping that wasn't an insulting question. No one had ever come out to her before!

"Well, I like them well enough," Stevie said. "I just don't want to, you know, do stuff with them."

"Oh. It's just that some people are bisexual."

Stevie laughed. "That sounds way too confusing to me!"

"Me too. Sheesh."

Suddenly, Clarissa stood up on Stevie's lap and began to make that freaky, clacking sound cats make when they spot likely prey. It made Cordelia wince.

"Maybe we'd better go," Stevie said, grabbing Clarissa to her chest. "Because in about one minute that seagull over there is going to be history."

Cordelia jumped to her feet. "Ugh! Come on!"

Stevie followed, clutching a very annoyed Clarissa very tightly.

Chapter 74

Sarah steeled herself. If she were going to make this offer, then she was going to have to mean it. She couldn't be a tease about it, suggesting an adoption and then backing out. She was going to have to stand by her word.

"Mom," she said, hoping her voice wasn't shaking. Her hands certainly were. "I've been thinking. A lot. And maybe . . . maybe adoption is the right thing to do."

Her mother dropped the dish towel she had been holding onto the floor. Sarah somewhat awkwardly retrieved it. Her mother's face wore an expression of shock.

"What?" she said. "But we've all decided . . . we've been making plans. We're making a quilt. We *want* the baby."

"I know, but . . ." Sarah pressed her lips together to stop them from trembling. *Come on,* she scolded silently. *You're doing this for your family.*

"What brought this on, Sarah?" her mother asked.

"Nothing. It's just that I've been thinking about how difficult it's going to be for you and Dad, and it seems like the only reasonable way to handle things is to . . ." Sarah found she couldn't go on, no matter how hard she tried to.

Her mother took Sarah's arms and held them tightly. She looked searchingly, almost imploringly into her daughter's eyes. "Answer me honestly," she said. "Promise?"

Sarah nodded. It was an automatic gesture. She wasn't quite sure what words might come out of her mouth next.

"Do you really want to give up your child?" her mother asked.

Sarah hesitated. She wasn't sure there was any point in lying at this point. "No," she said. "But—"

"But nothing. Please, *please* trust me, Sarah. Everything will be all right. I promise."

Sarah laughed, but it was a wild and unhappy laugh. "You can't promise that, Mom. No one can."

"Yes," Cindy said forcefully, tightening her grip on Sarah's arms. "I can promise and I do. I will make everything all right."

Sarah just stood there, silent. Had her mother become delusional? Had she become so desperate to keep the family intact that she would ignore a difficult reality—like a new baby to feed, clothe, and rear—until it was too late to defend against it?

Sarah closed her eyes. This had been a huge mistake. She had probably caused more grief by proposing an adoption at this point when it was clear that for better or worse none of them wanted to let the baby go. At least, her mother didn't want to let him go, and neither did she.

"Sarah?"

She opened her eyes. Her mother released her hold.

"You look tired. Why don't you lie down for a while? I'll call you for dinner."

Sarah didn't have the strength to answer or to argue. She nodded and turned to leave the kitchen.

"Sarah?"

Sarah looked over her shoulder.

"Don't tell your father we had this conversation, all right? I'll speak to him."

Sarah nodded and left.

Chapter 75

It was a little after ten o'clock in the evening when Adelaide put the cooking magazine she had been pretending to read on her bedside table.

"I've been thinking," she said.

Jack, in the bed next to her, raised an eyebrow. "Often a dangerous thing."

"This is serious, Jack. I've been thinking that now might be a good time to tell Cordelia about the adoption."

"Really?" Jack put aside the book he had been enjoying, a classic espionage novel set during the Cold War. "Why now? Isn't she still a little young?"

"I don't think so, no. And," she said, "I can't help but think that knowing about my experience when I was seventeen will help Cordelia come to terms with Sarah's situation."

"Maybe," Jack said, but he sounded dubious. "Just remember that once that news is out there, you can't take it back."

Adelaide sighed. "I know."

"On the other hand," Jack pointed out, "there's no obligation ever to tell Cordelia, is there? Unless, and this is a macabre thought, someday in the future Cordelia falls in love with someone who turns out to be this young man and then . . ."

"God, Jack, don't even think that!" Though Adelaide herself had considered the awful possibility more than once, to hear it voiced aloud was doubly horrifying.

"Sorry," Jack said. "I have an imaginative mind."

"Am I being selfish?" she asked her husband, after a moment in which she recalled her conversation with Maggie Collins at the library. "Wanting Cordelia to know?"

"I don't see how, unless you're hoping to gain something from it. Are you?"

"I don't think so." *Not even sympathy?* a little voice in her head asked her. "No," Adelaide said firmly. "I don't want anything. I guess it's just that I'm not one hundred percent sure I'm doing the right thing."

"Then, don't tell her yet. Maybe a better time will come."

"Hmm. Maybe." Was there ever a good time for the revelation of a secret so big? And really, *were* her motives so pure and unselfish? How could anyone ever really know if she was doing something for the right reasons?

"How did you feel after you told Cindy about the adoption?" Jack asked.

"Relieved, mostly," Adelaide admitted. "Of course, I had no choice but to tell her. I'd really upset her by pushing the idea of an adoption. I felt I had to explain my—my insistence. And to apologize."

"And how did Cindy feel?"

"Terribly sad."

"And she's an adult. Cordelia's only a kid. Think about it a bit more, okay?" Jack suggested.

"I will," she promised.

"Remember that old adage: When in doubt, don't."

Adelaide smiled. "You and your old adages!"

"Yes, well, my old adages and I are going to sleep now if this conversation is over."

"It is. Good night, Jack."

He leaned over and kissed her. "Good night, Adelaide."

Adelaide turned off the light on her bedside table and lay staring into the dark for a long time. She had promised Jack she would think more about her decision to tell Cordelia about the adoption. But by the morning, she didn't need to give the subject any further thought. She knew what she was going to do.

Chapter 76

Cindy was alone in the shop. Adelaide had an appointment with her dentist and wouldn't be in until after lunch. The girls had the day off but would be coming to the shop around four to do some work on the baby's quilt. Truth be told, often enough the girls spent more time chatting than sewing, but Cindy figured that any activity that kept women together was important.

It had been a slow morning. Only one person had come by the shop, a regular who knew exactly the thickness and color of thread that she wanted. She had been in and out within three minutes, tops. Cindy would have been happy if a big tour bus of people came by, each person loudly demanding personal attention. It would help take her mind off that fraught encounter with Sarah.

Poor child. She had been ready to make an enormous sacrifice for the sake of her family. It must have taken an awful amount of courage to come forward like that and suggest a path her deepest instinct told her not to take.

Cindy rubbed her eyes. She and Joe must have been indiscreet. Sarah must have overheard one of the conversations in which they had been talking about money. They would have to be more careful. They would have to talk and plan when Sarah wasn't at home. Sarah, or Stevie.

Cindy stuck by her very firm opinion that keeping Sarah's baby was the right thing for the family to do. Still, she wondered if she should have been so *forceful* with Sarah. She did not want to be a bully with either of her children. And what had she been thinking, promising that the future would be rosy? Sarah was right. No one could promise that, *no one*, not even the most loving parent or devoted spouse or dedicated friend.

Sarah had admitted that she didn't really want to give up her baby. So she must have been motivated solely by guilt at the thought of putting such a burden on her parents. Cindy wondered. Was a motive of guilt ever sufficient and genuine enough to be respected and acted upon? Maybe. But not in this case. No.

Cindy caught a glimpse of a woman peering into the shop from the sidewalk. She waved, but either the woman didn't see her or she wasn't in a friendly mood. She moved on and Cindy shrugged.

There was another thing. She had told Sarah not to tell her father about their conversation; she had said that she would tell him herself. But she had lied. The truth was that Cindy was afraid Joe would encourage an adoption now that Sarah had mentioned the possibility. This was the third secret she was keeping from her husband. Somehow, in the space of a few months, she had become a person of silence and deception.

Cindy sighed. She had to keep reminding herself that this unborn child was not her own. It was *Sarah's*. And Sarah was Cindy's child. It was Cindy's job to show support and loyalty to her daughter before her grandson. Wasn't it? Or did the baby now take precedence because he was an utterly dependent being? Where did Cindy's responsibility end and Sarah's begin?

The bell over the shop's door rang. Cindy sighed in relief. Finally. Customers, three of them together. And by the look of them, these women were serious quilters. Even if Cindy hadn't had an instinct for such things, their bags—identical and with the words Kittery Kquilters Klub stitched on the side—would have given them away. Thankfully, the next half an hour or so would involve her in matters that had nothing to do with doubtful motives, blatant lies, and false promises.

Chapter 77

"It's nice out here," Stevie said. "Quiet. Pretty."

The girls were on the deck at the Kane house. There had been a sun-shower and now the grass was twinkling with raindrops and there was a coolish breeze.

Cordelia was stretched out on a lounge chair. Stevie was cross-legged in an upright folding chair, sewing a bit of their quilting project with her deft hands. (Cordelia's latest efforts had been ruined when she spilled her soda all over the fabric.) Clarissa was stalking the deck, acting like the director of homeland security against unwanted bugs and mice.

"Yeah," Cordelia said. "It would be perfect if we had a pool."

"Clarissa wouldn't like it. She hates the water. Most cats do."

"Mmm." Cordelia squirted more sunblock onto her legs. You could never be too careful. Skin could get burned and icky very quickly.

"Did anyone ever ask you questions about Sarah?" Stevie asked suddenly. "You know, when everybody first found out?"

"Yeah," Cordelia said, "back before school ended, a few girls asked me some stuff."

"Did they say mean things about Sarah?"

Cordelia tossed the tube of sunblock aside. She had no problem with lying to Stevie about this. "No," she said. "No one said anything mean." Boy, one girl had been such a bitch! "They seemed genuinely concerned. There was this one girl though who's got a bad reputation as a gossip. Let's just say I shut her down."

Stevie smiled. "You don't look tough at all, but I totally believe that you can be."

Cordelia thought that anybody could be tough, given the right provocation. "What do your friends say about Sarah being pregnant?" she asked.

Stevie shrugged. "They don't say anything."

"Really? Still nothing?"

"Well, Marly wanted to know a bunch of stuff at first. Like, if Sarah was going to marry Justin. But I just told her I didn't want to talk about it. After that, no one's said anything. It's kind of weird."

Cordelia thought about that. It *was* a little weird. "Are you going to tell them that you're gay?" she asked.

"I don't know," Stevie said. "Probably someday they'll find out. Anyway, I haven't been spending as much time with Marly and Tara and Shannon as I used to."

Cordelia had suspected as much. She wondered if Stevie was afraid that her friends might react badly if she told them the truth about herself. "They're being nice to you, aren't they?" she asked. "I mean, no one's giving you a hard time?"

"No, no. They're totally nice. It's just—" Stevie shrugged.

"Stevie, I'm your friend. What's going on?"

Stevie put down her sewing. "It's just that one time at Tara's house I overheard her mother saying something—not nice—about Sarah. She was on the phone. I didn't purposely listen, but I couldn't help but hear her."

Cordelia shot upright on the lounge. "What a bitch! Sorry, but that's what she is." It was especially awful, Cordelia thought, for an adult to say hurtful things about a child. That was downright cowardly.

"And Shannon's brother is kind of a creep," Stevie said. "He's, like, seventeen, and he's always, I don't know, watching me. A few times he's touched me, like put his arm around my shoulders."

Cordelia felt her face flush with anger. "Oh, my God, Stevie, the next time he touches you, just yell, 'Get off me!' And I mean yell loud. He's so totally wrong. And you should tell Shannon you don't like it when he touches you. She's your friend. She should tell her idiot brother to back off!"

Stevie shrugged and looked down at her lap.

"And if that doesn't do the trick, then you tell your father and let him handle the creep!"

"Sometimes it's just—too much. I can't . . ." Stevie began to sob. "I don't feel safe anywhere," she cried. "I feel like bad things are happening all around me and if I'm not really careful . . ."

Clarissa leaped from the ground and onto Stevie's lap where she began to whimper and circle in distress.

Cordelia got up and went over to Stevie. She put her arm around her slim shoulders. "You're safe with me, always," she said firmly. "And look, you know you can go to my mom and dad anytime, right? They're pretty awesome as far as parents go." *And Mom already knows that you've been sad and worried,* Cordelia added silently.

Stevie nodded and wiped her eyes with the back of her hand. "Sorry," she said.

Cordelia laughed kindly. "Why?"

"I hardly ever cry."

"I cry all the time!"

Clarissa put her front paws on Stevie's chest and began to lick the tears from her cheeks.

"Besides," Cordelia pointed out, "if anyone tried to hurt you, they'd have to answer to Clarissa, as well as to me."

Stevie smiled. "I think I have cat hair in my mouth."

Chapter 78

"I like being in charge of the shop," Cordelia said. "Well, in co-charge."

Sarah smiled. "Me too. It's really good of your mom to trust us."

Adelaide and Cindy had gone to the home of a woman who had a family quilt to sell. They would examine the quilt, assess its value, and possibly make an offer. Sarah thought of them as good cop and bad cop. Mrs. Kane was, of course, as the shop's owner, the bad cop, and Sarah's mother was, as the employee and sidekick, the good cop. The thought amused her—but not enough to erase the memory of the awful dream she had had the night before.

In the dream, she had died giving birth to the baby. She didn't remember a lot of the details now, but she did remember hearing a doctor say, "She's gone," and struggling to sit up and show him that no, she was *not* gone, she was still very much *alive*. Then someone, maybe a nurse, had laid the baby's quilt over her face and suddenly, Sarah knew she was completely alone in the hospital room. Finally, she had woken up, whimpering and trying desperately to raise her arms, each of which felt like a thousand pounds. She had stayed awake for the rest of the night, terrified of falling back into the clutches of her unconscious.

"I had this terrible dream last night," she said to Cordelia suddenly, though in fact she hadn't planned on telling anyone about it.

"Me too!" Cordelia cried. "I was late for a class, but I couldn't remember which class and I couldn't find my notebook and I forgot where my locker was and then, when I found it, I couldn't remember the combination! I was frantic. And then I woke up."

"Oh."

"What happened in your dream?" Cordelia asked.

"Well," said Sarah, "actually, it was more of a nightmare. Maybe I shouldn't—"

"No, you *have* to tell me now! If you don't tell me, I'll be wondering for the rest of the day."

"Okay. I died. In the hospital, giving birth."

"A nightmare is right!" Cordelia shrieked. "Thank God they aren't real!"

"Well, you know, there is actually a slim chance that I could die. In real life."

Cordelia leaped to her feet and clutched her head. "How could you even think such a thing? Oh my God, of course you're not going to die!"

Sarah shrugged. "Oh, I know that. It's just, you know, sometimes things go wrong."

"But they won't go wrong. You're young and healthy and strong and . . ."

Sarah laughed. "Okay! Nothing will go wrong!"

Cordelia sank back onto the stool behind the counter. "You almost gave me a heart attack."

"Sorry."

"Anyway, you've been going to those childbirth prep classes, right?"

"Yeah."

"Well, they should help put your mind at ease, right?"

Sarah shrugged. "Actually, they're kind of weird."

"How?"

"Well, everyone's sitting around on the floor with their legs spread. It's not very—private." *Nothing about pregnancy is very private,* Sarah added silently. *Not much, anyway.*

"Oh. Your mom is there with you, right?"

"That's another thing," Sarah said. "I'm the only one in my class without a male coach. It kind of makes me—obvious."

"Big deal. I'd trust your mom over some pimply guy any day!"

Sarah laughed. "Actually, one of the guys looks like he's only about fifteen. Poor thing has the worst acne I've ever seen."

"Fifteen! Is he the father?"

Sarah shrugged. "I guess. The girl he's with looks about fifteen, too. And they look nothing alike, so I don't think it's her brother. Anyway, I can't really see asking your brother to be your birthing coach!"

"Or your annoying cousin or the smelly guy who sits next to you in math class!"

"Can you imagine?"

"Do you know," Cordelia said, "that some men go through terrible shock after they witness their wife or girlfriend give birth? I read this recently. There's, like, official counseling for these men. They're traumatized! Post-traumatic stress disorder or something."

Sarah laughed. "Then it's a good thing women do the birthing!"

"Yeah, well, it's not exactly something I'm looking forward to," Cordelia said with a grimace. "Back like fifty years ago, women were just knocked out. Think about it. You go into labor, someone pumps you full of drugs, you wake up, and voilà! You're handed a nice clean baby. And you don't even know what went on!"

"I think it sounds horrible," Sarah said, "like something out of a creepy sci-fi movie. You could be handed an alien baby for all you know, or even just some other woman's baby."

"I don't know," Cordelia said, "I think it sounds kind of cool. Too bad that's not an option anymore. Now you have to go through the whole thing wide-awake. Ugh."

"But then it's over and you have a lifetime of happiness." Sarah paused after saying these words. Did she really believe that sentiment? Did anyone?

The tinkling of the bell above the door diverted Sarah's thoughts and the conversation.

"Hi!" Cordelia said brightly to the two women who had come in. They were obviously a mother and daughter; you could always tell a mother and daughter team, even when they didn't look all that much alike. "Let us know if we can help you with anything."

Sarah turned to reviewing the morning's receipts. Cordelia was far better with the customers than she was, and far less interested in the financial part of the business.

One of the customers let out a peal of laughter so loud that Sarah jumped. So loud and so at odds with the tenor of Sarah's thoughts. No matter what Cordelia—or her own mother—might say, something bad *could* happen, to either her or to the baby. And there might be nothing she or anyone else could do to prevent it.

Chapter 79

Adelaide felt very nervous but very determined. She had told Jack her intentions the night before. His response was, "I respect your choice." Not exactly the most encouraging response, but it was better than him telling her that she was being an idiot.

Cordelia stomped into the kitchen. "Where's Dad going?" she asked. "I saw him drive away a few minutes ago."

"He went to play golf with that old friend of his, the one who lives in Arizona during the winter."

"Oh, you mean Mr. Benson."

"Yes."

"He's nice."

"Yes. Cordelia, I want to talk to you about something."

"What?" Cordelia's eyes widened. "Am I in trouble? Did I do something wrong?"

Adelaide smiled. "I don't know. Did you?"

"I don't think so. No. Definitely not."

"Then of course you're not in trouble. Come, sit down."

"What is it, Mom?" Cordelia asked, joining her mother at the table.

"I want to tell you about something that happened to me a long time ago."

And she did. When she was finished, Adelaide noted that Cordelia looked paler than normally. And she seemed oddly calm, too. After a full two minutes, she still had said nothing and would not meet her mother's eye.

"Cordelia, please, say something," Adelaide pleaded.

Cordelia looked now at her mother and shook her head. "I don't know what to say. I can't believe it. You. And Sarah."

Adelaide half rose from her seat. "Let me get you something to drink."

"I'm fine," Cordelia said quickly.

"Do you have any questions?"

"Yes. Did you ever regret it? Giving your baby up for adoption?"

Adelaide sighed and sank back into her chair. "The answer to that question is yes, and then no, not always. Though it took a good deal of time to reach a state of only occasional regret."

"Are you still sad about it?"

"Yes." That answer was easy enough to give.

"Who was the father? I mean, had you been going out with him for a long time?"

"Not really," Adelaide said, embarrassed. "Just a few months."

"Did you love him?"

"I don't know," Adelaide admitted. "I suppose I did, in the way that you can talk yourself into believing you love someone at seventeen."

"Did he love you?"

How relentless she is, Adelaide thought. She had never seen Cordelia like this. She felt as if she were on trial without a good defense attorney. "Most definitely not," she answered. "But I didn't know that for sure until I got pregnant."

"Do you know where the baby is now?"

"He's not a baby anymore. And no, I don't."

"Did you see him when he was born?"

Adelaide's heart contracted, and it was a moment before she could speak. "I couldn't bear to," she said finally.

"What did his new parents name him?"

"I have no idea."

"What if someday he decides to find you?" Cordelia pressed. "What if he calls you or just shows up at the door? What then?"

"I don't know," Adelaide said. "It's something that terrifies me, but at the same time I almost long for it. Your father and I have talked about the possibility. And he's vowed to support me in whatever decision I make about a relationship with—with my son."

"So Dad knows?" Cordelia asked, her eyes wide.

"Of course he knows. He's my husband."

"Was he angry with you when he found out?"

Adelaide bit back a sigh of annoyance. Was her daughter really so naive? "He didn't 'find out,' Cordelia. It wasn't like that. I told him while we were dating. I knew I was falling in love with him, and I wanted everything about me to be out in the open. And of course he wasn't angry. He was sympathetic."

"Does he know you're telling me this?" Cordelia asked.

"Of course. We discussed it. We both know this is an important piece of our family's history. Difficult, but important. Do you understand that?"

Cordelia shrugged. "What would you have named him—your son—if you had kept him?" she asked.

Adelaide shook her head. "I don't know. I forced myself not to think about that. Giving him a name would have made it impossible to give him up. At least, that's how it felt at the time. It was bad enough I found out he was a boy. I thought that if I didn't know the sex it would make losing my baby a little bit easier."

Cordelia seemed to be absorbing this. Then she said: "And Grandma and Grandpa really wanted nothing to do with their own grandchild?"

"A baby changes everything," Adelaide said carefully. "For everyone, especially when there's only a single parent who needs to rely on help from family. My parents had raised their child already. They simply were too tired to raise another one."

"Too selfish, you mean."

There was vehemence in her daughter's words. Adelaide felt them as a blow. "Do you think I was selfish in giving up my son for adoption?" she asked, dreading the answer Cordelia might give.

"I don't know," Cordelia said after a long moment. "Maybe."

"I'm sorry you think that. I hope that maybe someday you can better understand." And maybe, Adelaide added silently, feel some sympathy for me. *Oh, God,* she thought, *is that really why I told Cordelia this? Because I* did *need her sympathy after all?*

Cordelia opened her mouth as if to say something more, but then closed it, got up from her seat, and left the kitchen without a word.

Adelaide put a hand to her suddenly aching head. She felt overwhelmed with guilt. It had been a mistake to tell Cordelia. It had been a bad judgment call. She should have listened to Jack and kept quiet. And now it was too late. The proverbial cat was out of its bag, and this cat was a particularly sharp-clawed and dangerous one.

Chapter 80

Joe had had a tough day at work. He had been forced to fire a new employee, a nineteen-year-old named Frank O'Donnell. He had given Frank the requisite three warnings, of course, but Frank hadn't taken them to heart.

"The guy had it coming," Joe said, shaking his head. "He was just too careless. He was putting himself and the other men at risk. Still."

Cindy put the carton of milk into the fridge. "I know. But it's a difficult thing to disappoint someone. Just keep in mind that he disappointed you first. If he hadn't, he'd still have a job."

Joe nodded. "It's a good thing he only has himself to worry about. No wife, no kids."

"Will you give him a reference? What if a prospective employer calls you for a good word?"

Joe seemed to consider. "Doubt that will happen," he said after a moment. "Frank would want to erase his time with Bauer Construction. But off the record? I could say he's a nice kid without telling a lie."

"That's something. Oh, Sarah saw Dr. Westin this morning. Everything is just fine."

"Good."

"Oh, and I wanted to ask you if we had any of that paint left over from when we last touched up the bathroom. I'm afraid part of the baseboard looks a bit rough. I'd say it was Clarissa's doing, but I know she's too smart for that."

"Got half a can in the workshop. I'll bring it in."

"Thank you, Joe."

Cindy turned away from her husband to put on a pan of water to boil. She had gotten a bag of small red potatoes at the farm stand and thought they would be nice with the salmon she was making for dinner.

"Sometimes I think I want to kill him."

Cindy spun around. "Who? Frank?"

"No. Morrow."

Cindy put her hand to her heart. "Oh, Joe, don't say that. You know you don't mean it."

But the raw anguish she saw in her husband's eyes almost took her breath away.

"Yes," he said. "I do."

Cindy didn't for one moment think that Joe would act on his anger, but the very fact that he had admitted it to her was worrisome enough. She was protective of her husband. That someone could get through his usual calm and good nature and inspire such negativity was appalling to her. It made her furious, more furious, she thought, than Joe would ever be capable of feeling.

"Joe—" she began.

"Shouldn't have said that. Forget it."

Cindy nodded. Best, she thought, to let his outburst go without further remark. "I'm making salmon for dinner," she said.

"Sounds good. You work hard for us, Cindy."

"I enjoy it," she said, and she meant it.

"And I appreciate it. We all do, the girls, too. I just wish . . . I wish I could provide more for us."

Cindy thought of the quilts she hadn't been able to let go of and felt a stab of guilt. "I believe everything's going to be okay, Joe," she said, more strongly than she felt. "I really do."

Joe rose from the table and gathered her into his arms. She rested her cheek on his shoulder and sighed.

Chapter 81

Cordelia drifted into the kitchen. She didn't quite know why she was there. She wasn't even that hungry. But there she was, and there, too, was her father.

"Hey, Dad."

"Hey, Cordelia." He nodded toward the carton of ice cream he held. "Do you want some ice cream?"

"I shouldn't."

"That's not an answer to my question."

"Okay, then, yes, I want some. But I'm not going to have any."

"Okay," he said, dropping a large scoop into a bowl. "How's the quilt project coming along?"

"Fine. It's almost done. Sort of."

"That's good."

"Mom told me," Cordelia blurted. "About her—about her son."

"Yes," her father said, returning the ice-cream carton to the freezer. "I know. How are you feeling about it?"

Cordelia shrugged. "I don't know. Weird. It's like we have this big family secret now."

"It was always a part of our family's story, Cordelia. All that's changed is that now you know the story, too. There is no more secret."

"Except that maybe her son—my half-brother—doesn't know he's adopted or if he does, maybe he doesn't know about

Mom. That her name is Adelaide Kane and that she's married and has a daughter and lives in Maine."

"That's true," her father admitted. "But we don't really know for sure what he knows or doesn't know."

Cordelia considered. What would it be like to live in the dark about your origins? She tried, but she failed to imagine such a state. How could she? She had always known exactly who she was. At least, she thought that she had. She had not known that she was a sister, a sibling. For all she knew she might even be a sister-in-law or an aunt!

"I wish I could meet my brother," she said. "What if we look a lot alike? What if we like the same movies and food and, I don't know, what if we have some of the same habits? What if he has really bad eyesight, like I do?"

"What if you *did* share all those things?"

Cordelia shrugged. "I don't know. It's just strange thinking there's someone out there with a bunch of my DNA and he doesn't even know it. It feels somehow unfair."

"To you or to him?" her father asked.

That, Cordelia thought, *was a good question.* "To us both," she said after a moment.

"I'm sorry this is so hard for you," her father said.

"Why did she have to tell me, Dad? It would have been better if I'd never known."

Her father put his empty bowl and spoon into the dishwasher. "Give it some time, Cordelia," he said then. "Let this information sink in a bit. And know that your mother didn't mean to hurt or upset you by telling you about the adoption. She was hoping that in some way it might help you deal with Sarah's situation."

Cordelia shook her head and laughed. "How?"

"I don't quite know," her father admitted. "But her intentions were good."

Cordelia sighed. "I suppose so. But what I really can't understand is why she was pushing the idea of Sarah putting her baby up for adoption when she knows how hard it was to do."

"Again, her intentions were good. Maybe they were a bit—emotional—but she only wanted what she thought would be best for Sarah."

"Why would Mom think that she knew what was best for Sarah? She's not Sarah's mother! And it's not her baby!" Cordelia frowned. "It's all very confusing. Maybe I will have some ice cream after all."

Her father smiled. "I ate all of the pistachio, I'm afraid. But there's still chocolate."

"That'll do."

Chapter 82

The moment Sarah appeared in the doorway to the kitchen her mother leaped up from her seat at the table. She was clutching a magazine. "There you are!" she said. "I've been dying to talk to you."

Sarah repressed a sigh. Her mother had been poring over parenting magazines since Sarah had announced her pregnancy. They were all over the house. Occasionally, Sarah leafed through one. Mostly, she found them repetitive and faddish. Too often they seemed to be making outrageous efforts to create alarm. A lot of times the writing wasn't very interesting, either. The pictures of the babies were cute, though. Everybody liked looking at pictures of babies.

Anyway, after Sarah had gone to her mother with the offer of putting her baby up for adoption, her mother had gotten even more—well, even more annoying.

"What is it?" Sarah asked.

"I just read an article about teaching your child a second language right along with English. It sounds very exciting, doesn't it? I think we should send away for this introductory package and learn more about what's involved. I mean, I think that you should send away for it. It's your child, after all. It's just that all these language experts are saying it's the right thing to do, so it seems to me we should take their advice. I mean, that *you* should take their advice."

Sarah bit back an impatient reply.

"I don't know," she said, as evenly as she could manage. "I'll think about it."

Her mother frowned. "I'm not sure there's much to think about. It seems to me that—"

"Mom. I said, I'll think about it."

Her mother compressed her lips into a tight line. "All right."

"Thanks, Mom," Sarah said, a tiny little bit of guilt niggling at her. "Really. I know you're just trying to help, and I appreciate it."

"Well, at least read the article. Information is always a good thing."

Except, Sarah thought, *when it isn't because it isn't really substantial, or is misleading, or unproved.*

"Okay," she said. "I'll read it."

"Good." Her mother handed the magazine to Sarah. "I've turned down the corner of the page on which the article starts so it'll be easy to find. Oh, and there's another good article in this issue. It's about vaccinations. They're very important, you know."

"Yes, I know. Thanks."

Her mother left the kitchen. Sarah resisted rolling her eyes, but she did toss the magazine onto the table. She had an unhappy feeling that she would have to fight her mother on every single decision regarding the baby. If that were the case, life in the Bauer house would be miserable for everyone until she could afford to move out with her son and start a life of her own with him. And that might be years from now.

Sarah sighed. She was not naive enough to imagine that life alone with her baby would be idyllic. She would have the burden of worrying all to herself, no husband or partner with whom to share it. At least, living with her parents, she would have the comfort of knowing that if for some reason she couldn't be there for her child, someone else would be. If a fire broke out in the middle of the night and she was overcome by smoke, then her mother or her father or even Stevie could rescue the baby. If she lost her job, her son would still have food and shelter. And if something even worse happened . . .

Sarah sat in the chair her mother had abandoned. A while ago Dr. Westin had given her an article on postpartum depression. Women suffering from postpartum depression did terrible things to their babies. At least once a year, you heard about some distraught, wild-eyed woman who drowned her children in a bathtub or strapped them inside the family car and sent it into the deep end of the local lake for all sorts of fantastical reasons, from voices in her head commanding her to save her children from the horrors and evils of life to revenge on the hated father of the children.

Sarah toyed with the edge of the magazine her mother had given her. What if after the birth of her baby she became so depressed that she couldn't even handle basic feeding? Would her parents take her baby away? Would they go to court to gain legal control of him? Would they keep the baby and throw her out of the house? They could do that; it was their house after all. It was hard to imagine her parents ever doing something so—so drastic—but then again, it was hard to imagine, to accept, even now, that she had gotten pregnant.

Such morbid thoughts often assailed Sarah in the dark hours of the night. Daytime wasn't necessarily much better, except, she found, when she got lost in her work on the baby's quilt. Otherwise, she was intensely aware at almost every moment of the enormity of her situation. Almost every time she found herself smiling at the thought of the life growing within her, feeling calm and even pleased, a jolt of panic or guilt would assail her and the peaceful, joyous moment would be gone.

Like what had happened today. She had walked into the kitchen feeling just fine. And now, only a few moments later, she felt anything *but* fine.

Sarah picked up the magazine and went up to her room. She would read the article because she had promised her mother she would, but what was the point in following every rule and doing everything just the way the "experts" told you to do them? You could make every possible preparation, but the reality was that everything changed and would continue to go on changing and you would never know—you *could* never know—what exactly was going to happen next.

Chapter 83

Adelaide was alone in the shop when a young man passing along the sidewalk outside caught her attention. She hurried forward to the window to get a closer view as he continued on. *What was it?* she wondered. *Was it the length of his stride or maybe the set of his shoulders? Was it the dark hair?* Whatever it was exactly, the young man had reminded her an awful lot of Michael Baker. Well, of the Michael Baker she had known twenty-one years earlier.

The young man passed out of sight, and Adelaide, heart racing, turned away from the window. She hated when this sort of thing happened. *Would* she recognize her son if she saw him on the street? Would he somehow recognize her, blood calling out to blood? Or did that only happen in novels and the movies?

Adelaide went back to man the counter. Maybe she *had* seen her son, maybe she even had talked to him, and not known that the person she was speaking to was her own flesh and blood. The thought made her head spin. So many possibilities . . . The one possibility she had never entertained was that her son might be dead. She *needed* the fantasy of being able to look into his eyes someday. Without that, well, she wasn't sure what might happen to her.

Not that the fantasy of meeting her son was helping her much at the moment. Her thoughts were mostly mired in memories of that awful conversation with her daughter.

What a disaster. Jack had been a great comfort, but even her husband's reassuring words could not erase Adelaide's memory of Cordelia leaving the kitchen, her shoulders stiff. And, a day later, he told Adelaide that Cordelia had come to him. She had been upset, he told Adelaide, angry and confused and very curious about her half-brother.

Jack had urged Adelaide to remember that Cordelia was in many ways a typical naive, self-righteous, unsympathetic young person for whom life is black and white, decisions right or wrong. It was clear that she was only now coming to understand how dreadfully complicated and nuanced the world was. And how difficult it was to negotiate each and every day and still feel good about yourself as a productive and caring and decent person.

That helped a little.

The door to the shop opened, and Cindy came in. She held a folded quilt over her arm.

"The repair won't be difficult," she told Adelaide, indicating the quilt. "I can get it done in a week. Seems Mrs. Gallagher's grandson is undergoing a fixation with scissors. Poor woman thought the quilt was ruined."

"Good. I mean, good about the repair, not about the child from hell."

"What's up?" Cindy asked, placing the quilt on a table next to one of the frames. "You look upset."

"I am upset," Adelaide admitted. "I told Cordelia about the adoption. I mean, about my son."

"Oh. How did she take the news?"

"Not well, I'm afraid."

"It *is* a lot to absorb," Cindy said carefully. "And Cordelia is an emotional girl."

"Yes. But, Cindy, I'm scared that for the rest of her life every time she looks at me she's going to see—well, someone disappointing."

Cindy shook her head. "She loves you. Give her time to come to terms with the fact that her mother had a life before her."

"And to think I convinced myself I was telling her because the news might help her to, I don't know, have more sympathy for Sarah. But Cordelia already *had* sympathy for Sarah! She was dealing with things just fine until I opened my big mouth. Look at how much she's been enjoying working on the baby's quilt! What have I done?"

Cindy squeezed Adelaide's hand. "Do you want me to talk to her?"

Adelaide sighed. "No. I think that maybe she needs to be left alone for a while." Adelaide laughed bitterly. "But what do I know?"

"What did Jack say?"

"Honestly, he wasn't really keen on my telling Cordelia from the start. She went to him after our conversation. She wasn't happy."

"Both Sarah and Cordelia are facing some major growing-up lessons this summer, aren't they?"

"Our poor girls."

"Growing up is bound to happen," Cindy pointed out. "If you're lucky."

Adelaide gave a halfhearted laugh. "Then I guess they're lucky. But wait, there's something else. I know you didn't want Sarah to know about my past. But things were going so badly with Cordelia I didn't remember to ask her not to tell Sarah. I'm so sorry, Cindy."

"It doesn't matter now," Cindy said. "It won't hurt her to know."

"Are you sure?"

"I'm sure. Now, let me make you a cup of coffee."

"Thanks," Adelaide said. "And if there's a doughnut back there I'll take that, too."

Chapter 84

You didn't have to be particularly sensitive, Cindy thought, to feel the tension in the room.

They were at The Busy Bee after hours to work on the quilt. This evening their task was to sew several of the shapes they had each created—fish, roses, seashells, and lobsters—onto the background fabric with a variety of interesting stitches.

At least, Cindy thought the stitches were interesting. No one else at The Busy Bee seemed particularly happy to be there or interested in the work at hand. Cordelia was clearly upset with her mother. She hadn't looked directly at Adelaide since they had entered the shop. Well, she *was* absorbing some pretty big and upsetting news. As for Adelaide, she wore a pained expression, and her hair, usually so perfectly styled, was almost messy.

Stevie seemed on edge and was uncharacteristically klutzy. She had dropped her needle twice and tripped over a leg of the stool behind the counter. Cindy found it disturbing to see her younger daughter, who usually moved with such grace, be so awkward. *Something must be on her mind,* Cindy figured, *but what?* There was never much use in quizzing Stevie about her feelings.

Sarah was pensive, not unusual for her, but these days, Cindy watched her like a hawk watching a mouse. No. More accurately, like a fierce mother lion watching her cub when the hyenas were on the prowl.

Maybe, Cindy thought, working on the quilt together this evening would help heal the pain and hurt or just plain irritability everyone but her seemed to be feeling. And if it didn't, she might have to suggest they call out for pizza.

"Is there such a thing as chocolate soda?" Sarah asked suddenly.

"What on earth made you think of chocolate soda?" Cindy asked with a laugh. "And yes, I think that there is such a thing. Though I'm not sure I've seen it around for some time."

"I don't know. It just sounds like it would be a really delicious thing."

Cordelia nodded. "Mmm. I agree. Especially with whipped cream on top."

Adelaide looked from Cordelia to Sarah. "Next time I'm at the store I'll look for some if you'd like."

Cordelia just shrugged.

"Thanks, Mrs. Kane," Sarah said. "But don't go out of your way."

"There's such a thing as cream soda," Cindy said. "I think it's actually vanilla flavored. One time a woman visiting from New York City told me about it. I can't for the life of me remember how the topic of soda came up! I do know she bought one of my smaller quilts."

"I think they both sound awful," Stevie said. They were the first words she had spoken in almost an hour. "Probably all gross artificial chemical flavoring."

No one had a reply for that comment.

"The baby is kicking," Sarah announced, putting her hand to her side. "You can feel if you want. It's just when strangers . . ."

"Yeah," Cordelia said. "People should know better. They're always saying and doing things that they shouldn't."

Cindy saw Adelaide flinch. Clearly, neither of the adults had any doubt as to whom Cordelia's remark was aimed.

"Stevie?" Sarah asked. "Do you want to feel?"

"No, thanks. Ow!"

She had stabbed herself with her needle.

"Are you okay?" Cindy asked.

Stevie nodded. And then she said, "No. I'm not. I got my period this morning and I feel . . . awful."

Cindy put a hand on her daughter's head and smoothed her hair. Her purple hair. "Growing up," she said, "isn't always fun."

"No," Adelaide said carefully, her eyes on her work. "It isn't. Sometimes you have to accept some difficult truths about the people you love."

Sarah looked up and frowned. "Like what, Mrs. Kane?"

There was a moment of awkward silence. Cindy opened her mouth to say something, anything, but Cordelia cut her off.

"Like nothing," she said. She put down her work and placed the flat of her palm against Sarah's belly. "It's so hard. I mean, your stomach. It's kind of weird. Sorry. I didn't mean that in a bad way."

Sarah smiled. "Do you want to feel, Mrs. Kane?"

"Oh," Cordelia said quickly, "my mother doesn't need to feel it. She knows all about being pregnant."

Cindy felt her cheeks flush. Really, Cordelia was acting badly, tempting her mother to show anger, to fight back. Cordelia was punishing her mother in the only way she knew how—by being a brat.

Cindy walked over to where Adelaide sat bent over her work and put a hand on her shoulder. Adelaide looked up and gave a small smile of thanks. *How our children hurt us so,* Cindy thought. *It was a wonder that a mother could bear it.*

"I think we've done enough work for this evening," Cindy announced, admitting to herself that sometimes, even quilting together couldn't soothe hurt feelings. "I'm going to call for a pizza."

Chapter 85

Cordelia spread the blanket under her with her hands. She was at the beach alone. Stevie was taking a turn working at the shop, and there had been no point in asking Sarah to come along. Sarah loved the beach but lying around on a blanket with hundreds of other sunbathers wasn't her thing. She preferred to come off-season or after hours and hunt for shells in the sand, and look for eagles overhead, and poke around at smelly seaweed that had washed ashore.

Cordelia lay back on the blanket, her bag close to her side. Fully packed, she guessed it weighed close to ten pounds. In it were a towel, a pair of backup sunglasses, two bottles of water, a large tube of sunblock, a small tube of lip balm, the latest issues of *Elle* and *InStyle* and *Vogue,* and two apples, in case she got hungry. Come to think of it, the bag probably weighed closer to fifteen pounds once you added the blanket, which meant that carrying it around amounted to weight-bearing activity, which was the same as exercise. And *that* meant that she could treat herself to dessert after dinner that night.

If, that is, her mother served anything really good.

Cordelia had been avoiding meeting her mother's eyes since her big revelation. It was as if things were too close now, too intimate between them. Her mother had become something other than a mother. She had become an individual with a past that had nothing to do with Cordelia or her father. So, at the same time, her mother had become a stranger to her. Their relationship had sustained a rift.

At least, that's how it felt to Cordelia, and she felt resentful and sad and a little bit angry. Her life had suddenly become like the plot of a soap opera! What other crazy secrets would her mother reveal? Were her parents in actuality circus performers (a lion tamer and an acrobat?) on the run for having robbed banks all across the Midwest? Was she, Cordelia, in actuality a Swedish princess, stolen as an infant by an anti-royalist faction bent on causing domestic heartache among the nobility and whisked away to the United States where she was subsequently . . .

Cordelia almost laughed aloud. No. None of that was real. There was no point in abandoning reason in favor of the ridiculous. Though the ridiculous could be kind of fun.

But nothing about her mother's story was even remotely fun, certainly not the part about Cordelia's grandparents pretty much forcing their daughter to give up her baby. *Why had they acted so badly?* Cordelia wondered. *How could they have turned their back on their only child?* It seemed beyond mere cruelty. It seemed like—indifference. Wasn't it true that the opposite of love wasn't hate, it was indifference? Cordelia only knew her grandparents vaguely. Maybe they were mean-spirited, cold-hearted people who thought of other people only as nuisances to be endured!

Well, Cordelia couldn't blame her mother if she still harbored angry feelings toward her parents for their lack of support all those years ago. She hadn't *sounded* angry when she told Cordelia her story, but maybe she had been acting. And Cordelia wondered if her grandparents still harbored feelings of disappointment in their daughter. What a mess all around!

And no one was safe from messiness; that was the really terrifying part. Anyone could get pregnant, even levelheaded Sarah, because passion could make even the most reasonable person do crazy things. Personally, Cordelia knew very little about sexual passion. She didn't think she was a cold person—

she hoped that she wasn't—but for some reason, she hadn't yet felt any really intense emotion in her life. Crushes didn't count. And what she felt for her parents, though real, wasn't—overwhelming. Her love for them just *was*. It was just *there*. She knew it. She lived it more than she felt it, if that made any sense.

Cordelia sat up on her elbows. A group of four girls about her age were strutting by, tossing their hair and giggling. Each was wearing a bikini that was unbelievably tiny. Cordelia grimaced. Really, she was hardly a prude (or was she?), but those bathing suits bordered on X-rated! She shifted her gaze to the right only to see a couple making out on a blanket. She was both embarrassed and fascinated by their public display of affection. Or lust, which wasn't the same thing. Affection wasn't dangerous. Lust was very dangerous.

Cordelia looked away from the couple, embarrassed now by her voyeurism. She was almost seventeen, and she had never even made out with a guy. Well, she had kissed a little at a party last year, but nothing more. Maybe there was something wrong with her. Why weren't her hormones raging like everyone else's? Why wasn't she strutting and giggling?

Suddenly, Cordelia felt very young and very naive. The truth was that in spite of the bad stuff about Sarah's situation, she was a tiny bit in awe of her friend for having moved on toward maturity—well, toward sexual experience—without her.

Cordelia glanced again at the amorous couple and wondered what John Blantyre was doing with his last summer in Maine before heading off for college. She bet he looked good in a bathing suit. He wasn't one of those muscle-head types, but he was slim and fit.

Idly, she wondered what he would say if she called him and maybe asked him out. He might very well say yes. Things between them might very well click. She might even . . . and here her thoughts became more focused. She might even be able to catch up with Sarah, get back to sharing the same level of experience.

John *was* really nice. And he *had* been going to ask her out that time at school when she had run away.

Cordelia sat up abruptly. Her face was burning, and it had nothing to do with the sun. Oh, my God, she thought, how insane to even *consider* losing her virginity and risking pregnancy or a disease just to—to what? Fit in? Feel a part of Sarah's life again? Kill the pain of loneliness?

Wow, Cordelia thought, holding her bottle of water to her flaming cheeks. *I just dodged a very big bullet.*

After a moment, she lay back down on the blanket and closed her eyes. *Think of fluffy bunnies,* she told herself. *Think of those lace-up boots you want for fall. Think of gold, glittery nail polish. Just think of anything but boys.*

Chapter 86

"Finally!" Cordelia cried, the moment the door had closed behind the most recent customer. "I thought she would never stop talking!"

"Yeah, but she did buy a lot of stuff," Sarah pointed out. "She spent almost one hundred dollars. That's pretty major."

"I guess. But I would so rather be at the beach or lying out on my deck or shopping," Cordelia grumbled.

Sarah bit back a smile. "Don't you appreciate the money? You can't go shopping without money."

"Well, there is that," Cordelia admitted. "But working is so boring! Doing inventory is boring. Wrapping packages and stocking shelves is boring!"

"Okay, not all of it is—stimulating. But it could be a lot worse. We could be working for awful bosses instead of our moms."

Cordelia rolled her eyes. "All right, there is that, too. Still."

"And it is kind of fun, working on the quilt for the baby when there are no customers. Don't you think so?"

"Yeah, quilting isn't half as bad as I thought it would be, except when I drop the needle! The quilt's going to be really pretty. I love how we're doing the white beach roses against the cream background."

"And the customers, most of them anyway, are pretty pleasant."

Cordelia laughed. "Okay, you convinced me! Working at

The Busy Bee is a lot nicer than working for, say, some big grocery store. You know Willy, from Mr. Davis's class? He bags at Hannaford. He told me that one time this customer made him repack her groceries three times before she was satisfied. Can you imagine? And he couldn't say anything to her because the customer is always right, or at least, they're supposed to be."

"Well, if a customer here was obnoxious, we couldn't say anything in protest, either," Sarah pointed out.

"But we could tell my mom and then, look out! She's banned people from the store, you know."

"Really?"

"Oh, yeah. One summer there was this woman who came in every single day for a week. She would spend almost twenty minutes browsing and never buy a thing. Then on the Friday, she came in, but about two minutes later she kind of hurried to the door. I don't know how my mom knew, but she was sure the woman had lifted something so she shouted after her and then ran to the door and blocked it."

"Oh my God," Sarah said. "What happened?"

Cordelia laughed. "I was terrified there was going to be a fight—like, what if the woman was crazy?—but all that happened was that the woman handed over a package of needles she had stuffed in her bag. My mom told her never to come back or she would call the police."

"So she never came back."

"Right. The really weird thing was that she didn't look like a criminal or a troublemaker. She looked like a perfectly respectable middle-aged woman. She was wearing nice clothes and had this big diamond ring."

"Maybe she was a kleptomaniac," Sarah suggested.

"Or maybe it was a dare! Maybe her perfectly respectable friends put her up to it!"

"It just goes to show that you can't judge a book by its cover."

"Appearances are deceiving. I know."

Sarah smiled ruefully. "Like me. I know some people,

maybe most people, look at me and think I'm a stupid, irresponsible kid."

"Which you are not!"

"Well, maybe I am, in some ways. But I don't really believe that about myself, not entirely. Anyway, I want people to look at me and see a person who's sworn to be a good mom, someone who's smart and someone who's really sorry for making a stupid mistake."

Cordelia groaned. "Oh my God, Sarah, you've got to stop blaming yourself, really! Accidents happen."

"But a lot of times they can be prevented."

"Life isn't a commercial for an insurance company, Sarah."

Sarah laughed. "What?"

"You know what I mean. You've seen those ads on television that say, do this and your house won't go on fire and your insurance rates won't go up. Don't do that because you'll run your car into a tree and your insurance rates *will* go up. In real life, well, sometimes you can do everything the way you're supposed to, and stuff can still mess up."

"Yes," Sarah said. "You're right. Life *is* random. But that doesn't mean people don't feel guilt. It doesn't mean that people *shouldn't* feel guilt. People are responsible for the majority of their lives."

"Maybe. But you still have to give yourself a break sometimes. Like, okay, I made a mistake, I forgive myself, I won't do it again, move on."

"You sound like a life coach or one of those self-help gurus."

"So what if I do?" Cordelia said a bit defensively.

"So nothing. Thanks, Cordelia. I *do* appreciate your support. Really."

Chapter 87

"Rats."

Adelaide had brought her laptop to the kitchen table to read her e-mail. She frowned at her in-box. There was a message from her mother in Florida, occasioning the all too familiar stab of guilt. When had she last spoken to her mother? It had to have been at least two months ago. Then again, she hadn't heard from either of her parents in that time. But wasn't it the duty of the adult child to make the contact?

With a sigh, Adelaide opened the e-mail. There was the usual update about life in Palm Hills. Her parents had won first place in a couples' tennis tournament. Her father had a cold, nothing serious. The neighbors to the right had put up an illegal awning and the neighbors to the left had brought the matter to the condo board. Adelaide felt a sort of unpleasant lethargy descend over her as she read the uninteresting details of her parents' life in retirement.

The next paragraph proved far more interesting.

"Oh," her mother wrote, "I thought you might be interested to know this. Last week I saw a piece in the *New York Times* about the father of your son. I'm sure you could still find the article online. He seems to have made quite a good job of his life, which he certainly could not have accomplished if he had been burdened with a wife and child at the age of eighteen. Smart man."

Adelaide's hands began to shake, and she felt hot all over.

She knew without a doubt that she should not read on, that she should immediately delete her mother's e-mail. But, as with a gruesome accident that tempts viewing, Adelaide read on.

"After having seen that article," her mother wrote, "I can't help but think that without that unfortunate incident in your past burdening your progress like some dead weight you might have chosen to marry someone with Michael's drive and talent. But then again, that's just a mother's opinion, and the past is the past."

Adelaide sat back in her chair. The cruelty of her mother's remarks hit her like a sharp slap across the face. She didn't feel angry—that would come later, no doubt. What she felt was the nauseating shock that comes when someone you thought loved or even simply liked you lashed out at you without obvious provocation. It undermined so much of what you took to be true—that you were a decent person and that other people knew and acknowledged that you were a decent person.

To bring up that awful, painful time in her daughter's life and in such a seemingly casual but obviously deliberate way seemed to Adelaide like something impossible to forgive. Like something impossible, too, for her mother to explain or to justify. What purpose could it possibly have served other than to wound? And why did her mother, after all these years, feel the need to wound her daughter? Adelaide had done what she was told and had given up her baby. Her mother had not been inconvenienced. Her lifestyle had not been disturbed.

Adelaide closed her eyes and took a deep breath. At that moment she couldn't imagine sharing this shame and her hurt with anyone, not even with Jack. Amazingly, stunningly, her own mother had succeeded in intruding into her marriage, damaging the emotional intimacy she usually shared so easily with her husband. Her mother had hit the send key in Florida, and the bullet had hit its target all the way up north in Maine.

Finally, Adelaide opened her eyes and hit the delete button. She felt that she might never be able to talk to her mother again. What was there to say, after that missive? "Thanks, Mom, for your opinion"?

It was ridiculous of course, to allow her mother to disturb her peace of mind so badly. She was an adult with a husband and child to care for and a business to run. She was no longer that frightened seventeen-year-old, desperate for someone to help her, desperate for someone to save her from having to make a very tough decision.

But a mother, especially an unkind one, was a powerful force to defend against. Adelaide got up from the table to make a cup of tea. As she was spooning sugar into her cup, she remembered Cordelia's anger at her grandparents for their part in pushing the adoption. Could she have contacted her grandparents to reproach them? Could Nancy Morgan's e-mail be an act of retaliation?

No. Adelaide dismissed the idea. Cordelia would never take a step that might backfire on her mother, no matter how angry she felt. It wasn't in Cordelia to want to wound. She was suffering right now, but Adelaide was sure she would get past the pain or the confusion or whatever it was she was feeling.

Adelaide dropped the spoon and put her hand to her head. Although sometimes, as she knew all too well, pain and confusion could last forever.

Chapter 88

Cindy stood at the living room window, peering down at the end of the road. It was a very hot and very humid day. She was worried about Sarah being out under the burning sun. She hoped she had put on plenty of sunblock. She hoped she had worn a wide-brimmed hat and high socks for protection against the tics. She hoped she had thought to bring water with her. Dehydration was a real possibility.

Cindy checked her watch yet again. It was close to two; Sarah had been gone for almost three hours. She was now absolutely convinced that something terrible had happened. She was certain that Sarah was in trouble, sprawled at the bottom of a ravine with a broken leg and smashed ribs. She could not banish the terrible image of Sarah huddled in the back of a lunatic's van, kidnapped for gruesome purposes. A bear, made mad by fear or some dread disease, had attacked Sarah, leaving her a bleeding mess with only the squirrels as chattering witnesses.

"Stop, stop, stop," Cindy murmured to the window, but the outrageous thoughts kept pounding at her brain. What if, in a moment of extreme panic over the upcoming birth and all that would result, Sarah had gone off to commit suicide? Cindy's stomach heaved. She was horrified to have for one moment considered such a tragic possibility, but there it was, lodged in her overheated mind.

She couldn't stay still any longer. She snatched her car keys from a peg just inside the front door and raced outside to the car she had left parked in the driveway. But just as she was lowering herself into the driver's seat, she saw Sarah, coming around the bend at the end of the road. Feelings of relief warred with feelings of anger. Tears of all sorts threatened to blind her. She closed the door of the car with more force than was necessary and stood waiting until Sarah was close enough to hear her.

"Where were you?" she called. "I was frantic with worry."

Sarah frowned, as if puzzled. "I went for a walk. I told you that before I left."

"But you were gone for almost three hours!"

"So? That's not unusual."

"You could have called to tell us you were okay."

Sarah half laughed. "I never call when I'm out for a walk. You've never asked me to."

"Do you at least have your phone with you when you go out?" Cindy demanded.

"Of course," Sarah replied, an edge of annoyance in her tone.

"Well, you didn't this time because I called you."

Sarah stuck her hand in the back pocket of her jeans. "Oh, sorry. I guess I forgot to bring it. I must have left it charging in my room."

"Lord," Cindy cried. "Sarah, you can't just go wandering off like that. You have a responsibility now to someone other than yourself. You have a responsibility to your baby."

Sarah laughed. "I don't believe this! How is taking a walk in the woods behind my own home hurting my baby?" she asked, her voice shrill. "And how dare you imply I'd do something to put my baby in danger! I'm a good person. I'm a responsible person. Just because I forgot my phone one time doesn't mean I'm stupid."

"I didn't say that you were."

"You implied it."

Cindy was caught short. Had she indeed? Suddenly, she became aware that Stevie was standing in the driveway, witness to the scene. She looked very small and alone.

"I'm sorry," she said. "I was just worried, that's all."

"Worried about what? What the neighbors would say if—" Sarah sighed heavily. "Never mind. Look, I'm sorry, Mom. Can we please just—forget it?"

Cindy pressed her lips together tightly. She didn't want to forget it. But she knew that to prolong the conversation at this point would be pointless. It would only make them both angrier. "Do you want something to eat?" she said finally. "It's past lunchtime."

Sarah lowered her eyes. "All right," she said. "I'll be inside in a minute."

Chapter 89

Pinky was perched against the pillows on Cordelia's bed. He looked a bit worse than he had back in the winter. Well, Cordelia thought, he had been a great help to her since then and she loved him more than ever. Appearances really didn't count for much in the end.

Cordelia plopped down at her desk and opened her laptop. She had been thinking about what she had told Sarah the other day, that accidents happened, that you shouldn't always be hard on yourself. She believed that. But if she believed that people should be forgiven for their mistakes, why was she still being so harsh about her mother?

Cordelia shook that question away. She was not ready to make peace with her mother. She still felt too—too wound up by what she had learned. There was still too much noise in her head, obstructing a way to forgiveness and understanding.

Women having babies. *Blah!* Sometimes Cordelia felt as if Sarah's pregnancy (and her mom's first one?) had taken over her own life. It occupied so much of her thoughts. Even her dreams, when she remembered them, were now often peopled with random babies and toddlers and once even a stunningly handsome boy about eighteen who came up to her in a mall and said, "I'm Sarah's baby. Tell her I liked the quilt." Talk about bizarre.

And here was more proof that her life was no longer her own! What was she doing on a sunny summer afternoon? Not shopping. Not reading a fashion magazine. Not hanging out at the beach. No, she was sitting in her bedroom researching teen pregnancy! Fun!

That was sarcasm, because not a bit of it was fun. There was all this information on how badly things would probably turn out for Sarah and her child. This one site said that approximately seven hundred and fifty thousand teenage girls became pregnant each year. Eighty-two percent of those pregnancies were unplanned. More than half of the pregnancies continued on to birth. That was a heck of a lot of children being born to children!

And it all only confirmed what her mother had told her months before, when she had been urging Mrs. Bauer to talk Sarah into putting her baby up for adoption. (Was *that* why she had been so pro adoption? Did she want Sarah to have the good life she had made for herself? Or did she only want another person to experience her pain?)

Scariest bit of all to Cordelia was the danger inherent in childbirth. The statistics were startling. In the United States, women were currently dying from childbirth at the highest rate in decades. *What!* Some experts felt this was due to obesity and the increase in voluntary C-sections. There was another dread statistic. Every year more than half a million women worldwide died of pregnancy or childbirth. It was horrifying.

And then there was this: Teenage mothers were reported to be at a higher risk for birth complications, toxemia, anemia, and death.

Death!

Suddenly, finally, Cordelia felt a pang of sympathy for the pregnant seventeen-year-old her mother had been. Had she lain awake at night, petrified of dying? Had she gone to the hospital scared that she would never come out?

It was all very, very frightening, and she wondered if Sarah knew how dangerous the natural act of giving birth could be. If she did know, how did *she* sleep at night? How did she get through the day—eating meals, working at the shop, taking those long walks—without being totally preoccupied with the thought of death?

A chill ran through Cordelia. Sarah had had that awful nightmare about dying. Could it have been a premonition? No, Cordelia decided immediately. Absolutely not. Sarah wasn't the sort of person who was visited by spirits of the past or haunted by ghosts of the future. Her feet and her head were firmly planted in *this* world.

Sarah, Cordelia told herself firmly, would be fine. She wasn't even a little bit overweight, and she was planning a vaginal birth, not a C-section, and in spite of that awful news about so many women dying in childbirth, this was still *the United States of America!* And some of the best medical care in the country was available right there in Maine. There was no way Sarah's life would be in danger. No. Way. Sarah was the proverbial picture of health. In a way, Cordelia realized, she looked better now than she ever had. That old cliché about pregnant women having a glow was true after all! It was probably just hormones doing whatever it was they did, but still.

Cordelia shut down her laptop. Sometimes, she thought, getting up from her desk, information could be a bad thing, especially when taken in large doses when you were all alone. Fortunately, there were several very effective antidotes to information overload.

Food was one of them, especially when it was of the cheese variety.

Chapter 90

"Was it a nice walk?" Stevie asked when their mother had gone into the house.

"Yeah," Sarah said. "I saw some really grotesque mushrooms, the kind that look like gargoyles. And I saw a mother deer and her fawn in the distance."

"That sounds cool."

Sarah smiled in spite of the fact that she felt embarrassed that Stevie had been a witness to the fight with their mother. She realized she knew so little about Stevie's life these days, what she was thinking, how she spent the time when she wasn't working with everyone else on the baby's quilt. Now that she thought about it, she hadn't seen Stevie's friends, Marly and Tara and Shannon, around in months. And when was the last time she had watched a movie with her sister or made ice-cream sodas or talked about a book they had both read? Was Stevie unhappy? Not knowing made Sarah unhappy.

"I'm sorry you had to hear that," she said now. "Mom and I never used to fight. Now it seems like we're always at each other's throats."

"Yeah. Mom's been a bit hyper lately. She probably didn't mean anything, you know, critical."

"Maybe," Sarah admitted. "It's just that she's become so overprotective lately. Anyway, I'm sorry. This all must be so hard on you."

Stevie shrugged and stuck her hands in the back pockets of

her black-and-white-striped pants. Sarah thought that they were new; at least, she hadn't noticed them before.

"And I've only been thinking about me and my problems. I'm sorry, Stevie. I hope you're not feeling ignored around here."

Stevie shook her head now. "It's no big deal. Well, what I mean is don't worry about me. I'm fine."

"Are you sure, Stevie?"

"Yeah. You know, I could go on a walk with you sometime."

Sarah smiled. She was touched by her sister's offer. "You wouldn't rather hang out with your friends?"

"Well, I like hanging out with my friends, but I like hanging out with you, too. Besides, maybe Mom won't freak out so much if she knows someone's with you."

"You'll be my protector?" she asked with a smile. "My knight in shining armor?" *Well,* she thought, *Justin certainly hadn't been.*

Stevie straightened her shoulders. "I'm pretty tough when I need to be."

"Well, I hope you wouldn't need to be! By the way, are those new pants? They're really nice."

"Sort of new. I made them about a month ago. I've worn them a few times."

"I'm sorry. I guess I just never noticed them before."

"I've been spending some time with Cordelia," Stevie said suddenly. "But I guess you know that."

"Really?" Sarah was genuinely surprised at this news, and also, she realized, a tiny bit jealous. "No, I didn't know. That's great. I mean, what with me being so . . . so preoccupied and all. I guess I haven't been a very good friend to her."

"She never complains." Stevie smiled. "She's really kind of fun."

"I know! She's so different from me in some ways. But I guess maybe that's why we're friends. Though sometimes I think she must find me boring."

"No. I think she finds you kind of fascinating. I think she admires your being so smart. She says you're an intellectual."

Sarah smiled ruefully. "Maybe someday," she said. But when? How could she focus on training her mind with a child to support? She might not make it to college until her thirties, if ever. She would definitely never make it to law or nursing school. A wave of depression washed over Sarah. It was something that happened so often, every halfway pleasant moment interrupted by a rush of fear and sadness.

"I should apologize to Mom," she said now. "I guess someday I'll be just like her. I mean, crazy worried about my child. Maybe it's inevitable."

Stevie smiled. "That's kind of a scary thought. But isn't it one of those clichés, that we all turn into our parents eventually?"

"Well, things could be worse. Mom and Dad are pretty great."

"Yeah, we really don't have anything to complain about, do we? Well, not much. There was that time when Mom got that really awful haircut, remember?"

Sarah pretended to shudder. "That really was terrible, wasn't it? And I was so embarrassed to be seen with her! How mean of me. But I was only twelve. I guess most twelve-year-olds are embarrassed by their parents no matter what they do or how cool they are."

Sarah paused, stunned, because it had just occurred to her that before too long, *she* would have a child who would be embarrassed by her very presence in the room. Sarah didn't know how she would possibly handle being hated by the very person she loved the most, even if that "hate" was just a passing adolescent mood.

"What's wrong?" Stevie asked. "You look kind of weird suddenly. Are you sure you weren't bit by some evil poisonous insect on your walk?"

Sarah forced a smile. "No evil poisonous insect. Let's go in. I'm starved."

"And," Stevie said, "we don't want Mom to start freaking again."

Chapter 91

They had finished dinner some time ago. Cordelia had gone off to watch a few episodes of *Fashion Foot Soldiers* she had taped (the show had to do with shoes and boots, of course), and Jack had lingered at the kitchen table with Adelaide, where she had finally told him about her mother's e-mail. Not the part that had criticized him but all the rest. Understandably, he was furious.

"Will you let me confront her?" he asked. "She has some colossal nerve treating you so badly."

"But what could you possibly say?"

"I could tell her to leave my wife the hell alone."

Adelaide smiled sadly. "I don't think it will do any good, Jack. She's not going to change at this point in her life. But thank you. Thank you very much."

There was another reason Adelaide didn't want Jack getting involved. She was afraid that her mother might turn her nastiness on *him*, too. Jack's ego was pretty tough, but still, he did not need that sort of grief.

"Cordelia's still not meeting my eye," she said now. "It's like I told her I'd been in jail for murder."

"She'll come around."

Adelaide laughed a little wildly. "What is it about me, Jack? My mother hates me. My daughter hates me."

"No one hates you, Adelaide," Jack said, taking her hand. "Your mother is just deficient in the maternal instinct department. Sorry, but it's true. Cordelia is just being a teenager. Be patient with her."

"I'm trying, really."

"Good. On another topic, I tried to talk with Joe earlier."

"About what?" Adelaide asked.

"Plans for Sarah to finish high school. Plans for her going on to college."

Jack was well positioned to know a lot about Sarah and her potential. She was very smart and a very good student, and even though there was little academic bent to her home life, Jack had always felt certain that with a little encouragement Sarah could get into an academically sound college. As for the cost, well, he and the school counselors would help her with applications for financial aid and scholarships. If necessary, they would encourage her to attend a junior college for the first two years and then transfer to a four-year school.

But now, Sarah's future was in jeopardy.

"And?" she asked.

"And he politely but firmly declined to discuss his daughter's future. And since we were in his workshop surrounded by implements of destruction, I let it drop."

"Well, he is a classic old-time Mainer," Adelaide pointed out. "Private and self-sufficient and proud."

"That man might prove too proud for his own good one day."

"He's not stupid, Jack."

Jack sighed. "I didn't say that he was. But sometimes it's a lot smarter to ask for help than to try to tackle a complicated problem on your own. It's a lot smarter to admit you don't have all the answers before things get out of hand."

"That's true. But it's also smart to know when you can't force someone to face a problem on your time line or to do what *you* think is best for them to do. I learned my lesson with Cindy when I tried to push the idea of an adoption."

"Yeah. You're right. Interesting, isn't it?" Jack mused. "Sarah gets pregnant, and we all wind up learning some tough lessons."

"No person is an island."

"And it takes a village. Well, I don't know about you but I could stand a little levity. How about we watch an episode of *Arrested Development*?"

Adelaide smiled. "Good idea. We'll laugh at the absurdity, and our own lives will seem so much more normal."

Chapter 92

Cindy was poaching a chicken bought from a local farm in order to make a curry chicken salad for dinner. It was a family favorite. (Even Clarissa liked it, though she avoided the raisins by picking them out with one long, needlelike nail.) The carcass and assorted vegetables would go toward making chicken stock. Her mother had taught her the beauty and value of a good homemade stock, and not just for making soup.

"Yum, curry chicken salad!"

Cindy looked around to see Sarah coming in to the kitchen. "Someday," she said, "you'll probably be bored with it."

"Never."

Sarah had apologized after their latest conflict. Cindy had apologized as well. Neither was one to hold a grudge.

"Mom?" Sarah asked, taking a seat at the table. "Be honest, okay."

"Okay." Cindy never liked it when people began a conversation by extracting this promise. She always hoped that she *could* be honest, but sometimes, well, sometimes honesty was not the best policy.

"What would my grandmother have thought about my situation?" Sarah asked.

Thankfully, Cindy didn't have to lie. "Oh, well," she said promptly, "I think she'd be worried about your future, and the baby's future. But she would have loved to work on the baby's quilt, and she would have been fully supportive of you. Of that I'm entirely sure."

"Unlike Grandpa?"

"Well . . . your grandfather is different."

"I never asked what he said when you told him I was pregnant."

"He said that he wished you luck."

"That's all?"

"Yes." It was the truth.

"Oh." Sarah attempted a smile. "I guess it could have been worse."

"He's not a bad man, you know. He's just—different from your father."

"I know. I wonder what Grandma would think about his being married to someone so much younger than he is. Someone with teenagers."

Cindy had often pondered the very same question. "I think," she said, "that she would want your grandfather to be happy. But I also think she would want him to spend some time with his grandchildren."

"And his daughter?" Sarah asked with a small smile.

"I guess she would want that, too. I do miss him, even though he was never very demonstrative with either my mother or me." And maybe, Cindy thought, that was why she had married a man who, though quiet, was also very generous with his affection.

"I wonder if he'll come to see his great-grandchild."

"I hope so," Cindy said, but she wondered if she meant that.

"I'll ask him to visit. His wife too. She could come if she wants to."

"Of course," Cindy said.

"They would probably have to stay in Stevie's room. The baby will be with me, of course. We'd have to borrow a sleeping bag or an air mattress for Stevie . . ."

"Well, I wouldn't worry about that now," Cindy suggested.

"I'm not worried. Just thinking ahead. I'd like the baby to know his uncle Jonas, too, and his aunt Marie. Maybe they would visit us sometime."

"And his cousins in Brunswick? Ben and Jill and their children?"

"Of course," Sarah said. "Maybe the baby will bring everyone in the family closer together. Or do you think I'm being silly? Is that just wishful thinking?"

Cindy was pretty sure that it *was* wishful thinking, but what she said was, "No. A baby can work all sorts of miracles."

Sarah smiled. "Thanks, Mom," she said. "I'll set the table for dinner."

Chapter 93

"What do you have?" Sarah asked.

The girls were sitting on a bench at the top of the beach; it was their lunch break. Cordelia unwrapped her sandwich.

"Turkey and Swiss cheese. With Miracle Whip, of course. Mayonnaise is totally boring."

"I've got peanut butter and grape jelly. Lately, I can't get enough peanut butter and grape jelly. Talk about boring!"

"At least it's good for you," Cordelia said. "My mom has this brownie recipe that uses peanut butter. It's awesome. Seriously fattening, though."

"Mmm," Sarah mumbled. "She made them for my birthday last year."

For a few minutes, Cordelia ate her sandwich and watched an adorable little boy, about two she guessed, playing in the sand. He was wearing a blue bonnet to protect his wee head from the sun. His arms and legs were adorably chunky, and he had a little Buddha belly. Cordelia wanted to squeeze him. She wondered if her half-brother had been that awesomely cute when he was little.

"I found out something really big," she blurted. "About my mother."

Sarah looked over at her. "Is she okay?"

"Oh, she's fine. It's something that happened a long time ago."

"How did you find out?" Sarah asked. "And don't say you were snooping through her things!"

"I would never do that," Cordelia protested, even though she had been tempted once or twice, just out of natural curiosity. But her mother kept her stuff so orderly, Cordelia knew she would be found out in a minute. "She told me."

"Is it a secret? I mean, does anyone else know?"

Cordelia's conscience pricked at her. She knew that she should say yes, it's a secret, because she felt that it was. It was so big that it had to be. Instead, she said, "No, it's okay if I tell you. You just can't tell anyone else, okay? Not even your mother."

Sarah, mouth full again, nodded.

Cordelia looked again at the little boy in the blue hat. "When my mom had just graduated from high school she had a baby," she said. "A boy. And she gave him up for adoption."

The moment the words had left Cordelia's mouth, her conscience did more than prick at her. It stabbed at her. She knew she had done wrong. The secret had absolutely not been hers to reveal. Telling Sarah about her mother's past was an act of betrayal; it was an act of childish anger. But it was too late to take back the words that had been spoken.

"Wow," Sarah said after a moment. "Your poor mother."

"Yeah, well, poor me, too!" Cordelia was aware that she sounded sulky, but she couldn't seem to help it. Besides, somehow sand had gotten into her sandwich. That was always really annoying.

"What do you mean?" Sarah asked.

"I could have had a brother! I mean, a brother I could have actually known!"

Sarah laughed. "Doubtful. If your mother had kept the baby, she probably never would have met your dad and you never would have been born. Do you think she'd have had the freedom to take a vacation in Ogunquit—that's how she met your dad, right?—if she was supporting a child all on her own?"

Cordelia brushed aside this objection, though it had the ring of sense to it. A lot of what Sarah said had the ring of truth to it. Sometimes, Cordelia found this as annoying as sand in her sandwich.

"It's different for every person," Sarah went on, with, Cordelia thought, a very smug air of wisdom. "You can't judge another's choice. You weren't there. It was a different time and place. And you're not her."

"I can't believe you're defending my mother in this!"

"I'm not defending her," Sarah argued. "That would imply she had done something wrong and needed defending."

Cordelia frowned. Why did Sarah always have to have a reasonable answer to other people's unreasonable behavior?

"I mean, if she could give away one baby, what was to stop her from giving away another? Like me?" Cordelia winced at her own words. She knew that her mother had not done what she had done lightly. She knew she had suffered and was probably still suffering.

"Yeah, but that didn't happen, did it? Come on, Cordelia. Don't be silly."

Cordelia looked back to where she had last seen the toddler. He and his mother were gone. Suddenly, it all felt like too much. Too much change, too much sadness, too much loss. "I wish you weren't having this baby," she blurted. "I wish you had—"

"What?" Sarah asked quietly. "You wish I had what?"

Cordelia bit her lip. There was no way she could bring herself to say, "I wish you had had an abortion. I wish you had had a miscarriage." It would be too, too cruel. Instead, she said, "I wish that you had never gotten pregnant."

"But I did. And there's no point in wishing for something you can't have. Besides, now that I am pregnant, now that I know there's this little person in me, I don't want it any other way. I wouldn't turn back time. He's mine now. Can you understand that? We're bonded forever, no matter what happens."

"Yeah," Cordelia said. "I understand." But she wasn't sure that she could understand, not really, not like Sarah could.

They finished their lunch in a slightly uncomfortable silence. Cordelia supposed she should get used to uncomfortable silences. There would always be a river of difference between them now. Well, it was better than not having Sarah as a friend at all. And, it was inevitable that their lives would go in different directions; she knew that well enough. She had just never expected it to happen so soon.

"We'd better get back to the shop," Sarah said. "Help me up?"

Cordelia smiled, stood, and reached for Sarah's hand. "With pleasure," she said. "How about I buy us each a cookie on the way back?"

"As long as mine has peanut butter in it."

Chapter 94

"Thanks for having us over to work on the quilt, Mrs. Bauer," Cordelia said. "I always love being here."

The five women were gathered around the kitchen table. Sarah's mother had made her infamous butterscotch chip cookies and already—not that Sarah was counting—Cordelia had eaten three. Well, she thought, reaching for her second cookie, they were pretty hard to resist.

Stevie was absorbed in her work, her face a mask of concentration. Clarissa sat on the table, carefully watching every move of Stevie's skilled hands. Mrs. Kane and her mother were chatting idly about the exploits of some impossible neighbor while they sewed, and Cordelia, when she wasn't eating, was leafing through a magazine devoted to needlecraft, the pile of material before her largely ignored.

As for Sarah, her work was going slowly as her mind was mostly elsewhere. (Unlike her mother, she wasn't skilled enough to multitask.)

It was odd, but in the past few days or so, Sarah had realized that she no longer felt *any* connection to Justin whatsoever. She felt—and this was weird—almost as if she had generated the baby on her own. She wondered if this was a common feeling among women who were pregnant by men they didn't love or by men who didn't love them. Or maybe *all* pregnant women experienced this feeling of exclusivity on some level, even if they were happily partnered. She glanced over at her mother and Mrs. Kane. She supposed she could ask them about what she was feeling, and Dr. Westin might have some insight, too.

Besides, no matter how alien Justin *seemed*, he *was* always there with her, one half of the baby growing inside her. She knew all about the nature versus nurture argument, an argument that could never be fully resolved. A child was not born a blank slate. At the same time, the experiences a parent or caretaker provided counted enormously toward creating the adult that child would become.

So what traits *had* Justin contributed to their baby? Who *was* Justin Morrow, anyway? It was frustrating to know so little about him, but maybe there just wasn't all that much to know. Maybe he really *wasn't* a person of any nuance or complexity. And maybe, in spite of her very best efforts—and this was a scary thought—her child would grow up to have a shallow personality and a weak character just like his father. Maybe he would grow up to exhibit Justin's lack of moral fiber. Maybe, in spite of her encouragement, he would barely be able to finish high school without flunking out due to sheer laziness.

Sarah wondered now if that really was why Justin had barely managed to graduate. Maybe he had a learning disorder that had never been identified. Maybe it *had* been identified, but his parents had ignored the doctor's findings out of embarrassment or simply a lack of concern. Sarah figured she would never know the answers to any of these vexing questions.

Anyway, she thought now, eyeing the rapidly dwindling supply of cookies, hopefully her son would be more like his mother simply because *she* would be the primary influence on him. Maybe he would love the harsh cry of seagulls and enjoy walks through the woods and rambles on the beach and the glorious sight of the sun setting over the marshes at the end of the day. And all because *she* would have taught him to love and appreciate those things. She would have introduced him to the natural world through her own eyes of wonder.

Sarah's mother laughed at something Mrs. Kane had said. Well, Sarah thought, if she would be the primary person in her child's life, her wonderful parents and her amazing sister would not be far behind in importance. It would be a very good thing for her son to grow up with a strong male figure like Joe Bauer. It wasn't strictly necessary to have a good male role model in the home—lots of people went without this and did just fine in life—but it certainly couldn't hurt. She would be giving her son the gift of a superlative grandfather. That was something to feel good about.

As if summoned by her thoughts, the back door to the house opened and Sarah's father came in, closing the door carefully behind him.

"Ladies," he said, and was greeted by a chorus of welcome. "Hard at work, I see."

Cordelia laughed. "Well, some of us are!"

He indicated the brown paper bag he was holding. "I brought some ice cream, but I see you already have cookies so . . ."

"Dad!" Sarah laughed. "What kind did you get?"

Joe Bauer smiled. "Maple walnut, of course."

"Sarah's current favorite," Stevie explained. "She eats so much maple walnut ice cream the baby is probably already addicted to it."

"Well," Sarah said, putting down her sewing. "He *is* my son!"

Chapter 95

Adelaide was at The Busy Bee alone. Cindy had the afternoon off, Sarah would be in after two, and Jack was taking Cordelia for her annual checkup. And, after that, they were going for nachos at her favorite Mexican place. Going to the doctor made Cordelia a nervous wreck, and she claimed to need nachos as part of her recovery.

If things at the shop got busy, Adelaide might feel pressed, but otherwise she enjoyed the times she was on her own. She felt a bit like the queen of her very own kingdom. True, she hadn't made the business a success entirely on her own, but she *was* the guiding spirit of The Busy Bee.

And Adelaide was in a good mood. That very morning, Cordelia had complimented her mother on a new blouse. She said that it brought out the brilliant blue of her mother's eyes. Brilliant blue! Adelaide saw the compliment as a gesture of reconciliation, a pretty big step in the right direction. Maybe Cordelia had told Sarah about the long-ago adoption, and maybe Sarah had helped her come to terms with it. There was no point in Sarah *not* knowing; even Cindy had said so.

The bell over the door announced the arrival of a customer. *Well,* Adelaide thought, *maybe.* He didn't exactly look like her usual customers. He looked to be about sixty, wearing a clean but frayed plaid shirt, old jeans held up with suspenders, work boots, and a John Deere cap.

"Hello," Adelaide said with a smile. "May I help you?"

The man nodded. "I saw an ad for your shop in the paper," he said. "That's down in New Hampshire. My wife, Betty, loves quilts. Can't get enough of 'em. She's been feeling poorly lately, can't even leave the house some days. Thought I'd come up here while her sister's visiting—don't like to leave her alone—and buy her something nice. Cheer her up. Problem is, don't know what I'm lookin' at!"

Adelaide came out from behind the counter. "Well, then," she said, "let's see what I can do for you." Talking budget to men buying a gift for their wives could be delicate. She didn't want to insult him by suggesting a very expensive item or, conversely, by suggesting one that he might see as costing suspiciously little.

She asked the man about his wife's favorite colors. He thought for a moment and came up with blue and "that red that's like brown."

"Maroon?" Adelaide suggested. He nodded. She asked him if anything in the store looked like the kind of quilts his wife already owned, and after examination he pointed out a few pieces. She asked if a quilt was what he would like to give her or if supplies were more what he had in mind. "Her hands are pretty shaky at the moment," he said. "It better be something finished."

Adelaide thought she had just the right quilt for this devoted husband. She went to one of the shop's long, flat drawers and carefully opened it. "This," she said, lifting a quilt from the drawer, "is a piece your wife might like. It's a sampler quilt. The design is called 'Farmer's Wife.' It was made by my dear friend Cindy. She and her family live right here in Yorktide."

"It's pretty," the man said. "Colors are right. Looks like it might perk her up some. And she is a farmer's wife."

"I don't know what you had in mind to spend," Adelaide said. By now she was determined to let this nice man have the quilt at whatever price he could afford.

Without taking his eyes off the quilt he mentioned a dollar

figure. Adelaide smiled. "Well," she said, "you'll have change in your pocket on the way home."

The man smiled now. "Can you wrap it up?" he asked. "Truck's not as clean as it should be."

Adelaide completed the purchase and handed the man the quilt carefully wrapped in layers of tissue paper. "I hope your wife loves it," she said. "And I hope she feels better soon."

"Thank you kindly," the man said, and took his leave.

Adelaide realized that she was smiling. The encounter with that loving husband had been the icing on what was already a good day. She decided she would give the entire amount he had paid to Cindy, forgoing The Busy Bee's usual cut. There were more important things in life than money. Like the fact that her daughter didn't hate her after all!

Chapter 96

It was almost four o'clock. Joe would be home soon. At least, Cindy hoped that he would. He had taken on another new client even though he was already stretched. "We need the money," he had argued, and Cindy couldn't deny that. Still, she was concerned that he not work too hard and become careless. Accidents on a job site could be minor, but they also could be major. Just the previous year, a guy Joe knew pretty well had fallen off a ladder while doing some repair work to a roof and had broken both legs. He was still on disability, and his family was really feeling the pinch.

Well, assuming Joe would walk through the door under his own steam, Cindy had decided to make brownies for him. (And for her.) Brownies from a box mix were all well and good, but Cindy enjoyed the process of making them from scratch. There was something very soothing about carefully measuring the flour and slowly melting the chocolate, and finally, about spreading the gooey mixture into a pan. And, of course, there was the eating part.

"Hi."

Cindy smiled. "Hi, yourself." Sarah's body was very clearly a woman's body now. Not once had she complained to her mother about swollen feet or an aching back. Maybe she really wasn't feeling any discomfort. Maybe she felt she didn't have a right to complain. Unfortunately, that sounded a lot like Sarah.

"Mmm, that smells so good. When are they going to be ready?"

"Soon," Cindy said. "In about ten minutes."

"Good. I can't wait."

"You'll have to let them cool a bit first."

"Why?" Sarah said. "It's just you and me. Who cares if I've got brownie goo running down my chin?"

Cindy laughed. "Good point."

Sarah took a seat at the table. "So guess what, Mom?" she said. "I've decided on a name for the baby."

"I can't wait to hear it!"

"It's Henry. Henry Joseph."

"Oh." Cindy was immediately aware that her tone had been less than enthusiastic. She had been hoping that Sarah would choose the name David. It was a good, strong biblical name. She had planned on naming her second lost child David.

Sarah's face fell. "You don't like it?"

"It's not that," she said quickly. "But no one in our family is named Henry. At least, as far as I know."

"That doesn't matter, does it? I just really like the name. Henry."

"It's a fine name," Cindy said with a nod. "Old. Traditional. And not something silly like some of the names these celebrities are calling their children."

"Not only celebs, Mom. You know Maureen Ross, who works at the Dunkin' Donuts on River Street? She just had a girl and named her Cognac."

Cindy cringed. "I know Maureen's mother. She's one of the shop's most loyal customers. I wonder what she thinks of having a granddaughter named after an alcoholic beverage."

"I hope she's not a teetotaler. Can you imagine?"

"No. But I just thought. Brandy is a girl's name. Maybe Cognac will sound normal someday."

"How about Kahlúa? Mint Julep? Oh, I know! Sloe Gin Fizz!"

"How do you know all those names of drink?"

Sarah smiled. "I read a lot."

"What are you reading, exactly?"

"Oh, Mom, you can't honestly think I drink!"

But Cindy had, for a split second. She had thought: *Is that why Sarah got pregnant? Had she been drunk when it happened?* "Of course not," she said firmly.

"I've never even had a beer though Justin—" Sarah looked away.

Cindy tensed. Every time his name was mentioned, and thankfully that wasn't often these days, she felt a surge of pure anger. She hated that she couldn't seem to get control over her emotions where Justin was concerned. "Justin what?" she asked, keeping her tone even with effort.

"Nothing," Sarah said, turning back to her mother. "I feel absolutely nothing for him anymore so I wish . . . I wish I could just forget about him completely, have my memory erased or something."

Don't we all, Cindy answered silently. "Well," she said, "that's not going to happen. But maybe over time . . ."

"No." Sarah's tone was firm. "Every time I'll look at Henry, I'll see Justin, won't I? At least, I'll think of him."

"Not necessarily," Cindy argued, but she wasn't sure she believed what she was arguing. "You'll see Henry first and foremost and that's who you'll love, just Henry, for who he is all on his own."

Sarah looked doubtful. "I hope you're right, Mom."

Cindy hoped she was right, too. The oven timer went off then, and she reached for a dish towel. "Brownies are done."

"Excellent. I feel like I could eat the whole bunch."

Cindy took the hot pan from the oven and put it on top of one of the burners on the stove. "I remember being ravenous all the time when I was pregnant with you," she said. "Not with Stevie, though. I had all sorts of weird reactions to different foods with that pregnancy." Cindy gestured to the pan of cooling brownies. "Like chocolate. I love chocolate, but for some reason it nauseated me when I was pregnant with your sister. It's funny how every pregnancy can be so unique."

Sarah laughed shortly. "I doubt I'll ever know."

"What do you mean?" Cindy asked.

"Come on, Mom. I'm having a baby at seventeen. Who knows how I'll be able to afford things in the future? Who knows if I'll even be able to go to college, let alone travel like I had planned? It would be stupid to have another baby when I'll be struggling to handle the first one for the rest of my life. After all, I can't be relying on you and Dad forever. It wouldn't be fair."

Cindy felt immeasurably saddened by her daughter's attitude of defeat. "Oh, Sarah, don't talk like that," she pleaded, joining her at the table. "Your entire life is still ahead of you. You just have some challenges now that you didn't have before. You could still go to college someday and get married and have more children and—"

"Mom," Sarah said, taking her mother's hand. "Thanks, but I know the reality. I've read the statistics. They're pretty grim. And I know, I know, I'm not a statistic, I'm an individual, but still. There's a lot stacked against me. It would be silly to deny it."

My poor baby, Cindy thought, fighting the urge to sob. Was there really to be no mystery or magic left in her world, no innocence or possibility of simple joy? It couldn't be. It wouldn't be fair.

Then again, who ever said that life was fair?

Cindy gave Sarah's hand a squeeze. "I think we should eat a brownie now."

Chapter 97

Sarah was lying on the second bed in Cordelia's room. It was still kind of odd to see her pregnant, Cordelia thought, with breasts that actually needed a bra. It made her a little uncomfortable. The pregnancy was so blatant now. It was so much a reminder to Cordelia that Sarah had actually had sex. And that she, Cordelia, had not.

Not that she was in any rush to have sex, now that she was witness to Sarah's challenges. Her one ultra brief and entirely lunatic notion about asking John Blantyre to have sex with her had been a serious aberration, a moment of sheer, well, lunacy! That, or sunstroke.

"Here, I got something for the baby. For Henry." She held out a glossy blue gift bag, a profusion of red tissue paper poking out of it.

Sarah took the bag, reached inside, and pulled out a plush lion toy. "It's adorable," she cried. "I'm sure he'll love it—after he drools all over it. But why a lion?"

"Because he's going to be a Leo," Cordelia explained, stretching out on her own bed. "It's his sun sign. King Henry."

"Oh, right. That means he's going to be sociable, right? And popular."

"And have a big personality."

"And a lot of hair, too, like a lion's mane?"

Cordelia frowned. "Hmm. I don't think it works that way."

"I know. I was only teasing. I don't believe in any of that astrological stuff. But the lion is cute."

"You know, you're a Leo, too. But you don't act much like one."

"See?" Sarah said with a nod. "It's all nonsense."

"Hmm. I just thought of something. If the baby is late, he'll be a Virgo. I don't think I'll be able to find a stuffed—what? Virgin?"

Sarah laughed. "Let's stick with the lion either way. So what's your sign?"

"Sagittarius, of course."

"The archer? The half man, half horse? Funny, you don't look anything like a man or a horse."

"Ha. But I have a passion for travel—I mean, I will have a passion for travel when I have the money to do it right—and I can be blunt, and I change my mind a lot."

"You do change your mind a lot," Sarah agreed.

"All the time. But it's normal for a Sag."

"I see," Sarah said, raising her eyebrows dramatically.

"Go ahead, laugh if you want to. But it hurts no one to be into sun signs and all. It's fun."

"I suppose. As long as you don't give all your money to those bogus psychics, the kind who advertise in the back of cheesy magazines."

Cordelia grinned. "How would you know anything about cheesy magazines? You read *National Geographic*!"

"There was this old issue of something called *AWAKE!* in my doctor's office," Sarah explained. "I couldn't resist flipping through, and there were all these ads in back for obviously fake psychics and people who do cupping and sell these weird herbal concoctions. Every single ad promised your life would be totally changed for the better after you forked over your hard-earned cash. There were all these phony testimonials, too. Like, 'my hair grew in thicker than ever when I poured this mustard and ground crystal tonic over my head.' And, 'after years of searching for my soulmate, I finally found him when I tuned into my Otherworld Healer, thanks to Reverend Rainbow Dewdrop.' That sort of thing."

"Rainbow Dewdrop?"

"Well," Sarah said, "something like that."

"Well, there are a lot of legitimate psychics and alternative healers," Cordelia argued. "They just don't advertise in the back of cheesy magazines. They're too honest."

"I guess. It's just that those ads for phony professionals make me feel bad for the people who believe them."

"You feel bad for everybody. You'd feel bad for a robber who didn't get away with enough of your money! You'd be like, here, take another five dollars."

Sarah laughed. "I would not! Well, maybe I'd feel bad that he probably had had a terrible, deprived childhood that led him to become a criminal in the first place."

"See what I mean?"

"But you *have* to try to understand people's motives, their history, what makes them do what they do," Sarah argued. "It matters if we're going to have a fair society."

Cordelia shrugged. "I guess. But that still doesn't mean I'm personally going to feel bad for someone who tries to rob me!" She was silent for a moment, thinking. And then she said, "Sarah, you're going to make a really great mom."

"Why?"

"Because you're a very good person. You're smart, and you have a big heart. What more do you need? And don't say money or education or any of those other things. A brain and a heart are pretty awesome all on their own."

"You're a really great friend," Sarah said quietly. "For having such faith in me. Some days I don't have a whole lot of faith in myself at all."

"Well, do yourself a favor and get some! I'll be right back." Cordelia hauled herself off the bed. "I'm going to get us some food."

"Awesome," Sarah said.

Cordelia laughed. "Hey, that's my word!"

Chapter 98

Sarah had eaten three peanut butter and jelly sandwiches and two large oatmeal cookies. Now she was stretched out on Cordelia's second bed with the stuffed lion sitting atop her stomach. It really was adorable. Maybe, she thought, they should add the image of a friendly lion to Henry's quilt.

"So are you going to breast-feed?" Cordelia asked. "Pretty much everyone does these days, right?"

"I don't know about that, but yeah, I'm going to breast-feed. I'm a little worried about it, though."

"Why? Like, if it will hurt?"

"No," Sarah said. "I don't care about that. It's the logistics of it all. I'll have to pump enough milk so that while I'm at school my mother can feed the baby."

"Oh. What about, you know, when you're out at a restaurant or something. Or at the beach."

Sarah felt herself blush. "I know it sounds silly, but I'm pretty sure I'd feel too embarrassed to breast-feed outside of my home. It's just that, you know . . ."

Cordelia laughed. "I do know! You've never even worn a two-piece bathing suit, no matter how many times I've tried to talk you into buying one. If you're not comfortable showing your naked stomach to total strangers, how are you going to handle showing your naked breast—even a part of it—to the world?"

"Yeah. And forget about breast-feeding when my father is

in the room. He comes from farm stock; he probably sees it as perfectly natural and practical. But I think I inherited a modesty gene, probably from my mother's side of the family."

"Well, I wouldn't breast-feed in front of my father, either," Cordelia said. "What's wrong with going into another room?"

"Some people would say that feeling embarrassed about breast-feeding is anti-feminist," Sarah pointed out.

"Whatever! What ever happened to live and let live? I thought it was a free country!"

"Really. Do you know that back in May some girl in my French class asked me if I had posted pictures of my 'bump' on my Facebook page?"

Cordelia laughed again. "First of all, you don't have a Facebook page!"

"And second, the whole obsession people have with posting 'selfies' totally puzzles me. Well, to be honest, it actually kind of repulses me."

"I know!" Cordelia cried. "And believe me, with all the time I spend online I see a lot of 'selfies.' Half the time they're posing as if they're porn stars or something, pursing their lips and zooming in on their boobs. What's the point? Who are they trying to impress?"

Sarah smiled. "Boys, of course."

"Boys who are going to expect them to be porn stars? Isn't that false advertising? My mother would call it being a tease."

"I wonder how all those girls are going to feel about those selfies when they're older," Sarah said musingly. "Are they going to be embarrassed? Or are they just going to think, hey, we were kids having fun, no big deal?"

Cordelia shrugged. "I have no idea. All I know is that I'm not advertising my cleavage on social media."

"It all seems so frivolous," Sarah said, "except that I suspect it's much more damaging than frivolous in the end."

"Yeah," Cordelia said. "Maybe."

"Not that I have any right to criticize. I might not be into making suggestive poses and taking selfies, but I am pregnant.

Sixteen and pregnant and not once in my life have I shown the tiniest bit of cleavage or bared my stomach or stuck out my butt other than to sit in a chair."

"Hey. Be nice to yourself, Sarah."

Sarah shrugged. "And I really hate when people call a woman's unborn baby a 'bump'! I don't know, it somehow demeans the whole thing. I mean, sometimes being pregnant is unpleasant or inconvenient, but the *fact* of pregnancy is amazing and beautiful. It's a miracle."

Cordelia smiled. "I'm so glad you feel that way, Sarah."

"I really do. At least, now I do. At first, well, not so much."

"Hey!" Cordelia cried. "I just had a great idea!"

"What?" Sarah asked.

"I know what the baby can dress as for Halloween! A lion! With a hat like a big fuzzy mane!"

Sarah laughed. "That would be adorable. And we'll definitely have to post *that* picture online!"

Chapter 99

Adelaide and Cordelia were spending the day in Portland. It was the first time they had spent any significant amount of time alone together in a while. Adelaide had been thrilled that Cordelia had met her suggestion of a day out with such enthusiasm. It was, she hoped, another step toward healing.

They visited the museum in the morning and then had lunch at DiMillo's right on the water. After, they spent some time on Exchange Street, going into almost every one of the shops until Adelaide was exhausted from saying, "No, you can't have that pair of earrings," and "No, we can't afford to pay three hundred dollars for a pair of shoes." In a shop called Se Vende Imports, Cordelia had found a brass ring she declared she absolutely could not live without and, mercifully, it was only ten dollars. Ten dollars was not too much to pay for her daughter's happy smile.

Now they were sitting down by the ferry dock, watching the private sailboats, speedboats, and small excursion vessels bobbing at their moorings. The Old Port was jammed with tourists, some from the enormous cruise ship that had sailed into town that morning, but here, by the water, it was relatively quiet.

"I like playing tourist for a day," Cordelia said. "Especially since we didn't get to go away this summer."

"I'm really sorry about that," Adelaide said. "We'll go next summer."

"It's not a big deal. It's not like we live somewhere gross. Anyway, I wouldn't have wanted to leave Sarah for a whole week."

Adelaide was so proud of the way Cordelia had stuck by her friend. She and Jack had raised—were still raising—a good person. They were very, very lucky.

"I really love my new ring. Thanks, Mom."

"You're welcome. It looks good on your hand. And what's that nail polish color you're wearing?"

"Spanish Moss. Do you like it?"

"Ordinarily I wouldn't opt for green on nails. But yes, I do like it."

"I was kind of bummed at first that I had to keep my nails shorter than I like because of the quilt. I mean, it's hard enough to sew with *short* nails!"

"But now?" Adelaide asked.

Cordelia shrugged. "Now, I don't really care. It was worth it. Besides, once the quilt is finished, I'll let my nails grow long again."

Adelaide smiled. "Making the quilt *has* been a worthwhile thing, hasn't it?"

"Should we bring Dad something from Portland?" Cordelia said after a moment.

"Like what?"

Cordelia shrugged. "I don't know. Like, maybe a goofy hat or something."

"Or maybe a cupcake from that place on Fore Street he likes."

"Oh my God," Cordelia cried, "that means I'll have to get one for myself, too, and I swore I wasn't going to eat dessert this week!"

"Okay then," Adelaide said, biting back a smile, "a hat it is. But maybe something he'll actually wear."

Cordelia frowned. "On second thought, he really does love those cupcakes . . ."

"And one cupcake isn't going to kill you, you know."

Cordelia grinned and jumped up from the bench. "What are we waiting for?"

God, Adelaide thought, following her daughter. *I am so lucky. I wouldn't trade this child for anyone or anything, ever.*

Chapter 100

Cindy and the girls were out shopping at the outlets in Kittery. They had stopped for lunch at a tiny clam shack, with only three tables inside and four picnic tables outside. They sat at one of those now, with one crab roll, one order of fried clams, one order of fish and chips, and three bottles of water. Eating out had always been a big treat and soon would probably be a thing of the past, at least until . . . Well, at least until things settled into place.

Cindy enjoyed these rare mother-daughter excursions and was glad that Adelaide had pressed her into taking the day off. Especially since the day before Adelaide and Cordelia had gone to Portland while Cindy and Sarah had manned the shop on what had turned out to be one of the busiest days of the season.

A tall, middle-aged woman in a lightweight tracksuit passed their table, carrying a tray of food. She stared blatantly at Sarah and continued to shoot glances at her after she was seated at the next table with a man in a similar tracksuit.

Cindy bristled but held her tongue. Maybe Sarah hadn't noticed the woman's rude interest.

"Doesn't that bother you?" Stevie asked. "When people give you weird looks?"

So much, Cindy thought, *for discretion.*

"I'm used to it," Sarah said. "I don't like it, but I'm used to it."

"I mean, how do they know you're not married or engaged?

How do they know you're not a really young-looking twenty-one? Why is it any of their business?"

Sarah shrugged.

"If Clarissa were here," Stevie said, shooting a scowl in the direction of the overly curious woman, "she'd probably leap over there and scratch that woman's eyes out!"

"Then I'm glad she's not here!" Cindy declared. "So what's left on our list besides a new paper towel holder? I can't believe that old one finally broke."

"Well," Stevie said, "it *was* plastic. Maybe we should get a metal one or maybe a wooden one."

"If we came home with a wooden paper towel holder, your father would be—well, he wouldn't be angry, but he would point out that he could easily have made one himself."

Sarah shook her head. "I'm always amazed at how many things he's good at. I mean, how did he learn to do so much?"

"He's smart," Cindy said.

"He pays attention," Stevie added. "He watches things closely to see how they're done. You know, we should get Dad something while we're here."

Cindy frowned thoughtfully. "I don't think he needs anything."

"But that's what will make it special. He won't be expecting anything. He'll be surprised."

"Stevie's right," Sarah said. "We have to find something perfect. He's always doing nice things for us."

"Not that you don't do nice things for us, too, Mom."

Cindy laughed. "No, you're right. Your father deserves a treat. But—what?"

"I got it!" Stevie cried. "Last week I saw his favorite Bruce Springsteen CD in the recycling bin. It was broken. Let's get him a new one."

"Perfect," Sarah said. "I wonder why he didn't say anything about it."

"Because he didn't want one of us spending money on him," Cindy said. "Well, we'll show your father!"

Chapter 101

The Busy Bee had been quiet for twenty minutes or so after a flurry of customers that had kept both Cordelia and Sarah scurrying around, answering questions, and wrapping packages. Not every person had bought something, but most had and Cordelia had happily counted their intake at close to two hundred and fifty dollars. Now, the girls were enjoying the break. Sarah was perched on one of the stools behind the counter, and Cordelia was leaning on it. (If her mother had been there, she would have told Cordelia not to lean on it because she would dirty the glass.)

"I almost did a really stupid thing," Cordelia said suddenly. "Well, I thought about doing it. I wouldn't actually have done it."

"What?" Sarah asked. "And don't say, 'I was going to jump off a bridge into the river to see if I could survive.' "

"Me? Take a physical risk? Sewing is the only sport I can handle—barely! No, nothing like that, but you still can't tell anyone."

"All right."

"I don't even know why I'm telling *you*. Maybe—"

"Cordelia."

Cordelia sighed and told Sarah about her nanosecond idea of losing her virginity to John Blantyre. "I don't know what I was thinking, really," she said, shaking her head. "Well, yes, I do. I was feeling so stupid and naive compared to you. And . . . and left out. I know, I know, it's crazy. But that's how I felt."

Sarah looked horrified. "And you thought that getting someone to have sex with you would what? Make you like me? Like we'd be members of the same club or something? And after what your poor mother went through all those years ago?"

Cordelia cringed. "Okay, okay, I said I know it was dumb. And I didn't actually *do* anything. I just thought about it, for like, half a minute."

"Well, I have no right to judge. But, Cordelia, trust me, you don't know what you have until you lose it," Sarah insisted. "Freedom. Your childhood. Don't be stupid, Cordelia. Just don't."

"I'm not a child," Cordelia argued. "I'm only a few months younger than you."

"Yes," Sarah said. "Yes, you *are* a child. And so am I still, in a lot of ways. It's nothing to be ashamed of, it's just the way it is."

Reluctantly, Cordelia agreed. It would be stupid to be ashamed of something neutral like your age. Besides, it wasn't as if it was something you could change. Lie about, maybe, but not change. Time and only time would make you older, never younger.

Cordelia sighed. "My mother always says, 'don't be in a rush to grow up. You'll be an adult soon enough and adulthood lasts a long time.' "

"She's right," Sarah said. "You're an adult a lot longer than you're a child. If you're lucky."

"But adulthood seems exhausting, doesn't it? When was the last time any of our parents did something really fun or wild or outrageous?"

Sarah smiled. "My parents? Probably never."

"You know what I mean. I know there are perks to being an adult, but sheesh, all those bills to pay and toilets to clean and jobs to go to and tough decisions to make, like what health insurance plan you can afford!"

"What's the alternative?" Sarah said. "Besides, I think the

perks probably far outweigh the annoying stuff. Like, being *allowed* to make your own decisions."

"Ha! About *everything*. No one to make up your mind for you! I mean, you even have to figure out what you want to have for dinner every night!"

"Well, that's probably one of the good things about a relationship," Sarah pointed out, "like marriage. Teamwork. You can share the responsibilities."

Cordelia frowned. "Maybe. But you still have a lot more responsibilities than you had as a kid! I don't see either of my parents slacking off, ever."

Sarah's expression darkened.

"What's wrong?" Cordelia asked quickly. "Did the baby kick you in a rib?"

"No. I was just thinking that my childhood will officially end the moment the baby is born."

Cordelia reached across the counter and took Sarah's hand. "Oh, Sarah, I'm sorry! Here I am complaining about—well, about what amounts to nothing. I mean, about something that everyone goes through at some point. Growing up."

Sarah managed a smile. "If they're lucky."

"Yeah. If they're lucky."

Chapter 102

Sarah held the cold glass of lemonade against her forehead. She was at Cordelia's house again. Her own was too unbearably hot, even with the window units going. She had considered asking Mrs. Kane if she could sleep there at night but decided her parents might feel bad about it, like they weren't providing their child with something basic like a comfortable place to rest.

"God, it's so hot!" Cordelia cried. She was dramatically sprawled across her bed. "I can feel the heat even through the air-conditioning. It's, like, lurking. It must be horrible to be pregnant when it's ninety degrees in the shade," she said sympathetically.

Sarah smiled ruefully. "Well, if I had planned things out, I wouldn't be in this mess."

"I just hope that if I ever decide to get pregnant I look at the calendar first. I mean, who would want to be due in the middle of January when you could wind up being stranded by a blizzard on your way to the hospital! I can't imagine giving birth in the backseat of a car. Gross!"

"And no drugs. Though I hope I can keep the drugs to a minimum. But I don't think I can be a total hero and do without anything."

"You'd better not even try!" Cordelia cried. "You're going

to be exhausted afterward, that's what my mom says. Why should you be in pain, too?"

"Well, I think I'll be in pain no matter what. But I know what you mean. Maybe if things were different, I'd feel braver. Like if I had a husband and the pregnancy was planned and I had money." Sarah sighed. "Maybe not."

"I'll never feel brave about giving birth. I'm totally freaked out by the idea. Maybe I'll have a planned C-section. A lot of people have them these days."

Sarah frowned. "That's major surgery, you know. And it can be risky."

"I know, but at least I won't feel anything."

"I'm not sure that's entirely true. I mean, I think you feel a lot of pressure."

"Pressure, I can handle. It's excruciating pain that frightens me."

"Thanks," Sarah said with a laugh. "I feel so calm and reassured now!"

"Oh, I'm sorry! Don't listen to me. I'm just a big coward. You're so much braver than I am about everything."

"Am I?" *Brave* was not the first word Sarah would use to describe herself.

"Yeah. You're going through with this. If it were me, I . . . well, I don't know what I might do. Die of fright, probably."

"It will never be you," Sarah said firmly. "You've been scared straight by me."

"I guess I probably have been. How weird. I always thought I was the—"

"The what? The one who would screw up?"

"No, I mean—I just—" Cordelia's face was flushed with embarrassment.

Sarah laughed. "It's okay. I'm just teasing. Anyway, it only goes to show that life is full of surprises."

"I hate surprises. Unless they're under the Christmas tree. Then you can be pretty sure they're good surprises."

"I hate surprises, too," Sarah said. "I used to think that I liked them. But not anymore."

"Yeah. I can see that. Do you want more lemonade?" Cordelia asked, swinging her legs off the bed.

"What I want is more ice. In a bucket and dumped over my head."

Chapter 103

Adelaide was in the kitchen making a pitcher of iced tea when Cordelia came in with a rare pensive look on her face.

"Hi," Adelaide said. "Something on your mind?"

Cordelia sat on a stool at the counter. "Yeah. Mom, can we talk about something?"

"We can talk about anything."

"I've been thinking a lot about what you told me. About the adoption. And I'm sorry I was such a jerk to you. You did what you had to do, and it must have been so hard."

Adelaide fought back tears of joy and relief. "Thank you, Cordelia," she said. "And you weren't a jerk."

Cordelia shrugged. "I guess it was just such a shock. I mean, it was the last thing I ever expected to hear. Well, maybe not the very last, but still."

"I'm so sorry. I realize now that my timing was awful."

"You could have decided never to tell me."

"I suppose I could have," Adelaide admitted. "Your father pointed that out to me."

"But I'm glad that you did tell me. I wasn't at first, but now I am."

"Good. I guess no one really likes to learn that her parents had past experiences that weren't—pleasant. But maybe it's important we find out that our parents are flawed. Sometimes, seriously flawed."

But Adelaide wondered. Was it *really* better that she knew

her mother's true nature? Or would she be happier if she still believed that her mother was a kind and caring person? No. That would mean she was living under a delusion, and delusions were never a good idea.

"Well, I don't think giving your baby up for adoption was a sign of being flawed," Cordelia said. "It was a brave thing to do. As brave as Sarah's keeping her baby."

"Yes. Two acts of courage, keeping a child and giving away a child. Each requires a big leap of faith."

"Life is really hard, isn't it?" Cordelia said. "I mean, I guess on some level I kind of knew that, but until Sarah got pregnant I was really pretty innocent. Not to say that I'm totally mature now!"

"I think," Adelaide said, "that no matter how mature you are, life can always surprise or shock you. Or challenge you."

Cordelia frowned. "So it doesn't get easier?"

"Is that what it sounded like?"

"Yeah! Like, no matter how much experience you have it doesn't necessarily matter because something so bad or weird or unexpected could happen that you're left with—I don't know, with your mouth hanging open."

Why deny it? Adelaide thought. "That's when it helps to have friends and family to turn to," she said. "No one can really live life alone, not successfully, anyway."

"What about monks and nuns and people like that?" Cordelia asked.

"Most people in religious orders live in communities. Community members care for one another. But maybe there are some who live alone. . . . Except they're not alone because they have their god."

"See? Nothing is simple! How can anyone ever say, 'This is a fact,' when in the next half a second someone else can say, 'But what about this other fact that contradicts your fact?' "

Adelaide smiled fondly at her daughter. "Cordelia, you're a lot more mature than you give yourself credit for being!"

"Yeah, well, mature or not, I am sooooo hungry. What are we having for dinner?"

Chapter 104

"Burgers are ready," Joe announced from his place at the charcoal grill.

It was August tenth, Sarah's birthday, and there was a small birthday party slash baby shower in progress in the Bauers' backyard. Joe had hung blue streamers from the big maple tree by the shed, and there were blue balloons tacked to the edge of the picnic table. (Clarissa had immediately popped the first three Joe had blown up.) Sarah had collected wildflowers and put them in several mason jars now lined up and down the center of the table. The weather had cooperated. It was sunny and warm but with hardly a trace of humidity.

In addition to burgers, there was potato salad and corn on the cob and pigs in a blanket. (Clarissa had already made off with two of them.) Cindy had made Sarah's favorite carrot cake with pineapples and cream cheese frosting. The women were drinking wine. The men were drinking beer. The girls were drinking homemade lemonade.

At Sarah's request they had opened the presents for the baby first. (The quilt was not quite finished; that presentation would have to wait for another moment.) Joe had made a cradle for the baby out of pine. Cindy thought it was the most elegant thing he had ever crafted. Needless to say, it was also perfectly constructed. No grandchild of Joe's was going to tip over and be dumped on the floor while being rocked to sleep with a lullaby!

Adelaide and Cordelia had put together an enormous basket of baby products—lotions and powder, wipes and diapers, onesies and supersoft towels for after Henry's bath. The basket was decorated with blue and yellow ribbons and bows and lollipops in the shape of stars.

Stevie presented Sarah with a mini trousseau for her nephew. It consisted of a cap, a jacket, and a pair of pants, all in a supersoft, blue, wide-wale corduroy. "For fall and winter," she had explained. "I estimated how big he might be by then. The woman in that specialty kids' shop in Ogunquit helped me."

Cordelia smiled as Sarah exclaimed over Stevie's work. "I'm really looking forward to being the fun aunt," she announced. "You know, the aunt who spoils him rotten and lets him do things he's not supposed to do. Like, I don't know, eat candy right before dinner."

"What about me?" Stevie asked.

"You can be the cool aunt. You can . . . you can do whatever it is cool aunts do!"

"Like, make him fun clothes and teach him how to dye his hair!"

Cindy, seeing the expression on her husband's face at the mention of a boy using hair color, intervened. "Let's stick to making him clothes," she said.

The presents for Sarah were no less special. Stevie had made Sarah a denim shirt that she could wear now as well as after the baby was born. "It's sort of boho," she explained. "I know it's not your style, but I thought it would look really good on you."

Sarah had thanked her and put it on over her T-shirt. It did look good on her. Cindy thought her younger daughter might someday have a very successful career in fashion design. Imagine that. Then again, there was her skill with cats. . . .

Adelaide and Jack gave Sarah a gift certificate to the day spa in Ogunquit. "I know it's not something you would ever do for yourself," Adelaide explained. "But trust me, as a new mother you're going to need an afternoon of pampering. And I'll watch the baby for you."

Cindy and Joe had invested in a small silver circle charm with the initials HJB engraved on it. It was hung on a slim silver chain. Cindy fastened it around her daughter's neck. "I'll never take it off," Sarah declared.

"I was stumped," Cordelia told the group. "I had no idea what to get Sarah for her last birthday as a—well, is there a word for it, like pre-mother? I really wanted to get something special. But I just couldn't think of anything perfect. So . . ." She handed Sarah an envelope. "I hope it's okay."

Sarah opened the envelope. "It's a gift card for The Bookworm. Thank you, Cordelia. Really."

Cordelia shrugged. "But do you think you're even going to have time to read once the baby comes? I keep hearing that new parents are sleep deprived and that they never have the time to do the things they love to do, like go to the movies. I've even heard that they barely have the time to take regular showers! It sounds like a nightmare. Personally, if I couldn't shower daily, I'd go mad."

Cindy thought she saw a flicker of worry cross Sarah's face. "Don't worry," she said firmly. "We'll make sure Sarah has the opportunity to take a shower. And to read."

"And to go to the spa," Adelaide added.

"And to study for exams." Jack grinned. "Well, I am an educator. I have to mention school, don't I?"

Joe cleared his throat. "I think it's time we cut the cake."

They sang "Happy Birthday." Jack's lovely tenor made up for Joe's mumbling and Cordelia's off-key screech. Cindy noted that Clarissa had run off the moment the voices had been raised.

"Make a wish, make a wish!" Stevie and Cordelia chanted when the song had ended.

Sarah closed her eyes for a moment. When she opened

them, she blew out the seventeen candles in one breath. There was applause all around. Cindy wiped tears from her eyes and saw Adelaide do the same.

"Thanks, everyone," Sarah said, her eyes shining. "You've made this the best birthday ever."

Chapter 105

"Only a few weeks to go," Cordelia said. She and Sarah were in Cordelia's bedroom again. Sarah practically lived at the Kane house these days. Cordelia wondered why she didn't just sleep there, too. She had suggested as much, but Sarah had said no thanks.

"Assuming I actually make the due date," Sarah replied. She was lying on the second bed, her feet up on a stack of pillows. "I feel as if I could explode."

"I know you, Sarah. You're the most punctual person ever. You'll have the baby exactly on time."

"I might be punctual," Sarah argued, "but that doesn't mean my body is. The body has a mind of its own. I might not even have the baby until a week or two after my due date."

"Oh, I know, I know. I'm just being—"

"A good friend."

"You know, I've been thinking. There are advantages to being a young mother."

"Like what?" Sarah asked, raising an eyebrow.

"Like, you won't be one of those forty-year-old moms running after a toddler and complaining about all the stuff older moms complain about. You'll be healthy and strong and have a lot more energy. When the baby is ten, you'll only be twenty-seven. When he's eighteen and goes off to college you'll only be—wait, um . . ." Cordelia did a quick, eye-squinting mental count. "Thirty-five. You'll have a whole life ahead of you."

"You're sweet, trying to find the bright side."

"Well, someone has to!"

"Just don't say that people will think we're brother and sister."

"They might," Cordelia said, "if he looks a lot like you. What would be wrong with that?"

Sarah shrugged. "Nothing, I guess. It would just be a reminder that I was a teenage mom. It might embarrass him."

"Oh." Cordelia hadn't thought about that. "What if he looks a lot like Justin?"

"That'll be a bit weird, I guess. But I'll love him no matter what. And it's not like Justin isn't attractive."

Cordelia thought that point was debatable. "Do you think you'll go to the senior prom next spring?" she asked.

"I doubt it. I mean, who would ask me? Who would want to go to a prom with a *mom?*"

"We could go in a group," Cordelia suggested. "Not everyone goes with a date."

"Maybe. But something tells me I just won't care about the prom."

"Oh. Because you'll have this adorable baby at home."

"I hope I feel that way," Sarah said fervently. "I hope I'm head over heels in love with him."

"Why wouldn't you be?"

"Some women aren't. I can't imagine how horrible that must be, not to feel madly in love with your baby."

This was news to Cordelia. Aside from those mentally ill women who killed their children, she thought that all women loved their children as a matter of course. "So all that stuff about maternal instinct isn't always true?"

"From what I've read, no, it's *not.*"

Cordelia remembered what her mother had told her about how painful it had been to give up her baby. *She* had had plenty of maternal instinct. Cordelia felt a stab of pity for her mother. She had been so young and so alone, having to make a decision no teenager should have to make, the sort of decision that would affect the shape of her future. And now, there was Sarah. . . .

"What about applying for college?" she asked. "Will you wait a year or two?"

Sarah sighed. "I'm not really sure. I guess I won't know until the baby is here and we all have time to get used to our new life. So much is going to change. . . ."

"So much has already changed."

"Like my body! I can hardly see my feet. Do you know how weird that is?"

"You're not fat, you know," Cordelia pointed out.

Sarah laughed. "I know that! Besides, do you think I'd care about something as trivial as an extra few pounds, especially now?"

"No. I'm the one who freaks about weight!"

"You shouldn't. But you know that."

Cordelia shrugged.

"You know, when the condom broke, my first reaction was sheer terror."

Cordelia was startled. Sarah had never talked about—specifics. "Oh," she said.

"I've never been so scared in my life as I was at that moment. I felt sick to my stomach. I thought I would faint. I thought I would—die. Right there in Justin's shabby little apartment, just drop dead."

"What did Justin say?" Cordelia asked, though she wasn't sure she really wanted to know what the Idiot had said.

Sarah kind of laughed. "He told me to stop crying. He told me that everything was okay. He told me that nothing had, you know, happened. He told me to take a shower and wash really thoroughly. So I did."

Cordelia felt her cheeks flame. How could Sarah, a straight-A student, the most reasonable person Cordelia knew, have been so naive? "You believed him?" she asked, hoping her tone didn't betray the tiniest bit of the disappointment she felt in her friend.

Now Sarah blushed. "Yes. I did. I was petrified, Cordelia. I guess at that moment I *had* to believe him."

"You poor thing," Cordelia said, and she meant it.

Each girl lay quietly for a while. Cordelia felt that there was so much still to say and yet, nothing more to be said. It was a weird feeling.

Sarah finally broke the silence. "I feel like that me, back in January, was an entirely different person from this me," she said. "I feel as if I've aged ten years in the past few months."

"Matured, you mean?" Cordelia asked.

Sarah laughed softly. "Well, I hope so, but I did mean aged. Like as in getting older. And I feel—peaceful. For the first time since I found out I was pregnant. No. Maybe for the first time ever. Really and truly peaceful. It's amazing."

Cordelia's eyes widened. "You'd think that you would feel anything but peaceful, with what's about to happen!"

"I know. Maybe it's just that I've finally accepted the inevitable. No, it's more than that. It's like I feel—happy. Calm."

"Well, I'm glad for you," Cordelia said. "Because I'm still a nervous wreck!"

Sarah turned her head to look at Cordelia. "Why? All you have to do is get ready to be the fun aunt. And you'll be the best fun aunt ever."

Cordelia grinned. "I know," she said. "I am good at fun."

Chapter 106

Sarah had fallen asleep for a while. When she woke, she turned her head to see Cordelia where she had last been, on her own bed and flipping through a fashion magazine.

"Sorry I dozed off," she said.

Cordelia turned another page. "It must be exhausting, growing an entire person inside you. Besides, you were only asleep for, like, fifteen minutes."

Sarah adjusted her position and stretched her legs. She thought she had been dreaming about Justin. Could you actually dream when you had only been asleep for fifteen minutes? Maybe Cordelia was wrong about the time. Anyway, images of Justin had been floating around in her head.

"I never talked to you about this," she said now, aware that on some level she was talking to herself. "In fact, I never talked to *anyone* about it. I think that was one of the problems."

Cordelia sighed dramatically. "Sarah," she said, "I have no idea where you're going with this!"

Sarah looked over at her friend. "My feelings for Justin," she said. "The, um, passion I felt for him."

Cordelia closed the magazine. "Oh."

"I didn't think there was anyone I *could* talk to about how I felt. I didn't think anyone would understand the strength of my attraction to Justin, how much I—how much I wanted him. I'm sorry. Is this making you uncomfortable?"

"No," Cordelia said quickly. "Well, a little. But you should talk, Sarah. What's there to hide now?"

"The truth was I was really embarrassed about how I felt. It—it isolated me."

"I never . . ." Cordelia shook her head. "It never occurred to me that you were so *into* Justin."

"Well, I was. And the odd thing was that keeping those feelings to myself made them grow even more powerful."

"Really?"

Sarah nodded. "Absolutely. I didn't know it at the time, but I've figured out that keeping everything such a secret from you and my mom gave all those feelings an irresistible strength. It was like I was cherishing the sense of my feelings being forbidden. Okay, *I* was the one who decided they were forbidden in the first place, but still. Forbidden fruit is so much sweeter than the fruit it's okay to eat."

"Wow," Cordelia said. "That's a pretty deep thing to realize about yourself."

Sarah laughed. "I've had a lot of time to think this summer. I figured I should put it to good use. You know, get smarter. If I'm going to be responsible for another human being, I need to be as smart as I possibly can be."

"I don't think I'll ever be smart enough to be a mother. A good one, I mean."

"Yes, you will," Sarah said. "You're a natural."

Cordelia made a face. "Sarah, my priorities are food, fashion, and fun. In that order. I'm not exactly mature."

"You're way more mature than you think, trust me."

"Whatever. If I do have a baby someday, you can tell me what I'm doing wrong. But it will be way, way in the future."

"Deal. Do you know," Sarah said thoughtfully, "that my mom got married when she was eighteen? Actually making the decision to get married so young seems so—impossible. My pregnancy was an accident. But my mother *made* that huge conscious decision to commit to spending the rest of her life with my father. How did she know she was doing the right thing? It could have been a disaster."

Cordelia shrugged. "She was in love. Love makes you do silly things and totally heroic things. That's what my dad always says, anyway."

"I really admire her, you know. I think she's an incredibly strong person."

"She is," Cordelia said. "And she's so talented, too. Henry's quilt wouldn't be half as awesome if it weren't for her."

"And look at your mom," Sarah added. "Running her own successful business. We both lucked out. We both got a good role model."

Cordelia raised an eyebrow. "Yeah. Talk about pressure!"

Chapter 107

Adelaide rarely took advantage of the deck and now, stretched out on a recliner, she wondered why. Really, you could pretty easily convince yourself you were on vacation at a fancy resort. Okay, the Kanes didn't have a swimming pool, but they did have several large planters each spilling a profusion of flowers. Another long, low planter held her thriving herb garden. There was a glass of cold lemonade on the pretty little table at her right. And the view wasn't bad at all. The Kanes' backyard and deck faced the backyard and deck of their closest neighbors, Stan Lancaster and Mike Perez. Stan was a magnificent gardener, and Mike was a hardscape designer. Together they had created a gorgeous space complete with a bubbling fountain, an orderly herb garden, and a sweep of flowers in blocks of orange and purple—and Adelaide got to gaze at it for free.

Daydreaming was also free and not a bad way to spend her afternoon off from The Busy Bee. And right now, Adelaide was daydreaming about adopting another child. A baby, preferably, someone who would grow up knowing only Jack and Adelaide as his parents, someone they could cherish from the moment he was born. How fun it would be to have a fat, healthy, giggly baby to hold and to love!

Adelaide took a sip of lemonade. Of course, she thought, bringing another person into their household at this point would entail huge changes for all three of them. There were Cordelia's feelings to take into consideration. She was a sensitive person and had already battled troubled feelings regarding her mother's past. She might feel as if the baby were a replacement child, now that she would soon be going off to college.

And Jack would be under more pressure to make money, especially when the baby was little and Adelaide couldn't work on expanding her own business. And making money wasn't enough. It had to be saved, too, and invested. There wasn't only college to consider. There was retirement, too. They had talked about doing some traveling when they both stopped working. Nothing elaborate, maybe just long car trips, but still, travel would take money.

Adelaide's back hurt. She shifted on the recliner until the pain eased somewhat. *And*, she thought, there was the fact that neither of them was as young as they used to be. Starting over with a new baby meant midnight feedings, and erratic hours and . . . huh. It was pretty much what Cindy and Joe would be doing. If she and Jack acted quickly, their new child could be raised along with Sarah's child and the families could share some responsibilities. . . .

But that didn't address the fact that Jack might be opposed to the idea. Adopting a child just wouldn't work unless both partners were one hundred percent behind the idea. You couldn't force your partner to accept the reality of a child, not if you wanted to keep your relationship intact.

There were so many obstacles and difficulties. . . . Adelaide choked on another sip of lemonade. What, she wondered, had she been thinking? She didn't really want another child, did she? What she wanted was her first child back! Of course that was what she wanted.

One child could not be used as a substitute for another child. It would be completely unfair to everyone, an enterprise bound to fail, an entirely selfish act.

No. An adoption wasn't going to happen. Her family was already complete. She would remain content with the wonderful child she had been lucky enough to keep.

Adelaide was surprised to find tears streaming down her cheeks.

Chapter 108

Stevie smiled. "This feels like a ceremony."

"It *is* a ceremony!" Cordelia announced. "Why else would we be having champagne?"

"Sparkling cider, you mean," Sarah pointed out.

Cordelia shrugged. "Anything fizzy means a celebration."

The Kane and Bauer women were at The Busy Bee to celebrate the fact that Henry's quilt, measuring an impressive five feet by five feet, was finally finished. It was spread out on one of the quilt frames to show off the colorful images (including a last-minute lion with a shaggy mane), the impressive stitching, and, across the bottom, the baby's name, Henry Joseph, in big block letters.

Everyone took a turn having her photograph taken standing next to the quilt, and then Adelaide had attempted a group selfie. The result was a little wobbly, but it would do.

"Let's toast our accomplishment." Adelaide raised her glass. "To a job well done."

"To a job well done!"

"And just in time!" Cordelia added.

Cindy put her arm around her daughter. "I'm so proud of you, Sarah."

"But I hardly did anything but prick my finger a lot," Sarah protested. "And make weird-looking starfish. You guys did most of the creative stuff."

"What I meant," Cindy said, wiping a tear from her eye,

"was that I'm proud of you for *everything*. For your being Sarah."

Sarah blushed. "The quilt is really lovely," she said. "It's amazing to see it finished."

"You're going to use it, I hope," Adelaide said. "I mean, not just hang it on the wall."

"Oh, no, I'm definitely going to use it! Though I guess I'll have to learn how to clean it properly. You can't just stuff it in the washing machine with the sheets!"

"And you can't store precious things in the attic in case there's a big storm and the roof leaks."

Sarah looked inquiringly at Cordelia. "Why would I be storing Henry's quilt instead of using it?"

Cordelia shrugged. "It was just something I read in one of Mom's magazines."

"I suppose you'll have to keep Clarissa away from the quilt," Adelaide said.

Stevie shook her head. "Oh, no, Mrs. Kane. Clarissa is way too smart to destroy something so valuable."

"It's true," Sarah added. "In fact, I'm kind of expecting her to be a babysitter for little Henry. The little kitty guarding the little Leo. How cute would that be!"

"Maybe Henry will learn to quilt someday," Cordelia said, taking a sip of the sparkling cider.

"Why not?" Stevie said. "Quilting shouldn't be just for women. Lots of guys knit these days. Why not quilt?"

"When I was a little girl," Adelaide added, "the tailor in our neighborhood was a man. He was very old. He'd learned the craft from his father before him, growing up in Italy."

Cindy smiled. "I wonder what your father would feel about his grandson wielding a needle and thread?"

"I think he'd be proud," Sarah said firmly. "After all, Dad builds things with wood. Why wouldn't he appreciate a boy building something useful out of fabric?"

"Well, he certainly wouldn't stand in anyone's way," Cindy affirmed. "Live and let live is what Joe would say."

"Jack wouldn't mind, either. He would say, let the boy do whatever makes him happy."

Cordelia cleared her throat. "Ahem. And what I would say is, can we please cut the cake now?"

Cindy picked up the knife. "That, we can all agree on."

Cindy busied herself cutting the chocolate iced cake she had made that morning. On top she had spelled out the baby's name in blue and yellow jimmies. She really *was* proud of Sarah. She had handled the pregnancy and all it entailed with such grace. She had soldiered through the tough emotional times and had, Cindy believed, come to accept with some peace the role she was about to be handed.

"For Sarah first," she said, handing her older daughter a paper plate. "A big piece."

"I want a big piece, too," Cordelia said; then, she reddened. "I mean, may I have a big piece?"

Adelaide shook her head, and Cindy laughed. "Yes," she said, "you may."

"You always had a sweet tooth," Sarah said. "I mean, more than me, anyway."

Cordelia shrugged. "Sugar is my vice. Everyone needs one vice, right?"

Adelaide raised an eyebrow at her daughter. "Who told you that?"

"I don't know if everyone *needs* a vice, but I think that probably everyone has one."

Cindy looked to her younger daughter. "Now how did we get on the topic of vices? This is supposed to be a happy moment. Let's talk about, I don't know, virtues!"

"Like the virtue of accepting what life brings you," Sarah said. "Honestly, when I first found out I was pregnant, I didn't know if I could handle it. Now, almost nine months later, here I am. Don't get me wrong, I'm nervous and all, but I'm also happy."

"Life is full of surprises," Cindy said.

"The human spirit is resilient," Adelaide added.

Cordelia nodded. "And cake always helps."

Chapter 109

Cordelia was alone at The Busy Bee. After the presentation of the quilt, Cindy and Sarah had gone home, and her mom had gone out to run an errand. There had been no customers for the past forty-five minutes, which gave Cordelia plenty of time to think about what Sarah had told her the other day about how in lust she had been with Justin.

She didn't know why she had been so surprised, but the whole passion thing did explain a lot. And when she gave it more thought, she realized that she felt closer to Sarah than she had since Sarah had gotten pregnant. Because the year before, she had had a crush on a senior on the basketball team. It wasn't the same as having a boyfriend, not at all, but still, she thought that now she could understand if only a little bit Sarah's infatuation with Justin.

She still sometimes thought of him—his name was Roddy—but without any of that sick-to-her-stomach feeling. In fact, now she couldn't understand what she had found so attractive about him. His ears stuck out more than a little bit and his hair wasn't that great. But for about two whole months, she had been possessed (that wasn't too strong a word) by thoughts of him. And it had come on *boom,* like that, like some cosmic ruler had snapped his fingers and suddenly, Cordelia had been smitten. She had spent hours fantasizing in minute detail about conversations they would have, kisses they would indulge in, and meaningful glances they would share across a crowded cafeteria. She had created entire scenes—no, complete movies!—in her head starring the two of them, movies in which they would run off in his car and drive across country and sleep wrapped in each other's arms, under a starry sky. In these movies Roddy and Cordelia were each other's everything; no one in the entire world understood Roddy like Cordelia did and no one in the entire world understood—and worshipped—Cordelia like Roddy did.

And then, *boom,* it was all over. She had walked in to the school's library one afternoon to find Roddy and a few other members of the basketball team goofing around at a table by the window. The librarian, a perpetually harried-looking woman, was busy at the desk, her back to the boys, when suddenly one of them (Cordelia hadn't seen who it was) threw a wadded-up piece of paper at her. It hit her square on the head, and the boys erupted in muffled hoots and guffaws.

And that had been the end of Cordelia's crush or infatuation or romantic disease. She remembered turning away and walking right out of the library, totally embarrassed by the fact that she had found Roddy Murphy the stuff of dreams. She was beyond glad she hadn't said anything to Sarah about her feelings for Roddy. Sarah wouldn't have made fun of her, but still, she might have pointed out, in her usual reasonable way, that Cordelia's feelings couldn't really be for or about Roddy because she didn't *know* Roddy. Cordelia understood that now. It was as if her free-floating romantic feelings, to which all teenagers were subject, had for some random reason attached themselves to Roddy Murphy though they might just as easily have attached themselves to another boy.

Love, at least, infatuation, really was like a sickness. It wasn't something you asked for. It was just something that, being human, you were vulnerable to contracting. And so maybe that's how even sensible Sarah Bauer had succumbed to Justin Morrow's dubious (his imagined?) charms.

And maybe that's what had happened with her mother, too, back when she was seventeen. Maybe that guy, whoever he was, had had a dizzying effect on her so that she had done something terribly careless and had had to pay a horrible price.

Cordelia realized that she was frowning. She still couldn't fully accept the weird fact that she was not her mother's only child. It made her feel a bit less special in the world. Still, she was absolutely certain of her mother's love. In fact, she wondered if her mother had spoiled her—and she *had* spoiled her, no doubt about that!—to make up for having given up her first child. Probably. Cordelia thought she would have done the same. It was something about guilt and atonement.

And it made no sense, really, but she kind of missed the brother she had never known. Maybe someday she might be able to find him . . . but would that be the right thing to do? What if he didn't know he was adopted? That seemed unlikely, didn't it? Or, what if he knew he was adopted but didn't want to be found, especially by his birth mother's daughter—the child she had kept?

The door of the shop opened, startling Cordelia out of her reverie.

"Was it busy?" her mother asked.

"Dead as a doornail," Cordelia said. "What is a doornail, exactly? A nail used in making doors?"

Her mother shrugged. "I guess so. Better ask your father or Mr. Bauer. I don't do carpentry."

Chapter 110

Sarah was stretched out on her bed, her feet propped on a pile of pillows. Henry's quilt was draped across the back of her desk chair. It made her happy to see it there. And in a matter of weeks, it would make her happy to see the quilt covering little Henry himself. (Though you had to be careful about blankets and pillows around infants!)

In the past weeks, she had thrown out most of the trinkets Justin had given her over the course of their relationship, but she had kept two, one for Henry and one for herself. The first was a little stuffed rabbit about the size of her hand. It was brown and black with a pink nose. The other was a bracelet with an inlay of iridescent seashell. She would never wear it—it was more Cordelia's style, a bit flashy—but she thought it was very pretty. No harm would come from it remaining in her sock drawer. If she was being sentimental about these two tokens of—well, of whatever it was that had existed between them—so be it. Because whatever it *had* been, it had resulted in the creation of a life. Whatever it had been, it had not been worthless.

No, the creation of a new life was not a waste. What mattered was what people made of that new life, how they cared for and nurtured it. That's where waste might come into play.

She remembered something she had read on the Internet a week or two ago. Every single day more than two thousand girls in the United States got pregnant. Girls, not women. And eight out of ten fathers—boys, not men—did not marry their girlfriends. And—this had really upset Sarah—the sons of teenage mothers were twice as likely to go to prison than the sons of older mothers.

Sarah wondered how much of that sort of information was meant to scare a girl away from sex. (Were boys ever scared away from sex?) If she had known then all she knew now, would she have resisted her desires? Would she have been smarter and gotten on the pill? It was impossible now to say.

Just like it was impossible to know what Justin had really seen in her. She wasn't the prettiest girl in town, nor was she the one with the best personality. But she had never questioned his attraction to her, not once during all the months they were together. He had made her believe that he found her beautiful and special. He had really listened to her when she talked. . . . Correction. Sarah had *thought* that he had listened. And she realized now that she had never told him anything important about herself. Maybe deep down she had known that he wasn't capable of a proper response. In fact, the more she thought about it, the more she believed that the entire relationship had been only smoke and mirrors, more a figment of her imagination than a mutual experience rooted in genuine emotion.

Sarah sighed and rested her hand on her stomach. She felt what she thought was a little foot and thought of all the joy Justin would be missing by rejecting his child. She sincerely hoped that he would grow up and mature. If he didn't—and some people never did—he might very well leave several more abandoned children in his wake.

And not all of them would be as lucky and as blessed as her little Henry.

Chapter 111

Adelaide was alone in the den after dinner. There was little chance she would be disturbed. Jack was watching a Red Sox game. Cordelia was watching *Down with Love* for about the sixth time.

Adelaide sat at her desk. She had been thinking about how at the gifting of the quilt Cindy had told Sarah that she was proud of her. Adelaide had been touched, but at the same time, she had felt a pang of intense jealousy in the presence of that warm, nurturing relationship.

She wondered now if her own mother had ever been proud of her, even before her "big mistake." She couldn't remember her mother ever praising her for anything—getting good grades, keeping a clean room, making the basketball team. But maybe her mother *had* praised her. Memory was a notoriously tricky thing. Maybe, after the pregnancy, and her mother's insistence that she "get rid of" the baby, Adelaide had obliterated any memories of her mother having been supportive and encouraging.

Maybe.

Adelaide took out a pen and a yellow legal pad (yes, she still used her handwriting skills). She thought she might draft a letter to her mother, expressing what she felt about that toxic e-mail. She wasn't sure it was something she would ever send, but she felt that the process of putting her feelings on paper might help her achieve some peace of mind. Certainly, Adelaide didn't expect anything in her relationship with Nancy Morgan to actually change.

Unless, of course, she decided to cut all ties with her mother.

The idea had never occurred to her before. But, why not? As it was, the relationship was an empty husk, kept up as a matter of form. At least, that's how it felt on Adelaide's end and she suspected her mother would agree.

But there was her father to consider. How would a final rift between his wife and his daughter affect him? Adelaide was certain her mother would forbid her father to contact her. And she didn't see him having the nerve or the energy to fight for a private relationship with his daughter.

What would Jack say to such an idea? Even though he was her fierce supporter, he would probably advise against such a dramatic option.

And what would Cindy say? Cindy didn't know about Nancy Morgan's last e-mail. In spite of how Adelaide felt about her mother, she still felt bound by the ancient commandment to honor her. There was a limit to the critical things she could reveal about her mother to anyone other than her husband.

So, knowing only the little she did, Cindy would probably point out that Adelaide's parents were geriatric and might not have that much longer to live. How would Adelaide feel when they died? she would ask. The regret at having abandoned the relationship might be unbearable.

Yes, Adelaide countered to the imagined voice of her friend. There *was* such a thing as filial duty, but how did you determine when a person was no longer worth your time and respect?

But cutting off a relationship entirely, even one that had been diseased for years, was not an easy thing to do. There might even be cases in which it was the *wrong* thing to do and this case, Adelaide's, might be one of them. It was hard to know for sure. After all, what had her mother done to her that was so wrong except to be her particular self?

Suddenly, Adelaide began to write. She only stopped twenty

minutes later when her hand was so cramped around the pen she had to use the other hand to release it.

She felt as if she had done something good. Still, she would not send the letter. She had rushed into telling Cordelia about the long-ago adoption, and the revelation had been painful for Cordelia to bear. She knew now to be more cautious. Words could not be unspoken or unwritten. They could only be suffered.

Adelaide folded the sheet of paper, put it in an envelope, and slid it into the top drawer of her desk. She suddenly felt like watching that Red Sox game.

Chapter 112

Joe was fast asleep. Cindy, however, was awake. A book lay unopened beside her as she thought back on what had been a very special and memorable day.

She and Stevie had helped Sarah pack a bag for the hospital. Clarissa had also helped. She had climbed into and out of the bag after each item was placed within.

"She wants her scent on everything," Stevie had explained. "She doesn't want you to feel lonely in the hospital. And she doesn't want you to forget her."

Sarah had laughed. "As if I could ever forget Clarissa for even one minute! I've never known such a small creature to make such a big impression."

Much of what Cindy had decided to pack might prove unnecessary, but she wanted Sarah to feel prepared and as at home as possible. A new cotton nightgown (though she would mostly be wearing a johnny), her slippers (the hospital would probably have her use their own socks with treads), a book (she probably wouldn't have time to read), a few hair bands (okay, those *always* came in handy), basic toiletries (the hospital would supply those, as well), and a bag of the cashew turtles from Harbor Candy that Sarah loved so much.

The process of packing had been a bittersweet experience for Cindy. Her daughter would be leaving the house a child and coming back a parent. That transformation seemed—revolutionary.

When the bag was packed, the three of them had made ice-cream sundaes. After a small bowl of vanilla ice cream, Clarissa had chased a plastic straw around the kitchen floor until it disappeared under the fridge.

Cindy smiled into the darkened room. If anyone asked for her definition of happiness, she would say that happiness meant being right here at home in this house on Maple Road with her children and her husband. And in a few days, that definition of happiness would expand to include a home that included her grandson.

Joe mumbled. Cindy turned out the light and lay down. She rested her hand on her husband's arm and drifted off to sleep.

Chapter 113

"This could be it," Cordelia said. "The big day."

She and her mother had just opened The Busy Bee. The air conditioner hadn't had time to cool the shop yet, and Cordelia was fanning her face with a flyer left by a member of one of the local summer theater troupes.

"Yes," her mother said. "Sarah's doctor thinks she's ready."

"What do you think we should do?"

Her mother laughed. "What can we do?"

Cordelia shrugged. She wasn't the praying type—her family only went to church at Christmas—but maybe she could try to say a prayer for everything to go well. *Um, God,* she said silently. *Please be with Sarah today. Let everything turn out okay. And please let little Henry be okay, too.*

And then, in typical Cordelia fashion, her mind switched its attention from Sarah, Henry, and God and landed on jewelry.

"Mom?" she said. "Did you ever consider selling some jewelry at the shop? I mean, beach glass stuff, necklaces, earrings? Beach glass is really popular."

"True, but it's not really our brand, is it?"

"But we sell other gifts," Cordelia pointed out, "like the soaps and the balsam cushions. And lots of local people make beach glass jewelry, and locally made stuff is an attraction. People think it's more genuine or something."

"You're right," her mother admitted. "I suppose we could

give it a try. Maybe I'll see about buying a small supply for next summer."

"Cool. I could model the jewelry while I'm here."

Adelaide laughed. "Ah, so is *that* your ulterior motive? Free jewelry?"

"Well, I wouldn't keep it! Remember when we were in Boston last year, and we went to the mall at Copley Place and I dragged you into that shop called Landau?"

"I do remember being dragged, yes."

"Remember how the saleswoman was wearing a bunch of the products? It's a very effective sales tool. If I'd had the money, I would have bought out the shop!"

"Well, it's a good thing you didn't have the money," her mother said. "As I recall, there were some pretty expensive items in those cases."

"*Gorgeous* items! Those rings!"

The store phone rang then and Adelaide hurried to the little office/kitchen space in back. Half a moment later, she had returned.

"Who was it?" Cordelia asked. "Was it them?"

Her mother smiled. "That was Mrs. Bauer. They're taking Sarah to the hospital! Boy, that girl is punctual!"

"Oh my God," Cordelia cried, "let's go right now! Come on!"

"Wait, Cordelia. There's no need to rush. Cindy says Sarah still has some way to go. It could be hours and hours before the baby comes."

"But—"

"But it will be much nicer to wait here at the shop than at the hospital. Trust me."

Cordelia frowned. "All right. But I'm not going to be able to do anything but worry in the meantime."

"Try not to worry. Sarah will be in good hands."

Cordelia burst out crying. "I'm just so happy and excited and scared and, and I don't know what!"

The bell above the door tinkled, and a customer came in to find Cordelia bawling.

"My best friend just went into labor!" she cried.

The woman seemed a bit taken aback. "Oh," she said, after a moment. "How wonderful. I wish her the best."

Cordelia nodded and ran to the kitchen from where she could hear her mother smoothly making a sale.

Chapter 114

The Bauer family was on its way to the hospital. Clarissa had seen the family off with a rousing chorus of meows. When Sarah had settled in the backseat, her mother next to her and Stevie in the front seat with her father, she had turned to see Clarissa sitting in the living room window, watching them, her eyes wide and serious.

"Are you okay, Sarah?" her mother asked now, squeezing her hand.

"I'm fine," she said. "I just can't wait to meet Henry. I just feel so happy!"

"And I can't wait to meet my grandson. I wonder if he'll call me Grandma or Nana. Well, I guess that's up to us, right?"

"Grandma," Sarah said. "That's what you'll be. And Dad will be Grandpa. And Stevie will be Aunt Stevie."

"This is the last time it'll just be the four of us," Stevie said suddenly. "Right here in this car, the very last time."

Sarah thought her sister sounded a bit sad. Maybe *nostalgic* was the better word. Well, she could understand Stevie's mood. In some ways, a new child in the house would have a bigger effect on Stevie than on anyone else.

"It will be better when there are five of us," Cindy replied firmly. "I'm sure of it."

"Six if you count Miss Clarissa," Sarah's father said.

"I count her," Stevie said.

"Me too, Stevie. Mom," Sarah asked. "Did you call the Kanes?"

"Before we left the house. Adelaide and Cordelia were at the shop."

"I can just imagine Cordelia! She's probably jumping up and down and driving her mother mad with questions she has no way of answering."

Sarah's mother laughed. "And begging to go to the hospital right this minute!"

Sarah smiled and looked out of the window. They were passing the Applewood Farm Stand and a bit farther along the road Sarah could see the veritable wall of lilac bushes that marked the edge of Mr. Chapel's property. At this time of the year, they were past flowering but they were still lovely. And there was Kountry Korner Antiques, which, in spite of the silly spelling of its name, was chock full of authentic and interesting items, and then there was the Barrys' lush pasture where there were always a few horses grazing. All landmarks Sarah had known since she was small. They were precious to her in a way she could never quite put into words.

And in a day or two she would pass these landmarks again, but this time with her son. He wouldn't be able to see the farm stand and the horses yet, but she would tell him they were there and promise to introduce him to the world that would soon be his. She was so, so happy that her mother had refused to let her consider an adoption. She was so, so happy to be having this baby.

This is the most important thing I have ever done, she said to herself. *Maybe the most important thing I'll ever do. Don't forget one moment. Don't ever forget!*

"Almost there, Sarah," her mother said, taking her hand.

"Good. Because—oh! Ow! Boy, that hurt."

"There's the sign for the hospital!" Stevie looked over her shoulder. "You'll be okay, Sarah."

Sarah smiled through another contraction. "I know I'll be okay," she said. "I have my family with me."

Chapter 115

They were in the kitchen making dinner. Correction. Adelaide, as usual, was doing the prep work, chopping, slicing, and defrosting. Cordelia was pacing the floor and being generally anxiety ridden.

"Why haven't we heard anything yet?" Cordelia asked for what had to be the fifth time in so many minutes.

Adelaide was wondering as well. There had been no word from Cindy or from Joe since that one call around nine that morning. "I don't know, but I'm sure everything is fine," she said, with an assurance she didn't quite feel. "Try to be patient."

"I'm just saying, it's been almost nine hours since Mrs. Bauer called to say they were going to the hospital."

"A woman can be in labor for days, Cordelia. You know that. Worrying about Sarah isn't going to help the process along."

"But what kind of friend would I be if I wasn't freaking out?"

She had a point, Adelaide thought. "Okay," she said. "Worry if you have to worry. I'll try to be calm for the both of us."

"Are you sure we can't call the hospital and ask them what's happening?"

"I doubt anyone would tell us anything, Cordelia. We're not technically family."

Cordelia fell into a chair at the table and crossed her arms across her chest. "It's not fair. We're as close as family. Maybe closer!"

The phone rang at that moment, saving Adelaide from having to confront the fraught topic of familial relationships.

"It's them!" Cordelia cried, leaping from her chair. "It's got to be!"

God, Adelaide thought, *I hope so.* She wiped her hands on a towel and reached for the receiver.

"Hello?" she said. She was aware of the mixture of fear and excitement in her voice.

She listened to Joe Bauer. She did not blink or frown or put her hand to her heart. She did not say a word.

"What, what, what?" Cordelia hissed, tugging at her arm. "Is everything okay? Can we go to the hospital now?"

Adelaide slowly replaced the receiver.

"Mom? Mom, I'm getting a weird feeling! What is it?"

"That was Mr. Bauer," Adelaide said, her voice barely above a whisper.

"And? Is everything okay?"

Adelaide did not reply. She did not look at Cordelia as she shrugged out of her grip. She walked to the door of the kitchen. "Jack!" she shouted. "Jack, come downstairs, quickly, please!"

Behind her, Cordelia was still saying plaintively, "Mom? Mom, what? What happened? Say something!"

Adelaide didn't move or speak again until her husband arrived a moment later. And then she fell heavily against him.

He stumbled backward with the suddenness of her collapse. "My God, Adelaide," he cried, grasping her tightly. "What's wrong? Are you sick?"

She opened her mouth and closed it again. The words, those dreaded words, threatened to choke her.

"Mom, what is it?" Cordelia shouted from across the room. "Mom!"

With supreme effort, Adelaide opened her mouth again. "Sarah," she said, her voice harsh, "is gone."

Jack tightened his grip on her. "What?" he demanded.

"She . . . she died. The baby is fine. But Sarah . . ."

Behind them, Cordelia screamed. And then she began to sob.

An animallike wail came from Adelaide then, a cry of pure pain. "Jack! Oh, God, Jack!"

She could hear Cordelia rushing across the kitchen, and a moment later felt her crash into them. Jack clasped his wife and his daughter tightly in his arms. Adelaide heard him begin to cry.

Chapter 116

Cindy was alone in the room. She stood at a distance from the bed on which Sarah lay, covered by a thin white sheet.

In the space of a moment, Cindy thought, feeling her brain struggle to break free of the shock. *In the space of a moment, everything could be lost. In the space of a moment, every plan you had made, large or small, every bit of the future you had looked forward to, from the next moment to the next ten years, could be entirely irrelevant.*

Cindy took a step closer to the bed and shuddered. *If only disbelief were strong enough to reverse the truth,* she thought. *If only I could say, "I don't believe that my daughter is dead" and then, she would not be dead.*

But that wasn't the way the world worked, not at all. Sarah almost—almost—looked as if she was sleeping, but she was not. This was only the shell of Sarah, her face pale and her hair damp, the plastic identification tag around her thin wrist, her poor body still swollen with evidence of the great thing she had just accomplished—and of the awful thing she had just endured.

Cindy took another step closer and leaned over her daughter. Gently, as if Sarah could still feel her mother's embrace, she put her arms around her and laid her head against Sarah's. If only the two of them could stay there forever. And why not? What was there to live for now? Her oldest surviving child, the child upon whom she had lavished so much love, the child from whom so much good was expected, was gone.

"Mrs. Bauer?"

The voice came from behind her. Cindy hadn't heard anyone come into the room.

"Are you all right?" the woman asked, her voice hushed. "Can I get you some water?"

With a sob, Cindy released her child and turned away from the bed. She shook her head. "No," she said, her voice rough. "I need to go to my family."

The nurse gently took Cindy's arm and led her from the room. Cindy did not look back. In a small, private waiting room down the hall, Joe and Stevie were waiting. The nurse left them alone. For a while, the grieving family stood with their arms around each other, their heads pressed together. Finally, Cindy sighed and pulled away a bit.

"We need," she said, "to see the baby. We need to see Henry."

Another nurse led Cindy, Joe, and Stevie to the NICU where seven-pound, two-ounce Henry Joseph lay swaddled in a crib.

"The poor mite," Joe murmured. "My grandson."

Stevie put out a hand as if to touch the sleeping baby and then, instead, put her hand over her eyes.

And the strangest feeling came over Cindy then. All of the sorrow and pain of Sarah's death was still with her, it always would be, but alongside it, there was something else, something a bit brighter. *This,* she thought, *is Sarah's child. And in Henry, Sarah still lives. This baby,* she thought, *is a miracle. And he is ours. He is our miracle.*

"He's beautiful," she said, putting her arm around Stevie's shaking shoulders. "Sarah gave us this precious gift. And we will care for him, won't we? We will love him like Sarah would have. Won't we?"

Through her tears, Stevie nodded. Joe gathered his family in his arms, and together, the Bauers welcomed their newest member.

Part 3

Great necessities call out great virtues.

—Abigail Adams

Chapter 117

It was late September. Adelaide was still keeping summer hours at The Busy Bee, though running the shop almost entirely on her own now was tiring. That said, she was grateful to have someplace to *go* every day.

It had been a month since Sarah had died. Adelaide still had trouble believing that she was gone. At least once a day, she relived that shattering phone call from Joe. She thought she would never be able to forget hearing those terrible words: "My daughter is dead."

Everything had been all right at first. The baby had been in some small distress, but Sarah had managed to give birth to him naturally.

And then, a moment later, disaster had struck. Sarah began to bleed heavily (exsanguination, or hemorrhage the doctors called it) and rapidly went into hypovolemic shock. The doctors had been just about to start a blood transfusion and intervene surgically when Sarah had died.

Just like that. Here one moment, gone the next.

The exact cause of the hemorrhage remained unknown. Even after an autopsy, the doctors explained, there might not be an answer to that most dreadful of questions: Why?

But the Bauers said they didn't need to know why. Knowing what had caused the fatal bleed wouldn't bring back their daughter. Besides, Joe had trouble with the thought of his child's body being cut apart even if it was in pursuit of the truth.

Adelaide hadn't dared to argue with her friend's decision not to have an autopsy performed, though she and Jack felt that if Cordelia had been the one to die on the operating table . . .

But their daughter was not the one who had died. They were the fortunate ones.

The door to the shop opened, and a young woman came in, holding the hand of a little girl around the age of five. The girl was clutching a baby doll around the neck, not a grip recommended in the real world.

"Good afternoon," Adelaide said. "Let me know if I can help you with anything."

The woman smiled and went over to the far wall on which two newly acquired quilts were displayed. The little girl marched over to Adelaide, who stood behind the counter, and held her doll up for inspection.

"This is my baby," she announced with unmistakable pride. "Her name is Belle. Like the princess."

Adelaide felt her heart contract. "She's a very pretty baby," she said. "You must love her very much."

The little girl grabbed the doll back to her chest. "Oh, yes," she said quite seriously. "Very much."

The young woman came to join them at the counter. "My daughter is obsessed with that doll," she whispered. "I can hardly pry it out of her hands at bath time. It's part fabric," she explained. "Water will ruin it."

Adelaide smiled weakly. "Yes," she said. "My daughter was the same way with a stuffed unicorn. She still has it, and she's almost seventeen."

It turned out that the woman was simply killing time and not interested in buying. Ordinarily, this sort of visitor didn't bother Adelaide in the least. But now, she prayed for the woman and her daughter to leave.

Girls and dolls, women and babies . . .

Finally, they did leave, and Adelaide sighed aloud in relief.

Every day since Sarah's passing presented a new challenge. And everyone was coping as best as he or she could. Jack, in his usual vigorous manner, was spearheading a scholarship in Sarah's name. Joe, in his usual stoic manner, had refused to take any time away from his work commitments.

And Cindy . . . every single day she visited Sarah's grave, most times with the baby. Sarah had been buried in the Bauer family plot in a beautiful old cemetery on the outskirts of Yorktide. "In a way, she's back home," Cindy had said. "I mean, really home, with her ancestors." She had put the hexagon quilt she made for baby Sarah seventeen years ago in the coffin with her daughter. "A quilt is a treasure which follows its owner everywhere," she told Adelaide, quoting a popular saying among quilters. "It will comfort Sarah on her journey."

Adelaide was glad that Cindy could find solace in that belief.

As for Adelaide, well, the way she was coping with the loss was by throwing herself into the care of her daughter. Cordelia had taken Sarah's death very badly. For the first two weeks she had barely been able to swallow water. She had been overcome by fits of sobbing that threatened to choke her. She had spent hours curled up on her bed, clutching her old stuffed unicorn. She couldn't sleep. She wouldn't talk.

Adelaide and Jack had felt it necessary to take Cordelia to a doctor who advised putting her on a prescription tranquilizer. They carefully monitored her dosage, and Cordelia was showing some small improvement but not enough for her parents' peace of mind. At least, she was eating again but without any real interest. The other day Jack had been able to raise the ghost of a smile when he did his infamous imitation of Bill Murray's character in *Caddyshack*.

She had gone back to school a week after its official start but without any of her usual enthusiasm. Teachers and administration had been trained in dealing with tragedies such as what had befallen Sarah, and as Sarah's only real friend, Cordelia was being looked after closely. Still, she was on her own when kids came to her with expressions of condolence or offers of friendship or, horribly, condemnation disguised as sympathy: "She got what she deserved." No one had actually *said* that to Cordelia, but there were ways in which critical comments could be couched in flowery, innocent-seeming language. Adelaide had heard some of them herself from a few nasty-minded people in town.

And on the topic of nasty-minded people . . .

The letter Adelaide had written to her mother just before Henry was born was still in her desk. Once Sarah died, Adelaide had realized that there were more important and more immediate concerns for her to handle than a coldhearted old woman.

Adelaide looked at her watch. Cordelia would be home from school soon, though Jack would be staying late for a meeting. Without debating the idea, Adelaide set about closing up The Busy Bee for the day. Losing a potential sale mattered nothing; being home with her grieving child mattered an awful lot.

Chapter 118

Cindy had just come back from visiting Sarah's grave. It was a nasty day in early November, damp and chill and overcast. Snow was predicted. Sarah had loved the snow so much. It would look pretty piled on her headstone.

Cindy put the kettle on to boil. The house was quiet. Henry was down for a nap, Joe was at work, and Stevie was at school. Unconsciously, Cindy put her hand to the silver charm she wore around her neck. It was the one she and Joe had given Sarah for her birthday back in August. She wore it in memory of the vital and special person Sarah had been—and always would be, in Cindy's memory.

A memory that was at times intensely, acutely detailed and clear; at other times, frustratingly vague; and at still other times, almost restfully nonexistent. Grieving, Cindy reflected now, was a very strange process. Some days, she thought she wouldn't survive it.

She had read somewhere, a long time ago, that the intensity of a really strong emotion could almost make you lose your memory of what had *caused* that really strong emotion—a person dying, a traumatic event. At the time, the idea had made no sense to her. But now . . .

Just that morning Cindy had realized she had forgotten the exact color of Sarah's eyes. The day before, try as hard as she might, she simply could not call up the last words she had heard Sarah speak or the last words she had spoken to her daughter. These experiences filled her with a desperate sadness, as well as with deep feelings of guilt. What sort of mother couldn't remember the color of her child's eyes? What right did that sort of mother have to live?

In the first weeks after Sarah's death, as she lay in bed, listening to the baby's tiny movements in the crib by her bed, Cindy had wondered if forgetting might be a good thing in the end, easier to bear, less awful than too precise and constant a degree of memory. She had wondered if she could pray for a state of relative emotional oblivion. Would her God grant such a request? Would any God?

And then she had wondered: How would a state of emotional oblivion affect those people in her life who were still here on earth—Joe, Stevie, and Henry? In the end, after weeks of near sleepless nights, she had come to realize that to feel nothing would be of no benefit to anyone at all. Like it or not, she was a deeply generous person and nothing could totally change that. She couldn't willingly abandon those Sarah had left behind. It would be a sort of penance for Cindy to push past the pain and guilt, the sorrow and the anger, and be present for her family. Her family—what remained of it—*had* to be her mission in life. It was what was going to keep her sane.

The teakettle whistled. Cindy poured the water into a cup and sank into a chair at the kitchen table. She might forget some things, even temporarily, but others could never be forgotten. There were too many witnesses, too many aides to memory. Sarah's funeral was one of them.

Every member of Joe's family had attended, Jonas and Marie from Chicago and the cousins from Brunswick. Cindy's father had come (and gone back to Augusta shortly after the church service), though his wife and her children had not. Cindy had been glad about this. She didn't know May well enough to feel comfortable sharing such an intimate grief. She would have liked to believe that May understood this and had chosen not to come because of it. But maybe May just hadn't been able to get the time off work.

It was different with the neighbors and other townsfolk who came to the church, people with whom the Bauers shared their daily lives in ways both large and small. Some had barely known Sarah herself; some were Joe's clients; some were members of Cindy's quilting workshops; others knew the family only by sight. But both Cindy and Joe were glad for their presence and support. There were major benefits to life in a small, tightly knit community, and the support of that community when tragedy struck was one of them. The amount of food that arrived at the Bauer home in the days and weeks following Sarah's death was astonishing. Neighbors had taken it upon themselves to mow the lawn and to take the garbage to the dump. Joe's employees had taken up a collection among themselves and Joe's repeat clients, and had presented him with a check to help with the funeral expenses. Cards and flowers were left for Cindy and Joe and Stevie at The Busy Bee.

And then there were Sarah's schoolmates. Every single member of Sarah's class had been at the funeral with the exception of one boy who was traveling in California with his parents. Many of Stevie's classmates had been there as well, as had their parents. The reverend had told them it was the most well-attended funeral The Church of the Savior had ever seen. It was a bittersweet distinction.

Cindy thought she heard Henry waking and hurried into the living room to check on him. But he was still asleep in the cradle Joe had made for him. Cindy looked down at her grandson. She loved him so very much. "Poor little thing," she whispered.

At some point in the future, Henry would probably want to know about his birth father. Now, the telling would be up to Cindy and Joe, and she figured they would cross that bridge when it loomed into view. To tell the naked truth—that Henry's birth father had wanted nothing to do with him—seemed a brutal choice. To disguise the reality with the intent of easing Henry's pain would be kinder: "Your father was very young; he wasn't able to help care for you." It wasn't far from the truth.

Cindy went back to the kitchen and poured more hot water into her cup. Thinking of Justin reminded her of the day the card from the Morrows had arrived. It was about a week after Henry's birth and Sarah's passing. She and Joe were in the kitchen. He was sitting at the table going through some paperwork from the hospital. Cindy was standing at the counter, separating the mail into bills, junk, and personal notes and letters.

She remembered thinking that the house seemed upsettingly quiet without Sarah's presence. Even though she had never been a loud or noisy person, her absence fairly screamed.

And then, she had come to the card.

She had opened the envelope with trepidation. At this terrible time, would June Morrow dare to attack or to blame? Cindy couldn't be sure what that despicable woman was capable of doing.

There was no salutation. The printed message was the usual sort of thing to be found in these cards. There was no personal note. Someone, probably June, had signed the card Mr. and Mrs. Morrow. It was as impersonal a gesture as it could possibly be. Cindy wondered why they had even bothered to send a card at all.

"We got a card from the Morrows," Cindy had said. "Do you want to see it?"

Without looking up from his work, Joe had laughed bitterly. "No."

Cindy had carefully torn the card into shreds and tossed it into the garbage can. "Not one word about the baby. They act as if he doesn't exist. It's—it's appalling. Their own flesh and blood . . . It's insulting. It's wretched behavior."

"Good riddance. At least they aren't fighting us for custody. Not that we would let them win. We're adopting that baby, and that's final."

Cindy hadn't replied. She harbored a secret worry that if the

Morrows did sue for legal custody of Henry they might win. She didn't know enough about the law to feel even a shred of Joe's confidence in the Bauers' rights to the baby. And Justin, as the father, still might stake a claim. . . .

But now, almost three months after Sarah's passing and the birth of his son, there had still been no word from Justin. He must have been told. He must not have cared. Or maybe, just maybe, he was too overcome with remorse to make himself known.

For the first few weeks after Sarah's death, Cindy's feelings of anger toward Justin had threatened to grow out of control. In her darkest moments, she blamed him for having killed her daughter. She fantasized about hurting him. Once she dreamed of killing him. She told no one of these feelings. She didn't want to be told that they were wrong or dangerous. In a way, she welcomed them.

But the demands of a baby—of Sarah's baby—had taken rightful precedence in her mind and in her heart. Increasingly, Justin was more of a distant and unpleasant memory than an object of loathing. She no longer feared him. She almost pitied him.

Cindy sighed and looked over to the fridge. The photographs of Sarah and Stevie through the years were still on the door. She would never take them down. She needed reminders of that idyllic past, when both of her surviving children were with her, happy and healthy. She missed Sarah dreadfully, in a very deep way she couldn't articulate, and in a million tiny ways, too. She missed Sarah's daily companionship. She found herself turning around from the stove and addressing the table, as if Sarah was sitting right there. "Do you know who I saw in the drugstore today?" Or, "Do you remember the Christmas we made that wonderful chocolate bark?" It was always, always a shock to find no one else in the room.

Cindy heard the front door open. Stevie was home from school. Cindy hurried to greet her daughter. Clarissa, always alert, was already perched on her shoulder.

"How was school?" Cindy asked. She thought that Stevie looked thinner than usual. It frightened her.

"Fine. Did you visit the grave today?" Stevie asked, unwinding her scarf without unsettling Clarissa.

"Yes."

"Was everything okay? I mean . . ."

"Yes," Cindy said. "I replaced the flowers. The caretakers had raked up most of the leaves."

"Good." Stevie walked over to where Henry lay asleep and peered down at him. "Is Henry okay?" she asked. "Did he eat well?"

Cindy felt her heart contract. This was a routine now, Stevie's coming home from school or Cordelia's house and checking to be sure that nothing bad had happened to the family in her absence.

"Yes, Stevie," she said firmly. "Everything is perfectly fine. Now, why don't we go into the kitchen for a snack?"

Stevie, Cindy's last surviving child, raised the ghost of a smile and followed.

Chapter 119

"We've got thirty people packed in here now. We're at code limit, I'm afraid, if we're not already over."

Cordelia glanced around The Busy Bee and nodded. Her mother was right. Things could get dangerous if they let any more people in.

"I'll stand at the door and explain that no one else can come in until some people leave. Who ever thought a quilt shop would need a bouncer?"

Cordelia managed a weak smile as her mother inched her way through the crowd.

She was the one responsible for this gathering of people on this cold winter evening. It had started when Sarah's headstone was put in place back in late October. It was a shiny pinkish marble. Cordelia figured it had cost a fortune, but how could you scrimp on your child's grave? Across the top, there was an engraved vine with flowers. Cordelia couldn't tell what kind of flowers they were, but Sarah would have known. Under Sarah's name there were the dates of her birth and of her death. Under that there were these words: *Beloved mother, daughter, sister.*

She assumed that Mr. and Mrs. Bauer had decided on the order of those words. Cordelia wondered. Were they supposed to remember Sarah primarily as a mother? And why wasn't the word *friend* there as well?

Everything about the headstone—the very fact of it, its very solidity—had bothered Cordelia. It made her feel physically nauseous. Sarah was not hard. She had never really liked pink. Sarah was—she was not that block of marble.

It was this visceral reaction that gave her the idea of making a different sort of memorial for her friend. So she had asked anyone who cared—kids at school, neighbors, regular customers of The Busy Bee—to make a square fabric patch in memory of Sarah. When all the patches were collected, they would be assembled into a pieced, free-form quilt.

Already, in mid December, they had enough patches to make *two* large quilts, one that would hang in the shop and the other that would hang in the halls of Yorktide High. Many of the patches depicted Sarah's favorite flowers and birds and seashells and wildlife. A few featured Sarah's name written in elaborate stitching. Some quoted poems or the Bible. Stevie's patch had an absolutely perfect profile silhouette of her sister. Another particularly amazing patch showed a full-length image of Sarah, all done in bits and pieces of cotton and velvet.

Only Cordelia hadn't been able to make a patch in honor of her friend. No matter how hard she tried, she just couldn't decide on one image or one set of words that could adequately express what she felt about Sarah, or what Sarah had meant to her. So while Mrs. Bauer busied herself with the overall design of the disparate patches, Cordelia focused on collecting them.

This evening, a surprisingly big group of serious, talented quilters had gathered to begin assembling the final products. (Who knew that the women would have to work in shifts?) Mrs. Bauer said it was just as women had gathered for centuries to work and socialize and help one another through tough times. Cordelia hoped *someone* was being helped, because *she* certainly didn't feel any better.

Cordelia smiled at a woman she vaguely recognized and adjusted her glasses. She didn't know why she had made such a big deal about not wearing them. Given what had happened to Sarah—that awful, awful thing—it really was kind of embarrassing to admit she had been worried about looking dorky.

She would rather be alive and the dorkiest person in the world than be dead.

Ever since Sarah had died—well, after the period of hysterical crying had passed—Cordelia had felt strangely subdued, as if there was a hazy coating on her feelings. She wasn't thinking properly, either; she had been unusually forgetful and distracted, even though she had been off the tranquilizers since October.

It was all supposed to be the result of grief—a counselor at school had told her that—and grief was something everyone experienced differently. Cordelia wished she were going through this grieving process much more quickly. Everything felt so—uncomfortable. She was very tired, physically and mentally, and she wanted very badly for life to feel normal again. It would be a new normal, she knew that, but still, it wouldn't be this feeling of *dis-ease*. She had found that term, used with the hyphen, in one of the articles she had read online about depression.

Ms. Todd, who owned the diner down the road, came over to where Cordelia stood by the refreshment table.

"I understand," she said, "that making these quilts was your idea."

Cordelia shrugged. "It seemed a nice thing to do."

"More than just nice," Ms. Todd said. "You're a good friend to remember Sarah in this way. Such a lovely young woman. Such a terrible waste."

Cordelia swallowed harshly. Why couldn't people just leave her alone?! Now she was going to cry again and . . .

A call from across the room made Ms. Todd nod good-bye and hurry away.

Cordelia squeezed her hands into fists at her sides. Why did bad things happen? She had spent an awful lot of time since Sarah's death pondering this eternal question, but so far all she could come up with was that bad things happened because they just *did*. Life was random. You could choose to believe there was some plan to it all, formed by some great being with a moral purpose in mind, and maybe that would bring you some peace. But Cordelia thought that was just fooling yourself. It was better to enjoy, if you possibly could, every decent moment for as long as it lasted and always be braced for the not-so-decent moments that were bound to come along.

Like spending your birthday without your best friend for the first time in forever.

Without Sarah, there hadn't seemed much cause to celebrate. Still, her parents had insisted they mark the occasion; her mother had made Cordelia's favorite cake, with maple syrup frosting, and they had given her a gift card to her favorite clothing store at the mall.

Stevie had made her a beautiful, intricately woven, leather friendship bracelet. Cordelia had burst out crying when Stevie gave it to her, and that had made Stevie cry, too, and that had set Clarissa howling and circling at Stevie's feet in sympathy.

Thanksgiving, two days later, had come and gone in much the same subdued and tearful way. Cordelia and her parents had eaten dinner together and then gone to the Bauers' for pie and coffee. Cordelia didn't like being in the Bauers' house now. She especially couldn't bear to go into Sarah's old room, now little Henry's. Some of Sarah's stuff was still there, but her books had been moved to the living room to make space for all the equipment a baby seemed to require. Sarah's clothes, Stevie had told her, had been packed up and brought to Goodwill.

"Well," Stevie had reasoned, "that's where she got most of them in the first place."

Cordelia was brought back to the moment by Mrs. Castle from the local dry cleaners exclaiming, "He looks just like his mama!"

"Isn't it amazing?" Ms. Robinson, a teacher at the local grammar school, answered. "He has Sarah's chin and the shape of his eyes are just the same as hers."

They were of course referring to Henry, who was strapped in his car seat atop the counter, watched over by Stevie. No one, Cordelia had noted, had said anything about the baby looking like his father.

Personally, Cordelia thought Henry looked pretty much like any four-month-old baby—cute and cuddly (now that he had gotten past that fragile space alien look of a newborn) and pretty much interchangeable with the next cute and cuddly baby. But she guessed it made people feel good to find a resemblance between a motherless child and his mother. And maybe someday Henry really *would* look a lot like Sarah. That would be wonderful. He could look at pictures of the mother he never knew and then look at his own reflection in the mirror and somehow, even a little bit, know her. And of course, she, Cordelia, would tell him all about Sarah, what a good friend she had been, how smart she was, and how she had someday wanted to be a nurse or a lawyer. Unless learning about his mother's unfulfilled dreams would make Henry upset. . . .

How would any of them ever know what to do or to say without causing pain?

Cordelia gulped back tears and busied herself with straightening the stacks of paper napkins on the refreshment table. She often thought about how just days before Sarah had died, she had told Cordelia how peaceful and happy she felt. And Cordelia couldn't help but wonder if Sarah had somehow *known* that she was going to die, if she had known that she would not be called upon to raise her child, that she would be, in a way, set free. It was a macabre thought, Cordelia knew that, and besides, Sarah hadn't believed in things like premonitions and the supernatural. Like that dream Sarah had had earlier in the summer, the one in which she had died giving birth to Henry. It was all only coincidence. It was all only a big sick joke.

Cordelia looked out at the crowd at The Busy Bee and sighed. She wondered if life was always going to be sad now that she knew what death felt like.

"Cordelia, dear, do you know if there's more hot chocolate?"

It was Mrs. Bates, one of the store's oldest and most loyal customers, and a very sweet woman with a very sweet tooth.

Cordelia smiled. "I'll make another pot right away, Mrs. Bates."

She hurried back to the tiny kitchen behind the shop, glad to be busy and hoping to escape her dis-eased thoughts.

Chapter 120

It was Christmas Eve day. Stevie was staring out the living room window at the snow-covered lawn. Clarissa was perched on the windowsill, eyeing with concentration two cardinals futilely hunting for food on the smooth expanse of white. For half a second, Stevie thought she saw her sister standing where the lawn met the road, wearing her navy parka and old boots. And then, she was gone.

Well, Stevie thought bitterly, *she hadn't been there in the first place, had she?*

Tomorrow morning the four of them—not five—would go to church. The Kanes would be there as well, and the two families would sit together. Stevie dreaded the minister mentioning Sarah in his sermon, but she half expected that he would. Sarah's death seemed to have affected just about everyone who had known her even a little bit. Stevie and her parents couldn't go anywhere without someone giving them a sympathetic nod or coming up to offer a word of condolence or worse, not so subtly pointing them out to a companion. "There's the Bauer family," Stevie imagined them saying. "You know, the ones whose *unmarried teenage daughter* died in childbirth."

Stevie sighed and looked over at the tree her father had gamely brought home the week before. Clarissa had immediately scampered up to the very top and sat swaying under her own weight for a moment or two. Then she had jumped straight down to the floor six feet below. Stevie had barely been able to raise a smile.

She and her mother had decorated the tree with the old family ornaments, but it was a somber undertaking, without the usual giggles and reminiscences of past holidays. Henry had lain in his car seat nearby, watching them intently. The way he stared at people, as if he were really listening and understanding what they were saying, reminded Stevie a bit of the way Sarah would focus when she found something really interesting. But maybe she was imagining the similarity.

Anyway, since Sarah's death, Stevie had come to realize that life was just too horribly short and unpredictable to keep an important truth about yourself a secret. So she had decided to come out to her parents right after the holidays. Cordelia had offered to be there for support, but Stevie didn't feel she would need any. Her parents were wonderful, loving people. She was not afraid. And once Stevie had told her parents, Cordelia would be free to share the truth with hers.

It did make her sad that Sarah would never know who she really was, as a whole person. But there was nothing she could do about that. Once or twice since Sarah had died Stevie had tried to talk to her, but it had been a failure. Sarah was gone forever. She was beyond reach. At least, Stevie didn't know how to find her, except for those few times her image would flash before her eyes and then flee.

Stevie heard Henry cry from his room—once Sarah's room—and then heard her mother call, "I've got it!" In a moment all was quiet again. Her mother might have given Henry the little stuffed bunny he loved so much. Stevie wished he didn't like Justin's toy more than Cordelia's stuffed lion. Maybe the lion was just too big for his little hands. Maybe before long Henry would reject the bunny his jerk of a dad had given his mom. One could only hope.

Stevie's gaze rested on a family portrait the Bauers had had taken a few years back. It was a nice enough photograph, but that family no longer existed. There was a new family now.

Stevie had gone from younger sister to older sister in seconds; her role in the family dynamic had drastically changed, and in a way she deeply regretted. She would give anything, *anything* to have Sarah back. She would never say it aloud, but she wished that Henry had been the one to die. That would have been terribly sad, but it would have been less heartbreaking, less earth-shattering than losing her beloved sister. She could see no reason, no *meaning,* no *purpose* in Sarah's death. Nothing was better for the Bauer family now. Who had decided it was time for Sarah to leave them?

No, it just didn't make sense.

Clarissa leaped from the windowsill and went bounding from the room. She had been intensely curious about the baby at first, even a bit frightened, but within weeks she was taking naps at the foot of his cradle, and crying when he cried, and watching intently when he was bathed or fed. In fact, Clarissa was doing a better job of accepting the fact of Henry than Stevie seemed capable of doing.

Stevie rubbed her eyes. She couldn't wait until this stupid holiday season was over and she could stop pretending that she believed in happiness.

Chapter 121

Jack and Cordelia had gone to a movie. Adelaide was alone in the house. She had just finished putting away the last of the holiday decorations. In other years, Adelaide had found the process of dismantling the tree and returning ornaments to their boxes a bit depressing. But not this year. The Christmas holiday had been an exhausting time of sorrow and tempered joy for both the Kanes and the Bauers, and Adelaide was not alone in being glad it was gone.

Stevie might have had things worse than anyone. She had broken down at church on Christmas morning. Cindy had taken her home immediately. Joe and the baby had remained for the rest of the service and Jack had driven them home afterward. A week later, Stevie had told her parents that she was gay. It must have been such a burden on the poor girl, coming to know herself for who she was while all attention was focused on Sarah and the pregnancy. And then losing her sister in such a sudden and unexpected way . . .

Thankfully, Stevie's mood seemed a bit lighter now. There was still a long road ahead, but Stevie was strong and she had her parents' full support. The Kanes' support, too. Adelaide *had* to believe that she would be all right. She didn't think any of them could bear the loss of another child.

Cordelia had been miserable through the Christmas season, too, but like Stevie, she seemed to be rallying a bit. She had regained a small amount of her old spark and had once even asked to be taken to the mall. Still, there were days when she could barely manage a smile, and too often Adelaide came across her daughter staring out a window or slumped on the living room couch. When asked what she was thinking about, the answer was invariably the same: Sarah.

Cindy had experienced a bad moment when she received a Christmas card from an old friend of her mother, listing Sarah's name right along with Cindy's, Joe's, and Stevie's. Clearly, word of Sarah's passing hadn't reached everyone. Opening that card had been, Cindy said, like learning of the death all over again, a painfully unnecessary reminder of their loss.

As for Joe and Jack, well, they were each soldiering on, expressing their grief in the way men of their kind did—privately and by being productive. Joe was handling the majority of the paperwork involved in the bid for adoption, and Jack continued his efforts toward setting up the scholarship in Sarah's name.

And Adelaide . . . well, it was what had happened after the holidays, in the second week of January, that had most significantly affected Adelaide.

Her son had contacted her.

She had sat at the computer for close to an hour, rereading the e-mail—an e-mail she had almost deleted, as she often did when she didn't recognize the sender. Extreme feelings of relief and happiness flowed through her, making tears turn to laughter and then turn back again. Only a few lines, but lines with the power to radically change Adelaide's life.

"I believe that twenty-one years ago a woman named Adelaide Morgan gave up a baby boy for adoption. If you are that woman, I am that boy.

If you have any interest in a correspondence, you can e-mail me at this address or call at the number listed below.

Sincerely, Eric Nixon"

She had told Jack first. He had held her for a long time, saying nothing, stroking her hair. Then she had told Cordelia. For all her earlier interest in her half-brother, Cordelia's excitement was subdued.

"You're not going to run off with him and leave me behind, are you?" she had asked only, Adelaide suspected, half jokingly.

Adelaide had taken Cordelia's feelings of fear and uncertainty quite seriously. So soon after losing Sarah, Cordelia was bound to feel concerned that she might also lose her mother to the half-brother she had never known.

"No," she had assured her. "I am not. You and your father are my priorities. I made that choice long ago. There's room for Eric in my life, if he wants to be there, but he'll never replace you."

"Oh, I know," Cordelia had replied with an elaborate shrug. "I'm just being silly. So does he know about me?"

"Not yet. But I'll tell him."

"I wonder if he'll want to get to know me."

"I don't know," Adelaide had admitted. "Is that something you'd like?"

"Yeah. I think. He'd just better turn out to be cool. I mean, not someone like Justin."

Adelaide had felt a twinge of anger. How could a son of hers have grown up to be a jerk? Then again, she hadn't raised him. She would have to trust the love and intelligence of his adoptive parents, and hope they had taught him all that she would have done about responsibility and respect.

One thirty. Adelaide had decided to place the call at two o'clock. It was a random time but setting herself a deadline had helped hone her determination.

She knew there was no guarantee that she and Eric—his name was Eric!—would ever develop a close relationship. But maybe a close relationship *would* evolve, one where Adelaide could follow his life on Facebook and send him birthday cards and maybe even visit him once in a while. (The area code he had given told her he lived in Massachusetts.) She couldn't imagine his inviting her to his wedding someday—that might be too hurtful to his adoptive parents—but she would *know* about the wedding and send a gift and then, in time, learn that his wife was pregnant and maybe someday she could meet her grandchild. Or maybe Eric was gay and when he and his husband were ready to adopt a child he would do so with joy, remembering how well things had worked out for him, knowing now what courage it had taken his birth mother, Adelaide, to offer him to another family.

Adelaide felt a bubble of nervous laughter escape her. She knew she shouldn't be thinking in these terms. They might have only one or two brief and awkward conversations before parting again for good. So much time had passed, so many questions must have accumulated. It might prove too much for Eric to handle. She hoped fervently that he wouldn't come to regret their reconnecting.

But, for Adelaide, the risk was worth the potential pain. Finally, she would hear her son's voice, maybe even get to touch his hand, look into his eyes. There were moments when she felt unable to bear the joy and excitement. She thought that before now she had never really understood that phrase "bursting with happiness."

Adelaide went into the den. She would call her son from there, the most comfortable room in the house. That mattered somehow. She sat in one of the high-backed armchairs, her cell phone in her lap. It was one forty-five.

Jack had asked his wife how Eric had found her. Adelaide had no idea. She would ask him when they spoke—or not. Did it really matter? Jack had also asked if she were going to look up her son on the Internet before contacting him. The answer to that was no, she was not, and for a variety of reasons, one of which was that she wanted to allow Eric to retain a degree of privacy for as long as he needed or wanted it.

Finally, Jack had asked if Eric had mentioned his father. He had not, and Adelaide wondered if her son had searched him out as well. If he hadn't—and there was a very good chance that he had not; Adelaide had given no one at the hospital or adoption agency his name—he might ask her about him. The thought worried her. She wasn't sure if she was under a moral obligation to keep Michael Baker's identity a secret. No, how could she be? Still, she wondered if it would be right to reveal his identity. Would it be right to *refuse* Eric this information? It most certainly would *not* be right to give Eric a false name or to tell him that his father had died long ago.

And her parents . . . she didn't want them to know anything about Eric—not that they would care to know! But again: Did Eric have the right to know who and where they were? One thing was for sure. If he did ask about other family, she would *not* paint Nancy and Tom Morgan as bad or malicious people. She would not burden her son with her own negative opinions, no matter how valid her reasons for having them.

Adelaide looked at her watch. One minute until two o'clock. She lifted her cell phone. Her fingers were trembling so violently she could not hit the right keys and had to begin again twice. Finally, the call went through.

"Hello?" The young man's voice was pleasant and warm.

"Hello, Eric?"

"Yes?"

Adelaide closed her eyes. "This is Adelaide Kane," she said, with an immense feeling of pride. "Your mother."

Please turn the page
for a very special Q&A
with Holly Chamberlin!

Q. Did you research the phenomena of teen pregnancy before writing *The Beach Quilt*?

A. Yes, extensively. In the end, I chose not to include what I had learned in too informational a way. I did try to infuse the characters with some of the habits and thoughts and emotions found to be typical in the situation. *The Beach Quilt* is a novel, not a scientific study.

Q. What was the most surprising thing you learned while doing research about teen pregnancy?

A. The most surprising and disturbing thing I learned was that a huge number of women in the United States die in childbirth. I was, of course, aware of the dangers so many women around the world face during pregnancy and childbirth—disease, starvation, lack of clean water and proper medical care—but to discover that right here in my own country so many women don't survive the birthing of their child, well, that set me to thinking.

Q. How close to your heart is the experience of teen pregnancy?

A. To be honest, I've never personally known a teenage girl who found herself pregnant. Well, if I did, I never knew about it. I grew up in a very Catholic environment, and much was never spoken about, especially in those days. But over the course of my life I certainly haven't been unaware of the problem. It can break your heart, thinking of what young parents and their children might have to face. Life is hard enough when you have a full support system in place—a steady partner, a good job, a nice home, a network of family and friends. To—possibly—find yourself largely alone and reliant on social services . . .

Q. With that in mind, some readers might take issue with the fact that *The Beach Quilt* tells a very different tale of teen pregnancy, one in which the young mother-to-be is nurtured and cared for—one in which her child's future also looks relatively rosy. In other words, your story isn't quite as gritty as it might be.

A. To those readers I would say, remember, this is a novel. *The Beach Quilt* tells the story of two particular families in a particular time and place, making a particular set of choices. If the Bauers' ready acceptance of their daughter's pregnancy strikes some as odd, well, so be it. If they had thrown Sarah out of the house, other readers would have protested. Others might argue that life as a single parent anywhere, city or country, and in any circumstances, nurturing or not, can be difficult, and I would never deny that. The suspension of disbelief is essential to the experience of a fiction, be it novel or TV show or film! Besides, at bottom what I really wanted to write was a story of love triumphant—and I hope that I did.

Q. Are you a quilter?

A. I am not. Unfortunately, my dexterity—and eyesight!—is increasingly poor, so I've given up any kind of detailed work I had once enjoyed, like embroidery or beadwork. But I love quilts and the fact that they are an art form pretty much owned by women. I've never forgotten one stunning exhibit of quilts made by African American women at the American Folk Art Museum in New York City way back in the eighties. And my husband's mother, Janet, was gifted at weaving and needlework; we're lucky to have some of her pieces still.

Q. Can you offer a clue as to your next book?

A. Well, I've got a rudimentary idea in mind. There'll be a family of three quirky, creative sisters, between the ages of thirteen and twenty. Their mother is either long dead or long gone off on some adventure. Their father is very much present and beloved. One summer the sisters, who live in the fictional town of Yorktide, Maine, encounter a girl who appears seemingly from nowhere. The girl turns out to be homeless. I've yet to construct the circumstances of her backstory. The dynamics among the members of the family and this homeless girl will be the focus of the book. And, of course, there will be a cat character!

Q. So is Clarissa, the cat in *The Beach Quilt*, based on a real animal?

A. Yes! Betty, our fourteen-year-old tortoiseshell, exhibits amazing physical and mental talents. Plus, she's my gallant protector. Which is taking nothing away from Cyrus, fifteen, who although blind and almost entirely deaf, lives life as if he's the king of the house. Which, of course, he is. Plus, he likes to hold my hand, which is heaven.

Q. What was the first book you read after completing *The Beach Quilt*?

A. In rapid succession I caught up on the latest in the Ian Rutledge and the Bess Crawford series, both by Charles Todd. And then I went on to a Charles Todd stand alone, *The Walnut Tree*. I'm now eyeing Julian Barnes's *The Sense of an Ending* and a rereading of *A Room with a View*.

Q. What do you do to celebrate the completion of a book?

A. Sleep.

A READING GROUP GUIDE

THE BEACH QUILT

Holly Chamberlin

ABOUT THIS GUIDE

The suggested questions are included to enhance your group's reading of Holly Chamberlin's *The Beach Quilt*!

DISCUSSION QUESTIONS

1. Sarah's sudden vulnerability awakens vulnerabilities in Adelaide, Cordelia, Cindy, and Stevie. More than ever each feels the need for succor, attention, support, and sympathy. Talk about how closely we adopt our friends' pain and experience it as somehow our own. Do you think this is something women experience more than men, a sort of sympathetic engagement in the lives of those we love? Do you think this tendency is something taught or inherent—or, perhaps, both?

2. Courageous actions come in many forms. Talk about the acts of courage each of the main characters perform. For example: Stevie's coming out to Cordelia and later, to her parents; Cordelia's care of Stevie, her habit of standing up to bullies, her willingness to share parts of her true self (Pinky with Stevie and her foolish thoughts about losing her virginity to John Blantyre with Sarah); Sarah's decision to keep the baby (was her brief attempt to offer him for adoption an act of courage or desperation?); Cindy's attempts to have a family and her willingness to adopt Henry; Adelaide's decision to give up her son and then her willingness to welcome him back into her life.

3. Do you think that Cindy's refusal to sell the quilts is an act of selfishness? If her original idea of selling them was made in haste, is she justified in changing her mind? The quilts are hers, though their sale would benefit her family. When is one justified in not making a sacrifice for loved ones?

4. Consider the notion of what it means to "act out of character." For example, Cordelia tends to underestimate

her strengths and abilities, almost playing to an image of the silly young girl. Why do you think she engages in this sort of self-deprecation? How much of it is conscious or chosen? How much of it is the result of an image she has allowed others to create for her? Sarah wonders if she was ever really the responsible person people thought she was, or if she had been like an actor assuming a role written by someone else. Cindy feels resentment at having been placed in her current situation and is surprised to discover there are limits to her willingness to sacrifice for her family. We see mild-mannered Joe express the desire to kill Justin. Does anyone ever achieve a perfect harmony between the person inside and the person perceived? Or is there always tension between two perceived halves—halves that are really one complicated whole?

5. Adelaide briefly contemplates cutting all ties with her parents. Do you think she would be justified in doing so? After all, she feels she gets nothing positive from the relationship. But how can she really know what (if anything) her mother gets from it—good or bad, conscious or unconscious? When is someone justified in saying, "I appreciate the good things you have done for me, but I cannot forget or forgive the bad things"? Do blood ties require loyalty, or is loyalty a choice?

6. At one point Jack reminds Adelaide that Cordelia is a typically naive and self-righteous teenager, for whom the world is black and white and actions right or wrong. How do Cordelia and Sarah and Stevie mature (become more nuanced) over the course of the book? After Sarah's death, Cordelia and Stevie are convinced that they will never be happy again. If they were older, do you think they would feel so sure of a dark future? How does age and experience change the process of

grieving and recovery? Consider Cindy. Though devastated by the loss of her older daughter, she knows she has a duty to her remaining daughter, husband, and grandchild—as well as to herself—to carry on. Consider Adelaide's process of recovery from the loss of her first child. How complete or successful has her recovery been, and how does Sarah's pregnancy affect her healing?

7. "No person is an island." How does Sarah's pregnancy affect the lives of each of the other main characters, in ways both mundane and psychological or emotional? Is anyone better off for the changes wrought by Sarah's getting pregnant? Is anyone worse off for having spent the final months of her life by her side? Stevie and Cordelia tell us they see no rhyme, reason, or good having resulted from Sarah's death. Could an argument be made against that opinion?

8. Consider Cindy's keeping secrets from Joe—the call from Mrs. Morrow; her decision to sell the heirloom quilts; and Sarah's offer to put her baby up for adoption. In the first case, Cindy feels she is protecting her husband from further grief. In the second and third cases, she is afraid that he will oppose her opinions and thwart her will. How do you think Joe would feel if he knew his wife was withholding information, thoughts, and feelings from him? How does stress cause a person to act in unexpected and perhaps less than fully honest ways?

9. Cindy has trouble remembering that Sarah's baby is not her own. Adelaide has trouble distancing her remembered teenage self from the pregnant teenage Sarah. Talk about why each woman might have difficulty establishing emotional boundaries in this situa-

tion. On a related note, Adelaide, tempted once again to search for the father of her son, suddenly rejects the notion as a betrayal of her relationship with her husband. Do you think this feeling of guilt is justified, given the fact that Jack knows all about her past? Or is something else keeping Adelaide from pursuing her former lover?

10. How might Sarah's being pregnant have influenced Stevie's decision to come out to Cordelia as gay? If Cordelia hadn't become a friend, do you think Stevie would have been able to come out to her friends from school? Would she have chosen to confide in Sarah instead?

11. Do you think the Bauers should have attempted to hold Justin accountable for his actions regarding Sarah? Do you think it would have been worth the time, effort, and emotional cost to urge him to take responsibility for his child? Do you think they acted against the best interest of their daughter and grandson? Or do you think that the Bauers, given their strong sense of independence, made the right call? (On a related note, what do you think of their decision not to have an autopsy?) What do you think the Kanes, given Adelaide's past and their own somewhat different character as a family, would have done if Cordelia had been the one to get pregnant?

Set in a picturesque Maine beach town, bestselling author Holly Chamberlin's heartwarming and insightful novel delves into the choices and changes faced by two families over the course of one eventful summer. . . .

Everyone in Yorktide, Maine, knows sixteen-year-old Sarah Bauer. She's a good student and a dutiful daughter, as well as a beloved best friend to Cordelia Kane. So it's a surprise to all when sensible Sarah reveals that she is pregnant.

Though shocked, Sarah's family is supportive. But while Sarah reconciles herself to a new and different future, the consequences ripple in all directions. Her father—a proud, old-time Mainer—tries to find more work to defray expenses. Her younger sister grapples with a secret she can't share. Cordelia feels abandoned, and Cordelia's mother faces the repercussions of a long-ago decision. As Sarah's mother, Cindy, frets about how she'll juggle childcare with her job at the local quilting store, she seizes on an idea: to band together and make a baby quilt. Piece by piece, a beautiful design emerges. And as it progresses, reflecting the hopes and cares of the women who create it, each will find strength in the friendship and love that sustains them, in hardship and in joy. . . .

Please turn the page for an exciting sneak peek of Holly Chamberlin's newest novel

A WEDDING ON THE BEACH

coming soon wherever print and e-books are sold!

Chapter 1

Bess Culpepper steered her white Subaru wagon past the First Congregational Church at the crossroads of North Street and Log Cabin Road, noting with pleasure the pristine whiteness of the stately old building. Just beyond the church was the serenely charming Arundel Cemetery with its well-tended stone grave markers. Not many moments later Bess turned left onto Main Street, making a right onto Western Avenue at the Village Baptist Church.

She didn't need to drive through Kennebunkport—a town founded in 1653—in order to reach her destination, but she so loved the quaint town with its charming boutiques, beautiful homes, and the famous, though unassuming, bridge over the Kennebunk River that she chose to do so, patiently inching her way through the heavy summer traffic. Kennebunkport's year-round community was small—only a few thousand people made their homes there through winter—but in summer the population swelled to much larger numbers.

As Bess drove through Dock Square—at an even slower pace; cars vied with heavy foot traffic—she recalled the many delicious dinners she had eaten at Hurricane Restaurant, and the excellent local musicians she had heard there as well. She vowed to stop into Abacus Gallery before long; there was always something special and absolutely essential to be found there. Bess loved to shop.

Once out of the center of town, she made a left and began

the final leg of her journey to Birmingham Beach along roads that were shady with the dark green leaves of trees and bordered by charming Colonial-style homes, their lawns colorful with blooming rhododendrons, their gardens bright with peonies and roses.

Summer had always been Bess's favorite time of the year. Winters in Maine were long and more often than not, brutal. Fall was gorgeous but too short, and many years spring came almost too late to be properly appreciated. But summer! Now there was a season to be cherished. The sun in the sky until nearly eight o'clock; temperatures that didn't call for layers of fleece and wool; the sound of local bands playing rock and blues at the restaurants with decks and patios. Summer provided an excuse (as if there needed to be one) to eat ice cream whenever the mood struck and to wear bright and happy colors with pretty names like Mint Froth and Petunia Pink, and to visit the beach without the risk of frostbite.

And this summer would be the most special of them all because this summer forty-two-year-old Bess would be getting married. Like many women, she had dreamed of her wedding day since she was a little girl, long before she had any conception of the real meaning behind the pomp and ceremony. She had pored over magazines and websites, and had spent just as many hours imagining scenarios based on the classic fairytales she had read and the movies she had watched throughout her childhood and adolescence. The magnificent wedding scene in *The Sound of Music*. Audrey Hepburn wearing Givenchy in *Funny Face*. Queen Victoria marrying her beloved Albert. Sigh.

The details of a wedding—from the dress to the veil, from the ring to the bouquet—had been easy to conjure, even as she progressed through varying moods and fancies. At twelve Bess had thought Princess Diana's frothy confection by David and Elizabeth Emanuel was the model for the perfect wedding gown. At twenty, she had considered the possibility of getting married at the top of Cadillac Mountain, a location that seemed to call for a lacy, prairie-style dress, like something a

Bohemian bride might have worn back in the 1960s. At thirty, a sleek frock like the one by Narciso Rodriguez that Carolyn Bessette had worn on her wedding day had seemed just the thing.

What had been more difficult to imagine through the years was the groom, that necessary figure who would make a wedding possible. But Bess hadn't been worried. Prince Charming would make an appearance at the right time as all romantic heroes did. He might come in an initially off-putting packaging like The Beast or in an all-around glossy form like—well, like Prince Charming—or somewhere in between the two, a Mr. Darcy complete with a bit too much pride or prejudice but an otherwise stellar character and on sound financial footing to boot. Bess had dated enough deadbeat guys to appreciate the value of financial health.

But as she approached her fortieth birthday Bess had begun, just a little, to doubt that her very own Knight in Shining Armor would ever show up to walk side by side with her through life. She needn't have worried. Less than a year later, Nathan Creek, a widower for the past twenty odd years, had spotted her across a crowd of partygoers, introduced himself, and asked if he might take her to dinner one evening. Bess had said yes; three months later, Nathan had proposed; in about two weeks' time they would be married.

For the past eleven years, Bess had owned a party and event planning company called Joie de Vivre. The business continued to flourish even in years when the economy was not as robust as anyone would like it to be. People needed to honor loved ones and to acknowledge milestones no matter how much or how little money they had. Bess strove tirelessly to create special occasions tailored for each client; she loved what she did and could think of no career for which she was better suited.

So, when it came time to plan her own wedding, Bess was in the perfect position to make her dream a reality. A wedding on the beach. That was what she wanted, and that was what she was going to have. And an essential component of that wedding was a charming vacation house from which Bess could hold court prior to the big day.

Her amazing assistant, Kara, had found just such a place. Driftwood House had cost Bess a fortune, as the owners quite wisely preferred to rent for a four-week minimum, Maine's short summer being prime time for discriminating vacationers. But nothing was too good for her wedding or, perhaps even more importantly, for her friends. And not just any friends. The friends she had made in college and had kept and cherished all the years since. Marta Kennedy, long married to Mike MacIntosh, another of the old gang. Chuck Fortunato, now husband to Dean Williams. And Allison and Chris Montague.

There was only one dark spot in the sunny scenario. Two of those dear friends, a couple since freshman year of college, were nearing the finalization of a divorce. Bess and the others were deeply puzzled. No explanation or excuse had been offered. Questions had been deflected or met with silence. Endless hours had been spent guessing at reasons why the seemingly golden marriage of two such perfectly matched people as Allison and Chris was about to be so decidedly broken.

The upsetting fact of the impending divorce hadn't put Bess off from wanting—indeed, from needing—both Allison and Chris at her wedding. Even the fact, recently uncovered by Mike through an unprofessionally chatty colleague in the law, that Chris had been the leader in the divorce proceedings hadn't put Bess off inviting him.

Marta, however, had strongly suggested that before extending Chris an invitation Bess ask Allison how she felt about her soon-to-be former husband attending the wedding. So, Bess had called Allison one evening and after a few minutes of small talk had broached the delicate subject. "I'm thinking of asking Chris to the wedding," she said. "But I wanted to check with you first. It's totally fine if you say you'd rather I didn't. The decision is yours."

After a long moment of silence Allison had given her permission if not exactly her blessing. "Of course, you should ask him if that's what you really want. It's your day, Bess. It's all about the bride."

For a split-second Bess had wondered if Allison had meant something snide by that last remark but dismissed her suspicion as ridiculous. Allison was never snide. Still, Bess had gone on to extract a promise from her old friend that she was one hundred percent sure that she was okay with Chris attending the wedding. "It's just that it would be a shame for him not to be there," she said. "Even knowing . . . even knowing that it was Chris who initiated the divorce."

Allison had laughed then, an unhappy laugh. "I suppose I should have known it would come out sooner or later," she said.

But she had offered no further information and ended the call quickly after that. Bess sent the wedding invitations the very next morning. Before a full week had passed Chris had returned the reply card with the WILL NOT ATTEND box firmly checked off and a brief note scrawled on the back of the card. *I wish you and Nathan the best,* it read.

"I'm sure he'd like to come to the wedding," Bess told Marta on the phone that night. "He probably just thinks that it would be awkward seeing Allison. I'll tell him that Allison is fine with his being there. He'll change his mind. You'll see." Marta had not been so sure.

Bess had gone on to pursue Chris with a vengeance, first with texts and e-mails and when they went unanswered, with a handwritten letter. When after two weeks Bess had received no reply to this missive, she had called his cell phone; the call had gone to voice mail and Bess had left a carefully rehearsed message in a determinedly chipper voice.

Still, Chris did not respond and finally, with both Marta and Nathan urging she back off, Bess agreed to leave the matter alone. But in spite of Marta's telling her that she was being dangerously naïve in thinking that by bringing Allison and Chris together under the same roof she would work a miracle of reconciliation—and that was indeed Bess's fond hope—Bess wasn't sure she had done the right thing by ending her campaign to get Chris to join his old friends at her wedding this summer.

Driftwood House! There it was just ahead. Bess turned into the drive and parked outside the three-car garage. The house really was lovely. Built about ten years earlier, the cedar shingles had softened to silver. Gables, a traditional aspect of the Shingle Style home, gave a soaring aspect to the two-story structure. A back porch looked out over a lawn that rolled gently down to a set of wooden stairs that led directly onto Birmingham Beach. There could be no more perfect setting for Bess's perfect wedding.

Bess got out of her car, pushed her wavy light brown hair from her face, and smiled up at the house. It was certainly large enough to accommodate her friends comfortably. Mike and Marta were due to arrive first, followed by Allison, and then by Chuck, Dean, and baby Thomas. He would be the only child in Driftwood House until the day of the wedding when Bess's nieces and nephews, all seven of them, would make their boisterous appearance. Though it would embarrass Bess to admit this, it always took her a moment to recall the children's names and to remember which child belonged to which of her two sisters. Dennis, Alan, and Gus Jr. belonged to Mae and her husband. Lily, Tildy, Jacob, and Little Owen belonged to Ann and Walt. Bess kept meaning to come up with a trick to help her keep straight her family members, but she never got around to it.

Bess had included Marta's three kids in her invitation to the wedding, but Marta had told Bess that she could use a vacation from her brood. It was the first time Bess had ever heard Marta say such a thing. In fact, imagining Marta without her children gathered around her was almost impossible to do. But everyone needed a bit of a break from responsibility, even a Super Mom.

The car unloaded, Bess brought her travel bags inside and

stowed them in the largest of the three bedrooms on the second floor. Then she returned to the car and began hauling the boxes she had packed at her office into the den, the room she had designated as her command center. A laptop and printer; charges for both of her cell phones; notebooks and pens; a framed photo of Nathan taken on the first long weekend they had spent together. In this pleasant room, *the* wedding of the year would take its final form.

Bess was no stranger to the fact that an outdoor wedding was a fairly big risk—even in the summer bad weather could be an issue—but she was prepared for all eventualities. Her backup plans had backup plans, and she had taken out insurance against every imaginable disaster that might disturb the perfection of her big day. She had even hired a children's performer to help keep her sisters' offspring occupied. Bored children could mean trouble.

Bess opened one of the boxes she had brought to the den and removed a handcrafted leather folio, a gift from an admiring colleague who would be out of the country at the time of the wedding. Indeed, many of the vendors and clients with whom Bess worked had sent her incredible gifts. The owner of a high-end boutique in Ogunquit had given her a gorgeous John Hardy bracelet. A new corporate client in Portland had sent a large cut-crystal dish from Tiffany's. There seemed no end to the arrival of baskets filled with caviar, pâtés, and cheeses, or those crammed with cookies, candies, and jams. One vendor who had been working with Bess for years had given her two tickets to the Boston Symphony Orchestra; Bess had passed them on to Kara, who loved classical music. She had, however, kept the gift certificate for dinner at The White Barn Inn right here in Kennebunkport; Nathan had never been to the venerable Maine institution and was sure to love it. Everyone did.

Bess's phone alerted her to a call from her fiancé. She smiled as she heard Nathan's familiar voice greet her. The proverbial "everyone" said that the initial excitement of a romantic relationship wore off, but Bess didn't believe that it had to. Ten, twenty, even thirty years from now she fully expected to find a smile on her face when she heard Nathan's voice on the other end of the line. Romance didn't have to fade and die. It just didn't.

"So, does the house measure up to your impossible standards?" he asked when Bess got through telling him how much she loved him and he had returned the sentiment.

"Pretty much," Bess admitted. "Though I haven't made a full inspection yet."

"You know your friends will love it, flaws and all."

"I know but . . ."

Nathan laughed. "But you won't be happy unless every tiny detail is perfect. Well, just be careful not to lift anything too heavy. I'll be there before you know it."

"And you're Mr. Universe!"

Nathan, while fit, was in fact fifty-three years old. He laughed. "No, but I do own a monster of a hand truck and a pretty heavy-duty dolly."

"Good. And be sure to bring bungee cords, too. And a screwdriver. Never go anywhere without a screwdriver. My father told me that once and he was right."

Nathan promised to bring a screwdriver and with another protestation of love he signed off.

Bess sighed in contentment. She felt so very lucky to have finally found The One. Even her family liked Nathan and they had never liked anyone she had dated, not that they had ever said as much. They were far too reticent a bunch to speak freely about tricky things like emotions. Bess had grown up in rural Green Lakes, Maine, as had generations of Culpeppers before her. Introducing the cosmopolitan Nathan to Owen Culpepper, a man who had never traveled farther north than the paper mill town of Madawaska on the Canadian border or farther south than the amusement park in Old Orchard Beach, and to Matilda (née Wade) Culpepper, a woman who had dropped out of high school in her junior year to help care for the first of several elderly relatives she was to care for in her life, was bound to be tricky. But Nathan had very quickly won over Bess's parents with his sincerity and good humor. Even Bess's sisters and their husbands had given him the thumbs-up.

The raucous caws of a seagull caused Bess to frown. She went out to the back porch and eyed with suspicion the giant bird staring at her from the lawn. Hmm. How to keep seagulls from swooping in on the food at the reception? It was a problem she hadn't considered. Maybe she could enlist her brothers-in-law to be on seagull patrol. They could shout and wave their arms when one of the birds came too close for comfort. But that could prove dangerous. What if the bird was made angry by loud noise and vigorous movement?

Still, the image of Gus and Walt shouting and waving made Bess smile as she turned back into the house. Both were good men, though decidedly lacking in anything remotely akin to glamour. Like Bess's sisters, Ann and Mae, neither had gone to college. Neither earned much money in spite of working long and arduous hours. Gus could not afford to replace two front teeth he had lost in a hockey accident back when he was a teen. Walt suffered from a degenerative disc issue that caused almost constant pain. But as far as Bess knew, neither man had ever expressed dissatisfaction with his life; neither man allowed personal hardship to get in the way of his being a dutiful husband and father. And not once had either Ann or Mae complained to their big sister about her husband; both women seemed full of genuine affection for their spouses. But would Bess's sisters, each other's BFFs, ever confide in her about anything vital? That was a question that possibly muddied the waters when looking for a clear vision of Mae's and Ann's married lives. Even assuming that neither of Bess's sisters were lying about their happiness, and taking into consideration all of the stellar qualities Bess's brothers-in-law exhibited, Bess still had never been able to identify the passion or romance in her sisters' marriages. Unlike the passion and romance at the heart of what was going to be her special marriage.

But Mae's and Ann's domestic bliss or lack thereof was of little concern at the moment. No doubt about it, there was a layer of dust on the living room's baseboards. Kara had ensured that the house was stocked with cleaning supplies; Bess located a duster and briskly went about the task of chasing dust. Not one little thing was allowed to mar what Bess was sure would be the best wedding ever.

Visit us online at
KensingtonBooks.com
to read more from your favorite authors, see books by series, view reading group guides, and more.

Join us on social media
for sneak peeks, chances to win books and prize packs, and to share your thoughts with other readers.

facebook.com/kensingtonpublishing
twitter.com/kensingtonbooks

Tell us what you think!

To share your thoughts, submit a review, or sign up for our eNewsletters, please visit:
KensingtonBooks.com/TellUs.